I0613272

John Selden

The Table Talk of John Selden

John Selden

The Table Talk of John Selden

ISBN/EAN: 9783337399214

Printed in Europe, USA, Canada, Australia, Japan

Cover: Foto ©Andreas Hilbeck / pixelio.de

More available books at **www.hansebooks.com**

THE

TABLE TALK

OF

JOHN SELDEN

EDITED

WITH AN INTRODUCTION AND NOTES

BY

SAMUEL HARVEY REYNOLDS, M.A.

LATE FELLOW AND TUTOR OF BRASENOSE COLLEGE

Oxford

AT THE CLARENDON PRESS

1892

CONTENTS

—◦—

INTRODUCTION

———•———

It is now more than thirty years since the late Mark Pattison suggested to me to prepare an edition of Selden's Table Talk, and gave me some valuable hints as to the way in which a work of the kind ought to be done. Pattison was an enthusiast for Selden ; he considered him a typical Englishman, at once a representative of the best points in the distinctively English character, and wholly free from its common prejudices and shortcomings. Selden had certainly what have been termed the three main interests of Englishmen, politics, business and religion. His Table Talk gives us specimens of his remarks on all three, but on matters of business not so many as on the other two. That the conversations which it reports were held between 1634 and 1654, the year in which Selden died, may be assumed with certainty. The reporter, Milward, says in his introductory letter that he had had the opportunity to hear Selden discourse twenty years together, and he thus fixes the range of time which his notes cover. Now the letters referred to in Tythes, sec. 6, bear date in the Autumn of 1653, so that the conversation about them must have come very shortly before Selden's death. The chief part of the discourse is about contemporary events, and Selden's remarks upon these throw an interesting light on the history of his opinions and on his attitude to the parties of his day.

The early history of the book must be left incomplete on many points. It seems clear, as Mr. Singer has pointed out, that the MS. of it was put together within a few years of Selden's death. He finds proof of this in Milward's introductory letter where he speaks of 'Mr. Justice Hale, one of the Judges of the Common Pleas.' Hale, afterwards Sir Matthew Hale, ceased to be a judge of the Common Pleas in 1658 on Cromwell's death. It is clear too from this introductory letter, that when the MS. was ready it was placed in the hands of Selden's Executors, probably in the hands of Hale, whose name stands first in the list. But what became of it afterwards I do not know. It is not to be found among Sir Matthew Hale's papers in the Lincoln's Inn Library. The collection includes several of Selden's own papers, some of them unpublished as yet, but no part of the Table Talk. I have to thank the Librarian for his courtesy in placing within my reach very full means of information on this point. Now the earliest printed edition did not come out until 1689, more than thirty years after the MS. had been prepared. Of the history of the book in the meanwhile we know little or nothing. In some form or other it must have been accessible, for it is certain that there were copies made from it or from some second-hand rendering of it. But the long time which was suffered to pass before it was sent to press, suggests that there were parts of it which its trustees did not approve, and there are some at which they may have taken very reasonable offence. Religious questions are handled with a freedom of expression not at all to Hale's mind: the political sentiments are not those of Hale himself, and the book is disgraced by the insertion of several indecent references and expressions, which add nothing to the force of the passages in which they occur, and which Selden himself could hardly have wished should go down to posterity as specimens of his every-day talk.

After the Restoration, and during the whole reigns of Charles II and James II, not even the remainder of the Table Talk could have been received with much approval. The course of opinion and of events was setting another way; and Selden's outspoken words, his attack on the divine right equally of kings and of bishops, his reduction of the Monarchy to a limited constitutional form, his love of liberty, his insistence on obedience to law as part of a contract by which kings and subjects were alike bound—all this would have been very unlike the theory that found favour under the Stuarts. When the book at length appeared, in 1689, it was in a form which leaves much to be desired, replete as it is with blunders and in more than one place making downright nonsense of the passage. The present edition does something to bring the text back to what it must originally have been, and it certainly clears away some gross faults of which neither Selden nor his reporter can have been the originating cause. The Harleian MS., No. 1315, in the British Museum Library, has been taken as the basis of the text. The Library has three MSS. of the Table Talk. To the earliest of these, the Harleian, No. 690, the date assigned by Mr. Warner, the Assistant Keeper of MSS., is circa 1670. Next in order of time and a little later comes the Sloane MS., No. 2513, and latest of the three is the Harleian, No. 1315, for which the posterior limit of date can (for reasons which I shall presently explain) be fixed with certainty as 1689. Mr. Warner's authority as a palaeographist is so high that his opinion may be taken as conclusive. It is certain, however, that no one of these MSS. can have been the original copy of the Table Talk. The Harleian 690, the earliest of the three, leaves blank spaces for all the Greek words under the heading 'Descent into Hell,' and besides numerous other faults, blunders badly with the French. The Sloane MS. is even more out of the question. Besides its later date, it abounds throughout with blunders, grammatical and others, of the most obvious kind. Some of these have been corrected by a later hand, but the paper on which the MS. is written is so very like blotting-paper that almost every correction or change involves a deletion of the original text. The Harleian 1315 is of much better stamp than the Sloane. It accords very nearly with the MS. 690, and it has a special authority of its own by reason of an inscription on the back side of the title, which, as Harley's Librarian says, was written in it by Harley himself. The inscription runs thus—'This book was given in 168 (the final figure is unfortunately wanting) by Charles erle of Dorset and Middlesex to a bookseller in Fleet Street, in order to have it printed: but the bookseller delaying to have it done, Mr. Thomas Rymer sold a copy he procured to Mr. Churchill, who printed it as it came out in 169 . . .' This inscription is dated February 17, 1697. It thus fixes the date of the MS. as not later than 1689, and gives it an authority of its own, since it stands as proof that, but for the printer's delay, it would have been the basis of the earliest printed edition. The inscription is incorrect on one point, since it implies that the edition of 169 . . . (presumably the edition printed in 1696, by Jacob Tonson and Awnsham and John Churchill) was the first that had appeared. This, as we have seen, is not so. The first printed edition came out in 1689.

For bringing back the text to some nearer approach to its original and correct form, the choice lay between the Harleian MSS. 690 and 1315. Both contain excellent readings, and the two together, with occasional help from

the Sloane MS. and from the early printed editions, supply
material for a fairly satisfactory revision. But where no
notice appears to the contrary, the text now printed is that
of the Harleian MS. 1315. In all three MSS. several
passages which have been detached from the body of the
book are misplaced, or are added in an Appendix at the
end. These, in the present edition, have been put back
to the places to which they properly belong, and as they
appear in the edition of 1689. This, and an occasional
change of the spelling where it was obsolete or obviously
incorrect, are the only changes which have been made
without notice. Those who set a value on the vagaries of
a half-lettered scribe, will find them in abundance and of
all sorts in the Sloane MS. 2513.

With all helps, but in the absence of any conclusive
authority, the settlement of the text has been a matter of
difficulty and doubt. In deciding between different readings, or in conjectural emendations, I have taken as my
guide Selden's own rule. 'A man,' he says, 'must in this
case venture his discretion, and do his best to satisfy himself and others in those places where he doubts.' It is
safe to assume that Selden did not talk nonsense, and that
he was not ignorant of matters with which his published
works prove him to have been perfectly conversant. For
example, when he is made to say that a suffragan was no
bishop, we may conclude with certainty that he did not say
this, although the MSS. and the early printed editions
agree in putting it into his mouth. When he is made to
speak of Sir Richard Weston as the Prior of St. John's,
and of Valentine's novels as laying down the limits of
episcopal jurisdiction, I have borne in mind Porson's
remark that no editor in his senses adopts a reading
which he knows to be wrong, and I have changed the text
accordingly. But in every instance the reader has notice
of the change.

Milward, in his introductory letter, requests the reader to distinguish times, and in his fancy to carry along with him the when and the why many of these things were spoken. The alphabetical arrangement of the matter of the book gives us no help here. There is no attempt at a chronological order. Times are confused throughout, and we pass from subject to subject with no notice of either when or why except such as we can gather from the contents of each paragraph. I have done what I could, in an imperfect tentative way, to supply the want. Out of the great stream of events and writings and speeches which formed, so to say, the environment of Selden's life, I have picked out, here and there, what seemed likely to have suggested some of his remarks. In some instances the reference has been clear and certain; in some his published writings have given the clue, and have served to supplement the imperfect information in the Table Talk as well as to correct mistakes which must have been due to his reporter not to himself. Of his very numerous works, his History of Tithes is the only one to which he makes direct reference in the Table Talk. (See Tithes, sec. 6.)

Selden was born in 1584. In 1600 he entered at Hart Hall, Oxford. In 1602 he was a law-student at Clifford's Inn, and thence migrated to the Inner Temple in 1604. He soon became known as a man of vast and exact learning. So great was his fame as a constitutional lawyer, that before he became a member of Parliament he was often called in to advise the House on questions of prerogative, and he is credited with having had a principal part in framing the Protestation of 1621—a service for which he paid the penalty of five weeks' imprisonment by order of the Council. He was thus already a marked man when, in 1624, he was elected a member of the House, a position which he held in several Parliaments, viz. in 1626, 1628, and in the second Parliament of 1640. It was not

long before he again became a prominent champion of
the Parliamentary cause and an opponent of the high-
handed acts of injustice done by the King or in the
King's name. His knowledge of past history and of
precedents made him a valuable ally, and when the
Petition of Right was drawn up, Selden was one of those
who had been appointed to give help in preparing it.
This, and his general outspokenness in his place in the
House, marked him out, a second time, as a proper object
for royal vengeance. In the spring of 1629 he was one
of what he terms the 'Parliament men imprisoned tertio
Caroli,' by a stretch of the prerogative, aided and rendered effective by the subservient temper of the judges
before whom the prisoners were brought. Denzil Holles,
Eliot, and Valentine were among his fellow prisoners—an
illustrious company, in which Selden may not have been
unwilling to find himself included. The charge against
them had to do with their conduct and language in Parliament—matters about which no challenge could legally
be made by any outside authority. The judges would
have bailed the prisoners if they would have given
security for their future good behaviour, but this at
Selden's instance they most properly refused to do. It
would have been a surrender of their privilege for the
past, and a check on their future liberty of deed or word.
They were accordingly committed to the Tower, and
though in Selden's case the confinement did not last
long, and his treatment was not harsh, yet the restraint
was an outrage which he did rightly to resent, and which
in his case and in that of his fellow sufferers was of grave
and lasting injury to the cause which it was intended to
serve. In politics, as in religion, it is useless to play at
persecution. Charles by his half measures succeeded
only in making enemies of those whom he had hoped
to terrify into submission. Selden was not the most

formidable or the most bitter, but neither then nor in the future was he an adversary whom it was at all safe to provoke.

But just as Selden started as a Parliamentary champion on strictly constitutional grounds, so it was not long before the proceedings of the second Parliament of 1640 forced him into more or less of an antagonism to his old allies. We have several traces in the Table Talk of his growing coolness towards the advanced section of the Parliamentary party. Not, indeed, that his breach with his old friends had gone so far as to drive him into the opposite camp, expectant as it was and ready to welcome him if he had come over to it. He still held that the original contract between king and people had been broken, and that the subjects had thus been released from their promise of obedience. The quarrel, he saw clearly, had gone so far that it must be settled by an appeal to arms. It was a contest now, in which the original issues had become obscured, 'a scuffle,' as he terms it, between two sets of opponents with neither of whom could he identify himself. They must fight it out between themselves, and leave decent quiet people to their own business or to their books.

The outbreak of the civil war accordingly found him lukewarm, if not indifferent. He could look with no satis-faction to the victory of either side, to the king's high-handed disregard of law, or to the puritans' zeal not according to knowledge, and for objects many of which he disapproved. With the authors of the revolution of 1689 he would have been more entirely in agreement. The declared policy of the new rule was just what he had himself stood up for in evil days when power was triumphant over right. The year for the publication of the Table Talk was thus well chosen. When the illegal rule of James II had been ended, and when the Bill of

Rights had settled the government of England after the type which Selden approved, then and not till then was his Table Talk given to the world. The day had at length come in which Selden's own principles were in the ascendant, it was the triumph of the only cause for which he had ever cared personally to contend.

After the beginning of the civil war, there is not much in Selden's public career that calls for notice here. The references in the Table Talk to the public events of the time are few and indistinct. We have no word about Charles' trial and execution, or about Cromwell's rise and administration. It is hardly possible that these should not have been frequent matters of table talk, but we have no record of them in Milward's report. Has Milward avoided keeping a record of them, or has the Table Talk, prior to publication, been curtailed and bowdlerised in a political sense? Or has Selden kept carefully to his rule that wise men say nothing in dangerous times (Wisdom, 3), and that the wisest way for men in these times is to say nothing (Peace, 1)? If he did say anything, we have certainly no record of it. The chief subject to which he again and again refers is of a very different class. In 1643 he was appointed one of the learned pious members of the Westminster Assembly of Divines, and the Table Talk abounds with proofs of the kind of interest which he long continued to feel in his new work. The Assembly was formed of all parties in the Church and out of it. The prelatical party were included in it, but they studiously did not attend. The rest were Presbyterians with a moderate infusion of Independents and Erastians. Selden, it is certain, had no great love for bishops and clergy, but he did not regard them with the contemptuous dislike which he felt for the main body of their non-conformist opponents. The lofty claims and the ignorance and

b

intolerance of the Presbyterian section; the ranting of
the more ignorant Roundhead under the influence of
what he termed the Spirit, were even less to his mind
than the prelatical party had been.

In the Westminster Assembly of Divines it was with
the Presbyterians that he came chiefly into conflict.
They formed a clear majority, and as far as votes went,
contrived to carry things pretty well in their own way.
This, however, was the limit of their success. The
House of Commons refused to ratify their claims to a
free spiritual jurisdiction, or to acknowledge the divine
right by which they claimed to hold their ministry. In
debate they were no less unfortunate. Selden, by the
evidence of friends and of enemies, was one of the chief
thorns in their side. It was his way to lead them on to
argue, to amuse himself with their mistakes and contradictions, and to bring to bear his formidable battery
of learning against their favourite doctrinal strongholds.
His services in this sort were, as we might suppose,
very variously regarded. His friend and fellow divine,
Mr. Whitelock, a sound Erastian like himself, writes—

'Divers members of both houses, whereof I was one,
were members of the Assembly of Divines, and had
the same liberty with the Divines to sit and debate and
give their votes . . . . In which debates Mr. Selden spake
admirably, and confuted divers of them in their own
learning.

'And sometimes when they had cited a text of Scripture
to prove their assertion, he would tell them, *Perhaps in
your little pocket Bibles with gilt leaves* (which they would
often pull out and read) *the Translation may be thus, but
the* Greek *or the* Hebrew signifies thus and thus; and
so would totally silence them.' (Memorials, p. 71.)

Anthony à Wood, in his Athenae, quotes Aubrey to the
same effect : —

'He was one of the Assembly of Divines in those days, and was like a thorn in their sides, for he was able to run them all down with his Greeke and antiquities.'

Fuller, in his Church History, speaks less approvingly of the work, but bears testimony to the skill with which it was done. 'The Assembly,' he says, 'met with many difficulties, some complaining of Mr. Selden, that advantaged by his skill in antiquity, common law and the oriental tongues, he employed them rather to pose than profit, perplex than inform the members thereof in the fourteen queries he propounded. Whose intent was to humble the *jure divinoship* of Presbytery ... This great scholar, not overloving of any (and least of all these) clergymen, delighted himself in raising of scruples for the vexing of others; and some stick not to say that those who will not feed on the flesh of God's word, cast most bones to others to break their teeth therewith.' (Church History, Bk. XI. sec. ix. § 54.)

But when we pass from friends and neutrals to Selden's opponents in the Assembly, we find more ample proof than ever of his prominence and of the vigour of his destructive work. Poor Robert Baillie, a worthy Scotch Presbyterian, who had come up from Glasgow to join the Assembly of Divines, bringing with him the pure light of the Gospel as it was understood in those parts, found Selden terribly in his way in the Assembly and afterwards in Parliament. Baillie speaks sadly of 'Selden and others who will have no discipline at all in any Church *jure divino*, but settled only upon the free will and pleasure of the Parliament.' (Letters and Journals, ii. 31.)

He rises presently to a more vigorous form of denunciation, after proof given of the effectiveness of Selden's antagonism.

'The Erastian party in the Parliament is stronger than the

Independent, and is like to work us much woe. Selden is their head. If L'Empereur would beat down that man's arrogance as he very well can . . . . if he would confound him with Hebrew testimonies, it would lay Selden's vanity, who is very insolent for his oriental literature.' (Vol. ii. p. 107.) Whether this call on L'Empereur to the rescue was heard, I do not know. I have found no trace that it was in any part of Selden's writings. In Book I. of his De Synedriis Veterum Ebræorum, Selden quotes L'Empereur and praises him as 'doctissimus vir.' On one point he disagrees with him, but on a wholly different matter from those about which Baillie was in need of help. (See Works, i. 874.) The De Synedriis was published in 1650, two years after L'Empereur's death.

In dealing with the successive religious questions of his day, Selden's language is substantially the same. The Table Talk, it will be seen, relates to two wholly distinct periods,—to that of the attempted High Church movement under Laud's impulse and guidance, and to the counter movement when the Presbyterians were in power. The former of these was recognised by the leaders of the Oxford movement of 1833 as in the main identical with their own, since Laud's claims for the Church served to bring into prominence just those principles and beliefs which they themselves advocated, and which the Reformation had tended to obscure. Laud's failure is explained in the Table Talk. The promoters of the movement were in too great a hurry. They forced things on too suddenly, and in such a way as to give offence to those whom it would have been easy to conciliate by more gradual and more gentle methods. With the aims and purposes of the movement Selden had no sympathy, nor had he any with those of its more violent and fanatical opponents. He is thus in almost equal antagonism to each of the two parties which became dominant by turns. If he sometimes defends the bishops, it is not because he has any love for them, but because there must be some form of Church government, and there was no body more to his mind that could be put into the bishops' place. On their claim to rule *jure divino*, he speaks with great scorn, but he is no less scornful to those who think them so anti-Christian that they must be put away. In such matters as these, 'all is as the State likes.' From first to last Selden shows himself firm and consistent as an Erastian.

His own personal religion has been a matter of some controversy. 'Gentlemen,' he remarks, 'have ever been more temperate in their religion than the common people, as having more reason; the others running in a hurry.' Selden himself was no exception to the rule. Temperate he certainly was ; indifferent or lukewarm he would have been termed by the more zealous. Baxter, indeed, reports, on the authority of Sir M. Hale, that Selden was 'a re-solved serious Christian, an adversary to Hobbes,' and that the opposition between them was sometimes so sharp that Selden either departed from Hobbes or drove him out of the room. But these alleged contests do not prove much. Both parties to them were men of strong opinions and of somewhat overbearing tempers. If they quarrelled occasionally, as they very probably did, it is much more likely that their quarrels were about politics than about re-ligion. Religion, they both held, was a matter to be settled by the State, and as the State settled it, so it was to be. In politics they were less at one. Selden, as the upholder of a constitutional monarchy based on an assumed contract which both parties were alike bound to observe, could never have been brought to agree with Hobbes, the champion of a monarchy in which no misconduct on the monarch's part could give the subjects any right to resist. For proof, then, of Selden's religious faith we must look elsewhere. We shall not find it in Clarendon, who with all his praise of Selden's learning, humanity, courtesy, affability, and delight in doing good, is silent on the point of his religion. Nor will Usher help us with his very laudatory funeral sermon, in which he finds every excellence in Selden, but says nothing of his piety, because, as his hearers thought, he could find nothing which he could say with truth. The discussions about religion in the Table Talk are not, indeed, in the language of a theoretical sceptic. They show, beyond doubt, that Selden constantly professed a belief in revealed religion. But they are not at all what we should expect from a resolved serious Christian. They are rather in the language of one who takes religion under his wing, and finds it—like the virtue of humility—very good doctrine for other people. Their author will show respect to the established religion of his country, but he has no great care what form it takes, except as far as it is a powerful political engine which must not be suffered to fall into hands which will turn it to a mischievous use. D'Ewes, who knew Selden personally, took such offence at his seeming want of religion that he did not seek to be intimate with him.

His death-bed scene—he died in November 1654—has, as we might expect, been very variously reported. Lord Berkeley [1] tells us of the pious friends whom he summoned to be with him at the last, and of his own expressed trust in the promises of Holy Scripture as his best and only comfort at so anxious a time. On the other hand, Aubrey's account, as quoted in Wood's Athenae, is that—'When he was neer death, the minister (Mr. Johnson) was coming to him to assoile him ; Mr. Hobbes happened then to be there : sayd he, "What, will you that have wrote like a man, now dye like a woman?" So the minister was not let in.' But death-bed stories are pro-

---

[1] See Historical Applications, &c., written by a Person of Honour, p. 32, and Josiah Woodward's Fair Warnings to a Careless World, p. 129.

verbially 'common form.' They tell us more often what
the narrator wishes to believe, than what he has any
good authority for. We find accordingly that Selden's
editor and biographer, Archdeacon Wilkins, accepts and
records Lord Berkeley's story, and says nothing whatever about Aubrey's. (Works, vol. i, Vita Authoris,
p. xlv.)

Selden's vast and varied learning was recognised in
his own day by the general testimony of scholars in
England and on the Continent, and the fame of it still
survives. But this is all that can be said. As a writer,
he has never been popular, and is never likely to be. His
reputation, like that of Johnson, depends more upon what
has been written about him or has fallen from him in conversation, than upon any writings of his own. This is
due, in Selden's case, about equally to the matter and
to the manner of his works. The subjects which he
treats relate, some of them to the questions of his own
day, others to points of real permanent interest, but only
to the antiquarian reader, nor had he the art of popular-
ising what he wrote. Much of what he has written is in
Latin, and his Latin style, correct as it is, is strangely
rough and inelegant. Not seldom it presents an involved
series of parentheses within parentheses, until at length
the grammatical structure with which we start is put out of
sight and lost. When this difficulty has been overcome, and
when the reader has at last succeeded in evolving order
out of the confused and disorderly mass, the result often
is that he finds after all that he has gained nothing for
his pains. Selden's digressions are so frequent and so
perplexing as often to make it really doubtful what his
drift can possibly have been in his Latin or in his English
works. He draws at random on his vast stores, until the
thread of his argument is lost by his many and prolonged
and wholly irrelevant discursions, each of which gives

rise to fresh discursions, one subject calling up another, under no guide but the chance association of ideas in the very learned author's mind. His enormous erudition thus frequently proves to be a weight too heavy for him, an encumbrance rather than a help to clear methodical arrangement.

This fault does not attach to the Table Talk. Selden, under the stimulus of society, was a different man from what he was when he took pen in hand and set himself down to write out an exhaustive account of some subject which he had made his special study, and to treat incidentally every other subject that suggested itself by the way. In writing, a man may go on unchecked to his own satisfaction and to the impatience of his readers. In the to-and-fro toss of conversation he is under more effective restraint, and he becomes short and incisive in just the degree in which he is possessed of the conversational art. In this art Selden unquestionably excelled. We do not need Clarendon's testimony that he was the most clear discourser, and had the best faculty in making hard things . easy, and presenting them to the understanding of any man that hath been known. The Table Talk is evidence enough. It is as lively as his written works are dull, as attractive as they are many of them repelling. The miscellaneous collection varies in interest of course. Some of it has to do with matters of mere research; some with matters of grave consequence at the time, but of little or none now. Nor is it free from mistakes and contradictions, or from what its critic in the Acta Eruditorum calls φορτικὰ ἀκούσματα. In one passage, for example, it speaks slightingly of the learning of the bishops; in another it declares that there never was a more learned clergy, and that no one taxes them with ignorance. In the discourse on Preaching, it first condemns and then recommends preaching often in the same sense. In its defence

of duelling, in its explanation of the ass's head story
(Christians, 3) and of the Descent into Hell, it is hardly
ingenious, much less convincing. Its repeated assertions
that moral rules are of no force without a theological
sanction, display Selden possibly as a good theologian,
certainly as an unsound moralist. Some of its remarks on
the obligation of an oath are even more open to question.
The discourse on Oaths might almost be headed—the art
of perjury made easy. But on all these points it is Selden's
reporter with whom the chief fault must rest. It was his
business to discriminate between what was worth and
what was not worth giving to the world ; and not to write
down and publish everything said, it might be, at random
or in a perverse mood, and forgotten as soon as it was
said, or as soon as the thing under discussion had ceased
to be a question which Selden had approached as a con-
troversialist rather than as a judge. But when all deductions have been made, enough remains to bear out the
very high repute in which the Table Talk has stood. Its
critic in the Acta Eruditorum [1] wishes it included among
the 'multa ingenii monumenta quibus (Selden) aeternam
famam meruit.' Johnson singles it out as the best book
of its kind in existence, better than any of the much be-
praised French anas. Coleridge, as a poet, quarrels with
it, but he still finds more weighty bullion sense in it than
in the same number of pages of any uninspired writer.
This is substantially the verdict which the world of
letters has accepted and has endorsed. Johnson, one of
the vouchers for it, has been termed the wisest and the
wittiest of Englishmen. The Table Talk shows us, so to
say, the figure in every-day dress of one who might not
unfairly take rank as his competitor for one distinction.

---

[1] Supplementa, Tom. 1 : see viii. p. 424.

. *The References in the Notes are to the following Editions:*—

ROGER BACON. *Opus Majus.* Jebb's ed. 1733. folio.

BAILLIE. *Letters and Journals.* Edinburgh. 1775. 2 vols.

BINGHAM. *Christian Antiquities and other Works.* Clarendon Press. 1855. 10 vols.

CLARENDON. *History of the Rebellion.* Clarendon Press. 1807. 6 vols.; paged as 3 and so referred to.

CLARENDON. *Life.* Clarendon Press. 1827.

DUGDALE. *Monasticon.* By Caley, Ellis & Bandinel. 1830. 6 vols.

FIGUIER. *Histoire du Merveilleux.* Paris. 1860. 8vo.

GIBSON. *Codex.* 1761. 2 vols.

HARDWICK. *History of the Articles.* 1851.

LAUD'S WORKS. *Library of Anglo-Catholic Theology.* 1854.

NALSON. *Collections.* 1682. 2 vols.

NEAL. *History of the Puritans.* 1822. 5 vols.

PEARSON. *On the Creed.* Clarendon Press. 1816. 2 vols.

Preuves des libertez de l'Eglise Gallicane. 1639. 1 vol. folio.

PRYNNE. *Histrio-mastix.* 1633. small 4to.

RUSHWORTH. *Historical Collections.* 1721. 8 vols.

SELDEN. *Works.* Wilkins' ed. 1726. 6 vols., paged and referred to as 3. folio.

STOW. *Chronicle.* 1631.

Traitez des droits et libertez de l'Eglise Gallicane. 1639. 1 vol. folio.

WHITELOCK. *Memorials.* 1732. folio.

WILKINS. *Concilia.* 1737. 4 vols. folio.

WOOD. *Athenae Oxonienses.* Bliss's ed. 1817. 4 vols. (Selden's Life is given in vol. iii. p. 366 ff.)

THE DISCOURSE

OF

JOHN SELDEN, Esq.

OR

HIS SENSE OF VARIOUS MATTERS OF WEIGHT AND HIGH CONSEQUENCE

RELATING ESPECIALLY TO

RELIGION AND STATE

—◆—

Distingue tempora

TO THE HON^{BLE}

MR. JUSTICE HALE,

ONE OF THE JUDGES OF THE COMMON-PLEAS

AND TO THE MUCH HONOURED

EDWARD HEYWARD,

JOHN VAUGHAN,

AND

ROWLAND JEWKS, ESQ^{RS}

Most Worthy Gentlemen,

Were you not executors to that person, who (when he lived) 10
*was the glory of the nation, yet I am confident any thing of his
would find acceptance with you, and truly the sense and notion here
is wholly his, and most of the words. I had the opportunity to hear
his discourse twenty years together, and lest all those excellent
things that usually fell from him might be lost, some of them from
time to time I faithfully committed to writing, which here digested
into this method, I humbly present to your hands: you will quickly
perceive them to be his by the familiar illustrations wherewith they
are set off: in which way you know he was so happy, that (with
a marvellous delight to those that heard him) he would presently* 20
*convey the highest points of religion, and the most important
affairs of state to an ordinary apprehension.*

*In reading be pleased to distinguish times, and in your fancy
carry along with you the* when *and the* why *many of these things
were spoken; this will give them the more life, and the smarter
relish. 'Tis possible the entertainment you find in them may render
you the more inclinable to pardon the presumption of*

Your most obliged and
most humble servant

RICH. MILWARD.   30

l. 2. *Mr. Justice Hale,* ⎱ Milward speaks of these as Selden's executors.
l. 5. *Edward Heyward* ⎰
I have therefore given the names as they stand in Selden's will (see Works,
vol. i, Vita Authoris, p. 53), and as Milward may be assumed to have given
them.

B .

THE

DISCOURSE OF JOHN SELDEN

———‡———

I.

ABBEYS. PRIORIES.

THE unwillingness of the monks to part with their lands
will fall out to be just nothing, because they were yielded
up to the king by a supreme hand, viz*t*. a parliament. If
a king conquer another country, the people are loth to
lose their lands; yet no divine will deny but the king
may give them to whom he please. If a parliament make
a law concerning leather, or any other commodity, you
and I, for example, are parliament-men; perhaps in respect
to our own private interests we are against it, yet the 10

Explanation of signs.

H. Harleian MS. 1315.   H. 2. Harleian MS. 690.   S. Sloane MS. 2513.

Line 3. *they were yielded up to the king* &c.] The lands were taken from
the monks by two Acts of Parliament. The earlier, that of 27 Henry
VIII, cap. 28, gave the king the properties of the smaller houses, below
a clear annual value of £200. The next Act, that of 31 Henry VIII,
cap. 13, confirmed the surrenders which the Abbots or Priors of the
larger houses had in the meantime been threatened or cajoled into
making. Selden's remarks, here, may have been suggested by any
one of the numerous attacks made on church property in his own
day.

B 2

major part concludes it; we are then involved, and the law is good.

2. When the founders of abbeys laid a curse upon them that should take away those lands, I would fain know what power they had to curse me. 'Tis not the curses that come from the poor, or from anybody, that do me hurt because they come from them; but because I do something ill against them, that deserves God should curse me for it. On the other side, 'tis not a man's bless-
10 ing me, that makes me blessed; he only declares me to be so; and if I do well, I shall be blessed, whether any bless me or not.

3. At the time of dissolution, they were tender in taking from the abbots and priors their lands and their houses, till they surrendered them, as most of them did. Indeed the prior of St. John's, Sir William Weston[1], being a stout

[1] *William Weston*] Richard Weston MSS. and early editions; probably through confusion with the name of the High Treasurer in the early years of Charles' reign.

l. 3. *when the founders of abbeys* &c.] This may be an objection to one of the arguments which Selden had heard used by Dr. Hacket in defence of the sacredness of cathedral revenues. On May 12, 1641, there was a special session of the House of Commons to hear a dispute between Dr. Burgess, as assailant, and Dr. Hacket, as defender of these revenues; and Hacket, in the course of his speech, urged that 'these' (sc. the chapter revenues and lands) 'are dedicated to God; the founders appoint the uses, and curse any that alter it.' See Verney, Notes on the Long Parliament, p. 75–76.

l. 15. *Indeed the prior of St. John's* &c.] The priory of St. John of Jerusalem, the chief English seat of the Knights Hospitallers, was not touched by the Act of 31 Henry VIII, since the prior (as Selden implies) had not at that time surrendered; nor does it appear that he ever did surrender. The priory lands were taken away by a special Act passed in the next year. The prior died in May, 1540, on the day on which the suppression took effect. In Dugdale's Monasticon (vol. vi. 800–805) there is a long list of the lands and farms which had belonged to the priory. When the Knights Templars were suppressed, all their lands were given over to the Hospitallers; see (7 Edward II) a letter De Terris quondam Templariorum Hospitalariis liberandis. The grant was confirmed by 6, 7, and 12 Edward III, and some tenements

man, got into France, and stood out a whole year; at last
submitted, and the king took in that priory also, to which
the Temple belonged, and many other houses in England.
They did not then cry no abbots, no priors, as we do now
no bishops, no bishops.

4. Henry the 5th put away the friars aliens, and seized
to himself £100,000 a year; and therefore they were not
the protestants only that took away church lands.

5. In Queen Elizabeth's time, when all the abbeys were
pulled down, all good works defaced, then the preachers
must cry up justification by faith, not by good works.

II.

THIRTY-NINE ARTICLES.

THE nine and thirty articles are much another thing in
Latin, in which tongue they were made, than they are

in London, which had been wrongfully seized by Hugh Despencer,
were restored and secured to the Hospitallers. Dugdale, Monasticon,
vi. 809, 810.

l. 6. *the friars aliens*] These were religious orders, domiciled abroad,
and holding land in England. They were pecked at several times
before Henry Vth's reign. Edward I began in 1285; Edward III followed in 1337. In 1361 their lands were restored, but their revenues
were still occasionally taken away for a while. They were sequestered
during Richard II, and were finally expropriated in 2 Henry V.
Dugdale, Monasticon, vi. 985 ff. See also Prioratuum Alienigenorum
Catalogus, qui Leicestrensi Parliamento suppressi sunt. Anno Henrici
Quinti secundo. An. Dom. 1414. Dugdale, Monasticon, vi. 1652-53.

l. 13. *much another thing in Latin* &c.] See e.g. Article 9, in which
'quamvis renatis et credentibus nulla propter Christum est condem-
natio,' is rendered by, 'although there is no condemnation for them
that believe and are baptized.' In Article 33, 'pœnitentia' is rendered
'penance'—an error to which Selden seems to refer in the discourse
on 'Penance.' The right claimed in Article 37, 'Christianis licet *justa*
bella administrare,' is enlarged into 'it is lawful for Christian men to
serve in the wars.' The older version of 1552 had translated the same

translated into English.   They were made at three several
convocations, and confirmed by act of parliament six or
seven times after.   There is a secret concerning them:
of late, ministers have subscribed to all of them; but by
the act[1] of parliament that confirmed them, they ought
only to subscribe to those articles which contain matters of
faith, and the doctrine of the sacraments, as appears by the
first subscriptions.   But Bishop Bancroft, in the convocation held in King James's days, he began it; that ministers
10 should subscribe to three things, to the king's supremacy,
to the common prayer, and to the 39 articles: Many of
them do not contain matter of faith.   It is matter of faith
how the church should be governed?   Whether infants
should be baptized?   Whether we have any property in
our goods?

[1] *Act*, H. 2 and S.] Acts, H.

words by 'to serve in laweful warres.'   There are some other minor
inaccuracies.

l. 2.   *six or seven times after*] If this reading is to stand, the word
'times' must be taken in a special sense—parliamentary sessions or
terms.   So, perhaps, in 'Confession,' sec. 1, 'In time of Parliament,' i. e. when Parliament had met.   The Articles were confirmed
once only, viz[t]. in 1571, by 13 Elizabeth, chap. 12.

l. 5.   *by the act of parliament that confirmed them* &c.]   The Act orders
that every minister (except certain specified persons) is to declare his
assent, and subscribe to all the Articles of Religion which only concern
the confession of the true Christian faith and the doctrine of the
Sacraments.

The obligation on the clergy to subscribe to the whole of the
Articles was imposed at a Synod of the province of Canterbury, held
in 1604, under the presidency of Bancroft, then Bishop of London.   It
was then settled that no one was to be ordained who had not stated in
writing—Quod libro de religionis Articulis, in quos consensum est in
Synodo Londinensi an. MDLXII. omnino comprobat, et quod omnes et
singulos Articulos in eodem contentos, qui triginta novem citra ratifi-
cationem numerantur, verbo Dei consentaneos esse agnoscit (Wilkins,
Concilia, iv. 386).

III.

BAPTISM.

1. 'Twas a good way to persuade men to be christened, to tell them that they had a foulness about them, viz‡. original sin, that could not be washed away but by baptism.

2. The baptizing of children with us, doth only prepare a child, against he comes to be a man, to understand what Christianity means. In the church of Rome it has this effect, it frees children from hell. They say they go into *limbus infantum*. It succeeds circumcision, and we are sure the child understood nothing of that at eight days old. Why 10 then may not we as reasonably baptize a child at that age ? In England, of late years, I ever thought the priest baptized his own fingers rather than the child.

3. In the primitive times they had godfathers to see the children brought up in the christian religion, because many times, when the father was a christian, the mother was not ; and sometimes when the mother was a christian, the father was not ; and therefore they made choice of two or more that were christians, to see the children brought up in that faith. 20

l. 8. *it frees children from hell. They say they go* &c.] i. e. They say that unbaptized children go, &c. The *Limbus Infantum* was one of the divisions of hell. In the Church of Rome baptism is said to free children from this. See Canons, &c. of the Council of Trent, Session v. sec. 2, 3, 4. On the *limbus puerorum,* the place of eternal punishment for those *qui solo originali peccato gravantur,* and on the degree of punishment, the *mitissimam poenam* which they are alleged to suffer, see Aquinas, Summa Theolog. Supplementum 3^tiae partis. quaest. 69, art. 5 & 6. So, too, Moroni (Eccles. Dict. under title Limbo, Limbus) writes—Il secondo luogo, che chiamasi limbo o limbus puerorum, è quello in che vanno i bambini morti senza battesimo. Many various opinions are collected as to the nature and extent of their punishment. That it is to be eternal all the cited authorities agree. So, too, Dante writes of the occupants of the Limbo, or first circle of the Inferno, a vast crowd of infants, women, and men, there placed *perche non ebber battesmo,* and suffering only *duol senza martiri.* Inferno, Canto iv. 28–35.

IV.

BASTARD.

'TIS said, 23 Deuteron. 2, A bastard shall not enter into the congregation of the Lord, even to the tenth generation. *Non ingredietur ecclesiam Domini*, he shall not enter into the church. The meaning of the phrase is, he shall not marry a Jewish woman. But upon this ground, grossly mistaken, a bastard at this day in the church of Rome, without a dispensation, cannot take orders. The thing haply well enough, where 'tis so settled : but that 'tis[1] upon
10 a mistake (the place having no reference to the church) appears plainly by what follows at the 3 verse ; An Ammonite or Moabite shall not enter into the congregation of the Lord, even to the tenth generation. Now you know with the Jews an Ammonite or a Moabite could never be a priest ; because their priests were born so, not made.

[1] *But that tis*, S.] H. and H. 2, omit ' that.'

l. 5. *The meaning of the phrase is* &c.] Selden, in his De Successione in Pontificatum Ebraeorum, says that the sense which he gives here to the words is universally accepted among the Jews. Works, ii. p. 158.

l. 6. *But upon this ground*, &c.] That the rule in the Church of Rome was based on this text is stated, conjecturally, by Pope Gregory IX. In a letter addressed to the Archbishop of Canterbury on the appointment of a bastard to the see of Worcester, Gregory declares— Nos ergo cum fratribus nostris habito super hoc diligenti tractatu, relectis canonibus, quosdam invenimus qui non legitime genitos promoveri vetant ad officium pastorale, causam forte trahentes ex lege divina per quam spurii et manzeres usque in decimam generationem in ecclesiam Dei prohibentur intrare. The matter is then debated pro and con, and the Pope concludes that although, according to a canon of the Lateran Council, the appointment is irregular, yet he has a dispensing power. Decretales Gregorii IX, lib. i. tit. 6, cap. xx. Corpus Juris Canonici, vol. 2, pp. 61, 62 (ed. 2 by Friedberg, 1881).

So, too, Boniface VIII insists on the need of a dispensation, episcopal for the lesser orders, papal for the greater. Ibid. p. 977.

Aquinas cites the text as one among the arguments against the

V.

BIBLE, SCRIPTURE.

1. 'TIS a great question how we know Scripture to be
Scripture, whether by the Church, or by man's private
spirit. Let me ask you how I know anything? How I
know this carpet to be green? First, because somebody
told me it was green : that you call the church in your way.
And then after I have been told it is green, when I see that
colour again, 1 know it to be green, my own eyes tell me it
is green ; that you call the private spirit.

2. The English translation of the Bible, is the best trans- 10
lation in the world, and renders the sense of the original
best, taking in for the English translation the Bishops'
Bible as well as king James's. The translators [1] in king
James's time took an excellent way. That part of the
Bible was given to him who was most excellent in such a
tongue (as the Apocrypha to Andrew Downs) and then they
met together, and one read the translation, the rest holding
in their hands some Bible, either of the learned tongues, or
French, Spanish, Italian, &c. If they found any fault they
spoke ; if not, he read on.   20

---

[1] *Translators*, H. 2, corrected from 'translation'] 'translation,' H.

admission of bastards to orders. He concludes against their admission
without a dispensation, but on general grounds, and without further
reference to the text. Summa Theolog. Supplement, 3 part, quaest. 39,
art. 5.

l. 2. *'Tis a great question* &c.] This question is discussed very fully
in the course of the celebrated conference between Laud and the Jesuit
Fisher, the first complete account of which was published in 1639.
Laud handles the matter at greater length and with more unction than
Selden ; but for the most part substantially to the same effect. See
Laud's Works, vol. ii. p. 70 ff.

l. 10. *The English translation* &c.] For an account of the persons
employed in the translation, and of the rules which they were instructed to follow, see Wilkins, Concilia, iv. 432, and Fuller's Church
History, bk. x. sec. 3, § 1, with note *h* in Brewer's edition.

3. There is no book so translated as the Bible. For the purpose, if I translate a French book into English, I turn it into English phrase, not into French English. *Il fait froid*, I say, it is cold, not it makes cold ; but the Bible is translated into English words rather than into English phrase. The Hebraisms are kept, and the phrase of that language is kept: as for example, [He uncovered her shame] which is well enough, so long as scholars have to do with it ; but when it comes among the common people, lord, what gear do they make of it!

4. *Scrutamini scripturas.* These two words have undone the world. Because Christ spake it to his disciples, therefore we must all, men, women, and children, read and interpret the Scriptures.

5. Henry the 8th made a law, that all men might read the Scriptures, except servants ; but no women, except ladies and gentlewomen, who had leisure, and might ask somebody the meaning. The law was repealed in Edward the 6th days.

6. Laymen have best interpreted the hard places of the Bible, such as Joannes Picus, Scaliger, Grotius, Salmasius, Heinsius, &c.

7. If you ask, Which, of Erasmus, Beza, or Grotius, did best upon the New Testament? 'tis an idle question, for they did all well in their way. Erasmus broke down the first brick ; Beza added many things, and Grotius added much to him, in whom we have either something new, or

---

l. 1. *For the purpose*] i. e. for instance : for proof of what I say. A phrase used by Selden elsewhere. See 'Trade,' sec. 1, and— Eudoxus yet hath otherwise placed them ; as for the purpose, the spring equinox on the sixth day after the sun's entrance into Aries &c. Works, iii. 1415.

l. 10. *what gear*] i. e. what stuff.

l. 11. *Scrutamini*] Gk. ἐρευνᾶτε, probably the Present Indicative, and if so the words have been doubly misinterpreted.

l. 15. *Henry the 8th made a law*] This was 34 & 35 Henry VIII, ch. 1.

else something heightened that was said before ; and so 'twas necessary to have them all three.

8. The text serves only to guess by ; we must satisfy ourselves fully out of the authors that lived about those times.

9. In interpreting the scripture, many do, as if a man should see one have ten pounds, which he reckoned by 1, 2, 3, 4, 5, 6, 7, 8, 9, 10 ; meaning four was but four units, and five five units, &c., and that he had in all but ten pounds ; the other that sees him, takes not the figures 10 together as he doth, but picks here and there, and thereupon reports, that he has five pounds in one bag, and six pounds in another bag, and nine pounds in another bag, &c. when as in truth, he hath but ten pounds in all. So we pick out a text here and there to make it serve our turn ; whereas, if we took it all together, and considered what went before, and what followed after, we should find it meant no such matter.

10. Make no more allegories in scripture than needs must. The fathers were too frequent in them : they indeed, 20 before they fully understood the literal sense, looked out for an allegory. The folly whereof you may conceive thus ; here at the first sight appears to me in my window, a glass and a book, I take it for granted 'tis a glass and a book ; thereupon I go about to tell you what they signify ; afterwards, upon nearer view, they prove no such things ; one is a box made like a book, the other is a picture made like a glass. Where's now my allegory ?

11. When men meddle with the literal text, the question is, where they should stop ? In this case, a man must 30 venture his discretion, and do his best to satisfy himself and others in those places where he doubts. For although

---

l. 20. *The fathers were too frequent in them*] This is amply verified by the 120 closely printed pages of the Index de Allegoriis, in the second vol. of the Indices to Migne's Patrologiae Cursus Completus, p. 123 ff.

we call the Scripture the word of God (as it is) yet it was writ by a man, a mercenary man, whose copy either might be false, or he might make it false : for example, here were a thousand bibles printed in England with the text thus, [Thou shalt commit adultery] the word *not* left out. Might not this text be mended ?

12. The scripture may have more senses besides the literal, because God understands all things at once ; but a man's writing has but one true sense, which is that which 10 the author meant when he writ it.

13. When you meet with several readings of the text, take heed you admit nothing against the tenets of your church ; but do as if you were going over a bridge, be sure and hold fast by the rail, and then you may dance here and there as you please ; be sure you keep to. what is settled, and then you may flourish upon your various lections.

14. The Apocrypha is bound with the Bibles of all churches that have been hitherto. Why should we leave it out ? The church of Rome has her Apocrypha, viz[t]. 20 Susanna, and Bel and the Dragon, which she does not

l. 4. *here were a thousand Bibles* &c.] Mr. Barker, the printer. There is a cause begunne against him for false printing of the Bible in divers places of it, in the edition of 1631, viz[t] in the 20 of Exod[us] 'Thou shalt committ adultery'; and in the fifte of Deut[eronomy] 'The Lord hath shewed us his glory, and his great asse'; and for divers other faults. High Commission Cases, pp. 296 and 304 (Camden Society).

Barker was not the only sufferer. Laud's account is that—among them (i. e. the printers) their negligence was such as that there were found above a thousand faults in two editions of the Bible and Common Prayer-Book. And one, which caused this search, was that in Exod. xx. where they had shamefully printed, Thou shalt commit adultery. For this, the masters of the printing house were called into the High Commission, and censured, as they well deserved it . . . . And Hunsford, being hit in his credit, purse, and friends, by that censure for so gross an abuse of the Church and religion, labours to fasten his fangs upon me. History of the Troubles and Trial of Abp. Laud, Laud's Works, iv. 165 and 195.

This edition was known as ' the wicked Bible.'

l. 20. *Susanna, and Bel and the Dragon*] This is not so. Susannah

esteem equally with the rest of those books that we call
Apocrypha.

VI.

BISHOPS BEFORE THE PARLIAMENT.

1. A BISHOP, as a bishop, had never any ecclesiastical
jurisdiction : for as soon as he was *electus confirmatus*, that
is, after the three proclamations in Bow-church, he might
exercise jurisdiction, before he was consecrated ; but till
then [1] he was no bishop, neither could he give orders. Besides, suffragans were bishops, and they never claimed any
jurisdiction.   10

[1] *But till then*, H. 2, corrected] not till then, H.

and Bel and the Dragon are canonical in the Church of Rome.   They
are not specially named in the Decree of the Council of Trent, settling
the Canon of Scripture, because they are printed in the Vulgate as part
of the book of Daniel, and come, therefore, under the general rule that
the books named as canonical are to be received entire, with all their
parts, as they are contained in the old Latin Vulgate.   The only books
of the Apocrypha not received as canonical are the 3rd and 4th Books
of Esdras (printed in the English Apocrypha as Esdras 1 & 2) and the
Prayer of Manasseh.   See Canons and Decrees of the Council of
Trent, Session iv.

Accordingly, in the Douay version, the History of Susannah and
Bel and the Dragon stand in their appointed place as parts of the
canonical book of Daniel.

l. 4.   *A bishop as a bishop* &c.]   Selden discusses this very fully in
his De Synedriis veterum Ebraeorum, lib. I, ch. 13. vol. i. p. 1066.

l. 6.   *three proclamations*]   These were and are part of the ceremony
of confirmation.   Strype in his life of Archbishop Parker, bk. ii. ch. 1,
gives an exact account of the whole process in Parker's case, as it
was performed in the church of St. Mary de Arcubus [i. e. Mary le
Bow in Cheapside] . . .   The consecration—until which he 'was no
bishop, neither could he give orders'—came eight days afterwards.

l. 9.   *suffragans*]   These are expressly said to have 'no authority or
jurisdiction beyond that expressed in their licenses by a bishop or
archbishop to whom they are suffragans by commission under seal.'
26 Henry VIII, ch. 14, sec. 6.

2. Anciently the noblemen lay within the city for safety and security. The bishops' houses were by the water side, because they were held sacred persons, which nobody would hurt.

3. There was some sense for *commendams* at first ; when there was a living void, and never a clerk to serve it, the bishops were to keep it till they found a fit man ; but now 'tis a trick for the bishop to keep it to himself.

4. For a bishop to preach 'tis to do other folks' office. 10 As if the steward of the house should execute the porter's or the cook's place ; 'tis his business to see that they and all others about the house perform their duties.

5. That which is thought to have done the bishops hurt,

l. 5. *commendams*] It was one of Archbishop Laud's projects 'to annex for ever some settled commendams, and those, if it may be, sine curâ, to all the small bishoprics.' Laud's Works, vol. iii. p. 254.

That he had done this was one of the charges brought against him at his trial. In his history of his trial, he explains and defends his act, but he adds in the course of his remarks about it—' I considered that the commendams taken at large and far distant, caused a great dislike and murmur among many men. That they were in some cases *materia odiosa* and justly complained of.' Works, vol. iv. p. 177.

For further proof of the abuse of which Selden speaks, see Sir Ralph Verney's Notes of Proceedings in the Long Parliament, p. 14, giving the heads of a remonstrance of some of the clergy, referring *inter alia* to commendams. The remonstrance says, in Article 16, ' Bishops hold commendams and never come at them. As Mainwaring, Bishop of St. Davids, and the Bishop of Chester hold two of £1100 per annum.'

l. 9. *For a bishop to preach* &c.] That bishops did not preach is among the charges made against them by Nathaniel Fiennes (Feb. 1640). Nalson, Collections, i. 758.

See, too, Sir Benjamin Rudyard's speech on Sir E. Deering's Bill for the abolishing of bishops, &c. (May, 1641). Some of ours, as soon as they are bishops, *adepto fine, cessat motus*, they will preach no longer, their office is to govern. But in my opinion they govern worse than they preach, though they preach not at all, for we see to what a pass their government hath brought us. Nalson, Collections, ii. 249.

l. 13. *That which is thought* &c.] Clarendon, after speaking of the slovenly state into which many churches had fallen during Archbishop Abbot's time, and of the irregular way in which the services had in

is their going about to bring men to a blind obedience, imposing things upon them [though perhaps small and well
enough] without preparing them, and insinuating into their
reasons and fancies. Every man loves to know his commander. I wear those gloves, but perhaps if an alderman
should command me, I should think much to do it. What
has he to do with me? Or if he has, peradventure I do
not know it. This jumping upon things at first dash will
destroy all. To keep up friendship there must be little
addresses and applications; whereas bluntness spoils it 10
quickly. To keep up the hierarchy, there must be appl -
cations made to men, they must be brought on by little and
little; so in the primitive times the power was gained, and
so it must be continued. Scaliger said of Erasmus; *si*
minor esse voluerit, major fuisset; so we may say of the
bishops, *si minores esse voluerint, majores fuissent.*

many places been performed, adds—'This profane liberty and ur-
cleanliness the Archbishop [i. e. Laud] resolved to reform with all
expedition, requiring the other bishops to concur with him in so pious
a work.' He adds, presently, that—'The Archbishop prosecuted this
affair more passionately than was fit for the season; and had prejudice against those who, out of fear or foresight, or not understanding
the thing, had not the same warmth to promote it. The bishops who
had been preferred by his favour, or who hoped to be so, were at
least as solicitous to bring it to pass in their respective dioceses; and
some of them with more passion and less circumspection than they
had his example for, or than he approved; prosecuting those who
opposed them very fiercely, and sometimes unwarrantably, which was
kept in remembrance.' Clarendon, Hist. vol. i. 148 ff.

l. 9. *little applications*] i. e. (as explained at length by Bacon in the
Adv. of Learning)—'the observing carefully a man's manners and
customs, with the intention to understand him sufficiently whereby
not to give him offence.' Lord Bacon's Works (Ellis and Spedding),
vol. iii. 279.

l. 14. *Scaliger said* &c.] The nearest I can find to this is a passage in
J. J. Scaliger's Table Talk. Erasmus perspicacissimo vir ingenio, se
ipso haud dubie futurus major (quod scribit Paulus Jovius) si Latinae
linguae conditores imitari, quam petulanti linguae indulgere maluisset.
Prima Scaligerana, sub voce Erasmus.

l. 15. *voluerit,*] *voluit* MSS. and early printed editions.

6. The bishops were too hasty; else with a discreet slowness they might have had what they aimed at. The old story of the fellow that told the gentleman he might get to such a place if he did not ride too fast, would have fitted their turn.

7. For a bishop to cite an old canon to strengthen his new articles, is as if a lawyer should plead an old statute that has been repealed God knows how long.

VII.

BISHOPS IN THE PARLIAMENT.

10   1. BISHOPS have the same right to sit in Parliament as the best of earls and barons; that is, those that were made

l. 6. *For a bishop to cite* &c.] This was done in the Constitutions and Canons Ecclesiastical, put out in 1640 by the Synods of the two Provinces. See Canon v. 'Against Sectaries' and Canon ix on the summary or collection of visitatory articles which the Synod had caused to be made out of the rubric and the canons and warrantable rules of the Church. Wilkins, Concilia, iv. 548 and 550.

l. 10. *Bishops have the same right* &c.] The various objections, here stated and answered, to the right of bishops to sit in Parliament, to the nature of their seat by office and not by blood, and to the policy of allowing them to meddle with temporal affairs, were raised from time to time in the long series of discussions which led finally to the abolition of their right and then of their office.

See, especially, the reasons offered by the Commons in reply to the reasons offered by the Lords in favour of the bishops, June, 1641. They cover most of the points raised in this chapter of the Table Talk.

The Commons do conceive that bishops ought not to have votes in Parliament. First, because it is a very great hindrance to the exercise of their ministerial function.

(2) Because they do vow and undertake at their ordination, when they enter into Holy Orders, that they will give themselves wholly to that vocation.

(5) Because they are but for their lives, and therefore are not fit to have legislative power over the honours, inheritances, persons, and liberties of others.

(6) Because of bishops' dependency and expectation of translation to places of greater profit. Nalson, Collections, ii. 260.

by writ. If you ask one of them [Arundel, Oxford, North-umberland] why they sit in the house? they can only say, their father sat there before them [1], and their grandfather before him, &c.   And so says the bishop: he that was a bishop of this place before me, sat in the house, and he that was a bishop before him, &c.   Indeed your later earls and barons have it expressed in their patents, that they shall be called to the parliament.

Objection. But the lords sit there by blood, the bishops not.   .   10

Answer. 'Tis true, they sit not there both the same way, yet that takes not away the bishop's right.   If I am a parson of a parish, I have as much right to my glebe and tithes, as you have to your land, that your ancestors have had in that parish 800 years.

2. The bishops were not barons, because they had

---

[1] *Before them*, H. 2] so originally in H. 'him' is written over 'them.'

l. 16. *The bishops were not barons* &c.] What Selden here denies was among the statements made by Mr. Bagshaw, Reader of the Middle Temple, in his speech in Hall (1639) on the thesis Whether it be a good Act of Parliament that is made without the assent of the Lords Spiritual. He argues that it is good, because *inter alia* 'they do not sit in Parliament as bishops, but by reason of the baronies annexed to their bishopricks, which was done 5 W. I, and all of them have baronies . except the Bishop of Man, and he is not called to Parliament.' White-lock, Memorials, p. 33.

Selden explains his point more fully in his Titles of Honour, part ii. ch. 5, vol. iii. pp. 659, 724, 727. He shows that in the Saxon times the lay claim to be included in the Witenagemot was the holding of land of the king in chief by knight's service. Those who so held were, after the Normans, parliamentary barons, and their tainlands only were the parliamentary baronies. But in Saxon times, the bishops did not hold by this tenure, yet they were none the less summoned regularly to the Witenagemot, and had voice and place as bishops. And thus their freedom from that tenure . . . . continued it seems till the fourth year of King William I, when he made the bishopricks and abbeys subject to knight's service in chief, by creation of new tenures, and so first turned their possessions into baronies, and thereby made them barons of the kingdom by tenure.

baronies annexed to their bishoprics (for few of them had so, unless the old ones, Canterbury, Winchester, Durham, &c. the new erected we are sure had none, as Gloucester, Peterborough, &c. Besides, few of the temporal lords had any baronies). But they are barons, because they are called by writ to the parliament, and bishops were in the parliament ever since there is any mention or sign of a parliament in England.

3. Bishops may be judged by the peers, though in time of popery it never happened, because they pretended they were not obnoxious to a secular court; but their way was to cry, *Ego sum frater domini papæ*, I am a brother to my lord the pope, and therefore take not myself to be judged by you. In this case they impannelled a Middlesex jury, and dispatched the business.

4. Whether may bishops be present in case of blood?

l. 3. *as Gloucester, Peterborough* &c.] These were among the six bishoprics founded by Henry VIII out of part of the spoils of the monasteries. On the nature of their endowment see the king's grant to the bishopric of Gloucester: 'Damus .... habenda et tenenda omnia et singula praedicta, Aulas, Cubicula . . . . domos aedificia et caetera omnia et singula praemissa praefato episcopo Gloucestriae et successoribus suis imperpetuum, tenenda de nobis haeredibus et successoribus nostris in puram et perpetuam eleemosinam.' Rymer, Foedera, xiv. 727 (1712 fol.).

'So, too, in the case of Peterborough, the king (1542) grants to the bishop and his successors, various manors and rents (valued at £368 11s. 6d.), *in puram et perpetuam eleemosynam*, and subject to deductions only for tenths and first-fruits.' Willis, Survey of Cathedrals, iii. 493 (London, 1742, 3 vols.).

l. 9. *Bishops may be judged* &c.] Selden, in his treatise on the privileges of the baronage, lays it down as a rule of the common law that bishops, although unquestionably peers of the realm, were to be tried by common juries and were in fact so tried; no regard being paid to their claim as churchmen to be free from lay jurisdiction. He gives several instances in which this claim was made and disallowed, and the trial had by a common jury. Works, iii. 1538 ff.

l. 16. *Whether may bishops be present* &c.] This question became prominent and was hotly disputed at the trial of the Earl of Strafford.

Answer. That they had a right to give votes, appears by this; always when they did go out, they left a proxy; and in the time of the abbots, one man had 10, 20, or 30 voices. In Richard the 2d's time there was a protestation against the canons, by which they were forbidden to be present in case of blood. The statute of the 25th of Henry the 8th may go a great way in this business. The clergy were forbidden to use or cite any canon, &c. but in the later end of the statute, there was a clause, that such canons as were in usage in this kingdom, should be in force till the thirty- ᵗᵒ two commissioners appointed should make others; provided they were not contrary to the king's supremacy. Now the question will be, whether these canons for blood were in use in this kingdom or no? The contrary whereof may appear by many precedents in Richard 3 and Henry 7 and the beginning of Henry 8 [1] in which time there were more attainted than since, or scarce before. The canons of irregularity for blood were never received in England, but upon pleasure. If a lay lord was attainted, the bishops

[1] *Richard, Henry, Henry,* H. 2] initials only in H.

The bishops were denied all meddling even in the commission of preparatory examinations concerning the Earl of Strafford, as *causa sanguinis,* and they as men of mercy, not to deal in the condemnation of any person. Fuller, Church History, bk. xi. sec. 9, § 10.

That bishops were forbidden by the canons to pronounce sentence of condemnation at trials on a capital charge, is clear. See e.g. Wilkins, Concilia, vol. i. 112, 365 and 474.

On the authority of the canons, as law, it is laid down by 25 Henry VIII, chap. 19, that the canons are not to be pleaded or used if contrary to the king's prerogative or to the customs, laws and statutes of the kingdom—canons, not thus contrary, to be in force, as Selden states.

In the case referred to in Richard II's time, the exclusion of the bishops was a concession granted to them at their own request. The whole subject is discussed exhaustively in the opinion delivered by the Bishop of Lincoln (Williams) as to the right of the bishops to be present at Strafford's trial. Hacket, Life of Williams, part ii. p. 153 ff.

assented to his condemning, and were always present at the
passing of the bill of attainder : but if a spiritual lord, they
went out, as if they cared not whose head was cut off,
so none of their own. In those days the bishops, being
of great houses, were often entangled with the lords in
matters of treason ; but when d'ye hear of a bishop-
traitor now ?

5. You would not have bishops meddle with temporal
affairs. Think who you are that say it. If a Papist, they
10 do in your church ; if an English Protestant, they do among
you ; if a Presbyterian, where you have no bishops, you
mean your Presbyterian lay elders should meddle with
temporal affairs as well as spiritual. Besides, all jurisdiction is temporal, and in no church but they have some
jurisdiction or other. The question then will be reduced
to *magis* and *minus ;* they meddle more in one church than
in another.

l. 8. *You would not have bishops meddle with temporal affairs,* &c.]
So in 1641, a bill was introduced for the second time to forbid bishops
having votes in Parliament or holding any temporal office, 'the
greatest argument being that their intermeddling with temporal
affairs was inconsistent with, and destructive to, the exercise of their
spiritual function.' Clarendon, i. 470.

The same argument was used by Lord Say and Sele (June 1641),
who based it on the Scriptural rule that—' No man that warreth, en-
tangleth himself with the affairs of the world.' Nalson, Collections,
ii. 268.

Early in 1641, a committee of the House of Commons, appointed to
consider a remonstrance of some ministers, and the London petition
for the better government of the Church, voted, *inter alia,* that Article 6,
complaining that bishops were encumbered with temporal power and
state affairs, was material and fit to be considered by the House. Sir
R. Verney's Notes of Proceedings in the Long Parliament, pp. 4-14.

Most of the questions treated in the Table Talk, were raised in the
course of this inquiry.

See, too,—' It is not possible for one man to discharge two functions,
whereof either is sufficient to employ the whole man, especially that
of the ministry, so great that they ought not to entangle themselves
with the affairs of this world.' Speech of Nathaniel Fiennes, Feb.
1640-41. Nalson, Collections, i. 757.

6. *Objection.* Bishops give not their votes by blood in parliament, but by an office annexed to them ; which being taken away, they cease to vote; therefore there is not the same reason for them as for temporal lords.

Answer. We do not pretend they have that power the same way, but they have a right ; he that has an office in Westminster-hall for his life, the office is as much his, as his land is his that has land by inheritance.

7. Whether had the inferior clergy ever anything to do in the parliament ?   10

Answer. No, no otherwise than thus ; there were certain of the clergy that did use to assemble near the parliament, with whom the bishops, upon occasion, might consult ; (but there were none of the convocation, as it was afterwards settled, vizt. the dean, the archdeacon, one for the

Instances to the same effect will be found *passim* in the debates and speeches of the time.

l. 1. *Bishops give not their votes by blood* &c.] This was one of the stock arguments against the bishops. See, e.g.

'If they may remove bishops, they may as well next time remove barons and earls.

'*Answer.* The reason is not the same, the one sitting by an honour invested in their blood and hereditary, which though it be in the king to grant alone yet being once granted he cannot take away. The other sitting by a barony depending upon an office, which may be taken away; for if they be deprived of their office they sit not.' Speech of Lord Say and Sele, June, 1641. Nalson, Collections, ii. 268.

l. 14. *the convocation as it was afterwards settled*] In or about 1283, a canon was framed which may be regarded as settling historically the representation of the clergy in the convocation of the province of Canterbury. The rule laid down is ' ut in proximâ congregatione . . . . praeter personas episcoporum et procuratores absentium, veniant duo aut unus a clero episcopatuum singulorum.' The Archbishop's full writ, of which the canon is a copy, summons the attendance of bishops, abbots, priors, deans, and archdeacons throughout the province of Canterbury. Also ' de qualibet diocesi duo procuratores nomine cleri, et de singulis capitulis ecclesiarum cathedralium et collegiatarum singuli procuratores.' Stubbs, Documents illustrative of English History, pp. 452 and 456.

chapter, two for the diocese) but it happened by continu-
ance of time (to save charges and trouble), their voices and
the consent of the whole clergy were involved in the
bishops, and at this day the bishops' writs run, to bring all
these to the parliament, but the bishops themselves stand
for all.

8. Bishops were formerly of these two conditions; either
men bred canonists and civilians, sent up and down am-
bassadors to Rome and other parts, and so by their merit
10 came to that greatness; or else great noblemen's sons, or
brothers, or nephews, and so born to govern the state.
Now they are of a low condition, their education nothing
of that way; he gets a living, and then a greater living,
and then a greater than that, and so comes to govern.

9. Bishops are now unfit to govern, because of their
learning: they are bred up in another law: they run to the
text for something done amongst the Jews, that nothing
concerns England. 'Tis just as if a man would have a
kettle, and he would not go to our braziers to have it
20 made, as they make kettles; but he would have it made as
Hiram made his brass-work, who wrought in Solomon's
temple.

10. To take away bishops' votes, is but the beginning to

l. 23. *To take away bishops' votes* &c.] This was borne out by the
event. 'In 1646, by ordinance of Parliament, the name, title, style,
and dignity of archbishop and bishop were wholly taken away, from
and after September 5, and all and every person was disabled to hold
the place, function, or stile of archbishop or bishop.' Rushworth,
Hist. Collections, vol. vi. 373.

That they will 'always go for the king, as he will have them' was,
in effect, one of the arguments used against them in 1641. 'The Commons do conceive that bishops ought not to have votes in Parliament,
because . . . . of bishops' dependency and expectation of translation
to places of greater profit.' Nalson, Collections, ii. 261.

So, too, Lord Say and Sele, in the course of a debate in the same
year, urges that bishops 'have such an absolute dependency upon
the king that they sit not here as freemen . . . . For their
fears, they cannot lay them down, since their places and seats in

take them away; for then they can be of no longer use to
the king or state.   'Tis but like the little wimble, to let in
the greater auger.

Objection. But they are but for their life, and that makes
them always go for the king as he will have them.

Answer. This is against a double charity; for you must
always suppose a bad king and bad bishops. Then
again, whether will a man be sooner content, himself
should be made a slave, or his son after him? [when we
talk of our children we mean ourselves]. Besides, they 10
that have posterity are more obliged to the king than they
that are only for themselves, in all the reason in the
world.

11. How shall the clergy be in the parliament, if the
bishops be taken away?

Answer. By the laity; because the bishops, in whom the
rest of the clergy are included, assent to the taking away
their own votes, by being involved in the major part of the
house.   This follows naturally.

12.   The bishops being put out of the house, whom will 20
they lay the fault upon now? When the dog is beat out
of the room where will they lay the stink?

VIII.

BISHOPS OUT OF THE PARLIAMENT.

1. In the beginning, bishops and presbyters were alike;
like your gentleman in the country, whereof one is made

Parliament are not invested in them by blood, and so hereditary, but
by annexation of a barony to their office; and depending upon that
office and thereby of their places, at the king's pleasure they . . . .
sit . . . . but at will and pleasure.' Nalson, Collections, ii. 268.

l. 20. *The bishops being put out of the house &c.*]   This was done in
1642, when the king was at length induced to give his consent to the
Bill excluding them. Clarendon, i. 668.

l. 24. *In the beginning, bishops and presbyters &c.*]   The question

deputy-lieutenant, another justice of peace; so one is made a bishop, another a dean: And that kind of government by archbishops and bishops no doubt came in, in imitation of the temporal government, no *jure divino*. In time of the Roman empire, where they had a legatus, there they placed an archbishop; where they had a rector, there a bishop; that every one might be instructed in Christianity, which now they had received into the empire.

2. They that speak ingenuously[1] of bishops and presby-

---

[1] *Ingenuously*] MSS. ingeniously. The two words are confused in several places.

raised in the first three sections as to the identity of bishops and presbyters was one of the stock subjects of dispute in Selden's day. After the triumph of the Presbyterian party, it was answered by the legislature in the affirmative :—

'Whereas the word Presbyter, that is to say Elder, and the word Bishop, do in the Scripture intend and signify one and the same function, although the title of Bishop hath been by corrupt custom appropriated to one, &c.

'Nov. 8, 1645.'

Ordinance of Lords and Commons. Rushworth, Collections, vi. 212.

Selden's view agrees with, and was not improbably based upon, that of Archbishop Usher, to whom he was in the habit of referring, and for whose judgment he had a great and merited respect. Usher, his biographer Parr writes, was charged 'That he ever declared his opinion to be, that. Episcopus et Presbyter gradu tantum differunt non ordine—which opinion,' says Parr, 'I cannot deny to have been my Lord Primate's since I find the same written almost verbatim with his own hand, dated Nov. 26, 1655. And that the Lord Primate was always of this opinion I find by another note of his own hand, written in another book many years before this.' Parr adds some limitations and cautions; but subject to these, confirms the opinion from other writers. 'So that you see,' he adds, 'that as learned men, and as stout asserters of episcopacy as any the Church of England hath had, have been of the Lord Primate's judgment in this matter, though without any design to lessen the order of bishops or to take away their use in the Church.'—Life of Usher, Appendix, pp. 5–7.

l. 4. *In time of the Roman Empire* &c.] Bingham, Christian Antiquities, bk. ix. goes minutely into this, and shows in detail that the Church, in setting up metropolitan, patriarchal, and episcopal sees, commonly took the model from the civil divisions of the state.

ters say, that a bishop is a greater presbyter, and during the time of his being bishop, above a presbyter: as the president of the college of physicians, is above the rest, yet he himself no more than a doctor of physic.

3. The word [*bishop*] and [*presbyter*] are promiscuously used; that is confessed by all: and though the word *bishop* be in Timothy and Titus, yet that will not prove the bishops ought to have a jurisdiction over the presbyters, though Timothy or Titus had by the order that was given them. Somebody must take care of the rest: and that jurisdiction was but to excommunicate; and that was but to tell them they should come no more into their company. Or grant they did make canons one for another, before they came to be in the state: does it follow they must do so when the state has received them into it? What if Timothy had power in Ephesus, and Titus in Crete over the presbyters? Does it follow therefore our bishops must have the same in England? Must we be governed like Ephesus or Crete?

4. However some of the bishops pretend to be *jure divino*, yet the practice of the kingdom has ever been otherwise; for whatsoever bishops do otherwise than the

l. 20. *However some of the bishops pretend* &c.] This was and has ever been the claim of the High Church party. We find it e. g. asserted by Andrewes, and approved by Laud, and in express terms asserted by Laud himself. See 'Die Mercurii, ostendi rationes regi cur chartae Episcopi Winton. defuncti, de episcopis quod sint jure divino, praelo tradendae sint, &c.' Laud's Diary, Jan. 17, 1626; Works, iii. 199.

'We maintain that our calling of bishops is *jure divino*, by divine right... This I will say and abide by it, that the calling of bishops is *jure divino*, by divine right, though not all adjuncts to their calling.' Speech at the censure of Bastwick, Burton, and Prynne; Works, vi. pt. i. p. 43.

Selden's argument to the contrary seems to be based on the legal control exercised over bishops in the discharge of their functions, most notably in the matter of excommunications. See 'Excommunication.'

law permits, Westminster-hall can controul, or send them to absolve, &c.

5. He that goes about to prove bishops to be *jure divino*, does as a man that, having a sword, shall strike it against an anvil; if he strike it awhile there, he may peradventure loosen it, though it be never so well riveted; it will serve to cut flesh or strike another sword, but not against an anvil.

6. If you should say, you held your land by Moses' or
10 God's law, and would try it by that, you may perhaps lose; but by the law of the kingdom you are sure of it. So may the bishops by this plea of *jure divino* lose all. The pope had as good a title by the law of England as could be had, had he not left that, and claimed by power from God.

7. There is no government enjoined by example, but by precept: it does not follow we must have bishops still, because we have had them so long. They are equally mad who say bishops are so *jure divino* that they must be
20 continued; and they who say, they are so anti-christian that they must be put away. All is as the state likes.

8. To have no ministers but presbyters, 'tis as if in the temporal state, they should have no officers but constables, and justices of peace which are but greater constables. Bishops do best stand with monarchy; that as amongst the laity, you have dukes, lord-lieutenants, judges, &c. to send down the king's pleasure to his subjects; so you have bishops to govern the inferior clergy: these upon occasion may address themselves to the king, otherwise every
30 parson of the parish must come and run up to the court.

9. The protestants have no bishops in France, because

l. 31. *The protestants have* &c.] Probably suggested by Usher, who is quoted by his biographer Parr, as excusing or palliating the absence of bishops in the Churches of France on the ground that they are 'living under a popish power and cannot do what they would.' Parr's Life, Appendix, pp. 5 and 6.

they live in a catholic country, and they will not have
catholic bishops; therefore they must govern themselves
as well as they may.

10. What is that to the purpose, to what end bishops'
lands were given to them at first? We must look to the
law and custom of the place. What is that to any
temporal lord's estate, how lands were first divided, cr
how in William the Conqueror's days? And if men at
first are juggled out of their estates, yet they are rightly
their successors. If my father cheat a man, and he con- 10
sents to it, the inheritance is rightly mine.

11. If there be no bishops, there must be something else
which has the power of bishops, though it be in many;
and then had you not as good keep them? If you will
have no half-crowns, but only single pence, yet 30 single
pence are a half-crown; and then had you not as good keep
both? But the bishops have done ill. 'Twas the men,
not the function. As if you should say, you would have
no more half-crowns, because they were stolen, when the
truth is they were not stolen because they were half- 20
crowns, but because they were money, and light in a
thief's hands.

12. They that would pull down the bishops and erect a
new way of government, do as he that pulls down an old
house, and builds another of another fashion. There's a
great deal ado, and a great deal of trouble; the old rubbish
must be carried away, and new materials must be brought;
workmen must be provided; and perhaps the old one
would have served as well.

13. If the prelatical and presbyterian party should dis- 30
pute, who should be judge? Indeed in the beginning of
queen Elizabeth there was such a difference between the

---

l. 31.   *Indeed in the beginning of queen Elizabeth &c.*] Strype, in the
Annals of the Reformation, vol. i. chap. 5, gives a lengthy account
of this ' conference between some popish bishops and other learned

protestants and papists, and Sir Nicholas Bacon, lord chancellor, was appointed to be judge; but the conclusion was, the stronger party carried it.   For so religion was brought into kingdoms, so it has been continued, and so it may be cast out, when the state pleases.

14. 'Twill be a great discouragement to scholars, that bishops should be put down.   For now the father can say to the son, and the tutor to the pupil, Study hard, and you shall have *vocem et sedem in parliamento;* then it must be, Study hard, and you shall have an £100 a year if you please your parish.

Objection. But they that enter into the ministry for preferment, are like Judas that looked after the bag.

Answer. It may be so, if they turn scholars at Judas his age.   But what arguments will you use to persuade them to follow their books, when they are young?

men of that communion, and certain protestant divines, held in the month of March, 1559, by order of the Queen's privy council, to be performed in their presence, eight on one side and eight on the other.' The Queen orders it to be conducted in writing and the papists to begin.   The first day passed off quietly.   On the second day, difficulties were raised as to the course of the proceedings and the papists refused to go on, as it had been arranged that they should.   The conference thereupon broke up, after some ominous words from the Lord Keeper, Sir Nicholas Bacon.   ' For that ye would not that we should hear you, perhaps you may shortly hear of us.'   And so they did, for, as a punishment for their contempt, the Bishops of Winchester and Lincoln were committed to the Tower, and the others, except the Abbot of Westminster, were bound to make their personal appearance before the Council and not to depart the cities of London and Westminster until ordered.   They were afterwards compelled to dance attendance every day at the Council from April 5 to May 12, until at length their fines for contempt were settled; 'and so they were discharged, recognizances for their good abearing being first taken of them.'

In the Editor's Preface to the second volume of Laud's Works, numerous instances are given of oral and of written controversies and disputations in the sixteenth and seventeenth centuries, some of them between protestants and papists, others between the champions of different protestant sects.

IX.

BOOKS. AUTHORS.

1. THE giving a bookseller his price for his books, has this advantage; he that will do it, shall be sure to have the refusal of whatsoever comes to his hands, and so by that means get many things, which otherwise he should never have seen.   So 'tis in giving a bawd her price.

2. In buying books or other commodities, it is not always the best rule to bid but half so much as the seller asks.   Witness the country fellow, that went to buy two shove-groat shillings; they asked him three shillings, and 10 he offered them eighteen-pence.

3. They counted the price of the books (Acts xix. 19, and found it fifty thousand pieces of silver; that is, so many sestertii, or so many three-halfpence of our money; about three hundred pound sterling.

4. Popish books teach and inform; what we know, we

l. 10.   *two shove-groat shillings.*]   Shove-groat was one of the names of a game played by driving a smooth coin with a smart stroke of the hand along a table, at the further end of which nine partitions had been marked off, with a number inscribed on each of them. The score was reckoned according to the number on the partition in which the coin rested.   See Strutt, Sports and Pastimes, bk. iv. sec. 19. Nares (Glossary, sub voce 'shove-groat') adds that the shove-groat shilling, the coin with which the game was played, was sometimes a smooth shilling, sometimes a smooth groat, sometimes a smooth half-penny; and that any flat piece of metal would have answered the purpose, and would have passed, therefore, as a shove-groat shilling.

l. 16.   *Popish books* &c.]   By 3 James I, ch. 5, sec. 25 the importation is forbidden of popish primers, ladies' psalters, manuals, rosaries, popish catechisms, missals, breviaries, portals, legends and lives of saints containing superstitious matter, and the books themselves are ordered to be seized and burned.

It was one of the charges against Laud that he had connived at the importation of popish books, and had restored them to their owners when they had been seized by the searchers.   His answer to the charge is that great numbers of them had been burnt, and that if any of them had been re-delivered to their owners it was by order not from himself, but from the High Commission. Laud's Works, vol. iv. p. 347.

know much out of them. The fathers, church story,
school-men, all may pass for popish books ; and if you take
away them, what learning will you leave ? Besides, who
must be judge ? The customer or the waiter ? If he disallows a book, it must not be brought into the kingdom ;
then lord have mercy upon all scholars ! These puritan
preachers, if they have any thing good, they have it out of
popish books, though they will not acknowledge it, for fear

Whatever Laud may have done, or omitted to do, while he was in
power, the Act against popish books was strictly enforced afterwards.
See Nalson's Collections, vol. ii. p. 690, Dec. 1, 1641. This day the
Bishop of Exon reported to the Lords' House, 'That the Committee
formerly appointed by their House, have perused those books which
were seized on coming from beyond the seas . . . and finds them to
be of three several sorts.

'Such as are fit to be delivered to their owners and to be sold.

  The Holy Table, name and thing.

  Mr. Walker's Treaty of the Sabbath, &c.

'A second sort, fit to be sold to choice persons.

  Thomas de Kempis, Of the following of Christ, &c.

'A third sort of superstitious tablets and books, which are fit to be
burnt, as

  Missals, Primers, and Offices of Our Lady, &c. . . .

'Ordered . . . the second sort to be delivered over to safe hands, to
be sold to Noblemen, Gentlemen, and Scholars, but not to women.

'That the third sort be burned by the Sheriffs of London in Smithfield forthwith.'

Selden's remark was probably made about the date at which this
more strict rule was put in force.

l. 4. *The customer*] A collector and farmer of the customs. Conf.
Hakluyt's Voyages, i. 189-191 (ed. of 1809, 4to). 'In the ancient state
of Rome, the tenants of the empire paid for rent the tenth of their
corn, whence the publicans that hired it, as the customers do here the
king's custom, were called decumani.' Selden, Works, iii. 1098.

l. 4. *the waiter*] This probably means the tide-waiter, one of the
officers of the customs, whose duty it was to watch the landing of
goods arriving from abroad.

l. 6. *These puritan preachers* &c.] So the London Petition against
bishops, &c., complains of 'the Liturgy for the most part framed out
of the Romish Breviary, Ritualium, Mass Book, also the book of
Ordination, framed out of the Roman Pontifical.' Nalson, Collections,
i. 663.

of displeasing the people. He is a poor divine that cannot sever the good from the bad.

5. It is good to have translations, because they serve as a comment, so far as the judgment of one man goes.

6. In answering a book, 'tis best to be short; otherwise he that I write against will suspect I intend to weary him, not to satisfy him. Besides in being long I shall give my adversary a huge advantage; somewhere or other he will pick a hole.

7. In quoting of books, quote such authors as are usually ₁₀ read; others you may read for your own satisfaction, but not name them.

8. Quoting of authors is most for matter of fact; and then I write them as I would produce a witness; sometimes for a free expression, and then I give the author his due, and gain myself praise by reading him.

9. To quote a modern Dutchman where I may use a classic author, is as if I were to justify my reputation, and I neglect all persons of note and quality that know me, and bring the testimonial of the scullion in the kitchen. ₂₀

X.

CANON LAW.

IF I would study the canon-law, as it is used in England, I must study the heads here in use, then go to the practisers in those courts where that law is practised, and know their customs. So for all the study in the world.

XI.

CEREMONY.

1. CEREMONY keeps up all things; 'tis like a penny glass to a rich spirit, or some excellent water; without it the water will be spilt, the spirits lost.

2. Of all people, ladies have no reason to cry down ceremonies, for they take themselves extremely slighted without it[1]. And were they not used with ceremony, with compliments and addresses, with legs, and kissing of hands, they were the pitifullest creatures in the world: but yet (methinks) to kiss their hands after their lips, as some do, is like little boys, that after they have eat the apple, fall to the paring, out of a love they have to the apple.

XII.

CHANCELLOR.

10   1. THE bishop is not to sit with the chancellor in his court as being a thing either beneath him or beside him, no more than the king is to sit in the king's bench, when he has made a lord-chief-justice.

2. The chancellor governed in the church, who was a layman. And therefore 'tis false which they charge the bishops with, that they challenge sole jurisdiction. For the bishop can no more put out the chancellor, than the

---

[1] *Without it*, H. 2] without, H.

l. 4. *with legs*,] The 'leg' is an old-fashioned bow or courtesy, in which the leg is drawn back. The word occurs again in 'Poetry' sec. 4 and in 'Thanksgiving.' Conf. ' I think it much more passable to put off the hat and make a leg like an honest country gentleman, than like an ill-fashioned dancing master.' Locke, Some Thoughts concerning Education, § 196.

l. 10. *The bishop is not to sit* &c.] This seems aimed at Canon xi. of the Constitutions and Canons of 1640, which ordains ' that hereafter no bishop shall grant any patent to any chancellor ... otherwise than with express reservation to himself and his successors of the power to execute the said place, either alone or with the chancellor, if the bishop shall please to do the same.' Wilkins, Concilia, iv. 551.

The next clause in the Table Talk must have been spoken before this Canon had been put out. The Canon clearly gives the bishop a 'sole jurisdiction,' as often as he chooses to claim it.

chancellor the bishop. They were many of them made chancellors for their lives: and he is the fittest man to govern, because divinity so overwhelms all other things.

XIII.

CHANGING SIDES.

1. 'TIS the trial of a man to see if he will change his side; and if he be so weak as to change once, he will change again. Your country fellows have a way to try if a man be weak in the hams, by coming behind him, and giving him a little blow unawares; if he bend once, he will bend again.   10

2. The lords that fall from the king, after they have got estates by base flattery at court, and now pretend conscience, do as a vintner, that when he first sets up, you may bring your wench to his house, and do your things there; but when he grows rich, he turns conscientious, and will sell no wine on the sabbath-day.

3. Colonel Goring serving first the one side and then

---

l. 2. *for their lives*] Singer suggests that 'for their learning' would give a better sense here, but there is no authority for the change.

l. 17. *Colonel Goring* &c.] Goring, in 1641, gave evidence in Parliament about a real or alleged plot of the King for bringing up the army to London to surprise the Tower and overawe the Parliament. His disclosures were thought so important that he received public thanks 'for preserving the kingdom and the liberties of Parliament.'

In 1642 we hear of him as Governor of Portsmouth, 'having found means to make good impressions again in their Majesties of his fidelity.'

In the course of the same year, having come under the suspicion of the Parliament, and having been called to account by them, he contrived so to clear himself that 'they desired him to repair to his government, and to finish those works which were necessary for the safety of the place.' They supplied him with money for

D

the other, did like a good miller, that knows how to grind which way soever the wind sits.

4. After Luther had made a combustion in Germany about religion, he was sent to by the pope, to be taken off, and offered any preferment in the church, that he would make choice of: Luther answered, if he had

the purpose, and gave him a lieutenant-general's commission in the Parliamentary army. On his return to Portsmouth he declared for the King.

His next act was to surrender Portsmouth to the Parliament, treacherously according to Clarendon, but certainly not without having made strenuous efforts for its defence.

In 1643 he was appointed to a command in the King's army at York ' by the Queen's favour notwithstanding all former failings,' and from this date onwards he continued to serve the King. Clarendon sketches his character and conduct in terms of great bitterness, very unlike Selden's easy-going remark. See Hist. of Rebellion, i. 414-417, 651, 1114-1119; ii. 27, 212, 830 ff.

l. 3. *After Luther had made a combustion* &c.] The story of the offers made to Luther by the Pope's legate, and of Luther's reply to them, rests on the authority of Father Paul Sarpi. But Selden does not tell it quite fairly to Luther. What Sarpi says is that in 1535 the legate, Vergerio, had a special commission to treat with Luther and with other prominent persons among the reformers, and to make all sorts of promises to them, if only he could bring them to terms. Vergerio, accordingly, arranged a meeting with Luther at Wittemburg, and threw out some very clear hints of what the Pope, Paul III, would do to reward him if he would but cease from troubling the Church and the world. Luther's answer was that the offers had come too late, for he had been driven by the harshness with which he had been formerly treated, to make a more exact enquiry into the errors and abuses of the papacy, and knowing what he now knew he could not in conscience refrain from telling it out to the world. See Istoria del Concilio Tridentino, lib. i. sec. 53 (edition of 1835, in 7 vols.). Luther speaks of this interview in a letter to Jonas, written in the same year, but he says only that he met the Pope's legate by invitation,—' sed quos sermones habuerim non licet homini scribere.' (De Wette, Luther's Briefe, iv. 648.) Sarpi's story must be taken for what it is worth. His authority is not by any means unimpeachable, and Pallavicino (iii. c. 18) ridicules the tale as a romance.

I am indebted to the Bishop of Peterborough for all the above references.

offered half as much at first, he would have accepted it,
but now he had gone so far, he could not come back.
In truth he had made himself a greater thing than they
could make him ; the German princes courted him ; he
was become the author of a sect ever after to be called
Lutherans.   So have our preachers done that are against
the bishops, they have made themselves greater with the
people than they can be made the other way, and therefore there is the less probability of[1] bringing them off.
Charity to strangers is enjoined in the text.   By strangers 10
is there understood, those that are not of your own kir,
strangers to your blood, not those you cannot tell whence
they come; that is, be charitable to your neighbours
whom you know to be honest poor people.

XIV.

CHRISTIANS.

1. IN the church of Jerusalem, the Christians were but
another sect of Jews, that did believe the Messias was
come.   To be called, was nothing else but to become a
Christian, to have the name of a Christian, it being their
own language ; for among the Jews, when they made a 20
doctor of law, 'twas said he was called.

2. The Turks tell their people of a heaven where there
is a sensible pleasure, but of a hell where they shall suffer
they do not know what.   The Christians quite invert this
order ; they tell us of a hell where we shall feel sensible
pain, but of a heaven where we shall enjoy we cannot tell
what.

3. Why did the heathen object to the Christians, that

[1] *Less probability of.*   Singer conjecturally] less charity probably of, MSS.

l. 28. *Why did the heathen* &c.]   On the identification of Jews and
Christians, and on the reasons for it, Selden speaks in several places.

they worshipped an ass's head? You must know, that to a heathen, a Jew and a Christian were all one, that they

What he says in effect is that, since Christianity had its origin in Judæa, since the early Christians were in great part Jews by race, and worshipped the same supreme God as the Jews, and since they preserved for some time the civil rites and ceremonies of their nation, it was quite natural that the alien peoples, among whom they lived and from whose worship they both alike kept markedly aloof, should have seen no difference between them, and that in point of fact they habitually included them both under the common name of Jews. See Selden, Works, i. 59. II. Prolegomena, p. 10. II. 405 and 657.

The fiction about the ass's head was, Bochart says, started by Apion, an Egyptian grammarian of the first half of the first century, and he adds proof of the very wide credence which it received, about the Jews first, and about the Christians afterwards. The origin of the story he explains in several ways, but not very happily. See Hierozoicon, pt. 1, bk. ii. ch. xviii.

Morinus criticises Bochart and the authorities which Bochart quotes, and then with some hesitation tries his own hand on the problem. One of his conjectures is that the Hebrew words for a pot (sc. of manna) and for an ass are so nearly alike as hardly to be distinguished, and that the pot of manna, with its two handles or ears, preserved in the holy place, might itself be taken as an image of an ass's head.

Conf. Dissertationes Octo (Geneva, 1683), p. 157, on the question, ' Unde potuit venire in mentem gentium caput asininum esse Christianorum Deum?'

The story, as told by Apion, takes two forms, viz. that the head of an ass in gold, an object of worship among the Jews, was found in the holy place of the Temple by Antiochus Epiphanes; and again that a man named Zabidus, in the course of a war between the Jews and the Idumæans, managed to make his way into the Temple, and there found and carried away the golden head. See Josephus against Apion, bk. ii. ch. 7 and 10.

But if the calumny originated with Apion, and if the later versions of it can, as Bochart says, be traced to him as their source, it seems hardly worth while to enquire about it any further. Apion, it must be remembered, was notorious as a hater of the Jews. He not only wrote against them, but he was sent to Rome, on a special mission, as the most fit person to plead before the Emperor Caligula on behalf of the Alexandrian Greeks, in their quarrel with the Alexandrian Jews, and he did his work so effectively that the Emperor refused even to hear his opponent, Philo. The ass's head story, however started, and with whatever accessories it was adorned, would have

regarded him not, so he was not one of them. Now that
of the ass's head might proceed from such a mistake as
this. By the Jewish law, all the firstlings of cattle were
to be offered to God, except a young ass, which was to be
redeemed; a heathen being present, and seeing young
calves, and young lambs killed at their sacrifices, only
young asses redeemed, might very well think they had
that silly beast in some high estimation, and thence might
imagine they worshipped it as a God.

XV.

CHRISTMAS.

1. CHRISTMAS succeeds the Saturnalia, the same time,
the same number of holy days; then the master waited
upon the servant, just like the lord of misrule.

2. Our meats and our sports (much of them) have relation to church-work. The coffin of our christmas pies, in
shape long, is in imitation of the cratch; our choosing

gained ready credence at Rome about a people of whom they knew
little, and for whom they had no love. It was told first about the
Jews, and the identification of Jews and Christians explains sufficiently how it came to be told about the Christians afterwards.

l. 13. *the lord of misrule*] Strutt gives a full account of this 'mock
prince,' or 'master of merry disports,' of the manner of his appointment, of the length of his reign, and of the nature and privileges of
his office. He refers to and endorses Selden's opinion that all these
whimsical transpositions of dignity are derived from the ancient
Saturnalia, or feasts of Saturn, when the masters waited upon their
servants, who were honoured with mock titles and permitted to
assume the state and deportment of their lords. Sports and Pastimes, bk. iv. chap. 3, sec. 1–8.

l. 16. *the cratch*] An old English word for rack or manger. Fr.
crèche. It is frequently used for the manger in which Christ was
laid. Conf. 'And sche bare hir first borun sone, and wlappide hym in
clothis, and leide hym in a cratche.' Luke ii. 7; Wycliffe's Trans.
second version, as printed by Forshall and Madden.

king and queen on twelfth-night, has reference to the
three kings. So likewise our eating of fritters, whipping
of tops, roasting of herrings, jack of lents, &c. they were
all in imitation of church-work, emblems of martyrdom.
Our tansies at Easter have reference to the bitter herbs ;
though at the same time it was always the fashion, for a
man to have in his house a gammon of bacon, to shew
himself to be no Jew.

XVI.

CHURCH.

10 1. HERETOFORE the kingdom let the church alone, let
them do what they would, because they had something
else to think of, viz[t]. wars ; but now in time of peace, we
begin to examine all things, will have nothing but what we
like, grow dainty and wanton ; just as in a family, the heir
uses to go a hunting, he never considers how his meal
is dressed ; takes a bit[1], and away ; but when he stays
within, then he grows curious, he does not like this, nor
he does not like that, he will have his meat dressed his
own way, or peradventure he will dress it himself.

20 2. It hath ever been the gain of the church, when the

---

[1] *Takes a bit*, H. 2] take a bit, H.

l. 3. *Jack a lent*] Explained in Johnson's Dictionary as a puppet
formerly thrown at in Lent, like shrove-cocks. Conf.:
  ' Thou, that when last thou wert put out of service,
  Travell'dst to Hamstead-heath, on an Ash Wednesday,
  Where thou didst stand six weeks the Jack o' Lent,
  For boys to hurl three throws a penny at thee.'
                    Ben Jonson, Tale of a Tub, Act iv. sc. 2.
l. 5. *Our tansies*] 'Tansy, a herb : also a sort of pancake or pud-
ding made with it.' Bailey, Old English Dictionary.
l. 20. *the gain of the church*] I am not sure that this is the correct
reading. The MSS. give *gaine*, which may quite possibly have been
a mistake for *game*, a word better suited to the sense here. So, in
Bacon's Essay 'Of Usury,' the unquestionably correct reading, 'at

king will let the church have no power, to cry down the king and cry up the church. But when the church can make use of the king's power, then to bring all under the king's prerogative. The catholics of England go one way, and the court clergy the other[1].

3. A glorious church is like a magnificent feast, there is all the variety that may be, but every one chooses out a dish or two that he likes, and lets the rest alone. How glorious soever the church is, every one chooses out of it his own religion, by which he governs himself, and lets 10 the rest alone.

4. The laws of the church are most favourable to the church, because they were the church's own making; as the heralds are the best gentlemen, because they make their own pedigree.

5. There is a question about that article, concerning

----

[1] *The other*] corrected in MSS. from ' an other.'

the end of the game,' appears in some copies of the edition of 1625 as ' at the end of the gaine.' So, too, in the Table Talk (Power, State, end of sec. 7) the Harleian MS. 1315 reads, quite distinctly, 'comine,' instead of ' comme.'

l. 16. *There is a question about that article* &c.] The words in question—'The Church hath power to decree rites or ceremonies and authority in controversies of faith,' or, as they appear in the original Latin, 'Habet Ecclesia ritus statuendi jus, et in fidei controversi s auctoritatem'—were certainly part of the Latin text as printed in 1563, with the approval of the Queen. They were not in Archbishop Parker's preparatory draft of the articles, but they certainly were in the copy finally signed by the archbishop, the bishops and the clergy of the Lower House, at the convocation on January 29, 1562 (1563). Their subsequent history is not equally clear. They were not in the English MS. signed by the bishops in the convocation of 1571. They were in the Latin articles signed by the Lower House in the same year. It appears, too, that in 1571 there were copies of the articles printed in Latin and in English with the above words, and other copies, certainly in English, without the words. The whole question is discussed, and a summary of the arguments pro and con given, in Hardwick's History of the Thirty-nine Articles, p. 141. See also Laud's Works, vol. iv. 30, and vol. vi. 64 ff. A charge that the bishops had

the power of the church, whether these words (of having
power in controversies of faith) were not stolen in;
but 'tis most certain they were in the Book of Articles
that was confirmed, though in some editions they have
been left out: but the Article before tells you, who the
church is; not the clergy, but *cœtus fidelium.*

XVII.

CHURCH OF ROME.

1. BEFORE a juggler's tricks are discovered we admire
him, and give him money, but afterwards we care not for
them : so 'twas before the discovery of the juggling of the
church of Rome.

2. Catholics say, we out of our charity believe they of
the church of Rome may be saved: but they do not believe so of us; therefore their church is better according
to our own selves.   First, some of them no doubt believe
as well of us, as we do of them; but they must not say so.
Besides is that an argument, their church is better than
ours because it has less charity?

forged the clause and had foisted it into the articles, is dealt with
at length in Laud's speech at the censure of Burton, Bastwick, and
Prynne. Strype, in his Life of Archbishop Parker, bk. iv. chap. 5,
says that a Latin copy of the articles, printed in 1563, and containing
the disputed clause, 'is still extant in the Bodleian Library among
Mr. Selden's books . . . being found in Archbishop Laud's library,
from whence Mr. Selden immediately had it.' He adds, further, that
there were three editions of the Thirty-nine Articles in English,
printed in 1571 by Jugg and Cawood, all which have this clause;
'which three editions, with the said clause, I myself saw, as well as
other inquisitive persons, at Mr. Wilkins's, a bookseller in St. Paul's
Church-yard.' 'So that at length an edition that appeared abroad in
the same year, printed by John Day, wanting the clause, hath been
judged (and that upon good grounds) to be spurious.'

l. 17. *Besides is that an argument,* &c.] Dr. Prideaux makes this

3. One of the church of Rome will not come to our prayers. Does that argue he does not like them? I would fain see a catholic leave his dinner, because a nobleman's chaplain says grace. Nor haply would he leave the prayers of the church, if going to church were not made a note of distinction between a protestant[1] and a papist.

XVIII.

CHURCHES.

THE way coming into our great churches was anciently at the west door, that men might see the altar, and all the church before them ; the other doors were but posterns.

---

[1] *Protestant*, H. 2] protest, H.

point in the course of a series of lectures to which Selden refers elsewhere. See note on 'Predestination,' sec. 3.

l. 9. *The way coming* &c.] After the narthex (ante-temple) followed that part which was properly called ναός, the temple, and *navis*, the nave or body of the church … The entrance into it from the narthex was by the gates, which the modern rituals and Greek writers call πύλαι ὡραῖαι and βασιλικαί, the 'beautiful and royal gates.' Here their kings were wont to lay down their crowns before they proceeded further into the Church. Bingham, Christian Antiquities, bk. viii. ch. 5, sec. 1.

These royal gates were usually at the west, since the churches were usually built east and west, with the altar at the east end, but the rule was not always observed. See Christian Antiquities, bk. viii. ch. 3, sec. 2.

Bingham gives, in this chapter, the ground-plan of an ancient church, showing the royal gates at the west, with the altar and all the church in full view in front of them, and the other gates or posterns at the sides. See also Selden's letter to Usher of March 24, 1621 (22), asking 'whether we find that any churches in the elder times of Christianity were with the doors or fronts eastward' (Works, ii. 1707), and Usher's reply of April 16, showing that ancient churches were built in a variety of ways, some 'with the doors or fronts eastward,' some standing north and south ; but that for the most part they had the entrance at the west and the altar at the east end. R. Parr's Life of Usher. Letters, p. 81. Letter 49.

XIX.

CITY.

1. WHAT makes a city? Whether a bishoprick, or any-thing[1] of that nature?

Answer. 'Tis according to the first charter which made them a corporation. If they are incorporated by name of *civitas*, then they are a city; if by the name of *burgum*, then they are a borough.

2. The lord mayor of London by their first charter was to be presented to the king; in his absence to the lord chief justiciary of England; afterwards to the lord chancel-lor, now to the barons of the exchequer; but still there was a reservation, that for their honour they should come once a year to the king, as they do still.

---

[1] *Anything*, H. 2] any, H.

---

l. 8. *The lord mayor of London* &c.] The first notice of the presentment of the lord mayor to the King occurs in the fifth charter, granted by King John, 1215. It grants to the barons of the city of London that they may choose every year a mayor, 'so as, when he shall be chosen, to be presented to us or our justice, if we shall not be present.' By the sixth charter of Henry III, the mayor when chosen is to be 'presented to the Barons of the Exchequer, we not being at Westminster, so notwithstanding at the next coming of us or our heirs to Westminster or London, he be presented to us or our heirs, and so admitted mayor.' Edward I fixes the first presentation to be to the 'Constable of our Tower of London, but to us at our next coming to London.' See Noorthouck, Hist. of London, pp. 778, 782, 784. This rule is not varied in any later charters. For the practice, as it had afterwards been settled, see Maitland's Hist. of London, p. 1193 (fol. 1756). 'The Lord Mayor elect,' Maitland says, 'is presented first to the Lord Chancellor, and afterwards to the Barons of the Exchequer, when he has been sworn into his office.'

XX.

CLERGY.

1. THOUGH a clergyman have no faults of his own, yet the faults of the whole tribe shall be laid upon him, so he shall be sure not to lack.

2. The clergy would have us believe them against our own reason; as the woman would have had her husband against his own eyes, when he took her with another man, which she stoutly denied: What! will you believe your own eyes before your own sweet wife?

3. The condition of the clergy towards the prince, and the condition of the physician is all one: the physicians tell the prince they have agaric and rhubarb good for him and good for his subjects' bodies; upon this he gives them leave to use it; but if it prove naught, then away with it, they shall use it no more; so the clergy tell the prince they have physic good for his soul, and good for the souls of his people; upon that he admits them: but when he finds by experience they both trouble him and his people, then away with them, he will have no more to do with them. What is that to them, or any body else, if a king will not go to heaven?

4. A clergyman goes not a dram further than this: you ought to obey your prince in general. If he does he is lost: how to obey him, you must be informed by those, whose profession it is to tell you. The parson of the Tower (a good discreet man) told Dr. Mosely (who was sent to me, and the rest of the gentlemen committed 3d *Caroli*, to persuade us to submit to the king) that they found no

---

l. 6. *as the woman would have had* &c.] This seems to refer either to the story told in the first of the Adolphi Fabulæ (quoted in the Aldine ed. of Chaucer, vol. i. 232, Introductory Remarks), or to Chaucer's adaptation of the story in the 'Merchant's Tale,' of January and May.

such words, as parliament, *habeas corpus*, return, tower, &c. neither in the fathers, nor in the schoolmen, nor in the text; and therefore, for his part, he believed they understood nothing of the business. A satire upon all those clergymen that meddle with matters they do not understand.

5. All confess there never was a more learned clergy. No man taxes them with ignorance. But to talk of that, is like the fellow that was a great wencher; he wished God would forgive him his lechery, and lay usury to his charge.
10 The clergy have worse faults.

6. The clergy and treaty together are never like to do

---

l. 11. *The clergy and treaty*] This is the clear reading of the three MSS. which I have examined. The printed editions have 'the clergy and laity,' which gives an easier sense for the line, but does not suit so well with the general drift of the section. Selden seems to be referring to some attempted arrangement between two parties, in which the interference of the clergy, on the one side and on the other, was likely in his judgment to do harm by mixing up matters which had better have been left out. There were several attempted arrangements of which this might have been said. There was, e.g., the attempted treaty for peace between the King and the Parliament in 1643, in which one of the proposals was 'that religion might be settled with the advice of a synod of divines in such a manner as his Majesty, with the consent of both Houses of Parliament, should appoint' (Clarendon, History, ii. 477). Again, there was the abortive treaty of Newport, discussed in September, 1648, between the King, with some divines among his advisers, and the Parliamentary commissioners, attended by a body of their divines. In the course of this, questions about the church came prominently forward, and it was mainly on these that the negotiations finally broke down (Clarendon, History, vol. iii. 324, 327, 338-9). The remark in the text, in whichever form it stands, must clearly be limited to some such instance as the above. It is not to be taken as condemning in every case the joint action of clergy and laity. In 'Synod Assembly,' sec. 3, Selden distinctly approves this, and indeed insists upon it as necessary. He was himself a lay member of the Westminster Assembly of Divines, a mixed lay and clerical body, for which religious matters were the appointed business : so that 'the apothecary' was in place there, and his rhubarb and agaric were the proper ingredients of the sauce. The reading, therefore,—'the clergy and treaty'—though an awkward collocation of words, seems to give a sense best suited to

well. 'Tis as if a man were to make an excellent feast, and would have his apothecary and his physician should come into the kitchen : the cooks, if they were let alone, would make excellent meat ; but then comes the apothecary, and he puts rhubarb into the sauce, and agaric into another sauce and so spoils all. Chain up the clergy on both sides.

XXI.

HIGH COMMISSION.

MEN cry out upon the high commission, as if only clergymen had to do in it ; when I believe there are more laymen in commission there, than clergymen. If the laymen will not come, whose fault is that ? So of the star-chamber, the people think the bishops only censured Prynne, Burton, and Bastwick, when there were but two there, and one spoke not in his own cause.

the whole passage, and most in agreement with Selden's judgment elsewhere.

l. 8. *as if only clergymen* &c.] The Commissioners present in the High Commission Court on e. g. Nov. 17, 1631, were six clerics and four laymen ; on Nov. 24 there were seven clerics and five laymen ; on Jan. 26, 1634, six clerics and four laymen ; on Feb. 9 there were three clerics and eight laymen. See High Commission Cases (Camden Society), pp. 239, 245, 261, 264. On the popular dislike of the High Commission Court, and on the very good reasons for it, see Clarendon, Hist., vol. i. p. 439. His statement is, in effect, that it had come to meddle with things which did not properly concern it ; that it had extended its sentences and judgments, in matters tryable before it, beyond that degree which was justifiable, and had not only neglected prohibitions from the supreme courts of law, but had reprehended the judges for doing their duty in granting them. The growth of these abuses he ascribes to 'the great power of some bishops at court.'

l. 12. *people think the bishops only* &c.] They were tried, Clarendon says, ' in as full a court as ever I saw in that place.' The bishops present were ' only the Archbishop of Canterbury and the Bishop of London.' Hist. i. 310. The bishop who spoke was Laud, the arch-

XXII.

HOUSE OF COMMONS.

1. THERE be but two erroneous opinions in the House of
Commons; that the Lords sit only for themselves; when
the truth is, they sit as well for the commonwealth.   The
knights and burgesses sit for themselves and others, some
for more, some for fewer.   And what is the reason?   Because the room will not hold all; the Lords being few, they
all come; and imagine the room able to hold all the Commons of England, then the Knights and burgesses would
10 sit no otherwise than the Lords do.   The second error is,

bishop.   His speech is given at length in Laud's Works, vol. vi.
p. 41 ff.   The sentence was brutal, and it was carried out with brutal
and unusual severity.   'The report thereof,' says Rushworth, 'flew
quickly into Scotland, and the discourse among the Scots were, that
the bishops of England were the cause thereof.'   Historical Collections, ii. 385.   So Prynne, speaking from the pillory, ascribes the
whole business to the vexation of the bishops as the subjects of the
libels for which he and the others had been sentenced.   Cobbett,
State Trials, p. 747.   His statement is borne out by Whitelock's account
of the case.

'The King and Queen did nothing direct against him (Prynne) till
Laud set Dr. Heylin (who bore a great malice to Prynne for confuting
some of his doctrines) to peruse Prynne's book, &c.   The archbishop
went with these notes to Mr. Attorney Noy, and charged him to pro-
secute Prynne, which Noy afterwards did rigorously enough in the
Star Chamber, and in the meantime the Bishops and Lords in the
Star Chamber sent Prynne close prisoner to the Tower.'   Whitelock,
Memorials, p. 18.

The trial in the Star Chamber was in 1637.   That court and the
High Commission Court were abolished in 1640.   Selden's remarks
must therefore have been made at some time between the two dates.

l. 3.   *that the Lords sit only* &c.]   'If they (sc. the bishops) vote for
the clergy, then they are to be elected by the clergy, as the members
of the Commons House now are; but your Lordships, voting only for
yourselves, need no electors.'   Solicitor St. John's speech at a conference of the two Houses, 1641.   Nalson's Collections, ii. 501.

So, too, in Baillie's Letters and Journals, we find it stated that the
Lords represent none but themselves.   Vol. i. 369.

l. 10.   *The second error is* &c.]   That a money bill must originate with

that the House of Commons are to begin to give subsidies ;
yet if the Lords dissent, they can give no money.

2. The House of Commons is called the Lower House
in twenty acts of parliament : but what are twenty acts of
parliament amongst friends ?

3. The form of a charge runs thus, I accuse in the name
of all the Commons of England.   How then can any man
be as a witness, when every man is made an accuser?

XXIII.

COMPETENCY.

THAT which is a competency for one man, is not enough
for another ; no more than that which will keep one man
warm will keep another man warm : one man can go in

the House of Commons is admitted on all hands.   But whether the
opinion, that if the Lords dissent the Commons can give no money,
is, as Selden terms it, an error, is more than doubtful.   ' It is true that
the Bill of Subsidy is offered by the Commons only ; but before that
stage is reached, it is sent up to the Lords, is thrice read by them, and
is then sent back to the Commons, and there it remaineth to be carried
by the Speaker, when he shall present it.'   See Orders and Proceedings of the Commons, ch. xv. Harleian MS. v. 266.

Sir Erskine May says expressly that ' A grant from the Commons is
not effectual, in law, without the ultimate assent of the Queen and of
the House of Lords.'   Law, &c., of Parliament, p. 638 (9th ed.).

Indeed, that the Commons in Selden's day had a less independent
control over grants than they have gained since, appears from the fact
that although their right to originate grants was unquestionable, yet
bills of supply were, until 1671, liable to be amended by the Lords.
Ibid. p. 641.

l. 6.   *The form of a charge* &c.]   See, Message to the Lords re
Strafford, delivered by Mr. Pym at the command of the House : ' My
Lords . . . . I do here in the name of the Commons now assembled
in Parliament, and in the name of all the Commons of England, accuse
Thomas, Earl of Strafford, Lord Lieutenant of Ireland, of High
Treason.'   Nalson, Collections, vol. ii. p. 7.

There are other instances given at p. 796, and *passim.*

doublet and hose, when another man cannot be without a cloak, and yet have no more clothes than is necessary for him.

XXIV.

CONFESSION.

1. IN the time of parliament it used to be one of the first things the house did, to petition the king that his confessor might be removed ; as fearing either his power with the king, or else, lest he should reveal to the pope what the house was in doing, as no doubt he did, when the Catholic 10 cause was concerned.

2. The difference between us and the papists is, we both allow contrition, but the papists make confession a part of contrition; they say, a man is not sufficiently contrite, unless he confess his sins to a priest.

3. Why should I think a priest will not reveal confession ? I am sure he will do any other thing that is forbidden him, haply not so often as I. The uttermost punishment is deprivation. And how can it be proved, that ever any man revealed confession, when there is no witness ? And no 20 man can be witness in his own cause. A mere gullery. There was a time when 'twas public in the church, and that is much against their auricular confession.

XXV.

GREAT CONJUNCTION.

THE greatest conjunction of Saturn and Jupiter happens but once in eight hundred years, and therefore astrologers

l. 24. *The greatest conjunction* &c.] ' Conjonction en Astronomie se dit de la rencontre apparente de deux astres ou de deux planètes dans le même point des cieux, ou plutôt dans le même degré du zodiaque.

can make no experiments of it, nor foretell what it means ; not but that the stars may mean something, but we cannot tell what because we cannot come at them. Suppose a planet were a simple, or an herb; how could a physician tell the virtue of that simple, unless he came at it, to apply it ?

XXVI.

CONSCIENCE.

1. HE that hath a scrupulous conscience, is like a horse that is not well wayed[1]; he starts at every bird that flies out of the hedge.

2. A knowing man will do that which a tender con-

[1] *Wayed*, H. a] weighed H.

The conjunction of Saturn and Jupiter, placed by astronomers among the grand conjunctions, happens once in every twenty years. A less frequent conjunction, placed among the very grand, is that of Saturn, Jupiter, and Mars, which happens once in every five hundred years. See Diderot and D'Alembert, Encyclopédie, under heading Conjonction.

If Selden is writing of astrological conjunctions (as it would appear he is, from the remarks which follow) see, on the whole passage,— Planetarum prima diversitas est in virtutibus propriis. Nam Saturnus est frigidus et siccus, et omnis pigritiae et mortificationis et destructionis rerum causativus per egressum siccitatis et frigoris. Mars vero est corruptivus propter egressum caliditatis et siccitatis et isti duo planetae nunquam faciunt bonum nisi per accidens ; sicut aliquando venenum est bonum per accidens . . . .

Habent autem planetae virtutes alias a signis . . . . et iterum penes aspectus, qui sunt conjunctio, oppositio, etc. Conjuncti dicuntur planetae, quando sunt in eodem signo oppositi, quando unus est in septimo ab alio . . . . Quando vero malus opponitur aut conjungitur malo, tunc magnum malum est, &c. R. Bacon, Opus Majus, p. 237–8.

1.9. *well wayed;*] Explained in Bailey's Etymological English Dict. ' to way a horse is to teach him to travel in the way.'

'Way'd Horse (with horsemen) is one who is already backed, suppled and broken and shows a disposition to the manage.'

E

scienced man dares not do, by reason of his ignorance; the other knows there is no hurt: as a child is afraid to go in the dark, when a man is not, because he knows there's no danger.

3. If we once come to leave that out-loose, as to pretend conscience against law, who knows what inconveniency may follow? For thus, suppose an anabaptist comes and takes my horse; I sue him, he tells me he did according to his conscience; his conscience tells him all things are common amongst the saints, what is mine is his; therefore you do ill to make such a law, if any man take another's horse he shall be hanged. What can I say to this man? He does according to his conscience. Why is not he as honest a man, as he that pretends a ceremony, established by law, is against his conscience? Generally to pretend conscience against law is dangerous; in some cases haply we may.

4. Some men make it a case of conscience, whether a man may have a pigeon-house, because his pigeons eat other folks' corn. But there is no such thing as conscience in the business. The matter is, whether he be a man of such quality, that the state allows him to have a dove-house; if so, there's an end to the business; his pigeons have a right to eat where they list themselves.

l. 21. *The matter is, whether he be* &c.] The law seems to have been that—A lord of a manor might build a dove-cote upon his land, parcel of his manor, and this he might do by virtue of his right as lord thereof. It appears also from the obiter dicta in a case before the King's Bench, that the parson had a like right. But the tenant of a manor could not do it without licence, the reason assigned being that he can have no right to any privilege that may be prejudicial to others.

In every case, however, in which pigeons came upon a man's land, he might lawfully kill them, the quality of their owner notwithstanding. See Croke's Reports of cases in the reign of James I, pp. 382, 490, and Salkeld's Reports of cases in the reign of William and Mary, vol. iii. p. 248, sub voce ' Nuisance.'

XXVII.

CONSECRATED PLACES.

1. THE Jews had a peculiar way of consecrating things
to God, which we have not.

2. Under the law, God, who was master of all, made
choice of a temple to be worshipped in, where he was more
especially present: just as the master of a house, who owns[1]
all the house, makes choice of one chamber to lie in, which
is called the master's chamber; but under the gospel there
is no such thing; temples and churches are set apart for
the conveniency of men to worship in; they cannot meet 10
upon the point of a needle, but God himself makes no
choice.

3. All things are God's already, we can give him no right
by consecrating any that he had not before, only we set it
apart to his service. Just as a gardener brings his lord and
master a basket of apricocks, and presents them; his lord
thanks him for them, perhaps gives him something for his
pains, and yet the apricocks were as much his lord's before
as now.

4. What is consecrated, is given to some particular 20
man, to do God service; not given to God, but given to
man to serve God. And there's not anything, lands, or
goods, but some men or other have it in their power to
dispose of as they please. The saying things consecrated cannot be taken away, makes men afraid of consecration.

5. Yet consecration has this power, when a man has
consecrated anything unto God, he cannot of himself take
it away.

---

[1] *Owns*] owes, MSS.

l. 20.   *What is consecrated,* &c.]   See note on 'Tithes,' sec. 5.

XXVIII.

CONTRACTS.

1. If our fathers have lost their liberty, why may not we labour to regain it?

Answer. We must look to the contract; if that be rightly made, we must stand to it. If we once grant we may recede from contracts, upon any inconveniency may afterwards happen, we shall have no bargain kept. If I sell you a horse, and afterwards do not like my bargain, I will have my horse again.

10   2. Keep your contracts. So far a divine goes, but how to make our contracts is left to ourselves; and as we agree about the conveying of this house, or that land, so it must be. If you offer me a hundred pounds for my glove, I tell you what my glove is, a plain glove, pretend no virtue in it, the glove is my own, I profess not to sell gloves, and we agree for an hundred pounds; I do not know why I may not with a safe conscience take it. The want of that common obvious distinction of *jus præceptivum*, and *jus permissivum*, does much trouble men.

20   3. Lady Kent articled with Sir Edward Herbert, that he should come to her when she sent for him, and stay with her as long as she would have him; to which he set his hand: then he articled with her, that he should go away when he pleased, and stay away as long as he pleased; to which she set her hand. This is the epitome of all the contracts in the world, betwixt man and man, betwixt prince and subject; they keep them as long as they like them, and no longer.

l. 20. *Lady Kent articled* &c.] This probably means that Lady Kent retained, or sought to retain, Sir Edward Herbert, an eminent lawyer of the time, at a yearly salary, to do her legal work. Such arrangements were not uncommon. See Aikin, Life of Selden, p. 154, note.

XXIX.

CONVOCATION.

1. WHEN the king sends his writ for a parliament, he sends for two knights for a shire, and two burgesses for a corporation: but when he sends for two archbishops for a convocation, he commands them to assemble the whole clergy; but they, out of custom amongst themselves, send to the bishops of their provinces, to will them to bring two clerks for a diocese, the dean, one for the chapter, and the archdeacons; but to the king every clergyman is there present.   10

2. We have nothing so nearly expresses the power of the convocation, in respect of the parliament, as a court-leet, where they have a power to make bye-laws, as they call them; as that a man shall put so many cows or sheep in the common; but they can make nothing that is contrary to the laws of the kingdom.

XXX.

COUNCIL.

THEY talk (but blasphemously enough) that the Holy Ghost is president of their General Councils; when the truth is, the odd man is still the Holy Ghost.   20

XXXI.

CREED.

ATHANASIUS's creed is the shortest, take away the preface, and the force, and the conclusion, which are not part of the

l. 6. *they, out of custom amongst themselves,* &c.] See note on 'Bishops in Parliament,' sec. 7.

creed.   In the Nicene creed it is εἰς ἐκκλησίαν, I believe in
the church; but now our Common-prayer has it, I believe
one catholic and apostolic church.   They like not creeds,
because they would have no forms of faith, as they have
none of prayer, though there be more reason for the one
than for the other.

XXXII.

DAMNATION.

1. IF the physician sees you eat any thing that is not
good for your body, to keep you from it, he cries 'tis
poison.   If the divine sees you do any thing that is
hurtful for your soul, to keep you from it, he cries you are
damned.

2. To preach long, loud, and damnation, is the way to
be cried up.   We love a man that damns us, and we run
after him again to save us.   If a man had a sore leg, and
he should go to an honest judicious surgeon, and he should
only bid him keep it warm, and anoint with such an oil (an
oil well known), that would do the cure, haply he would
not much regard him, because he knew the medicine before-
hand an ordinary medicine.   But if he should go to a
surgeon that should tell him, your leg will gangrene within
three days, and it must be cut off, and you will die, unless

---

l. 1. *In the Nicene creed it is* &c.]   In the original Nicene creed
the words do not occur.   They were introduced in 381 at the Council
of Constantinople—πιστεύομεν . . . . . εἰς μίαν ἁγίαν καθολικὴν καὶ ἀποστολικὴν
ἐκκλησίαν.

On the distinction, to which Selden refers, between 'I believe in'
and 'I believe,' Bishop Pearson shows that 'Credo sanctam Ecclesiam,
I believe there is an holy church; or Credo in sanctam Ecclesiam is
the same; nor does the particle *in* added or subtracted make any
difference.'   See Pearson on the Creed, vol. i. pp. 28, 504, and vol. ii.
p. 421.

you do something that I could tell you; what listening there would be to this man! Oh, for the lord's sake, tell me what this is, I will give you any content for your pains.

XXXIII.

SELF-DENIAL.

'TIS much the doctrine of the times, that men should not please themselves, but deny themselves every thing they take delight in ; not look upon beauty, wear no good clothes, eat no good meat, &c. which seems the greatest accusa· tion that can be upon the Maker of all good things. If they be not to be used, why did God make them? The o truth is, they that preach against them, cannot make use of them themselves, and then again, they get esteem by seeming to contemn them. But yet, mark it while you live, if they do not please themselves as much as they can ; and we live more by example than precept.

XXXIV.

DEVILS.

1. WHY have we none possessed with devils in England? The old answer is, the protestants the devil has already, and the papists are so holy, he dares not meddle with them. Why then, beyond seas, where a nun is possessed, when 20

l. 20. *Why then, beyond seas*, &c.] The argument seems to be that the alleged holiness of the papists is no sufficient safe-guard to prevent the devil from daring to meddle with them, and that the hunting of huguenots out of church is a proof of enmity between the devil and his alleged friends or allies.

In the sixteenth and early in the seventeenth century, there were several outbursts of demoniacal possession. In 1609 the Basque

a huguenot comes into the church, does the devil hunt
him out? The priest[1] teaches him; you never saw the
devil throw up a nun's coats; mark that; the priest will not
suffer it, for then the people will spit at him.

2. Casting out devils is mere juggling. They never cast
out any but what they first cast in. They do it where, for
reverence, no man shall dare to examine it. They do it in
a corner, in a mortice-hole, not in the market-place. They
do nothing but what may be done by art. They make the
10 devil fly out at a window in the likeness of a bat, or a rat.
Why do they not hold him? Why, in the likeness of a
bat, or a rat, or some creature that is? Why not in some
shape we paint him in, with claws and horns? By this
trick they gain much, gain upon men's fancies, and so are

[1] *The priest*, H. 2] the devil, H.

country was the scene, and it was shifted, in the same year, to the
Ursuline convent at Aix. In 1613 the nuns of St. Brigitte, at Lille,
were tormented a second time by demons. They had suffered in the
same way about half a century before. But the most notorious of all
these attacks was the possession of the mother superior and some of
the nuns at the Ursuline convent at Loudun in 1632-4. The history of
this remarkable affair is given at length by Figuier. It appears to have
been the combined result of wild nymphomania and conscious fraud
on the part of the possessed nuns, probably aided by some sugges-
tive trickery on the part of other persons. It had, as it was intended
it should have, a tragical ending for the curé of Loudun, Urbain
Grandier, who was burnt alive in 1634, on a maliciously contrived
charge that he had introduced the devils into the bodies of the nuns.
For the full details of this awful story, see Figuier, Histoire du
Merveilleux, vol. i. pp. 81-257, and Bayle, Dictionnaire, under the
heading 'Grandier.'

I find no mention anywhere of the possessed nuns hunting a
huguenot out of the church. The nearest approach to it is in the
account of the possession in 1552 of the nuns of the convent of
Kintorp near Strasbourg, in the course of which—'Elles ne gouver-
naient plus leur volonté. Une fureur irrésistible les portait à se
mordre, à frapper et à mordre leurs compagnes, à se précipiter sur
les étrangers pour leur faire du mal.' Introduction to the Histoire du
Merveilleux, p. 47.

reverenced. And certainly if the priest can deliver me
from him, that is my greatest enemy, I have all the reason
in the world to reverence him.

Objection. But if this be juggling, why do they punish
impostors?

Answer. For great reason; because they do not play
their part well, and for fear others should discover them,
and so think all of them to be [1] of the same trade.

3. A person of quality came to my chamber in the
Temple, and told me he had two devils in his head; [I
wondered what he meant] and just at that time, one of
them bid him kill me, [with that I begun to be afraid, and
thought he was mad] he said he knew I could cure him, and
therefore entreated me to give him something, for he was
resolved he would go to nobody else. I perceiving what
an opinion he had of me, and that 'twas only melancholy
that troubled him, took him in hand, warranted him, if he
would follow my directions, to cure him in a short time.
I desired him to let me be alone for an hour, and then to
come again, which he was very willing to. In the mean
time I got a card, and lapt it handsomely up in a piece of
taffata, and put strings to the taffata, and when he came,
gave it him, to hang about his neck; withal charged him,
that he should not disorder himself neither with eating or
drinking, but eat very little of supper, and say his prayers
duly when he went to bed, and I made no question but he
would be well in three or four days. Within that time I
went to dinner at his house, and asked him how he did.
He said he was much better, but not perfectly well, for in
truth he had not dealt clearly with me: he had four devils
in his head, and he perceived two of them were gone with
that which I had given him, but the other two troubled him
still. Well, said I, I am glad two of them are gone; I make
no doubt but to get away the other two likewise. So I

---

[1] *Think all of them to be*, H. 2] all of them thought to be, H.

gave him another thing to hang about his neck.   Three
days after, he came to me to my chamber, and professed
he was now as well as ever he was in his life, and did
extremely thank me for the great care I had taken with
him.   I fearing lest he might relapse into the like dis-
temper, told him that there was none but myself and one
physician more, in the whole town, that could cure the
devils in the head, and that was doctor Harvey (whom I
had prepared) and wished him, if ever he found himself ill
10 in my absence, to go to him, for he could cure this disease
as well as myself.   The gentleman lived.many years, and
was never troubled after.

XXXV.

DUEL.

1. A DUEL may still be granted in some cases by the law
of England, and only there.   That the church allowed it

l. 14. *A duel may still be granted* &c.]   See Selden, Analecta Anglo-
Britannica, Works, ii. p. 949.
But he adds that there is hardly an instance to be found in which
this form of trial has been actually used in civil cases, and very few
instances in which it has been used in criminal cases.
Blackstone mentions it as still in force in his day.
'The next species of trial is of great antiquity, but much disused;
though still in force if the parties chose to abide by it; I mean the
trial by wager of battle . . . . a trial which the tenant or defendant in
a writ of right, has it in his election at this day to demand.' Blackstone,
Commentaries, bk. iii. ch. 22, sec. 5.   So too in criminal trials—bk. iv.
ch. 27, sec. 3.
These forms of trial, in civil and criminal cases, were done away
with by 59 George III, ch. 56.
l. 15. *That the church allowed it anciently*, &c.]   Ducange, Glossary,
sub voce 'Campiones' (champions), mentions the 'Campionum obla-
tiones, in Chartâ Manassis Episc. Lingonensis, ann. 1185, quas ii, prius
quam in arenam descenderent, Ecclesiis offerebant, quo in duellis Deum
sibi propitium conciliarent.'
Also, sub voce 'Duellum,' he shows that—'sacramenta quae in his

anciently, appears by this. In their public liturgies, there
were prayers appointed for the duellists to say; the judge
used to bid one of them go to such a church and pray, &c.
for the victory: and to the other go to such a prelate in
such a church, and pray, &c. But whether is this lawful?
If you grant any war lawful, I make no doubt but to con-
vince it. War is lawful, because God is the only judge
betwixt two that are supreme. Now if a difference happen
betwixt two subjects, and it cannot be decided by human
testimony, why may they not put it to God, to judge [10]
between them, by the permission of the prince? Nay,
what if we should bring it down, for argument's sake, to
the sword-men. One gives me the lie; 'tis a great disgrace
to take it, the law has made no provision to give remedy
for the injury, (if you can suppose any thing an injury for
which the law gives no remedy) why am not I in this case
supreme, and may therefore right myself?

2. A duke ought to fight with a gentleman. The reason
is this; the gentleman will say to the duke, 'tis true, you
hold a higher place in the state than I; there's a great [20]
distance betwixt you and me; but your dignity does not

occasionibus de more fiebant super sanctam crucem, sanctas reliquias,
aut sancta Evangelia, proferebantur coram sacerdotibus vel Ecclesiae
ministris.'

Canciani, in his Lex Costumaria Normannica, gives examples of
the oaths administered to the combatants that they are using no help
from sorcery or magical arts. Leges Barbarorum, vol. ii. p. 395, note.

Muratori shows that judicial combats were held anciently under the
full sanction of the Church, and that the clergy were sometimes parties
to them, either in person or more often by a champion chosen to
defend their cause. Antiq. Italicae, iii. p. 638, Dissert. 39.

Also, on p. 637, 'Tanta autem fuit divini patrocinii spes in abomi-
nandis hisce certaminibus ut (Johanne Sarisberiensi in Epistol. 169,
aliisque testibus) certaturi noctem praecedentem ducerent insomnem
in Templo ad tumulum alicujus sancti, ut eum in agone propitium
experirentur.' That they were again and again disapproved by the
Church and forbidden under heavy ecclesiastical penalties, hardly
needs proof. The proofs occur passim.

privilege you to do me an injury; as soon as ever you do me an injury, you make yourself my equal, and as you are my equal, I challenge you; and in sense the duke is bound to answer him. This will give you some light to under-stand the quarrel betwixt a prince and his subjects. Though there be a vast distance between him and them, and they are to obey him according to their contract; yet he has no power to do them an injury. Then, they think themselves as much bound to vindicate their right, as they are to obey his lawful commands. Nor is there any other measure of justice left upon earth but arms.

XXXVI.

EPITAPH.

An epitaph must be made fit for the person for whom it is made. For a man to say all the excellent things that can be said upon one, and call that his epitaph, 'tis as if a painter should make the handsomest piece that he can possibly make, and say 'twas my picture. It holds in a funeral sermon.

XXXVII.

EQUITY.

1. Equity in law is the same that the spirit is in religion, what every one pleases to make it. Sometimes they go according to conscience, sometimes according to law, some-times according to the rule of the court.

l. 3. *in sense the duke is bound*] i.e. in reality; in point of fact. Selden uses this phrase elsewhere, see 'Preaching,' sec. 3 and 'Vows.'

2. Equity is a roguish thing. For law we have a measure, know what to trust to; equity is according to the conscience of him that is chancellor, and as that is larger or narrower, so is equity. 'Tis all one as if they should make the standard for the measure we call a foot, a chancellor's foot[1]. What an uncertain measure would this be. One chancellor has a long foot, another a short foot, a third an indifferent foot; 'tis the same thing in the chancellor's conscience.

3. That saying, Do as you would be done to, is often so misunderstood; for 'tis not thus meant, that I, a private man, should do to you, a private man, as I would have you to me, but do, as we have agreed to do one to another by public agreement. If the prisoner should ask the judge, whether he would be content to be hanged, were he in his case, he would answer, No. Then says the prisoner, Do

---

[1] *We call a foot, a chancellor's foot.* Singer conjecturally] we call a chancellor's foot, MSS.

l. 1. *Equity is a roguish thing.* &c.] This has ceased to be true, as equity has come gradually to be administered under settled rules. On the conflict between law and equity in Selden's day, and on the general complaint about the aggressive and exorbitant authority of the Court of Chancery, see e. g. Chamberlain's letter to Carleton, November 14, 1616. 'On Tuesday, one Bertram, an aged gentleman, killed Sir John Tyndall, a master of the Chancery, with a pistol charged with three bullets, pretending he had wronged him in the report of a cause, to his utter undoing, as indeed he was not held for integerrimus. . . . Mine author, Ned Wymarke, cited Sir William Walter for saying that the fellow mistook his mark, and should have shot hailshot at the whole court, which indeed grows great, and engrosses all manner of cases, and breeds general complaint for a decree passed there this term, subscribed by all the king's learned counsel, whereby that court may receive and call in question what judgments soever pass at the common law, whereby the jurisdiction of that court is enlarged out of measure, and so suits may become as it were immortal. This success is come of my Lord Coke and some of the judges oppugning the Chancery so weakly and unreasonably that, instead of overthrowing that exorbitant authority, they have more established and confirmed it.' Court and Times of James I, vol. i. 439 (2 vols. 1848).

as you would be done to.   Neither of them must do as
private men, but the judge must do by him as they have
publicly agreed; that is, both judge and prisoner have
consented to a law, that if either of them steal they shall
be hanged.

———

XXXVIII.

EVIL SPEAKING.

1. HE that speaks ill of another, commonly, before he is
aware, makes himself such a one as he speaks against; for
if he had civility or breeding, he would forbear such kind
10 of language.

2. A gallant man is above ill words.   An example we
have in the old lord of Salisbury, who was a great wise
man.   Stone had called some lord about court, fool, the

l. 13. *Stone had called* &c.]   Doran (Court Fools, p. 196) says that this
remark is all that we know of Stone.   It seems to have been suggested
by the unseemly passages of arms between Archbishop Laud and
Archibald Armstrong, the Court Fool of the time (1637).   Their enmi-
ties had been of long standing.   The Fool had on several occasions
offered public affronts to the Archbishop, with the result (according to
Francis Osborn) that Laud 'managed a quarrel with Archie the King's
fool, and by endeavouring to explode him the court rendered him at
last so considerable . . . as the fellow was not only able to continue
the dispute for divers years, but received such encouragement from
bystanders as he hath oft, in my hearing, belched in his face such
miscarriages as he was really guilty of, and might, but for this foul-
mouthed Scot, have been forgotten; adding such other reproaches of
his own as the dignity of his calling and greatness of his parts could
not in reason or manners admit.'   Osborn goes on to speak of the
Archbishop as 'hoodwinked with passion' and as led by his too low-
placed anger into no less an absurdity than an endeavour to bring the
fool into the Star Chamber, and as having at last through the mediation
of the Queen got him discharged the Court.   Rushworth says, further,
that when news had come from Scotland that there had been tumults
about the new service-book, introduced at Laud's suggestion, 'Archibald, the King's fool, said to his Grace the Archbishop of Canterbury;

lord complained, and has Stone whipped: Stone cries, I
might have called my lord of Salisbury fool often enough,
before he would have had me whipped.

3. Speak not ill of a great enemy, but rather give him
good words, that he may use you the better, if you chance
to fall into his hands. The Spaniard did this when he was
a dying; his confessor told him (to work him to repentance),
how the devil tormented the wicked that went to hell: the
Spaniard replying, called the devil my lord; I hope my
lord the devil is not so cruel: his confessor reproved [10]
him. Excuse me for calling him so, says the Don; I
know not into what hands I may fall, and if I happen into
his, I hope he will use me the better for giving him good
words.

as he was going to the Council Table, 'Whea's feule now? doth not
your Grace hear the news from Striveling about the Liturgy?' with
other words of reflection. This was presently complained of to the
Council, and it produced an order from the King and the assembled
Lords that 'Archibald Armestrong, the King's fool, for certain scandalous words of a high nature, spoken by him against the Lord Archbishop of Canterbury, his Grace, and proved to be uttered by him by
two witnesses, shall have his coat pulled over his head and be discharged the King's service and banished the Court.'—Rushworth,
Collections, ii. 470.

It may be questioned whether Rushworth is correct in thus limiting
the occasion of Archie's disgrace. 'Archye,' writes Mr. Gerrard to
Lord Strafford (Strafford Papers, vol. ii.), 'is fallen into a great misfortune; a fool he would be, but a foul-mouthed knave he hath proved
himself; being at a tavern in Westminster, drunk as he saith himself,
he was speaking of the Scottish business, he fell a railing of my Lord
of Canterbury, said he was a monk, a rogue, and a traitor. Of this, his
Grace complained at Council, and the King being present, it was
ordered he should be carried to the Porter's Lodge, his coat pulled
over his ears, and kicked out of the Court,' &c.

We have also the well-known story of the fool's grace at dinner—
'Great praise be given to God, and little *Laud* to the devil.' See Doran,
Court Fools, 205-207.

XXXIX.

EXCOMMUNICATION.

1. THAT place they bring for excommunication, put away from among yourselves that wicked person, 1 Cor. v. 13, is corrupted in the Greek. For it should be τὸ πονηρόν, put away *that evil* from among you, not τὸν πονηρόν, *that evil person*. Besides, ὁ πονηρὸς is the *devil*, in Scripture, and it may be so taken there; and there is a new edition¯ of Theodoret come out, that has it right τὸ πονηρόν. 'Tis true the Christians, before the civil state became Christian, 10 did by covenant and agreement set down how they would live; and he that did not observe what they agreed upon, should come no more amongst them; that is, be excommunicated. Such men are spoken of by the Apostle, Romans i. 31, whom he calls ἀσυνθέτους καὶ ἀσπόνδους; the Vulgar has it, *incompositos, et sine fœdere*; the last word is pretty well, but the first not at all. Origen, in his book against Celsus, speaks of the Christians' συνθήκη, the trans-lator renders it *conventus*, as it signifies a *meeting*, when it is plain it signifies a covenant, and the English Bible 20 turned the other word well, *covenant-breakers*. Pliny tells us, the Christians took an oath amongst themselves to live thus and thus.

l. 2. *That place they bring* &c.] Stanley, in his notes on the Epistles to the Corinthians, remarks on this verse that—ἐξάρατε τὸν πονηρὸν is the usual formula for punishment on great crimes. See Deut. xiii. 5, xvii. 7, xxiv. 7, &c., also 2 Kings xxiii. 24. He adds, however, that Theodoret and Augustine read τὸ πονηρόν, and interpret it 'put away evil from amongst you.'

l. 16. *Origen, in his book* &c.] Οὕτω δὴ καὶ Χριστιανοὶ ... συνθήκας ποιοῦνται παρὰ τὰ νενομισμένα τῷ διαβόλῳ κατὰ τοῦ διαβόλου. Contra Celsum, bk. i. ch. 1. The word συνθήκη occurs several times in this chapter, and in the sense which Selden gives to it.

l. 20. *Pliny tells us*, &c.] He reports it, in a letter to Trajan, as a statement made to him by certain persons who had been brought

2. The other place [*dic ecclesiœ*] *tell the church* (Matt. xvi i. 17), is but a weak ground to raise excommunication upon, especially from the sacrament, the lesser excommunication; since when that was spoken, the sacrament was not instituted[1]. The Jews' *ecclesia* was their Sanhedrim, their court: so that the meaning is, if after once or twice admonition this brother will not be reclaimed, bring him thither.

3. The first excommunication was 180 years after Christ,

[1] *Was not instituted*] was instituted, MSS.

before him charged with being Christians, and who had ceased so to be. 'Adfirmabant autem, hanc fuisse summam vel culpae suae vel erroris, quod essent soliti stato die ante lucem convenire; carmenque Christo, quasi Deo, dicere secum invicem, seque sacramento non in scelus aliquod obstringere, sed ne furta, ne latrocinia, ne adulteria committerent, ne fidem fallerent, ne depositum appellati abnegarent.' Epistles, bk. x. 97.

l. 1. *The other place, dic ecclesiae* &c.] Selden, in interpreting this place, is following Erastus in his Explicatio gravissimae questionis &c. (1589) where he discusses it at great length. Conf. e.g. 'Clarior evadet tractatio si quae et qualis fuerit illa Ecclesia, cui jussit dicere, consideretur. In cujus rei declaratione hoc pro initio et fundamento pono . . . Christum scilicet de Ecclesia loqui quae tum esset.' Thesis 46.

'Dic ecclesiae, id est, Dic synedrio . . . Ego enim verba haec Dic ecclesiae idem significare assero, quod ista significant, Dic magistratui tuo, si non est impiae religionis defensor.' Confirmatio Thesium, p. 322. See also Thesis 45 and 56.

l. 3. *the lesser excommunication;*] There were two forms of excommunication—the lesser, involving mainly exclusion from the eucharist, and the greater involving also exclusion from all intercourse with the rest of the Christian body. See Erastus, Explicatio gravissimae questionis, &c., Thesis 7; and Selden's De Synedriis veterum Ebraeorum, i. ch. 9. Works, vol. i. p. 918.

l. 8. *The first excommunication* &c.] This is not clearly and probably not correctly reported. The excommunication in 180 A. D. and that by Victor are distinct. Victor's, too, was much more than what Selden is here made to term it. It was a wide sweeping sentence, cutting off the whole of the Asiatic churches from communion with the rest of the Church Catholic; and though not the first absolutely, was, in this respect, the first of its kind. See Selden, De Synedriis veterum Ebraeorum, bk. i. ch. 9. Works, i. 916. But

and that by Victor, bishop of Rome. But that was no more than this, that they should communicate and receive the sacrament amongst themselves, not with those of the other opinion: the controversy (as I take it) being about the feast of Easter. Men do not care for excommunication because they are shut out of the church, or delivered up to Satan, but because the law of the kingdom takes hold of them. After so many days a man cannot sue, no, not for his wife, if you take her from him. And there may 10 be as much reason to grant it for a small fault, if there be contumacy, as for a great one. In Westminster hall you may outlaw a man for forty shillings, which is their excommunication, and you can do no more for £40,000.

4. When Constantine became Christian, he so fell in love with the clergy, that he let them be judges of all things; but that continued not above three or four years, by reason they were to be judges of matters they understood

that there were excommunications earlier than this and earlier than 180 A. D. is clear from p. 920 and from the chapter *passim*.

l. 5. *Men do not care* &c.] See e. g. Nathaniel Fiennes' speech in Parliament (1640): 'Were it not for the civil restraints and penalties that follow upon it (sc. Excommunication) no man will purchase an absolution though he may have it for a half-penny. And I have heard of some that have thanked the Ordinaries for abating or remitting the fees of the Courts, but I never heard of any that thanked them for reclaiming their souls to repentance by their excommunications.' Nalson, Collections, i. 760.

l. 9. *there may be as much reason to grant it* &c.] This is the argument of the bishops in their answer to a book of articles in 1584. They urge that they do not excommunicate for two-penny causes, 'though indeed there be as much in 2*d.* as in £100,' but for disobedience to the order, decree, and sentence of the judge. So, in a temporal cause of 2*d*, a man is outlawed if he appear not or obey not; but he is not outlawed for 2*d*, but for his disobedience in a two-penny matter. Wilkins, Concilia, iv. 311.

l. 14. *When Constantine became Christian* &c.] The evidence for this is found in a rescript, purporting to be addressed by Constantine to the Prefect Ablavius. For the contents of this document, and for the discussions which have been raised about it, see Excursus A.

not ; and then they were allowed to meddle with nothing
but religion.   All jurisdiction belonged to him, and he
scantled them out as much as he pleased, and so things
have since continued.   They excommunicate for three or
four things, matters concerning adultery, tithes, wills, &c.
which is the civil punishment the state allows for such
faults.   If a bishop excommunicate a man[1] for what he
ought not, the judge has power to absolve, and punish the
bishop.   If they had that jurisdiction from God, why does
not the church excommunicate for murder, for theft ?   If 10
the civil power might take away all but three things, why
may they not take away them too ?   If this excommunication were quite taken away, the presbyters would be quiet ;
'tis that they have a mind to, 'tis that they would fain be at.

[1] *A man,* H. 2] omitted in H.

l. 2.   *he scantled them out*] i.e. simply—he measured them out.
The word involves no notion of a scanty measure, as the reading
in the printed editions—' scanted '—does.

l. 7.   *If a bishop excommunicate* &c.]   Selden, in his De Synedriis
veterum Ebraeorum, bk. i. ch. 10, gives numerous examples in
support of his assertion that in this country, as in other Christian
states, the power of excommunication was fixed and strictly limited
by the law of the land.   He shows that a sentence, illegally pronounced, was liable to be annulled by the King's order ; that punishment was threatened or inflicted on clerics who refused to obey the
order ; and that satisfaction in money was granted to the person
injured.   This he traces from William I to his own day.   Works,
vol. i. 977-990.   See also note on Power, State, sec. 7.

l. 14.   *'tis that they have a mind to,* &c.]   The Westminster assembly
of divines claimed for the Presbytery the uncontrolled right, *jure
divino,* to suspend from the sacrament such persons as they should
judge to be ignorant, or profane, or of scandalous lives.   This they
first settled by a majority vote among themselves, Selden and his
friends dissenting, and then again and again pressed upon Parliament
to admit and ratify their claim.   This, however, the Parliament refused
to do.   After some delay it granted them the power they sought, but
added a provision that if any person suspended from the Lord's Supper
found himself aggrieved by the proceedings of the local Presbytery,
he should have the right to appeal to the Assemblies, and thence, in

Like the wench that was to be married; she asked her
mother when 'twas done, if she should go to bed presently?
No, says her mother, you must dine first; And then to bed
mother? No, you must dance after dinner; And then to
bed mother? No, you must go to supper; And then to bed
mother? &c.

XL.

FASTING DAYS.

1. WHAT the Church debars us one day, she gives us
leave to take it out in another. First we fast, and then we
10 feast. First there is a carnival, and then a lent.

2. Whether do human laws bind the conscience? If
they do, 'tis a way to ensnare: If we say they do not, we
open a door to disobedience.

Answer. In this case we must look to the justice of
the law, and intention of the lawgiver. If there be not
justice in the law, 'tis not to be obeyed; if the intention of
the lawgiver be absolute, our obedience must be so too. If
the intention of the lawgiver enjoin a penalty as a compen-
sation for the breach of the law, I sin not if I submit to the
10 penalty; if it enjoin a penalty, as a further enforcement of
obedience to the law, then ought I to observe it; which
may be known by the often repetition of the law. The
way of fasting is enjoined unto them who yet do not observe
it. The law enjoins a penalty as an enforcement to obedience; which intention appears by the often calling upon

the last instance, to Parliament. See Whitelock, Memorials, pp. 129,
135, 164, 165, 169, 170; Neal's History of the Puritans, iii. 242, 246.
The exact words of the Parliamentary resolution are given in Rushworth, Collections, part iv. vol. i. 212. Selden's speech in the
debate, covering the same ground as his remarks in the Table Talk,
is given by Whitelock, p. 169. For the sequel of the dispute, see
'Presbytery,' sec. 4.

L 25. *which intention appears* &c.] See Gibson, Codex, tit. x. ch. 6,

us to keep that law by the king, and the dispensation to the Church to such as are not able to keep it, as young children, old folks, diseased men, &c.

XLI.

FATHERS AND SONS.

I t hath ever been the way of fathers to bind their sons. To strengthen this by the law of the land, every one, at twelve years of age, is to take the oath of allegiance in court-leets, whereby he swears obedience to the king.

XLII.

FAITH AND WORKS.

'Twas an unhappy division that has been made betwixt 10 faith and works; though in my intellect I may divide them, just as in the candle, I know there is both heat and light; but yet put out the candle, and they are both gone : one remains not without the other.   So 'tis betwixt faith and works.   Nay, in a right conception, *fides est opus.* If I believe a thing, because I am commanded, that is *opus.*·

p. 254, where the successive statutes on fasting, with the penalties for disobeying them and the provisions made for dispensations in case of need, are set out at length.

l. 7. *the oath of allegiance in court-leets*] 'The court-leet...is a court of record, held once in the year, within a particular hundred, lordship or manor, before the steward of the leet; being the king's court granted by charter to the lords of those hundreds or manors. . . . It was also anciently the custom to summon all the king's subjects as they respectively grew to years of discretion and strength to come to the court-leet, and there take the oath of allegiance to the king.' Blackstone, Comment., bk. iv. ch. 19, sec. 10.

That twelve was the age of discretion appears from the fact that persons under that age were excused attendance at the court-leet.

XLIII.

FINES.

THE old law was, that when a man was fined, he was to be fined *salvo contenemento*, so as his countenance might be safe ; taking countenance in the same sense as your countryman does, when he says, if you will come unto my house, I will shew you the best countenance I can, that is, not the best face, but the best entertainment. The meaning of the law was, that so much should be taken from a man, such a gobbet sliced off, that yet notwithstand-
10 ing he might live in the same rank and condition he lived in before. But now they fine men ten times more than they are worth.

l. 11. *But now they fine men* &c.] It was one of the grievances urged against the High Commission Court that 'they imposed great fines upon those who were culpable before them; sometimes above the degree of the offence .... which course of fining was much more frequent and the fines heavier after the King had granted all that revenue to be employed for the reparation of St. Paul's Church.' Clarendon, Hist., i. 439. So, too, in the Star Chamber, part of the sentence on Burton, Bastwick and Prynne was that they were fined £5000. Bishop Williams, for having received and divulged some libellous letters, was fined £8000. It was not paid, and could not have been, owing to what the bishop termed 'the vacuity of his purse.' Fuller, Church Hist., bk. xi. sec. 8, § 4.

Again, in 1641, when the High Commission Court and Star Chamber had been swept away, and when judges and accused had changed places, the fines were as heavy as before. Archbishop Laud, e.g. for his part in framing and putting out the Canons of 1640, was sentenced by Parliament to pay a fine of £20,000 ; Bishop Juxon of London, and Bishop Wren of Ely to pay £10,000 each ; the rest of the offending bishops to pay £5000. Rushworth, Collections, iv. 235.

A fine of £20,000 was imposed on Judge Berkley for his opinion in favour of ship-money, and £10,000 was actually paid by him and by his fellow-culprit Baron Trevor. Clarendon, Hist. ii. 566.

XLIV.

FREE-WILL.

THE Puritans who will allow no free-will at all, but God does all, yet will allow the subject his liberty to do or not to do, notwithstanding the king, the god upon earth. The Arminians, who hold we have free-will, yet say, when we come to the king there must be all obedience, and no liberty must be stood for.

XLV.

FRIENDS.

OLD friends are best. King James used to call for his old shoes ; they were easiest for his feet.

XLVI.

FRIARS.

1. THE friars say they possess nothing ; whose then are the lands they hold ? Not their superior's, he hath vowed poverty as well as they. Whose then? To answer this 'twas decreed they should say they were the pope's. And why must the friars be more perfect than the pope himself?

2. If there had been no friars, Christendom might have continued quiet, and things remained at the stay.

If there had been no lecturers [which succeed the friars in their way] the Church of England might have stood and flourished at this day.

l. 20. *If there had been no lecturers* &c.] See note on 'Lecturers,' sec. 1.

XLVII.

GENEALOGY OF CHRIST.

1. THEY that say, the reason why Joseph's pedigree is set down, and not Mary's, is, because the descent from the mother is lost, and swallowed up, say something, for so it was; but yet if a Jewish woman married with a Gentile, they only took notice of the mother, not of the father. But they that say they were both of a tribe, say nothing; for the tribes might marry one with another, and the law against it was only temporary, in the time while Joshua was in dividing the land, lest the being so long about it, there might be a confusion.

2. That Christ was the son of Joseph is most exactly true. For though he was the Son of God, yet with the Jews, if any man kept a child, and brought him up, and called him son, he was taken for his son; and his land (if he had any) was to descend upon him; and therefore the genealogy of Joseph is justly set down.

XLVIII.

GENTLEMEN.

1. WHAT a gentleman is, 'tis hard with us to define. In other countries he is known by his privileges; in West-minster-hall he is one that is reputed one; in the court of honour, he that hath arms. The king cannot make a

l. 7. *But they that say* &c.] This is a little obscure. It means, apparently, that whether Joseph and Mary had been of the same tribe, or of different tribes (as they might lawfully have been), the descent from the mother would equally have been ' lost and swallowed up.' An assertion, therefore, that the pedigree was set down on the father's side because they were both of a tribe would miss the real point.

l. 8. *the law against it*] Numbers xxxvi. 8, 9.

gentleman of blood; [what have you said ?] nor God Almighty; but he can make a gentleman by creation. If you ask which is the better of these two ; civilly, the gentleman of blood ; morally the gentleman by creation may be the better; for the other may be a debauched man, this a person of worth.

2. Gentlemen have ever been more temperate in their religion than the common people, as having more reason, the others running in a hurry. In the beginning of Christianity the fathers writ *contra gentes*, and *contra gentiles*, o they were all one ; but after all were Christians, the better sort of people still retained the name of Gentiles, throughout the four provinces of the Roman empire; as *gentilhomme* in French, *gentil-huomo* [1] in Italian, *gentil-huombre* in Spanish, and *gentle-man* [2] in English : and they, no question, being persons of quality, kept up those feasts which we borrow from the Gentiles ; as Christmas, Candlemas, May-day, &c. continuing what was not directly against Christianity, which the common people would never have endured.   20

XLIX.

GOLD.

THERE are two reasons given why those words, *Jesus autem transiens per medium eorum ibat,* were about our old

---

[1] *Gentil-huomo*] gentel-homo, H. and H. 2.
[2] *Gentleman*, H. 2] gentilman, H.

l. 22. *There are two reasons* &c.] The second reason given here is not what Selden gives elsewhere. After mentioning the alchemical reason for the inscription, he adds—' alii opinati sunt . . . amulcri vicem obtinuisse, et caedi et vulneribus averruncandis. Certe verba illa in iis quibus tortorum quaestioni subjecti interdum, dolori allevando abigendoque, utuntur locum habere ex jurisconsultis aliquot scimus.' Works, vol. ii. p. 1386.
Camden mentions the story told by the alchemists; but, with a

gold. The one is, because Ripley the alchymist, when he made gold in the tower, the first time he found it, he spoke these words, *per medium eorum*, that is, *per medium ignis et sulphuris*. The other is, because these words were thought to be a charm, and that they did bind whatsoever they were written upon, so that a man could not take it away. To this reason I rather incline.

L.

HALL.

The hall was the place where the great lord did use to
10 eat, (wherefore else were the halls made so big?) where he

disregard of dates, he gives Raymond Lully as the successful pro-
jector in the Tower. He adds that others say that the text on the
coins was only an amulet used in that credulous warfaring age to
escape dangers in battle. See Camden, Remains, sub tit. 'Money,'
p. 242 (ed. 7, London, 1674).

We learn, too, that the rose nobles of other nations, as well as of
ours, had these words stamped upon them. They were used in
England first by Edward III, and were copied on the coins of several
later reigns. Sometimes another passage of Scripture was used
instead of them; as e. g. 'A domino factum est istud, et est mirabile
in oculis nostris;' or 'per crucem tuam salva nos Christe redemptor.'
See Archbishop Sharpe, Dissertation on the Golden Coins of England, secs. 4 and 6.

l. 9. *The hall was the place* &c.] See e. g. Household Statutes
(first half of thirteenth century), framed for Bishop Grossetest. 'Make
ye your own household to sit in the hall, as much as ye may... And
sit ye ever in the middle of the high borde (table) that your face and
cheer be shown to all men. And all so much as ye may, without
peril of sickness and weariness, eat ye in the hall before your men.
For that shall be to you profit and worship.' Manners and Meals in
Olden Time, Part I, p. 329, 331 (Early English Text Society).

The Eltham Ordinances for the government of the royal household
under Henry VIII are framed in view of the King's dining in Hall,
and they give special permission for private meals when the King
does not dine in the Hall. See chh. 44, 45, and 52, pp. 151, 153.

saw all his servants and his tenants about him. He eat not
in private, except in time of sickness ; when once he became a thing cooped up, all his greatness was spilled.
Nay, the king himself used to eat in the hall, and his lords
sat with him, and then he understood men.

LI.

HELL.

1. THERE are two texts for Christ's descending into hell ;
the one, Psalm xvi. the other, Acts ii. where the Bible, that

But that the custom was ceasing to be observed appears from ch.
77, p. 160, which gives rules which had become necessary 'by reason
of the seldom keeping of the King's Hall.'

The above are printed in A Collection of Ordinances for the
Government of the Royal Household (1790, 4to).

l. 7. *There are two texts* &c.] This is incorrect. There are other
texts which have been, rightly or wrongly, interpreted to prove the
descent. Conf. Ephesians iv. 9 : 'Now that he ascended, what is it
but that he also descended first into the lower parts of the earth ?'
and 1 Peter iii. 19 : 'By which also he went and preached unto
the spirits in prison.' In the Forty-two Articles of 1552, the descent
into hell is explained and confirmed by a reference to this passage : 'Quemadmodum Christus pro nobis mortuus est et sepultus,
ita est etiam credendus ad inferos descendisse. Nam corpus usque
ad resurrectionem in sepulchro jacuit; spiritus ab eo emissus, cum
spiritibus qui in carcere sive in inferno detinebantur fuit, illisque
praedicavit, quemadmodum testatur Petri locus.' In the Thirty-nine
Articles of 1562, the Article on the descent ends with the words 'ad
inferos descendisse,' and omits all reference to the preaching to the
spirits in prison. At this date the authorised version of the Bible
was Cranmer's, or the great Bible (1539), in which (as in Tyndale's
earlier version) the reading in Acts ii. 27 is 'thou wilt not leave my
soul in hell.' The Thirty-nine Articles were confirmed or recognised
by Parliament in 1571, at which date, and up to 1611, the authorised
version was the 'Bishops' Bible' (1568). In this version the text
remains unchanged—'because thou wilt not leave my soul in hell';
and in the corresponding passage in Psalm xvi. 10 the word 'hell'
is marginally explained as 'in the state that souls be after this life.'

was in use when the Thirty-nine Articles were made, has
it (hell). But the Bible that was in Queen Elizabeth's time,
when the Articles were confirmed, reads it (grave), and so
it continued till the new translation in King James's time,
and then 'tis hell again. But by this we may gather the
Church of England declined, as much as they could, the
descent; otherwise they never would have altered the
Bible.

2. *He descended into hell.* This may be the interpretation
10 of it. He may be dead and buried, then his soul ascended
into heaven. Afterwards he descended again into hell, that
is, into the grave, to fetch his body, and to rise again. The
ground of this interpretation is taken from the Platonic

The text is changed in the Geneva Bible (1557) which reads 'grave'
for hell. This version was in common private use, and was most
favoured by the Puritan party, but it was not authorised or appointed
to be read in church. It does not appear, therefore, that the Church
of England at any time 'altered the Bible,' as Selden incorrectly says.
l. 13. *the Platonic learning*] That a metempsychosis was a Platonic
doctrine is certain. It appears in the story of Er, the son of Arminius,
in Rep. x. and in the Phaedrus 248, 249, where, in one passage, the
soul which is to take a new body is said to fall to the earth. So
among the later Platonists, Porphyry speaks of τὰς ψυχὰς εἰς γίνεσιν
κατιούσας (De Antro Nympharum, sec. 10), and again in his Ἀφορμαὶ
πρὸς τὰ νοητά, sec. 32. Conf. also Plotinus, Enneades, Enn. 4, lib. 8,
Περὶ τῆς εἰς τὰ σώματα καθόδου τῆς ψυχῆς, *passim*: and especially in § 4.
Εἴληπται οὖν (ἡ ψυχὴ) πεσοῦσα, καὶ πρὸς τῷ δεσμῷ οὖσα ... τεθάφθαι τε
λέγεται καὶ ἐν σπηλαίῳ εἶναι.
But that these views affected the language of the early Christians,
and that they understood the descent into hell in Selden's sense of
the words, there is nothing to show, and there is abundant evidence
to the contrary. On this subject the Greek and Latin fathers speak
with one voice. They understand Christ's descent into hell as a fact
distinct from his burial and resurrection. It is a literal visit to the
lower regions where the souls of the dead were detained, and from
which the souls of the old prophets and saints were liberated at
Christ's coming. Pearson, in his long and learned discussion on the
descent, puts the question, thus far, beyond all reasonable doubt.
Archbishop Usher, writing on the descent, shows out of Plato and
other philosophers and poets, that the word Hades is used to signify

learning, who held a metempsychosis, and when a soul did descend from heaven to take another body, they called it καταβασιν εἰς ᾅδην, taking ᾅδης for the lower world, the state of mortality. Now the first Christians, many of them, were Platonic philosophers, and no question spoke such language as then was understood amongst them. To understand by hell, the grave, is no tautology, because the creed first tells what Christ suffered, He was crucified, dead, and buried; then it tells us what he did, He descended into hell, the third day he rose again, he ascended, &c. 10

LII.

HOLY-DAYS.

THEY say the Church imposes holy-days. There's no such thing, though the number of holy-days is set down in some of our Common-prayer books [1]. Yet that has relation to an act of parliament, which forbids the keeping of any other holy-days. The ground thereof was the multitude of holy-days in time of popery. But those that are

[1] *Books*, H. 2] book, H.

a general invisible future state of the soul after it is separated from the body, and he interprets the descent accordingly. Conf. Parr's Life of Usher, Appendix 27. Selden's interpretation appears to be entirely his own. I can find no other authority for it.

l. 15. *an act of parliament, which forbids* &c.] This is the 5 and 6 of Edward VI, ch. 3, which enacts: 'that all the days hereafter mentioned shall be kept and commanded to be kept holy-days, and none other . . . and that none other day shall be kept and commanded to be kept holy-day, or to abstain from lawful bodily labour.' The list given corresponds with that now in the Book of Common Prayer. Selden's remark must have been made at some date before June 8, 1647, when an Ordinance was put out by Parliament that festivals called holy-days were no longer to be observed, any law, statute, custom or canon to the contrary notwithstanding. Rushworth, Collections, vol. vi. p. 548.

kept, are kept by the custom of the country; and I hope you will not say the Church imposes that.

LIII.

HUMILITY.

1. HUMILITY is a virtue all preach, none practise, and yet every body is content to hear. The master thinks it good doctrine for his servant, the laity for the clergy, and the clergy for the laity.

2. There is *humilitas quædam in vitio*. If a man does not take notice of that excellency and perfection that is in himself, how can he be thankful to God, who is the author of all excellency and perfection? Nay, if a man has too mean an opinion of himself, 'twill render him unserviceable both to God and man.

3. Pride may be allowed to this or that degree, else a man cannot keep up his dignity. In gluttony[1] there must be eating, in drunkenness there must be drinking; 'tis not the eating, nor 'tis not the drinking that is to be blamed, but the excess. So in pride.

LIV.

IDOLATRY.

IDOLATRY is in a man's own thought, not in the opinion of another. Put case I bow to the altar, why am I guilty of

---

[1] *Gluttony*, S.] gluttons, H. and H. 2.

l. 21. *Put case I bow* &c.] This practice had been attacked as idolatrous by Burton, in his Sermon for God and the King (p. 105), and had been described by Prynne, in his Histrio-mastix (p. 236), as 'our late crouching and ducking unto newly erected altars, a ceremony much in use with idolatrous Papists heretofore, and derived by them

idolatry? Because a stander-by thinks so? I am sure I do not believe the altar to be God, and the God I worship may be bowed to in all places, and at all times.

LV.

JEWS.

1. GOD at the first gave laws to all mankind, but afterwards he gave peculiar laws to the Jews, which they only were to observe. Just as we have the common law for all England, and yet you have some corporations that, besides that, have peculiar laws and privileges to themselves.

2. Talk what you will of the Jews, that they are cursed, 10 they thrive where'er they come; they are able to oblige the prince of their country by lending him money; none of them beg; they keep together; and for their being hated, my life for yours, the Christians hate one another as much.

LVI.

INVINCIBLE IGNORANCE.

'TIS all one to me, if I am told of Christ, or some mystery of Christianity, if I am not capable of understanding it, as if I am not told at all, my ignorance is as invincible; and therefore 'tis vain to call their ignorance only invincible, who never were told of Christ. The trick of it is to advance 20 the priest, whilst the Church of Rome says a man must be told of Christ by one thus and thus ordained.

from pagan practices.' Laud, in his speech at the censure of Burton, Bastwick and Prynne, justifies it at great length, and substantially for the same reasons as Selden. See Laud's Works, vol. vi. p. 55 ff. But he does not use Selden's phrase of bowing to the altar. What he defends is carefully guarded as bowing towards the altar.

LVII.

IMAGES.

1. THE papists taking away the second commandment, is not haply so horrid a thing, nor so unreasonable amongst Christians as we make it. For the Jews, they could make no figure of God but they must commit idolatry, because he had taken no shape ; but since the assumption of our flesh, we know what shape to picture God in. Nor do I know why we may not make his image, provided we be sure what it is : as we say St. Luke took the picture of the Virgin Mary, and St. Veronica of our Saviour. Otherwise it would be no honour to the king, to make a picture and call it the king's picture, when 'tis nothing like him.

2. Though the learned papists pray not to images, yet 'tis to be feared the ignorant do ; as appears by that tale of St. Nicholas in Spain. A countryman used to offer daily to St. Nicholas's image ; at length by a mischance the image was broken, and a new one made of his own plum-tree ; after that the man forbore. Being complained of to his Ordinary, he answered, 'tis true, he used to offer to the old image, but to the new he could not find in his heart because he knew it was a piece of his own plum-tree. You see what opinion this man had of the image; and to this tended the bowing of their images, the twinkling of their eyes, the virgin's milk, &c. Had they only meant representations, a picture would have done it without these

l. 2. *The papists taking away* &c.] The papists do not do this in terms. They read the second Commandment continuously with the first, and as forming part of the first. The first Commandment they take as—'Thou shalt have none other Gods before me, i. e. in my presence,' and they interpret the second as enlarging upon and explaining this. See e. g. the Douay Version—'Thou shalt not have strange Gods before me' (Latin Vulgate, coram me)—explained in the notes to Haydocke's edition of the version as ='in my presence. I shall not be content to be adored with idols.'

tricks. It may be with us in England they do not worship images, because living among protestants they are
either laughed out of it, or beaten out of it by shock of
argument.

3. 'Tis a discreet way concerning pictures in churches
to set up no new, nor to pull down no old.

LVIII.

IMPERIAL CONSTITUTIONS.

THEY say imperial constitutions did only confirm the
canons of the Church; but that is not so, for they inflicted
punishment, which the canons never did. Viz*. If a man
converted a Christian to be a Jew, he was to forfeit his
estate, and lose his life. In Valentinian's [1] novels, 'tis said
Constat episcopos [2] *forum legibus non habere, et judicant
tantum de religione* [3].

---

[1] *Valentinian's*] Valentine's MSS.   [2] *Episcopos*, H. 2] episcopus, H.
             [3] *Religione*, H. 2] religiones, H.

l. 8. *confirm the canons of the Church*] Θεσπίζομεν τοίνυν, τάξιν νόμον
ἐπέχειν τοὺς ἁγίους ἐκκλησιαστικοὺς κανόνας τοὺς ὑπὸ τῶν ἁγίων τεσσάρων
συνόδων ἐκτεθέντας ἢ βεβαιωθέντας. . . . Τῶν γὰρ προειρημένων ἁγίων συνόδων . . .
τοὺς κανόνας ὡς νόμους φυλάττομεν. Justinian's Novels, 131, ch. 1.
l. 10. *If a man converted* &c.] Conf. e. g. 'Judaeus servum Christianum nec comparare debebit nec largitatis titulo consequi . . .
Verum ceteros, quos rectae religionis participes constitutos in suo
censu nefanda superstitio jam videtur esse sortita . . . sub hac lege
possideat, ut eos, nec invitos, nec volentes, caeno propriae sectae con-
fundat: ita ut, si haec forma fuerit violata, sceleris tanti auctores
capitali poenâ, prescriptione comitante, plectantur.' Codex Theodosianus, lib. 16, tit. 9, sec. 4.
l. 12. *In Valentinian's novels* &c.] See the novels of Valentinian
the Third, tit. 34.

LIX.

IMPRISONMENT.

Sir Kenelm Digby was several times taken and let go again, at last imprisoned in Winchester house. I can compare him to nothing, but to a great fish that we catch and

l. 4. *I can compare him to nothing, but to a great fish* &c.] This comparison seems to refer to Sir Kenelm Digby's bodily size and bearing. 'He was a man of very extraordinary person and presence, which drew the eyes of all men upon him, which were the more fixed by a wonderful graceful behaviour, a flowing courtesy and civility, and such a volubility of language as surprised and delighted; and though in another man it might have appeared to have somewhat of affectation, it was marvellous graceful in him, and seemed natural to his size and mould of his person, to the gravity of his motion, and the tune of his voice and delivery.' Clarendon's Life, vol. i. p. 38. (Oxford 1827.) 'His person,' says Anthony à Wood, 'was handsome and gigantic, and nothing was wanting to make him a complete chevalier.' Athenae, iii. 689.

In 1638 Sir Kenelm Digby had been induced by Queen Henrietta Maria to write a circular letter to the Roman Catholics of the country, urging them to contribute liberally to the King's expenses in the matter of the war with the Scotch. Rushworth, Collections, iii. 1327. In January, 1640 (1641), he was called to account for this by the Parliament, and a Committee was appointed to prepare questions about what he and others had done. Commons Journals, ii. 74. In March, the two Houses presented a joint petition, praying that he and certain others be removed from the Court, as popish recusants, ii. 106. In May, 1641, six members were appointed with power to call before them Sir Kenelm Digby and others, and to offer them the Oaths of Allegiance and Supremacy, and if they refuse to take them, to give orders that they shall be proceeded against according to law, ii. 158. In June, 1641, a peremptory order was made for Sir Kenelm Digby to attend the Committee for Recusants Convict, ii. 182. That he was, at length, committed to Winchester House, appears by a letter, read in Parliament from the Lord Mayor of London, concerning his committal, and enclosing his petition for release. This petition the House refused to grant. Journals, ii. 978. His release was due to the intercession of the Queen Regent of France, as appears by a letter from the two Houses.—'We are commanded to make known to your Majesty that, although the religion, the past behaviour, and the abilities of this gentleman might give just umbrage of his practising

let go again ; but still he will come to the bait ; at last
therefore we put him into some great pond for store.

LX.

INCENDIARIES.

FANCY to yourself a man sets the city on fire at Cripple-
gate, and that fire continues by means of others, till it come
to Whitefriars, and then he that began it would fain quench
it ; does not he deserve to be punished most that first set
the town on fire ? So 'tis with the incendiaries of the state.
They that first set it on fire, [by monopolies, forest business, imprisoning of the parliament-men 3° *Caroli*, &c.] are 10
now become regenerate, and would fain quench the fire.
Certainly they deserved most to be punished, for being the
first authors of our distractions.

LXI.

INDEPENDENCY.

1. INDEPENDENCY is in use at Amsterdam, where forty
churches or congregations have nothing to do one with
another. And 'tis, no question, agreeable to the primitive
times, before the emperor became Christian. For either
we must say every church governed itself, or else we must

to the prejudice of the constitutions of this realm, yet nevertheless,
having so great regard to the recommendation of your Majesty, they
have ordered him to be discharged. Biographia Britannica, vol. iii.
p. 1706, note f.

I find no more distinct references to what Wood terms his 'activity
for the King's cause at the beginning of the civil wars,' or, as Selden
puts it, 'his coming again and again to the bait.'

l. 3. *Incendiaries.*]   See Excursus B.

fall upon that old foolish rock, that St. Peter and his. successors governed all. But when the civil state became Christian they appointed who should govern whom ; before, they governed by agreement and consent; if you will not do this, you shall come no more amongst us. But both the independent man and the presbyterian man do equally exclude the civil power, though after a different manner.

2. The Independents may as well plead they should not be subject to temporal things, not come before a constable, or a justice of peace, as they plead they should not be subject in spiritual things, because St. Paul says, Is it so, that there is not a wise man amongst you ?

3. The pope challenges all churches to be under him. The king and the two archbishops challenge all the Church of England to be under them. The presbyterian man divides the kingdom into as many churches as there be presbyteries. And your independent would have every congregation [1] a church by itself.

---

[1] *Congregation*, H. 2] congration, H.

l. 15. *The presbyterian man divides the kingdom &c.*] This is an incomplete account. See the form of Presbyterial Church Government agreed upon by the Westminster Assembly of Divines in 1645.

'Of Synodical Assemblies, the Scripture doth hold out another sort of assemblies, for the government of the Church, besides classical and congregational, all of which we call synodical. Synodical assemblies may lawfully be of several sorts, as provincial, national, and œcumenical.

'It is lawful and agreeable to the word of God that there be a subordination of congregational, classical, provincial, and national assemblies for the government of the Church.' Neal, Hist. of Puritans, vol. v. app. ix.

l. 17. *your independent &c.*] The view of the Independents as stated by themselves was that 'Every particular congregation of Christians has an entire and complete power and jurisdiction over its members, to be exercised by the elders thereof within itself. Apologetical Narrative of Independents (1643), quoted by Neal, Hist. of Puritans, vol. iii. p. 118.

Their main platform, says Fuller (Church History, bk. xi.), was

LXII.

THINGS INDIFFERENT.

In time of a parliament, when things are under debate, they are indifferent; but in a church or state settled, there is nothing left indifferent.

LXIII.

PUBLIC INTEREST.

All might go well in the commonwealth, if every one in the parliament would lay down his own interest, and aim at the general good. If a man were sick, and the whole college of physicians should come to him, and administer severally, haply so long as they observed the rules of art, he might recover; but if one of them had a great deal of scamony by him, he must put off that, therefore he prescribes scamony; another had a great deal of rhubarb, and he must put off that, and therefore he prescribes rhubarb, &c. they would certainly kill the man. We destroy the commonwealth, while we preserve our own private interest, and neglect the public.

LXIV.

HUMAN INVENTION.

1. You say there must be no human invention in the church, nothing but the pure word.

that churches should not be subordinate, parochial to provincial, provincial to national (as daughter to mother, mother to grandmother), but co-ordinate, without superiority, except seniority of sisters, containing no powerful influence therein.

Answer. If I give any exposition, but what is expressed in the text, that is my invention: if you give another expo-sition, that is your invention, and both are human. For example, suppose the word [egg] were in the text; I say, 'tis meant an hen-egg, you say a goose-egg; neither of these are expressed, therefore they are human invention; and I am sure the newer the invention the worse; old inventions are best.

2. If we must admit nothing but what we read in the
10 Bible, what will become of the parliament? For we do not read of that there.

LXV.

GOD'S JUDGMENTS.

WE cannot tell what is a judgment of God; 'tis presump-tion to take upon us to know. In time of plague we know we want health, and therefore we pray to God to give us health[1]; in time of war, we know we want peace, and therefore we pray to God to send us peace. Commonly we say a judgment falls upon a man for something in him we cannot abide. An example we have in King James, con-

[1] *And therefore we pray to God to give us health,* H. 2] omitted in H.

l. 13. *We cannot tell what is a judgment &c.*] Suggested, possibly, by a book, published in 1636, under the title of 'A divine tragedie lately acted,' or 'A collection of sundry memorable examples of God's judgments upon Sabbath-breakers and other like libertines in their unlawfull sports.' It gives fifty-five examples of some misfortune to Sabbath-breakers in the course of two years, and it appeals confi-dently to these as proof of direct divine interposition. It ends with an account of the death of Mr. William Noy, closely following the execution of the Star Chamber censure on the 'well deserving gen-tleman, Mr. Prynne.' The book has been ascribed to Prynne, but it does not bear his name or signature. It is entered as Prynne's in the British Museum catalogue, and is so lettered on the cover.

cerning the death of Henry the IVth of France ; one said
he was killed for his wenching, another said he was killed
for turning his religion. No, says King James, (who could
not abide fighting) he was killed for permitting duels in his
kingdom.

LXVI.

JUDGE.

1. WE see the pageants in Cheapside, the lions, and the
elephants, but we do not see the men that carry them. We
see the judges look big, look like lions, but we do not see
who moves them. 10

2. Little things do great works, when great things will
not. If I would take a pin from the ground, a little pair of
tongs will do it, when a great pair will not. Go to a judge
to do a business for you ; by no means, he will not hear of
it ; but go to some small servant about him, and he will
dispatch it according to your heart's desire.

3. There could be no mischief done in the commonwealth
without a judge. Though there be false dice brought in at
the groom-porter's, and cheating offered, yet unless he allow
the cheating, and judge the dice to be good, there may be 20
hopes of fair play.

l. 17. *There could be no mischief* &c.] See note on 'The King,'
sec. 6.

l. 19. *groom-porter*] 'An officer of the royal household, whose
business is to see the king's lodging furnished with tables, chairs,
stools and firing : as also to provide cards, dice, &c., and to decide
disputes arising at cards, dice, bowling, &c.' Quoted by Nares (Glossary, sub voce) from Chamb. Dict. Nares adds that 'formerly he
was allowed to keep an open gambling table at Christmas. . . . He is
said to have succeeded to the office of the master of the revels, then
disused.'

LXVII.

JUGGLING.

'Tis not juggling that is to be blamed, but much juggling, for the world cannot be governed without it. All your rhetorick, and all your elenchs in logic, come within the compass of juggling.

LXVIII.

JURISDICTION.

1. There's no such thing as spiritual jurisdiction; all is civil, the church's is the same with the lord mayor's. Suppose a Christian came into a pagan country, how can you fancy he shall have power there? He finds fault with the gods of the country. Well, they will put him to death for it. Then he is a martyr; what follows? Does that argue he has any spiritual jurisdiction? If the clergy say the church ought to be governed thus, and thus, by the word of God, that is doctrine all, that is not discipline.

2. The pope, he challenges jurisdiction over all; the bishops, they pretend to it as well as he; the presbyterians, they would have it to themselves; but over whom is all this? The poor layman.

LXIX.

JUS DIVINUM.

1. All things are held by *jus divinum*, either immediately or mediately.

2. Nothing has lost the pope so much in his supremacy, as not acknowledging what princes gave him. 'Tis a scorn

upon the civil power, and an unthankfulness in the priest.
But the church runs to *jus divinum*, lest if they should
acknowledge what they have, they have by positive law, it
might be as well taken from them, as given to them.

LXX.

KING.

1. A KING is a thing men have made for their own
sakes, for quietness' sake. Just as in a family one man is
appointed to buy the meat. If every man should buy, or
if there were many buyers, they would never agree ; one
would buy what the other liked not, or what the other had 10
bought before, so there would be a confusion. But that
charge being committed to one, he according to his discretion pleases all. If they have not what they would have
one day, they shall have it the next, or something as good.

2. The word king directs our eyes. Suppose it had
been consul or dictator. To think all kings alike, is the
same folly, as if a consul of Aleppo or Smyrna, should
claim to himself the same power that a consul at Rome
had. What, am not I consul? Or a duke of England
should think himself like the duke of Florence. Nor can 20
it be imagined that the word βασιλεὺς did signify a king

l. 15. *directs our eyes.*] This seems to mean, the word catches our
eyes and suggests the notion that it bears everywhere the same
sense.

This and the next clause seem directed against the Constitutions
and Canons Ecclesiastical of 1640, framed by the Convocations of
Canterbury and of York, in which the most high and sacred order of
Kings is said to be 'of divine right, being the ordinance of God
himself, founded in the prime laws of nature, and clearly established
by express texts both of the Old and New Testaments.' Wilkins,
Concilia, iv. 545.

the same in Greece, as the Hebrew word כלר did with the
Jews.   Besides, let divines in their pulpits say what they
will, they in their practice deny that all is the king's.
They sue him, and so does all the nation, whereof they
are a part.   What matter is it then, what they preach or
talk in the schools?

3. Kings are all individuals, this or that king; there is
no species of kings.

4. A king that claims privileges in his own kingdom,
10 because they have them in another, is just as a cook, that
claims fees in one lord's house because they are allowed
in another.   If the master of the house will yield them,
well and good.

5. The text [Render unto Caesar the things that are
Caesar's] makes as much against kings as for them; for
it says plainly that some things are not Caesar's.   But
divines make choice of it, first in flattery, and then because of the other part adjoined to it [Render unto God
the things that are God's], where they bring in the
20 Church.

6. A king outed of his country, that takes as much
upon him as he did at home, in his own court, is as if
a man and I being upon different ground, I used[1] to
lift up my voice to him, that he might hear me, at length
should come down to me and then expect I should speak
as loud to him as I did before.

[1] *As if a man and I being upon
different ground, I used*, &c., H. a] as if
a man and I being upon the ground,
used, &c., H.   As if a man upon a tree,
and I being upon the ground used,
&c., S.   As if a man on high, and I
being upon the ground used, &c.   Early
printed editions.   No one of all these
is quite satisfactory.   I have chosen
what seems the least faulty.

l. 2.   *let divines in their pulpits* &c.]   See, e.g., Dr. Manwaring's two
Sermons on the King's prerogative, in which he insists that the
King's power is not bounded by law; that it is the duty of his
subjects to obey his illegal commands ; and that if they are deprived
of property in their goods they have no choice but to submit.   Fuller,
Church History, century xvii, bk. xi. secs. 61, 62, 63, in ann. 1628.

LXXI.

KING OF ENGLAND.

1. THE king can do no wrong: that is, no process can be granted against him, you can have no remedy against him. What must be done then? Petition him, and the king writes upon the petition *Soit droit fait*, and sends it to the chancery, and then the business is heard. His confessor will not tell him he can do no wrong.

2. There's a great deal of difference between head of

1. 2. *The king can do no wrong*] Explained by Blackstone as meaning only 'that in the first place, whatever may be amiss in the conduct of public affairs is not chargeable personally on the king; nor is he, but his ministers, accountable for it to the people: and secondly, that the prerogative of the Crown extends not to do any injury.' Commentaries, bk. iii. ch. 17, sec. 1. Selden's remark deals only with one incident of the maxim, and guards, in the last clause, against one possible misinterpretation of it.

1. 8. *There's a great deal of difference* &c.] By 26 Henry VIII, cap. i. it is declared and enacted that the King's Majesty is the only supreme head in erthe of the Church of England. This Act was confirmed, with penalties, by 1 Edward VI, cap. 12.

In 'our Canons,' i.e. in the Constitutions and Canons Ecclesiastical of 1640, sec. 1, Concerning the Regal Power, the words used are 'The most high and sacred order of Kings is of divine right. . . . A supreme power is given to this most excellent order by God himself in the Scriptures, which is that kings should rule and command in their several dominions all persons of what rank and estate soever, whether ecclesiastical or civil. . . .

'The care of God's church is so committed to Kings in the scripture that they are commended when the church keeps the right way, and taxed when it runs amiss, and therefore her government belongs in chief unto Kings.' Wilkins, Concilia, iv. 545.

The difference of which Selden speaks is that the King, as head of the Church, is the fountain or original of all spiritual authority in his dominions, in the full sense in which he is the fountain of honour and the fountain of law; while the words of the Canon mean no more than that the Church and its ecclesiastical rulers are subject to the civil power. This latter is all that was claimed by Elizabeth, and all that was expressed in Article 37. On the other hand, every Bishop in his Oath of Homage, taken when he obtains the tem-

the church, and supreme governor, as our canons call the king. Conceive it thus; There is in the kingdom of England a college of physicians, the king is supreme governor of these, because they live under him, but not head of them, nor president of the college, nor the best physician.

3. After the dissolution of the abbeys, they did much advance the king's supremacy, for they only cared to exclude the pope: hence have we had several translations of the Bible put upon us. But now we must look to it,
10 otherwise the king may put upon us what religion he pleases.

4. 'Twas the old way when the king of England had his house, there were canons to sing service in his chapel: so at Westminster, in St. Stephen's chapel, (where the House of Commons sits) from which canons the street Canon-row has its name, because they lived there; and he had also the abbot and his monks, and all these the king's house.

5. The three estates are the lords temporal, the bishops

poralities of his see, acknowledges 'that I hold the said Bishopric, as well the spiritualities as the temporalities thereof, only of your Majesty.' This appears to be a survival of the earlier view.

l. 12. *'Twas the old way* &c.] On the King's Chapel Establishment see Excursus C.

l. 19. *The three estates are* &c.] Who formed the three estates was one of the disputed questions of the time. See, e.g., a speech by Bagshaw (Feb. 9, 1640): '(It was said) that episcopacy was a third estate in Parliament, and therefore the King and Parliament could not be without them; this I utterly deny, for there are three estates without them, as namely the King, who is the first estate; the Lords Temporal is the second; and the Commons the third. Nalson, Collections, i. 762.

Nalson quotes, on the other hand, from the Parliamentary Roll, 1 Richard III, 'at the request and by the assent of the three estates of the realm, that is to say the Lords Spiritual and Temporal and the Commons of this land assembled in this present Parliament,' &c., i. 764. See, also, a proclamation by Queen Elizabeth (1588) which speaks of 'the estate of the prelacy, being one of the three ancient estates of this realm under her Highness.' Wilkins, Concilia, iv. 340.

are the clergy, and the commons. The king is not one of
the three estates, as some would have it, [take heed of
that], for then if two agree, the third is involved ; but he
is king of the three estates.

6. The king has a seal in every court ; and though the
great seal be called *sigillum Angliae*, the great seal of
England, yet 'tis not because 'tis the kingdom's seal, and
not the king's, but to distinguish it from *sigillum Hiberniae*,
sigillum Scotiae.

7. The court of England is much altered. At a solemn 10
dancing, first you had the grave measures, then the corar-
toes, and the galliards, and all this is kept up with ceremony ; at length they fall to Trench-more[1], and so to the
cushion dance, and then all the company dance, lord and
groom, lady and kitchen-maid, no distinction. So in our
court in Queen Elizabeth's time, gravity and state was
kept up ; in King James's time things were pretty well ;

[1] *Trenchmore*] Frenchmore, MSS.

Nalson, in his remarks on Lord Say and Seal's speech (1642)
against Bishops, points out, as Selden does, the consequence which
would follow from counting the King as one of the three estates. The
opinion, he says, that the Bishops are not one of the three estates, in
Parliament, has been deservedly exploded by all persons of sense
and honour ' except such as would therefore have the King to be the
third estate, that so by bringing in a co-ordinancy of power, they may
the better accomplish their anti-monarchical designs, or at least reduce
the ancient and imperial Crown of these realms to the condition of a
Venetian seigniory.' Collections, ii. 269.

l. 13. *Trench-more*] A kind of lively dance, in triple time, to which
it was usual to dance in a rough and boisterous manner. Nares,
Glossary.

The reading in the MSS. is ' Frenchmore,' but there is no dance
so named, while ' Trenchmore,' the reading in the early printed
editions, is, as Nares shows, a name in common use.

l. 14. *cushion dance*] ' A dance of a rather free character, used
chiefly, it would appear, at weddings.' Its character is distinctly
shown by a passage which Nares quotes from Taylor (1630) :—' There
are many pretty provocatory dances, as the kissing dance, the cushion
dance, the shaking of the sheets, and such like.' Nares, Glossary.

but in King Charles's time, there has been nothing but
Trench-more and the cushion dance, *omnium gatherum*,
tolly polly, *hoyte cum toyte*.

LXXII.

THE KING.

1. 'Tis hard to make an accommodation betwixt the
king and the parliament. If you and I fell out about
money, you said I owed you twenty pounds, I said I
owed you but ten pounds, it may be a third party allowing me 20 marks, might make us friends. But if I said,
10 I owed you twenty pounds of silver, and you said I owed
you twenty pounds of diamonds, which is a sum innu-
merable, 'tis impossible we should ever agree; this is
the case.

2. The king using the House of Commons, as he did
in Mr. Pym and his company; that is, charging them with
treason, because they charged[1] my lord of Canterbury
and Sir George Ratcliffe, it was just as much logic as the
boy, that would have lain with his grandmother, used to
his father: You lay with my mother, why should not I lie
20 with your's?

3. There is not the same reason for the king's accusing
men of treason, and carrying them away, as there is
for the houses themselves, because they accuse one of
themselves. For every one that is accused, is either a
peer or a commoner; and he that is accused has his consent going along with them; but if the king accuses, there
is nothing of this in it.

4. The king is equally abused now as before; then they
flattered him, and made him do ill things, now they would
30 force him against his conscience. If a physician should
tell me that every thing I had a mind to was good for

---

[1] *Because they charged*] 'because' omitted in MSS.

me, though in truth 'twas poison, he abused me; and he abuses me as much, that would force me to take something whether I will or no.

5. The king, so long as he is our king, may do with his officers what he pleases; as the master of the house may turn away all his servants, and take whom he please.

6. The king's oath is not security enough for our property, for he swears to govern according to law; now the judges they interpret the law; and what judges can be made to do we know.   10

l. 9. *what judges can be made to do we know.*] Selden had good reason to know this. He was one of the members committed to prison after Charles' third Parliament, having been refused bail by the judges unless he would find sureties for his future good behaviour. This he and the others rightly and manfully refused to do, and were remanded to the Tower. Whitelock, Memorials, pp. 13, 14.

Again, in 1635 the King was advised by the Lord Chief Justice Finch and others to require the opinion of his judges (on ship-money), which he did, stating the case in a letter to them.

'After much solicitation by the Chief Justice Finch, promising preferment to some, and highly threatening others whom he found doubting (as themselves reported to me) he got from them in answer to the King's letter and case, their opinion . . . that when . . . the whole kingdom is in danger, your Majesty may by writ command all your subjects to furnish ships with men, victuals and ammunition, and may compel the doing thereof. And that in such case your Majesty is the sole judge both of the dangers and when and how the same is to be prevented and avoided. This opinion was signed by twelve judges.' Whitelock, Memorials, p. 25.

Clarendon remarks on this that 'The damage and mischief cannot be expressed that the Crown and State sustained by the deserved reproach and infamy that attended the judges, by being made use of in this and other like acts of power.' Men heard the payment of ship-money 'demanded in a court of law as a right, and found it, by sworn judges of the law, adjudged so upon such grounds and reasons as every stander-by was able to swear was not law.' He traces the disregard of law afterwards as due very largely 'to the irreverence and scorn the judges were justly in.' History, pp. 108, 109.

But the day of reckoning was at hand. In 1640, Judge Berkley, one of the twelve, was impeached by the Commons for his opinion

7. The king and the parliament now falling out, are just as when there is foul play offered betwixt gamesters; one snatches the other's stake, they seize what they can of one another's. 'Tis not to be asked whether it belongs not to the king to do this or that: before, when there was fair play, it did, but now they will do both what is most convenient for their own safety. If two fall to scuffling, one tears the other's band, the other tears his; when they were friends they were quiet, and did[1] no such thing; they let one another's bands alone.

8. The king calling his friends from the parliament, because he had use of them at Oxford, is as if a man had use of a little piece of wood, and he runs down into

---

[1] *They were quiet, and did,* H. 2] and were quiet and did, H. The second 'and' is written over the original 'they.'

in favour of ship-money, and was taken from his seat to prison by black-rod 'which,' says Whitelock, 'struck a great terror in the rest of his brethren.' Memorials, p. 40. Their turn came next, p. 47.

l. 11. *The king calling his friends* &c.] In 1643 the King . . . summoned all the members of both Houses of Parliament (except only such as, having command in His Majesty's armies, could not be absent from their charges) to attend upon His Majesty at Oxford, upon a day fixed in January next. Clarendon, Hist. ii. 622.

Thither, accordingly, the King's friends went, and a Parliament at Oxford was opened in due form. Meanwhile work of a different kind was in progress elsewhere; so that the Earl of Essex, in reply to a long letter from the absentees, written in the interest of peace and assuring him of the King's gracious purposes and general good-will to his subjects, was able to enclose with his curt answer a copy of 'a national covenant solemnly entered into by both the kingdoms of England and Scotland, and a declaration passed by them both together with another declaration by the kingdom of Scotland.' Clarendon, Hist. ii. 666.

These documents, the effect of which was to bind the signatories to keep firm in their armed resistance to the King, are given by Clarendon—the first at full length, the others (passed and published about the very time that the overture for peace came from Oxford) in substance; pp. 560, 667, ff.

So true did Selden's words prove, that—'when his friends are absent, the King will be lost.'

the cellar, and takes the spiggot, in the meantime all the
beer runs about the house. When his friends are absent,
the king will be lost.

LXXIII.

KNIGHT'S SERVICE.

KNIGHT'S service in earnest means nothing, for the lords
are bound to wait upon the king when he goes to war with
a foreign enemy, with, it may be, one man and one horse;
and he that does not, is to be rated so much as shall seem
good to the next parliament. And what will that be? So
'tis for a private man that holds of a gentleman.   10

LXXIV.

LAND.

1. WHEN men did let their lands under foot, the tenants
would fight for their landlords, so that way they had their
retribution; but now they will do nothing for them; nay,
be the first, if but a constable bid them, that shall lay the
landlord by the heels; and therefore 'tis vanity and folly
not to take the full value.

2. *Allodium* is a law-word contrary to *feudum*, and it
signifies land that holds of nobody. So *regna allodiata*
are kingdoms that are not held in fee of any body. We 20
have no such lands in England. 'Tis a true proposition;
all the land in England is held, either immediately or
mediately, of the king.

l. 12. *under foot*] i.e. for less than their value. See Bacon, Essay
41, Of Usury: 'they would be forced to sell their means, be it lands
or goods, far under foot.'

H

LXXV.

LANGUAGE.

1. To a living tongue new words may be added, but not to a dead tongue, as Latin, Greek, Hebrew, &c.

2. *Latimer* is the corruption of *latiner*, it signifies he that interprets Latin; and though he interpreted French, Spanish, or Italian, he was called the king's latimer, that is, the king's interpreter.

3. If you look upon the language spoken in the Saxon time, and the language spoken now, you will find the difference to be just as if a man had a cloak that he wore plain in queen Elizabeth's days, and since has put in here a piece of red, and there a piece of blue, here a piece of green, and there a piece of orange-tawny. We borrow words from the French, Italian, Latin, as every pedantic man pleases.

4. We have more words than notions; half-a-dozen words for the same thing. Sometimes we put a new signification to an old word, as when we call a piece, a gun. The word gun was in use in England for an engine to cast a thing

l. 4. *Latimer*] sometimes spelt Latiner or Latinier, has the different senses of interpreter, herald, and secretary, all based on the original sense—one who knows several languages, and who is thus qualified to act in any one of the above three capacities. See Warton, Hist. of English Poetry, vol. i. p. 65, text and note (ed. 1840, in 3 vols.), where numerous instances are given of its use by early English and French writers.

l. 17. *The word gun*, &c.] Conf.:

'Theo othre into the wallis stygh (climb)
And the kynges men with gonnes sleygh.'

King Alisaunder, pt. i. chap. 12, l. 3268.

The date of this poem is very early in the fourteenth century and therefore before gunpowder was in use. See Warton, Hist. of English Poetry, sec. 6. Weber's note on the passage is:—

'As to the word *gonne*, we have here perhaps the earliest use of it that can now be adduced, and it certainly signifies a machine for expelling balls of some kind. . . . A gun might have originally been a machine of the catapult kind; and on the adoption of powder, having

from a man, long before there was any gunpowder found out.

5. Words must be fitted to a man's mouth. 'Twas well said of the fellow that was to make a speech for my lord mayor; he desired to take measure of his lordship's mouth.

LXXVI.

LAW.

1. A MAN may plead not guilty, and yet tell no lie; for by the law no man is bound to accuse himself: so that when I say, Not guilty, the meaning is, as if I should say by way of paraphrase, I am not so guilty as to tell you; if you will bring me to trial, and have me punished for this you lay to my charge, prove it against me.

2. Ignorance of the law excuses no man; not that all men know the law, but because 'tis an excuse every man will plead, and no man can tell how to confute him.

3. The king of Spain was outlawed in Westminster-hall;

changed its form, might still retain its name.' Metrical Romances, vol. iii. p. 306 (Edinburgh, 1810).

See also Chaucer, in his description of a battle between Antony and Augustus :—

  'With grisly soune out gooth the grete gonne,
  And hertely they hurtelen al attones,
  And fro the toppe downe cometh the grete stones.'
    Legend of Good Women. Legenda Cleopatrie, l. 58.

This may, of course, be an anachronism, as the use of gunpowder was known to Chaucer and is referred to by him elsewhere. But the general drift of the passage makes for the earlier sense of the word. That after the invention of gunpowder the word soon passed to the sense which it now bears, appears from a passage in Grafton's Chronicle in ann. 1380 : ' In this time, as saith Polidore in his boke De Inventoribus rerum, gonnes were first in use, which were invented by one of Germany. But, saith he, lest he should be cursed for ever that was the author of this invention, therefore his name is hidden and not known.' Chronicle, p. 429 (London, 1809).

I being of counsel against him. A merchant had recovered costs against him in a suit, which because it could not be got, we advised to have him outlawed for his not appearing, and so he was. As soon as Gondomar heard that, he presently sent the money; by reason, if his master had stood outlawed, he could not have had the benefit of the law; which would have been very prejudicial, there being then many suits depending betwixt the king of Spain and our English merchants.

10   4. Every law is a contract betwixt the king and the people, and therefore to be kept. An hundred men may owe me a hundred pounds, as well as one man, and shall they not pay me because they are stronger than I ?

Objection. Oh! but they lose all if they keep that law.

Answer. Let them look to the making of their bargains. If I sell my lands, and when I have done, one comes and tells me I have nothing else to keep me, I and my wife and children must starve, if I part with my land : must I not therefore let them have my land that have bought it, and 20 paid for it ?

5. The parliament may declare law, as well as any inferior court may, viz⁺. the king's bench. In this or that particular case the king's bench will declare unto you what the law is ; but that binds nobody but whom that case concerns : so the highest court, the parliament, may do, but not declare law, [that is] make law, that was never heard of before.

l. 25. *but not declare law* &c.] In a Declaration or Remonstrance of the Lords and Commons (May, 1642), an uncontrolled power of declaring law as they please is claimed for the Parliament in direct terms. See, 'If the question be, whether that be law which the Lords and Commons have once declared to be so, who shall be the Judge ? Not his Majesty; for the King judgeth not of matters of law but by his courts, and his courts, though sitting by his authority, expect not his assent in matters of law. Nor any other courts, for they cannot judge in that case because they are inferior, no appeal lying to them from Parliament, the judgment whereof is, in the eye of the law, the King's judgment in his highest court, though the King in

LXXVII.

LAW OF NATURE.

I CANNOT fancy to myself what the law of nature means, but the law of God. How should I know I ought not to steal, I ought not to commit adultery, unless somebody had told me so? Surely 'tis because I have been told so. 'Tis not because I think I ought not to do them, nor because you think I ought not; if so, our minds might change: whence then comes the restraint? From a higher power; nothing else can bind. I cannot bind myself, for I may untie myself again; nor an equal cannot bind me, for we may untie one another. It must be a superior, even God Almighty. If two of us make a bargain, why should either

his person be neither present nor assenting thereto.' Rushworth, Collections, iv. 698.

This can hardly be distinguished from a claim to do what Selden terms ' make law that was never heard of before.' Selden's restriction applies, of course, to Parliament sitting in its judicial, not in its legislative capacity. See ' Power, State,' sec. 8, where he lays it down that ' the Parliament of England has no arbitrary power in point of Judicature, but in point of making law.'

l. 2. *I cannot fancy to myself* &c.] This is Selden's position in his treatise De Jure Naturali, &c., apud Ebraeos. He there treats the Law of Nature as identical with certain precepts handed down by Noah to his descendants. These precepts were of Divine origin, communicated by God to Adam, and by Adam to Noah. The same theory will be found in Gratian's work on the Canon Law (written about 1150) known as the Decretum Gratiani, and long an accepted authority for the subject of which it treats. But it appears there in a different form and without the laboured proofs which Selden accumulates from Jewish traditional sources. See ' Humanum genus duobus regitur, naturali videlicet jure et moribus. Jus naturae est, quod in lege et evangelio continetur, quo quisque jubetur alii facere quod sibi vult fieri, et prohibetur alii inferre quod sibi nolit fieri. Unde Christus in Evangelio: "Omnia quaecunque vultis ut faciant vobis homines, et vos, eadem facite illis. Haec est enim lex et prophetae."

' Hinc Isodorus in V libro Etymologiarum [c. 2] ait. Omnes leges aut divinae sunt aut humanae. Divinae natura, humanae moribus constant.' Corpus Juris Canonici. Friedberg, vol. i. p. 1 (ed. 2, 1879).

of us stand to it? What need you care what you say, or what need I care what I say? Certainly because there is something about me that tells me *fides est servanda*, and if we after alter our minds, and make a new bargain, there's *fides servanda* there too.

LXXVIII.

LEARNING.

1. No man is the wiser for his learning; it may administer matter to work in, or objects to work upon, but wit and wisdom are born with a man.

2. Most men's learning is nothing but history dully taken up. If I quote Thomas Aquinas for some tenet, and believe it because the schoolmen say so, that's but history. Few men make themselves masters of the things they write or speak.

3. The Jesuits and the lawyers of France, and the Low Countrymen, have engrossed all learning. The rest of the world make nothing but homilies.

4. 'Tis observable, that in Athens where the arts flourished, they were governed by a democracy; learning made them think themselves as wise as anybody, and they would govern as well as others; and they spake, as it were by way of contempt, that in the east and in the north they had kings. And why? Because the most part of them followed their business; and if some man had made himself wiser than the rest, he governed them, and they willingly submitted to him. Aristotle makes the observation. And as

l. 26. *Aristotle makes the observation*] See Παρὰ ταύτην δ' ἄλλο μοναρχίας εἶδος, οἷαι παρ' ἐνίοις εἰσὶ βασιλεῖαι τῶν βαρβάρων. Ἔχουσι δ' αὖται τὴν δύναμιν πᾶσαι παραπλησίαν τυραννικῇ, εἰσὶ δ' ὅμως κατὰ νόμον καὶ πατρικαί· διὰ γὰρ τὸ δουλικώτεροι εἶναι τὰ ἤθη φύσει οἱ μὲν βάρβαροι τῶν Ἑλλήνων, οἱ δὲ περὶ τὴν Ἀσίαν τῶν περὶ τὴν Εὐρώπην, ὑπομένουσι τὴν δεσποτικὴν ἀρχὴν οὐδὲν δυσχεραίνοντες.—Politics, iii. 14. 6.

in Athens, the philosophers made the people knowing, and therefore they thought themselves wise enough to govern, so does preaching with us, and that makes us affect a democracy; for upon these two grounds we all would be governors; either because we think ourselves as wise as the best, or because we think ourselves the elect, and have the spirit, and the rest a company of reprobates that belong to the devil.

LXXIX.

LECTURERS.

1. LECTURERS do in a parish church what the friars did 10 heretofore; get away not only the affections, but the bounty, that should be bestowed upon the minister.

Καὶ διὰ τοῦτ' ἴσως ἐβασιλεύοντο πρότερον, ὅτι σπάνιον ἦν εὑρεῖν ἄνδρας πολὺ διαφέροντας κατ' ἀρετήν, ἄλλως τε καὶ τότε μικρὰς οἰκοῦντας πόλεις. Ἔτι δ' ἀπ' εὐεργεσίας καθίστασαν τοὺς βασιλεῖς, ὅπερ ἐστὶν ἔργον τῶν ἀγαθῶν ἀνδρῶν. Ἐπεὶ δὲ συνέβαινε γίγνεσθαι πολλοὺς ὁμοίους πρὸς ἀρετήν, οὐκέτι ὑπέμενον ἀλλ' ἐζήτουν κοινόν τι, καὶ πολιτείαν καθίστασαν.—iii. 14. 11.

He shows elsewhere how at Athens successive popular leaders and demagogues ὥσπερ τυράννῳ τῷ δήμῳ χαριζόμενοι τὴν πολιτείαν εἰς τὴν νῦν δημοκρατίαν κατέστησαν.—ii. 12. 4 and 5.

l. 10. *Lecturers do in a parish church* &c.] In the early part of Charles's reign, the lecturers were under the control of the bishops, and we have frequent proof of the trouble which they caused, and of the pains taken by Laud and by other bishops to keep a tight hand upon them, and to see that they did not abuse the somewhat anomalous position which they occupied as licensed trespassers on another man's ground. By the parliamentary party they were regarded with great favour, and were, so to say, established by an Order of the House (Sept. 6, 1641) 'that it shall be lawful for the Parishioners of any Parish in the Kingdom of England or Dominion of Wales, to set up a lecture, and to maintain an orthodox minister at their own charge, to preach every Lord's day where there is no preaching, and to preach one day in every week where there is no weekly lecture.'

'Thus (says Nalson) did they set up a spiritual Militia of those lecturers who were to marshall their troops . . . neither parsons,

2. Lecturers get a great deal of money, because they preach the people tame [as a man watches a hawk] and then they do what they list with them.

3. The lecture in Black-friars, performed by officers of the army, tradesmen, and ministers, is as if a great man should make a feast, and he would have his cook dress one dish, and his coachman another, his porter a third, &c.

vicars, nor curates, but like the order of the Friers Predicants among the Papists, who run about tickling the people's ears with stories of legends and miracles, in the meantime picking their pockets, which were the very faculties of these men.'   Nalson, Collections, ii. 447, 8.

l. 2.   *as a man watches a hawk*]   i.e. forces it to watch ; keeps it without sleep.   For this obsolete use of the word, conf.:

'Another way I have to man my haggard,
To make her come and know her keeper's call,
That is to watch her, as we watch these kites
That bate and beat and will not be obedient . . .
Last night she slept not, nor to-night she shall not,' &c.
                                                                        Taming of the Shrew, iv. sc. i.
                              'my lord shall never rest,
I 'll watch him tame.'   Othello, iii. sc. 3.

This is still a known method by which wild hawks are tamed : see 'I have trained haggards or wild hawks perfectly in three weeks. This is done by keeping them awake at night and during the day, until tame.'   Corballis, Forty-five Years of Sport.   Falconry, p. 463.

l. 4.   *The lecture in Black-friars* &c.]   By 1647, after a good deal of alarm had been caused to the Presbyterian party by the growing influence of the Independents, and after several efforts had been made to put down their unlicensed preaching in the army and elsewhere, 'liberty of conscience was now become the great charter ; and men who were inspired, preached and prayed when and where they would.   Cromwell himself was the greatest preacher ; and most of the officers of the army, and many common soldiers, shewed their gifts that way.'   Clarendon, Hist. iii. 175.

Walker, in his History of Independency, gives a specimen of a common soldier's sermon, preached in 1649; and tells how, on the Sunday after Easter day, six preachers militant at Whitehall tired the patience of their hearers, until at last the Spirit of the Lord called up Oliver Cromwell, who spent an hour in prayer and an hour and a half in a sermon.   Part ii. pp. 152, 153 (ed. of 1660).

LXXX.

LIBELS.

THOUGH some make slight of libels, yet you may see by them how the wind sits. As take a straw and throw it up into the air, you shall see by that which way the wind is, which you shall not do by casting up a stone. More solid things do not shew the complexion of the times so well as ballads and libels.

LXXXI.

LITURGY.

1. THERE is no church without a liturgy, nor indeed can there be conveniently, as there is no school without a grammar. One scholar may be taught otherwise upon the stock of his acumen, but not a whole school. One or two that are piously disposed, may serve themselves their own way, but hardly a whole nation.

2. To know what was generally believed in all ages, the way is to consult the liturgies, not any private man's writing. As if you would know how the Church of England serves God, go to the Common-prayer book, consult not this, or that man. Besides, liturgies never compliment[1], nor use high expressions. The fathers oft-times speak oratoriously.

LXXXII.

LORDS BEFORE THE PARLIAMENT.

1. GREAT lords, by reason of their flatterers, are the first that know their own virtues, and the last that know their

[1] *Compliment*] complement, MSS.

own vices. Some of them are ashamed upwards, because their ancestors were too great. Others are ashamed downwards, because they are too mean.

2. The prior of St. John of Jerusalem is said to be *primus baro Angliæ*, the first baron of England ; because being last of the spiritual barons, he chose to be first of the temporal. He was a kind of an otter, a knight half spiritual, and half temporal.

3. *Question.* Whether is every baron a baron of some place ?

Answer. 'Tis according to his patent. Of late years they have been made baron of some place, but anciently not, called only by their sirname, or the sirname of some family into which they have been married.

4. The making of new lords lessens all the rest. 'Tis in the business of lords as 'twas with St. Nicholas's image: the countryman, you know, could not find in his heart[1] to adore the new image, made of his own plum-tree, though he had formerly worshipped the old one. The lords that are ancient we honour, because we know not whence they were ; but the new ones we slight, because we know their beginning.

5. For the Irish lords here to take upon them in Eng-

---

[1] *In his heart*, H. 2] in his own heart, H.

l. 4. *The prior of St. John &c.*] See Excursus D.

l. 11. *'Tis according to his patent &c.*] See Selden's Titles of Honour, Part ii. ch. 5, sec. 28, where the whole subject is discussed at length, and illustrations are given of the earlier and later forms of patents of nobility. Works, iii. 774.

l. 23. *For the Irish lords here &c.*] In 1626 a petition was addressed to the King, complaining that Scotch and Irish Lords, presuming on a precedence which had been granted them by courtesy, ' do by reason of some late created dignities in those kingdoms of Scotland and Ireland, claim precedency of the peers of this realm, which tends both to the disservice of your Majesty and these realms, and to the great disparagement of the English nobility. . . .

'We therefore humbly beseech your Majesty that . . . some course may be taken . . . so as the inconvenience to your Majesty may be

land, is as if the cook in the friars[1] should come to my lady
Kent's kitchen, and take upon him to roast the meat there,
because he is a cook in another place.

LXXXIII.

LORDS IN THE PARLIAMENT.

1. THE lords' giving protections is a scorn upon them.
A protection means nothing actively, but passively.   He

[1] *In the friars*, H. original reading, 'friars' restored in the margin in a
with 'fayrs' written over it, and with different hand] faires, H. 2; fayers, S.

prevented, and the prejudice and disparagement of the Peers and
nobility of this kingdom be redressed.' Rushworth, Collections, i. 233.

Among the reasons given in support of the petition is a statement
that these Scotch and Irish Lords, whatever titles they bear, are 'in
the eye of the Law no more than mere Plebeians.'

l. 1. *cook in the friars*] After the death of the Earl of Kent, Selden
lived with the Countess Dowager, generally at her house in Whitefriars.
The obtrusive 'cook in the Friars' may be understood therefore as
the cook from some neighbour's house. The var. lec. 'fair' or 'fairs'
seems to have been put in by some one who did not bear in mind
where Selden had been domiciled.

l. 5. *The lords' giving protections* &c.] The effect of a protection was
that the person holding it could not be arrested for debt. It was rightfully given to a servant of a member of either House, and was sought
and obtained and used by many persons who had no rightful claim to it,
and who used it to evade payment of their just debts.

In 1641 a petition was delivered to the Commons by divers citizens
of London, against the abuses of Parliamentary protections, alleging
that if there were not some speedy order for the calling in or regu-
lating the same, they would occasion the undoing of many families.
Rushworth, Collections, iv. 279.

It appears from the Lords' Journals that this petition was addressed
to both Houses, and was considered by both. A few days afterwards
a Committee of the House sat, and concluded that divers protections
should be annulled, some being surreptitiously obtained, others procured by persons of ability, on purpose to defeat their creditors. iv. 282.
This abuse of protections was felt by London tradesmen as a greater
grievance than ship-money. iv. 396.

that is a servant to a parliament-man is thereby protected.
What a scorn is it to a person of honour to put his hand
and seal to two lies at once, that such a man is my servant,
and employed by me; when haply he never saw the man
in his life, nor before never heard of him!

2. The lords' protesting is foolish. To protest is properly to save to a man's self some right. But to protest
as the lords protest, when they themselves are involved,
'tis no more than if I should go into Smithfield, and sell
10 my horse, and take the money; and yet when I have your
money, and you my horse, I should protest this horse is
mine, because I love the horse, or I do not know why
I do protest, because my opinion is contrary to the rest.
Ridiculous! when they say the bishops anciently did

l. 6. *The lords' protesting is foolish*]. The first formal protest of the
Lords was on Sept. 9, 1641, against a resolution of the House for
printing and publishing a former order concerning Divine Service,
while a question was pending as to a conference between the two
Houses on the subject. Six lords protested, and their protest of dis-
assent to the vote was entered on the Journals of the House. Rogers,
Protests of the Lords, vol. i. p. 7.

There were two more protests in that year, and several in the year
following. Rogers defends the practice as being, at that time, a
courageous avowal of sympathy with the Parliamentary party. He
remarks, further, that under the old rules of the House of Lords, the
division lists were entered on the Journals, but that in 1641 this had
ceased to be done, so that a formal protest of dissent was then the
only method by which an adverse vote could be recorded.

l. 14. *when they say the bishops anciently did protest* &c.] This perhaps
refers to a speech which had been made by Hyde (better known as
Lord Clarendon) in defence of Geoffrey Palmer. After the vote of
the Commons in favour of the Remonstrance of 1641, and when the
motion before the House was that the Remonstrance should be
printed, Palmer, one of the minority, had, with others, claimed a
right to protest, in the event of the motion being carried. He was
called to account for this as a breach of privilege, and in the course of
the debate on the matter Hyde said : ' He was not old enough to know
the ancient customs of that House ; but that he well knew it was a
very ancient custom in the House of Peers, and leave was never there
denied to any man who asked that he might protest, and enter his

protest, it was only dissenting, and that in the case of the pope.

LXXXIV.

MARRIAGE.

1. OF all actions of a man's life, his marriage does least concern other people ; yet of all actions of our life, 'tis most meddled with by other people.

2. Marriage is nothing but a civil contract. 'Tis true 'tis an ordinance of God ; so is every other contract ; God commands me to keep it, when I have made it.

3. Marriage is a desperate thing. The frogs in Æsop 10 were extreme wise, they had a great mind to some water, but they would not leap into the well, because they could not get out again.

4. We single out particulars, and apply God's providence to them. Thus when two are married, and have undone one another, they cry it was God's providence we should come together, when God's providence does equally concur to everything.

LXXXV.

MARRIAGE OF COUSIN-GERMANS.

SOME men forbear to marry cousin-germans out of this 20 kind of scruple of conscience, because 'twas unlawful

dissent against any judgment of the House to which he would not be understood to have given his consent.' Clarendon, Hist. vol. i. 489.

l. 21. *because 'twas unlawful before the Reformation* &c.] The more ancient prohibition of the Canon Law was to the seventh generation : ' De affinitate consanguinitatis per gradus cognationis, placuit usque ad septimam generationem observari. And the same was the law of the Church of England . . . But in the 4th Council of Lateran, which was held in the year of our Lord 1215, the prohibition was reduced to the fourth degree . . . which limitation was also the rule of the Church of before the Reformation, and is still in the Church of Rome. And so by reason their grandfather, or their great grandfather did not do it, upon that old score they think they ought not to do it ; as some men forbear flesh upon Friday, not reflecting upon the statute, which with us makes it unlawful, but out of an old score, because the Church of Rome forbids it, and their forefathers always forbore flesh upon that day. Others forbear it out of a natural consideration, because it is observed (for example) in beasts, if two couple of a near kin, the breed proves not so good. The same observation they make in plants and trees, which degenerate being grafted upon the same stock. And 'tis also farther observed, those matches between cousin-germans seldom prove fortunate. But for the lawfulness, there is no colour but cousin-germans in England may marry, both by the law of God and man : for with us we have reduced all the degrees of marriage to those in the Levitical law, and 'tis plain there's nothing against it. As for that that is said, cousin-germans once removed may not marry, and therefore, being a further degree may not, 'tis presumed a nearer should not[1], no man can tell what it means.

LXXXVI.

MEASURE OF THINGS.

1. WE measure from ourselves, and as things are for our use and purpose, so we approve them. Bring a pear to

[1] *And therefore being a further degree may not, 'tis presumed a nearer should not*, S.] omitted in H. In H. 2 ‘it is’ is inserted after ‘being.’ The rest is as in S.

England ; as appears, not only by this Statute (i.e. by 32 Henry VIII, cap. 38, declaring as a new rule that all marriages are lawful if beyond the Levitical degrees) but also by the frequent dispensations for the fourth degree, and no further, which we meet with in our ecclesiastical records, as granted here by special authority from the see of Rome.’ Gibson, Codex, p. 411.

the table that is rotten, we cry it down, 'tis naught; but bring a medlar that is rotten, and 'tis a fine thing ; and yet I warrant you, the pear thinks as well of itself as the medlar does.

2. We measure the excellency of other men, by some excellency we conceive to be in ourselves. Nash, a poet poor enough (as poets use to be), seeing an alderman with his gold chain, upon his great horse, said by way of scorn to one of his companions, Do you see yon fellow, how goodly, how big he looks ? why that fellow cannot make a blank 10 verse.

3. Nay, we measure the excellency of God from our-selves. We measure his goodness, his justice, his wisdom, by something we call just, good, or wise in ourselves; and in so doing, we judge proportionably to the country-fellow in the play, who said, If he were a king, he would live like a lord, and have peas and bacon every day, and a whip that cried slash.

LXXXVII.

DIFFERENCE OF MEN.

THE difference of men is very great. You would scarce 20 think them to be of the same species, and yet it consists more in the affection than in the intellect. For as in the strength of body, two men shall be of an equal strength, yet one shall appear stronger than the other, because he exercises, and puts forth his strength ; the other will not stir nor strain himself. So 'tis in the strength of the brain; the one endeavours, and strains, and labours, and studies; the other sits still, and is idle, and takes no pains, and therefore he appears so much the inferior. 30

LXXXVIII.

MINISTER DIVINE.

1. THE imposition of hands upon the minister, when all
is done, will be nothing but a designation of a person to
this or that office or employment in the church. 'Tis a
ridiculous phrase that of the canonists, *conferre ordines*.
'Tis *cooptare aliquem in ordinem*, to make a man one of us
one of our number, one of our order. So Cicero would
understand what I said, it being a phrase borrowed from
the Latins, and to be understood proportionably to what
10 was amongst them.

2. Those words you now use in making a minister,
Receive the Holy Ghost, were used among the Jews in

l. 5. *conferre ordines.*] This is the phrase used by Aquinas
passim. Conf. e. g. Summa Theolog. Supplem. pt. iii. quaest. 34,
art. 3.

l. 12. *were used among the Jews* &c.] This seems to have been
somewhat loosely reported. Selden, in his In Eutychii Origines
Commentarius, treats at length of the process by which judges, and
elders, and chief doctors of the law, were appointed among the Jews.
'Quisquis in potestatem judiciariam seu causarum rite cognoscendarum
facultatem evehendus erat, is per manuum impositionem, verbis
insuper de creatione conceptis, dignitatem eam regulariter adipisce-
batur; adeo ut dein dignus seu idoneus haberetur qui in synedria,
sive vigintitriumviralia sive septuagintauniusvirale cooptari legitime
posset, ibique judiciis praeesse.' Works, vol. ii. p. 436.

He does not say that the words 'receive the Holy Ghost' were any
part of the ceremony, but only that it was believed that the Holy
Spirit rested on those who had been thus duly appointed. 'Internus
ordinationis effectus habebatur eis ejusmodi, ut Spiritus Sanctus ....
super ordinatos quiesceret. De LXX Senioribus Mosi ejusmodi
ordinatione adscitis, et de eis qui seculis sequentibus rite ordina-
bantur, aiunt Et quievit super eos Majestas divina, quam et Spiritum
Sanctum vocitant.' p. 438.

Alting, like Selden, traces the custom from very early days, from
the appointment by Moses of the seventy elders, and from the
appointment of Joshua as Moses' successor. Conf. 'Tertius (ritus)
est manûs impositio .... unde tota promotionis solennitas ....

making of a lawyer; from thence we have them; which is
a villainous key to something; as if you would have some
other kind of prefecture, than a mayoralty, and yet keep
the same ceremony that was used in making the mayor.

3. A priest has no such thing as an indelible character.
What difference do you find betwixt him and another man
after ordination? Only he is made a priest (as I said) by
designation; as a lawyer is called to the bar, then made a

χειροθεσία appellari consuevit.' Historia promotionum Academicarum
apud Hebraeos (1652), p. 108.

In an earlier part of the treatise, speaking of Joshua's appointment
per impositionem manûs, he adds 'Atque hic notandum venit Sym-
bolum secundum in Magistrorum promotionibus adhibitum, χειροθεσίας
ritus, a Deo ipso, si non usurpatus in Mosis inauguratione, saltem
huic praescriptus.' p. 82.

But there is no mention by Alting of the use of the words, 'receive
the Holy Ghost,' fully and particularly as he describes every detail of
the ceremony in use. Nor do the words in the text, 'in making of a
lawyer,' adequately express the rank and authority conferred. That
the imposition of hands was copied by the Christians from the old
Jewish rite Selden does say, and this is probably what he ought here
to have been reported as saying. Works, ii. p. 439.

l. 5. *an indelible character.*] Aquinas insists on the indelible character of orders of all ranks, of the minor not less than of the priestly.
Summa Theolog. Supplem. pt. iii. quaest. 35, art. 2.

'If anyone saith that in the three Sacraments, Baptism to wit,
Confirmation, and Order, there is not imprinted in the soul a character, that is, a certain spiritual and indelible sign . . . let him be
anathema.' Session vii. Of the Sacraments, Canon ix. Canons, &c.,
of the Council of Trent.

'Forasmuch as in the Sacrament of Order, a character is imprinted
which can neither be effaced nor taken away; the holy Synod
condemns the opinion of those who assert that those who have once
been rightly ordained can again become Laymen.' Session xxiii. ch. 4.

On the other hand, Bingham, a very safe authority, quotes Calvin
as saying that the indelibility of orders 'was a fable, first invented in
the schools of the ignorant monks, and that the ancients were
altogether strangers to it: and that it had more of the nature of a
magical enchantment than of the sound doctrine of the Gospel in it,'
&c. Bingham himself concludes against it as a Romish superstition.
The whole subject is gone into very fully in Part ii. of his Discussion
on lay-baptism. Bingham, Works, vol. ix. p. 150 ff.

serjeant.   All men that would get power over others, make themselves as unlike them as they can; upon the same ground the priests made themselves unlike the laity.

4. A minister when he is made, is *materia prima*, apt for any form the state will put upon him; but of himself he can do nothing.   Like a doctor of law in the university; he has a great deal of law in him, but cannot use it till he be made somebody's chancellor: or like a physician, before he be received into a house, he can give nobody 10 physic; indeed after the master of the house has given him charge of his servants, then he may.   Or like a suffragan, that could do nothing but give orders, and yet he was a bishop[1].

5. A minister should preach according to the articles of religion established in the church where he lives.   To be a civil lawyer, let a man read Justinian, and the body of law, to conform his brain to that way; but when he comes to practise, he must make use of it so far as it concerns the law received in his own country.   To be a physician, let 20 a man read Galen and Hippocrates; but when he practises, he must apply his medicines according to the temper of those men's bodies with whom he lives, and have respect to the heat and cold of the climate; otherwise that which in Pergamus (where Galen lived) was physic, in our cold climate may be poison.   So to be a divine, let him read the whole body of divinity, the fathers and the schoolmen; but when he comes to practise, he must use it and apply it according to those grounds and articles of religion that are established in the church, and this with sense.

30   6. There be four things a minister should be at; the con-

---

[1] *He was a bishop*] he was no Bishop, MSS.

l. 12.   *and yet he was a bishop*]   The reading in the MSS. and in the early printed editions is 'he was no Bishop.'   This spoils the argument and is untrue in fact.   See 'Bishops before the Parliament,' sec. 1.

cionary part, ecclesiastical story, school divinity, and the casuists.

(1) In the concionary part, he must read all the chief fathers, both Latin and Greek, wholly; St. Austin, St. Ambrose, St. Chrysostom, both the Gregories, and [1] Tertullian, Clemens Alexandrinus, and Epiphanius, which last have more learning in them than all the rest, and write freely.

(2) For ecclesiastical story, let him read Baronius, with the Magdeburgenses, and be his own judge; the one being [10] extremely for the papists, the other extremely for the protestants.

(3) For school divinity, let him get Cavellus's[2] edition of Scotus or Mayro[3], where there be quotations that direct you to every schoolman, where such and such questions are handled. Without school divinity, a divine knows nothing logically, nor will be able to satisfy a rational man out of the pulpit.

(4) The study of the casuists must follow the study of the schoolmen, because the division of their cases is according [20] to their divinity; otherwise he that begins with them will know little, as he that begins with the study of the reports

---

[1] *The Gregories and* H. 2] the Gregories, &c., H.

[2] *Cavellus*] Javellus, MSS.

[3] *Mayro*] Mayco, MSS.

l. 13. *Cavellus—Mayro*] The reading of the MSS. and of the early editions is 'Javellus' and 'Mayco,' which (as Mr. Singer has pointed out) must be incorrect. Some of Duns Scotus' writings were edited in 1620 by Hugo Cavellus (i.e. Mac Caghwell) a Roman Catholic Archbishop of Armagh. In 1639 there was a complete edition of Duns Scotus published with variorum notes, in which H. Cavellus is one of several commentators cited.

Mayro, or Franciscus de Mayronis, a voluminous ecclesiastical writer, belongs to the first half of the fourteenth century. He was a disciple of Duns Scotus, and was known among the Franciscans as Doctor Illuminatus. A complete list of his writings will be found in Wadding's Scriptores Ordinis Minorum.

and cases in the common law, will thereby know little of the law. Casuists may be of admirable use, if discreetly dealt with, though among them you shall have many leaves together very impertinent. A case well decided would stick by a man, they would remember it whether they will or no, whereas a quaint exposition dies in the birth. The main thing is to know where to search; for talk they what they will of vast memories, no man will presume upon his own memory for anything he means to write or speak in public.

7. *Go and teach all nations.* This was said to all Christians that then were, before the distinction of clergy and laity; there have been since men designed to preach only by the state, as some men are designed to study the law, others to study physic. When the Lord's Supper was instituted, there were none present but the disciples. Shall none then but ministers receive?

8. There is all the reason you should believe your minister, unless you have studied divinity as well as he, or more than he.

9. 'Tis a foolish thing to say, a minister must not meddle with secular matters, because his own profession will take up the whole man. May he not eat, or drink, or walk, or learn to sing? The meaning of that is, he must seriously intend his calling.

10. Ministers with the papists [that is, their priests] have much respect; with the puritans they have much, and that upon the same ground, they pretend to come both of them immediately from Christ; but with the protestants they have very little; the reason whereof is,—in the beginning of the Reformation they were glad to get such to take livings as they could procure by any invitations, things of

l. 25. *intend*] i.e. give his mind to.
l. 32. *things of pitiful condition*] Archbishop Parker, in a letter to the Bishop of London, written circa 1560, says that owing to the

pitiful condition.   The nobility and gentry would not suffer
their sons or kindred to meddle with the church, and therefore at this day, when they see a parson, they think him
to be such a thing still, and there they will keep him, and
use him accordingly ; if he be a gentleman born, that is
singled out, and he is used the more respectively.

11. That the protestant minister is least regarded,
appears by the old story of the keeper of the Clink.   He
had priests of several sorts sent unto him ; as they came
in, he asked them who they were ; who are you ? to the 10
first.   I am a priest of the Church of Rome.   You are
welcome, quoth the keeper, there are those will take care
of you.   And who are you ? A silenced minister. You are
welcome too, I shall fare the better for you.   And who are
you ? A minister of the Church of England.   O God help
me (quoth the keeper) I shall get nothing by you, I am
sure you may lie and starve, and rot, before anybody will
look after you.

great want of ministers, the bishops had 'heretofore admitted into the
ministry sundry artificers and others not traded and brought up in
learning ; and as it happened in a multitude some that were of base
occupations.'

These men are termed 'very offensive to the people ; yea, and to
the wise of this realm ; they were thought to do a great deal more
hurt than good ; the Gospel thereby sustaining slander.' Strype, Life
of Parker, bk. ii. ch. iv.

Even in Selden's day, the clergy were a mixed multitude, some of
them (according to Sir Edward Deering) 'so poor that they cannot
attend their ministry but are fain to keep schools, nay alehouses some
of them.'   Nalson, Collections, vol. i. 760.

1. 8.   *the Clink*]   The clink, according to Stow, was a prison,
adjoining the Bishop of Winchester's House in Southwark, used in
old time for such as should brabble, fray, or break the peace. Survey
of London, bk. iv. p. 8 (ed. of 1720, 2 vols. folio).

For the use to which it was put afterwards, see Foxe (Acts and
Monuments), who says that Bishops Hooper and Rogers, after being
questioned by the Bishop of Winchester, were 'carried to the Clink,
a prison not far from the Bishop of Winchester's house.' Vol. vi.
p. 650, and again, p. 691 (8 vols. 1849).

12. Methinks 'tis an ignorant thing for a churchman to call himself the minister of Christ, because St. Paul, or the Apostles called themselves so. If one of them had a voice from heaven, as St. Paul had, I will grant he is a minister of Christ, and I will call him so too. Must they take upon them as the Apostles did? Can they do as the Apostles could? The Apostles had a mark to be known by, spoke tongues, cured diseases, trod upon serpents, &c. Can they do this? If a gentleman tell me he will send his man to me, and I did not know his man, but he gave me this mark to know him by, he should bring in his hand a rich jewel; if a fellow came to me with a pebble-stone, had I any reason to believe that he was the gentleman's man?

LXXXIX.

MONEY.

1. MONEY makes a man laugh. A blind fiddler playing to a company, and playing but scurvily, the company laughed at him; his boy that led him, perceiving it, cried, Father, let us be gone, they do nothing but laugh at you. Hold thy peace, boy, says the fiddler, we shall have their money presently, and then we will laugh at them.

2. Euclid was beaten in Boccaline, for teaching his

l. 21. *Euclid was beaten*, &c.] See Boccalini, I Ragguagli di Parnasso (Advertisements from Parnassus), Century II. Advert. 3; p. 201 in the Earl of Monmouth's translation.

The book is a curious medley. The scene is laid at Apollo's court on Parnassus—a great central Academy, at which news arrives, from time to time, of all dates, and from all quarters of the world (as e.g. in the text), and where various characters, ancient and modern, poets, philosophers, politicians, and historians, come up to be judged and have their proper rank assigned to them. It is a court of universal reference, open perpetually to hear complaints and to settle literary disputes. Sentence is given sometimes by Apollo in person, sometimes by his deputies. See also 'War,' sec. 11 and note.

scholars a mathematical figure in his schools, whereby he shewed that all the lives both of princes and private men tended to one centre, *con gentilezza* handsomely to get money out of other men's pockets, and put it into their own.

3. The pope used heretofore to send the princes of Christendom to fight against the Turk; but prince and pope finely juggled together; the moneys were raised, and some men went out to the holy war, but commonly after they had got the money, the Turk was pretty quiet, 10 and the prince and the pope shared it betwixt them.

4. In all times the princes in England have done something illegally, to get money. But then came a parliament, and all was well; the people and the prince kissed and were friends, and so things were quiet for a while. Afterwards there was another trick found out to get money, and after they had got it, another parliament was called to set all right, &c. But now they have so outrun the constable——

XC.

MORAL HONESTY.   20

THEY that cry down moral honesty, cry down that which is a great part of religion, my duty towards God, and my duty toward man. What care I to see a man run after a sermon, if he cozen and cheat me as soon as he comes home? On the other side, morality must not be without religion, for if so, it may change, as I see convenience. Religion must govern it. He that has not religion to govern his morality, is not a dram better than my mastiff-dog; so long as you stroke him, and please him, and do 30 not pinch him, he will play with you as finely as may be, he's a very good moral mastiff; but if you hurt him, he will fly in your face, and tear out your throat.

XCI.

MORTGAGE.

In case I receive a £1000, and mortgage as much land as is worth £2000 to you, if I do not pay the money at such a day. I fail; whether you may take my land and keep it in point of conscience?

Answer. If you had my land as a security only for your money, then you are not to keep it; but if we bargained so, that if I did not repay your £1000, my land should go for it, be it what it will, no doubt you may with a safe
10 conscience keep it; for in these things all the obligation is, *servare fidem.*

XCII.

NUMBER.

All those mysterious things they observe in numbers, come to nothing, upon this very ground; because number in itself is nothing, has nothing to do with nature, but is merely of human imposition, a mere sound. For example, when I cry one o'clock, two o'clock, three o'clock, that is but man's division of time, the time itself goes on; and it had been all one in nature, if those hours had been called
20 9, 10, and 11. So when they say the seventh son is fortunate, it means nothing; for if you count from the seventh backwards, then the first is the seventh; and why is not he likewise fortunate?

l. 14. *number in itself is nothing*] Numbering, Hobbes says, is an act of the mind; and by division of space or of time 'I do not mean the severing or pulling asunder of one space or time from another (for does any man think that one hemisphere may be separated from the other hemisphere, or the first hour from the second?), but diversity of consideration.' Hobbes, Computation or Logic, pt. ii. ch. 7, secs. 3 and 5.

XCIII.

OATHS.

1. SWEARING was another thing with the Jews than with us, because they might not pronounce the name of the Lord Jehovah.

2. There is no oath scarcely, but we swear to things we are ignorant of: for example, the oath of supremacy: how many know how the king is king? what are his right and prerogative? So how many know what are the privileges of the parliament, and the liberty of the subject, when they take the protestation? But the meaning is, they will defend them when they know them. As if I should swear I would take part with all that wear red ribbons in their hats; it may be I do not know which colour is red; but when I do know, and see a red ribbon in a man's hat, then will I take his part.

3. I cannot conceive how an oath is imposed, where there is a parity, vizt. in the House of Commons; they are all *pares inter se*, only one brings a paper, and shews it the rest, they look upon it, and in their own sense take it. Now they are but *pares* to me, who am one of the house[1], for I do not acknowledge myself their subject; if I did, then, no question, I was bound by oath of their imposing. 'Tis to me but reading a paper in my own sense.

4. There is a great difference between an assertory oath

---

[1] *One of the house*] none of the house, MSS.

l. 9. *when they take the protestation*] The form of oath agreed upon, and taken by the members of the House of Commons, was as follows: 'I, A. B., do, in the Presence of Almighty God, promise, vow, and protest, to maintain and defend . . . . the Power and Privileges of Parliament, the lawful rights and liberties of the Subject, and every person that maketh this protestation, in whatsoever he shall do in the lawful pursuance of the same' (May 3, 1641). Commons Journals, ii. 132.

and a promissory oath. An assertory oath is made to man before God, and I must swear so, as man may know what I mean. But a promissory oath is made to God only, and I am sure he knows my meaning. So in the new oath it runs [*Whereas I believe in my conscience*, &c. *I will assist* thus and thus]; that *whereas* gives me an outloose, for if I do not believe so, for aught I know, I swear not at all.

5. In a promissory oath, the mind I am in is a good interpretation; for if there be enough happened to change my mind, I do not know why I should not. If I promise to go to Oxford tomorrow, and mean it when I say it, and afterwards it appears to me that 'twill be my undoing, will you say I have broken my promise if I stay at home? Certainly I must not go.

6. The Jews had this way with them concerning a promissory oath or vow; if one of them had vowed a vow, which afterwards appeared to him to be very prejudicial, by reason of something he either did not foresee, or did not think of, when he made his vow; if he made it known to three of his countrymen, they had power to absolve him, though he could not absolve himself; and that they picked out of some words of the text. Perjury has only to do

l. 3. *a promissory oath is made to God only*] There seems no reason for this limitation, nor does it agree with what Selden says elsewhere. See 'All oaths are either promissory or assentatory (assertatory?); the first being that which binds to a future performance of trust; the second that which is taken for the discovery of a past or present truth. The first kind they . . . . used in taking the oath of all the Barons for the maintenance of the great charter,' &c. &c. Works, iii. p. 1533.

The statement in the text must be understood, therefore, as part and parcel of the argument in sec. 3, which, so helped out, seems to run thus—that since the oaths imposed by Parliament are promissory oaths, and since only a superior can rightfully impose such oaths or can give his own sense to them, it follows that any member of Parliament taking a Parliamentary promissory oath, takes it to God only, and in any non-natural sense which he himself chooses mentally to put upon it.

with an assertory oath, and no man was punished for perjury by man's law till Queen Elizabeth's time; 'twas left to
God as a sin against him. The reason was, because 'twas
so hard a thing to prove a man perjured; I might mis-
understand him, and he swears as he thought[1].

7. When men ask me whether they may take it in their
own sense, 'tis to me, as if they should ask whether they
may go to such a place with their own legs. I would fain
know how they can go otherwise.

8. If the ministers that are in sequestered livings will 10
not take the engagement, threaten to turn them out and
put in the old ones, and then I'll warrant you they will
quickly take it. A gentleman having been rambling two or
three days, at length came home, and being abed with his
wife, would fain have been at something that she was unwilling to, and instead of complying, fell to chiding him for
his being abroad so long: Well, says he, if you will not,
call up Sue (his wife's chambermaid); upon that she
yielded presently.

9. Now oaths are so frequent, they should be taken like 20
pills, swallowed whole: if you chew them you will find them
bitter: if you think what you swear, 'twill hardly go down.

XCIV.

ORACLES.

ORACLES ceased presently after Christ, as soon as nobody
believed them. Just as we have no fortune-tellers, nor

[1] *As he thought*, H. 2] as the thought, H.

l. 1. *no man was punished for perjury till Queen Elizabeth's time*]
This was by 5 Eliz. ch. 9, sec. 2. Earlier statutes had dealt only with
the suborning of false witnesses, and had left the false witnesses
themselves untouched.

wise men, when nobody cares for them. Sometime you
have a season of them, when people believe them ; and
neither of these, I conceive, wrought by the devil.

XCV.

OPINION.

1. OPINION and affection extremely differ. I may affect
a woman best, but it does not follow I must think her the
handsomest woman in the world. I love apples best of
any fruit ; it does not follow that I must think apples to be
the best of fruit. Opinion is something wherein I go about
10 to give reason why all the world should think as I think,
Affection is a thing wherein I only look after the pleasing
of myself.

2. 'Twas a good fancy of an old Platonic : the gods which
are above men, had something whereof man did partake,
[an intellect, knowledge] and the gods kept on their course
quietly. The beasts, which are below men, had something
whereof man did partake [sense, and growth] and the
beasts lived quietly in their way ; but man had something
in him, whereof neither gods nor beasts did partake, which

---

l. 13. '*Twas a good fancy* &c.] This bears some resemblance to a
passage in the Phaedrus (p. 247–249), in which the Gods are described
as borne aloft by winged horses of pure and noble breed, and as thus
keeping steadily in their course and in the possession of true knowledge. Other souls, whose horses are unequally yoked, one noble and
the other ignoble, cannot easily follow the upward movement of the
Gods, but are troubled and confused by the wild tricks of the ignoble
horse ; and if they are thrown out of their course, and fall to earth,
they suffer many disadvantages and are fed with opinion (τροφῇ δοξαστῇ
χρῶνται) in the place of true knowledge. If Selden's reference is to
some later Platonist, this must have been the original which he had
in mind. It is one out of many variations on the regular Platonic
theme of the distinction between real and phenomenal existence and
between the faculties by which they are severally known.

gave him all the trouble, and made all the confusion we see in the world; and that is opinion.

3. 'Tis a foolish thing for me to be brought off from an opinion in a thing neither of us know, but are led only by some cobweb-stuff; as in such a case as this, *Utrum angeli invicem colloquantur?* If I forsake my side in such a case, I shew myself wonderfully light, or infinitely complying, flattering the other party. But if I be in a business of nature, and hold an opinion one way, and some man's experience has found out the contrary, I may with a safe 10 reputation give up my side.

4. 'Tis a vain thing to talk of an heretic, for a man for his heart can think no otherwise than he does think. In the primitive times there were several opinions; nothing scarce but some or other held: one of these opinions being embraced by some prince, and received into his kingdom, the rest were condemned as heresies[1]; and his religion, which was but one of the several opinions first, is said to be orthodox and to have continued ever since the Apostles.   20

XCVI.

PARITY.

THIS is the juggling trick of parity; they would have nobody above them, but they do not tell you they would have nobody under them.

---

[1] *Heresies*, H. 2] heretics, H.

l. 5. *Utrum angeli invicem colloquantur?*] This is a point which Aquinas discusses at length, and on which he concludes in the affirmative. Summa Theolog. pt. i. quaest. 107, art. 1 and 2.

l. 21. *parity*] A term, in general use, for a form of Church government by a body of Presbyters or elders and lay assessors all equal in power, as opposed to Church government by bishops. It is so ex-

XCVII.

PARLIAMENT.

1. ALL are involved in a parliament. There was a time when all men had their voice in choosing knights. About Henry the Sixth they found the inconvenience; so one parliament made a law, that only he that had forty shillings per annum should give his voice, they under should be excluded. They made the law who had the voices of all, as well under forty shillings as above; and thus it continues at this day. All consent civilly in a parliament; women
10 are involved in the men, children in those of perfect age, those that are under forty shillings a year in those that have forty shillings a year, those of forty shillings in the knights.

2. All things are brought to the parliament, little to the courts of justice; just as in a room where there is a banquet presented, if there be persons of quality there, the people must expect, and stay till the great ones have done.

plained, e.g. by Laud, in his sermon before Charles' second Parliament:
'I know there are some that think the Church is not yet far enough beside the cushion; that their seats are too easy yet and too high too. A parity they would have; no bishop, no governor, but a parochial consistory, and that should be lay enough too. Well, first, this parity was never left to the Church by Christ. He left Apostles, and disciples under them. No parity. It was never in use with the Church since Christ; no Church ever, anywhere, till this last age, without a bishop. . . . And there is not a man that is for parity—all fellows in the Church —but he is not for monarchy in the State.' Laud's Works, vol. i. pp. 82, 83.

l. 4. *so one parliament made a law* &c.] The Act 8 Henry VI, ch. 7, recites that elections of knights of shires have been made by large and excessive numbers of persons of small substance, and that riots and disturbances are likely thence to arise. It enacts, accordingly, that knights of shires to come to Parliament be chosen by residents in the shire having free land or tenement worth at least a clear forty shillings by the year.

By 10 Henry VI, ch. 2, it is further expressly said that the qualifying estate must be a freehold.

3. The parliament in flying upon several men, and then letting them alone, does as a hawk that flies a covey of partridges, and when she has flown them a good way, grows weary and takes a tree; then the falconer lures her down, and takes her to his fist; on they go again, *hei ret*; up springs another covey; away goes the hawk, and as she did before, takes another tree, &c.

4. Dissentions[1] in parliament may at length come to a good end, though first there be a deal of do, and a great deal of noise, which mad wild folks make; just as in brewing of wrest-beer, there is a great deal of business in grinding the malt, and that spoils any man's clothes that comes near it; then it must be mashed; then comes a fellow in and drinks off the wort, and he's drunk; then they keep a huge quarter when they carry it into the cellar, and a twelvemonth after 'tis delicate fine beer.

5. It must necessarily be that our distempers must be worse than they were in the beginning of the parliament. If a physician comes to a sick man he lets him blood, it may be he scarifies him, cups him, puts him into a great disorder, before he makes him well; and if he be sent for to cure an ague, and he finds his patient has many diseases, a dropsy, and a palsy, he applies remedies to them all, which makes the cure the longer, and the dearer: this is the case.

6. The parliament men are as great princes as any in the world, when whatever they please is privilege of parliament; no man must know the number of their privileges, and whatsoever they dislike is breach of privilege. The

[1] *Dissentions.* H. 2, written above the line] dissenters, H. and S.

l. 14. *drinks off the wort*] i. e. drinks some from the wort.

l. 15. *they keep a huge quarter*] i.e. they make a great noise or disturbance. See Halliwell, Glossary of Archaic Words; *sub voce* 'Quarter.'

l. 29. *breach of privilege*] Clarendon remarks, with instances, on the extent to which this claim was made, and condemns, as Selden

duke of Venice is no more than the speaker of the house of commons; but the senate at Venice are not so much as our parliament men, nor have they that power over the people, who yet exercise the greatest tyranny that is any-where. In plain truth, breach of privilege is only the actual taking away of a member of the house; the rest are offences against the house. For example, to take out process against a parliament man, or the like.

7. The parliament party, if the law be for them, they call for law; if it be against them, they will go to a parliamentary way: if law be for them[1], then for law again: like him

---

[1] *If law be for them*] if no law be for them, MSS.

does, the notion 'that their being judges of their privileges should qualify them to make new privileges, or that their judgment should create them such.' This he terms 'a doctrine never before now (i. e. before 1641) heard of.' Hist. vol. i. 618-620.

l. 9. *if the law be for them* &c.] This seems to refer to the pro-ceedings at the trial of the Earl of Strafford. As Clarendon tells the story, his accusers began in due form of law, and when there were difficulties in the way of obtaining a conviction, they then resolved to proceed by attainder. Later, when the Bill of Attainder had been sent up to the Lords, and his accusers had promised 'to give their Lordships satisfaction in the matter of law,' Mr. Solicitor St. John, speaking on behalf of the Commons, urged *inter alia*, 'That, in that way of bill, private satisfaction to each man's conscience was sufficient, although no evidence had been given in at all, and as to pressing the law, he said, it was true we give law to hares and deer because they are beasts of chase, but it was never accounted either cruelty or foul play to knock foxes and wolves on the head as they can be found, because they are beasts of prey.' Clarendon, Hist. i. 337 ff.

St. John's speech, as Nalson relates it, points no less clearly to a 'Parliamentary way' of overriding the law: 'My Lords, in judgment of greatest moment, there are but two ways for satisfying those that are to give them, either the *lex lata*, the law already established, or else the use of the same power for making new laws, whereby the old at first received life. . . . The same law gives power to the Parliament to make new laws, that enables the inferior court to judge according to the old. . . . What hath been said is, because that this proceeding of the Commons by way of Bill implies the use of the meer legislative power, in respect new laws are for the most part passed by Bill.' Nalson, Collections, ii. 162.

that first called for sack to heat him; then small drink to cool his sack; then sack again to heat his small drink.

8. The parliament party do not play fair play, in sitting up till two of the clock in the morning, to vote something they have a mind to. 'Tis like a crafty gamester that makes the company drunk and then cheats them of their money. Young men and infirm men go away. Besides, a man is not there to persuade other men to be of his mind, but to speak his own heart; and if it be liked—so: if not, there's an end.   10

XCVIII.

PARSON.

1. Though we write [parson] differently, yet 'tis but person; that is the individual person set apart for the service of such a church, and 'tis in Latin *persona*, and *personatus* is a parsonage. Indeed with the canon lawyers, *personatus* is any dignity or preferment in the church.

l. 3. *in sitting up till two of the clock*] This was done in the debate on the Remonstrance (1641). The Remonstrance was carried shortly after midnight by 159 to 148 votes. Then came a new debate whether the Remonstrance should be printed, and it was finally resolved that it was not to be printed without the particular order of the House. The attempt to introduce a further restriction that it was not to be 'printed or published' did not succeed, the adverse votes being 124 to 101. The House rose at two in the morning. See Cobbett's Parliamentary History, and Forster's Grand Remonstrance, §§ 17 and 18. The Commons Journals, ii. 322, record the debates and their result, but say nothing about the hour at which a division was taken or at which the House rose. Clarendon's account is exact as to the hours. Hist. i. 485.

l. 12. *yet 'tis but person*] 'Those words *universae personae regni* I interpret all Abbots, Conventual Priors, and the like ... which yet time and use with us hath long since confined only to the Rectors of Parish-churches.' Selden, Titles of Honour, ii. 5, sec. 20; Works, iii. 732.

l. 14. *personatus is a parsonage*] 'Personatus et dignitas vere supponunt pro eodem; licet in aliquibus locis rectores ecclesiarum

K

2. There never was a merry world since the fairies left dancing, and the parson left conjuring. The opinion of the latter kept thieves in awe, and did as much good in a country as a justice of peace.

XCIX.

PATIENCE.

PATIENCE is the chiefest fruit of study. A man by striving to make himself a different thing from other men by much reading, gains this chiefest good, that in all fortunes he hath something to entertain and comfort 10 himself withal.

C.

PEACE.

1. KING James was pictured going gently down a pair of stairs, and upon every step was written *peace, peace, peace;* the wisest way for men in these times is to say nothing.

2. When a country-wench cannot get her butter to come, she says the witch is in her churn. We have been churning for peace a good while, and 'twill not come ; surely the witch is in it.

20   3. Though we had peace, yet 'twill be a great while ere things be settled : though the wind lie, yet after a storm the sea will work a great while.

vocantur Personae et sic habent personatum non tamen dignitatem.' Ducange, Glossary, Personatus ; and see Selden, iii. 732.

That parson and person were once used indifferently, appears from e. g. 'An Acte that no parson or psons shall susteyne any prejudice by means of the attaynder of the Lord Cardinall.' 21 Henry VIII, cap. 25. So, too, in 1 Edward VI, cap. 12, sec. 5.

CI.

PENANCE.

PENANCE is only the punishment inflicted, not penitence, which is the right word; a man comes not to do
penance, because he repents him of his sin, but because
he is compelled to it; he curses him, and could kill him
that sends him thither. The old canons wisely enjoined
three years' penance, sometimes more; because in that
time a man got a habit of virtue, and so committed that
sin no more, for which he did penance.

CII.

PEOPLE.   10

1. THERE is not anything in the world so much abused
as this sentence, *Salus populi suprema lex esto;* for we
apply it, as if we ought to forsake the known law when
it may be most for the advantage of the people, when it
means no such thing. For first, 'tis not *salus populi suprema lex est,* but *esto,* it being one of the laws of the
twelve tables; and after divers laws made, some for punishment, some for reward, then follows this, *salus populi
suprema lex esto;* that is, in all the laws you make, have
a special eye to the good of the people; and then what 20
does this concern the way they now go?

l. 2. *penitence, which is the right word*] This probably refers to
the English version of Article 33, in which the original Latin 'donec
per poenitentiam publice reconciliatus fuerit,' is wrongly rendered by
'until he be openly reconciled by penance.' Penitence would clearly
be 'the right word' here.

l. 16. *it being one of the laws of the twelve tables*] The words, as
Selden states them, occur in Cicero de Leg. iii. 3, sec. 8; but, like the
other laws in the treatise, they are said not to be quoted from the
twelve tables; ii. 7, sec. 18.

K 2

2. *Objection.* He that makes one, is greater than he that is made; the people make the king; *ergo*, &c.

Answer. This does not hold. For if I have £1000 per annum, and give it you, and leave myself ne'er a penny, I made you; but when you have my land, you are greater than I. The parish make the constable, and when the constable is made, he governs the parish. The answer to all these doubts is, Have you agreed so? If you have, then it must remain till you have altered it.

CIII.

10

PHILOSOPHY.

WHEN men comfort themselves with philosophy, 'tis not because they have got two or three sentences, but because they have digested those sentences, and made them their own. So, upon the matter, philosophy is nothing but discretion.

CIV.

PLEASURE.

1. PLEASURE is nothing else but the intermission of pain, the enjoying of something I am in great trouble for till I have it.

l. 14. *upon the matter*] i.e. in strict fact, really. See 'Subsidies,' sec. 1, and: 'It was upon the matter an appeal to the people, and to infuse jealousies into their minds.' Clarendon, Hist. i. 485. 'So that upon the matter, in a great wit, deformity is an advantage to rising.' Bacon, Essay 44, Of Deformity.

l. 17. *Pleasure is nothing else* &c.] This agrees with one of the accounts of pleasure which Aristotle criticises in the 7th Book of the

2. 'Tis a wrong way to proportion other men's pleasures to ourselves. 'Tis like a child's using a little bird,
[O poor bird, thou shalt sleep with me] so lays it in his
bosom, and stifles it with his hot breath; the bird had
rather be in the cold air: and yet too 'tis the most pleasing flattery, to like what others like.

3. 'Tis most undoubtedly true, that all men are equally
given to their pleasure; only thus, one man's pleasure lies
one way, and another's another. Pleasures are all alike,
simply considered in themselves. He that hunts, or he 10
that governs the Commonwealth, they both please themselves alike, only we commend that, whereby we ourselves receive some benefit; as if a man place his delight
in things that tend to the common good. He that takes
pleasure· to hear sermons, enjoys himself as much as he
that hears plays; and could he that loves plays endeavour
to love sermons, possibly he might bring himself to it as
well as to any other pleasure. At first it might seem
harsh and tedious, but afterwards 'twould be pleasing
and delightful. So it falls out in that which is the great 20
pleasure of some men, tobacco; at first they could not
abide it, and now they cannot be without it.

4. While you are upon earth enjoy the good things
that are here, (to that end were they given) and be not
melancholy, and wish yourself in heaven. If a king
should give you the keeping of a castle, with all things
belonging to it, orchards, gardens, &c. and bid you use

Nicomachean Ethics, and which he proves to be incomplete by
showing that there are some kinds of pleasure to which it does
not apply. Conf. "Ετι ἐπεὶ τοῦ ἀγαθοῦ τὸ μὲν ἐνέργεια τὸ δ' ἕξις, κατὰ
συμβεβηκὸς αἱ καθιστᾶσαι εἰς τὴν φυσικὴν ἕξιν ἡδεῖαί εἰσιν. "Εστι δ' ἡ ἐνέργεια
ἐν ταῖς ἐπιθυμίαις τῆς ὑπολύπου ἕξεως καὶ φύσεως, ἐπεὶ καὶ ἄνευ λύπης καὶ
ἐπιθυμίας εἰσὶν ἡδοναί, οἷον αἱ τοῦ θεωρεῖν ἐνέργειαι, τῆς φύσεως οὐκ ἐνδεοῦς
οὔσης..... Διὸ καὶ οὐ καλῶς ἔχει τὸ αἰσθητὴν γένεσιν φάναι εἶναι τὴν ἡδονήν,
ἀλλὰ μᾶλλον λεκτέον ἐνέργειαν τῆς κατὰ φύσιν ἕξεως, ἀντὶ δὲ τοῦ αἰσθητὴν
ἀνεμπόδιστον. Eth. Nicom. vii. 13 (12), sec. 2 and 3.

them, withal promise you after[1] twenty years to remove you to the court, and to make you a privy councillor; if you should neglect your castle, and refuse to eat of those fruits, and sit down, and whine, and wish that I was a privy councillor, do you think the king would be pleased with you?

5. Pleasures of meat, drink, clothes, &c. are forbidden those that know not how to use them; just as nurses cry, pah! when they see a knife in a child's hand; they will never say any thing to a man.

CV.

POETRY.

1. OVID was not only a fine poet, but, as a man may speak, a great canon lawyer, as appears in his Fasti, where we have more of the festivals of the old Romans than any where else: 'tis pity the rest were lost.

2. There is no reason plays should be in verse, either in blank or rhyme; only the poet has to say for himself, that he makes something like that which somebody made before him. The old poets had no other reason but this, their verse was sung to music, otherwise it had been a senseless thing to have fettered up themselves.

3. I never converted but two, the one was Mr. Crashaw from writing against plays, by telling him a way how to understand that place, *of putting on women's apparel*, which

----

[1] *Promise you after*] promise you that after, H. and H. 2. In S. so originally, with ' that ' deleted.

l. 24. *that place, of putting on women's apparel*] Deuteron. xxii. 5. This text is explained by Selden, after Moses Maimonides, as intended to forbid certain magical or idolatrous rites, in the course of which females appeared in male dress, males in female dress, and as having no reference, therefore, to the representation on the stage of female

has nothing to do with the business [as neither has it, that the fathers speak against plays in their time, with reason enough, for they had real idolatries mixed with their plays, having three altars perpetually upon the stage]. The other was a doctor of divinity, from preaching against painting, which simply in itself is no more hurtful than putting on my clothes, or doing anything to make myself like other folks, that I may not be odious or offensive to the company. Indeed if I do it with an ill attention it alters the case. So, if I put on my gloves with an intention to do 10 a mischief, I am a villain.

4. 'Tis a fine thing for children to learn to make verse, but when they come to be men they must speak like other men, or else they will be laughed at. 'Tis ridiculous to speak, or write, or preach in verse. As 'tis good to learn to dance, a man may learn his leg, learn to go handsomely; but 'tis ridiculous for him to dance when he should go.

5. 'Tis ridiculous for a lord to print verses; 'tis well enough to make 'em to please himself, but to make them public is foolish. If a man in a private chamber twirls his 20 bandstring, or plays with a rush to please himself, 'tis well

characters by male actors. See Works, ii. p. 365, De Venere Syriacâ; and p. 1690, where Selden discusses it at length in a letter to Ben Jonson. The text was used by Tertullian (e. g. De Spectaculis, cap. 23) and by Cyprian (Epist. 61, sec. 1) in the sense which Selden disallows; and Prynne, in his Histrio-mastix, quotes and endorses both these authorities, and adds reasons of his own against the practice which they and he condemn. See, especially, p. 208 ff. (in the small 4to. ed. of 1633). It is clear that the objections to the practice do not depend only on what the text in question may or may not mean.

l. 1. *as neither has it, that the fathers* &c.] The objections urged against stage-plays by the fathers were on account of their indecency even more than of their idolatry, and were continued as forcibly as ever at a time when the idolatry had ceased. See Bingham, Christian Antiquities, bk. XI. ch. v. §§ 6 and 9; and, especially, bk. XVI. ch. xi. § 12. Prynne, in his Histrio-mastix, quotes numerous passages from the fathers in condemnation of stage-plays, some of which are clearly open to Selden's remark, while others are not.

enough; but if he should go into Fleet-street, and sit upon a stall, and twirl a bandstring, or play with a rush, then all the boys in the street would laugh at him.

6. Verse proves nothing but the quantity of syllables; they are not meant for logic.

CVI.

POPE.

1. A POPE's bull and a pope's brief differ very much, as with us the great seal and the privy seal, the bull being the highest authority the pope can give; the brief is of less. The bull has a leaden seal upon silk, hanging upon the instrument; the brief has *sub annulo piscatoris* upon the side.

2. He was a wise pope, that when one that used to be merry with him, before he was advanced to the popedom, refrained afterwards to come at him, (presuming he was busy in governing the Christian world) the pope sends for him, bids him come again, And [says he] we will be merry as we were before; for thou little thinkest what a little foolery governs the whole world.

3. The pope in sending relics to princes, does as wenches do by their wassail at new year's tide; they present you with a cup, and you must drink of a slabby stuff; but the meaning is, you must give them moneys, ten times more than it is worth.

4. The pope is infallible where he has power to command; that is where he must be obeyed; so is every supreme power and prince. They that stretch this infallibility further, do but they know not what.

5. When a protestant and a papist dispute, they talk like two madmen, because they do not agree upon their principles. The only way is to destroy the pope's power; for

if he has power to command me, 'tis not my alleging reasons
to the contrary can keep me from obeying: for example, if
a constable command me to wear a green suit to-morrow,
and has power to make me, 'tis not my alleging a hundred
reasons of the foolery of it, can excuse me from doing it.

6. There was a time when the pope had power here in
England, and there was excellent use made of it; for 'twas
only to serve turns, as might be manifested out of the
records of the kingdom, which divines know little of. If
the king did not like what the pope would have, he would 10
forbid his legate to land upon his grounds. So that the
power was truly in the king, though suffered in the pope.
But now the temporal and the spiritual power (spiritual so
called because ordained to a spiritual end) spring both from
one fountain; they are like two twists that—

7. The protestants in France bear office in the state,
because though their religion be different, yet they
acknowledge no other king but the king of France. The
papists in England they must have a king of their own,
a pope, that must do something in our king's kingdom; 20
therefore there is no reason they should enjoy the same
privileges.

8. Amsterdam admits of all religions but papists, and
'tis upon the same account. The papists where'er they
live, have another king at Rome; all other religions are
subject to the present state, and have no prince elsewhere.

9. The papists call our religion a parliamentary religion,
but there was once, I am sure, a parliamentary pope.
Pope Urban was made in England by act of parliament,
against pope Clement. The act is not in the book of 30

l. 15. *they are like two twists that—*] We may perhaps add here—
'are spun out of the same stuff.' If the metaphor of the one fountain
is to be continued, some other words must be used. The early printed
editions read 'they are like to twist that,' an unmeaning remark here.

l. 30. *the act is not in the book of statutes*] It is given in the folio
edition of the Statutes (1816), in the original Norman French, and

statutes, either because he that compiled the book, would not have the name of the pope there, or else he would not let it appear that they meddled with any such thing, but 'tis upon the rolls.

10. When our clergy preach against the pope, and the Church of Rome, they preach against themselves; and crying down their pride, their power, and their riches, have made themselves poor and contemptible enough; they did it at first[1] to please their prince, not considering 10 what would follow. Just as if a man were to go a journey,

---

[1] *They did it at first*] altered in H. and H. 2 from ' they dedicate first,'— a reading which stands in S., and in the early printed editions.

---

translated. A few words in the following extract have been changed where the translation does not quite agree with the original text :

'Because our Sovereign Lord the King hath perceived, as well by Letters Patent newly come from certain Cardinals, rebels against our Holy Father Urban now Pope, as otherwise by common fame, that division and discord was betwixt our said Holy Father and the said Cardinals, which afforced them with all their power to depose our said Holy Father from the state papal, ... our Sovereign Lord the King caused the said letters to be showed to the Prelates, Lords, and other great men of the realm being at the said Parliament .... and it was pronounced and published by the said Prelates, by great and notable reasons there showed in the full Parliament, ... that the said Urban was duly chosen Pope, and that so he is and ought to be true Pope, and ought to be accepted and obeyed as Pope and chief of Holy Church. And this to be done all the Prelates, Lords and Commons in the said Parliament do accord.' 2 Richard II, stat. 1, ch. 7.

It appears from Walsingham's History that the interference of the English Parliament had been expressly sought by both parties to the dispute.

'Ad idem Parliamentum venerunt solemnes ex Italiâ papales nuntii .... declarantes injurias et damna quae idem dominus Papa pertulit insolentiâ apostatarum cardinalium, qui nitebantur eundem cum universâ Ecclesiâ subvertere et infirmare. Venerunt et nuntii eorumdem cardinalium .... allegantes fortiter pro iisdem. Sed Domino Deo avente, qui cuncta juste disponit, repulsi sunt apostatici, et admissi Papales, promissumque subsidium Domino Papae.' Thomas Walsingham, Hist. Angl. p. 216, as printed in Camden's Anglica, Normannica, &c., Script. (Francfort, 1603).

and seeing at his first setting forth the way clean, ventures forth in his slippers, not considering the dirt and the sloughs that are a little further off, or how suddenly the weather may change.

CVII.

POPERY.

1. THE demanding a noble for a dead body passing through a town, came from hence. In time of popery, they carried the dead body into the church, where the priest said dirges ; and twenty dirges at fourpence a-piece come[1] to a noble ; but now 'tis forbidden by an order from my lord marshal, the heralds carry[2] his warrant about them.

2. We charge the prelatical clergy with popery to make them odious, though we know they are guilty of no such thing : just as heretofore they called images mammets, and the adoration of images mammetry ; that is Mahomets and Mahometry, odious names ; when all the world knows the Turks are forbidden images by their religion.

[1] *Come*, H. 2] comes, H.   [2] *Carry*, H. 2] carrying, H.

l. 10. *but now 'tis forbidden* &c.] That it continued or was revived after Selden's day appears from the register of St. Clement's parish, Oxford : 'The Earl of Conway being carried through the parish in a hearse, and the minister of St. Clement's appearing in his surplice to offer burial, he received for the same 6s. 8d. The same he received for Sir Lionel (Leoline ?) Jenkins, whose corpse was brought through the parish, and interred in Jesus College Chapel.' See Peshall's Wood's City of Oxford, p. 284 (1773, 4to). The first and only Earl of Conway died without issue in 1683. Sir Leoline Jenkins died in 1685, and was buried in Jesus College Chapel. I am indebted to Mr. C. H. O. Daniel for the above reference.

CVIII.

POWER. STATE.

1. THERE is no stretching of power. 'Tis a good rule, eat within your stomach, act within your commission.

2. They that govern most, make least noise. You see when they row in a barge, they that do the drudgery work, slash, and puff, and sweat; but he that governs sits quietly at the stern, and scarce is seen to stir.

3. Syllables govern the world.

4. *All power is of God* means no more than *fides est servanda*. When St. Paul said this, the people had made Nero emperor. They agreed, he to protect, they to obey. Then God comes in, and casts a hook upon them, *keep your faith;* then comes in *all power is of God*. Never king dropped out of the clouds. God did not make a new emperor, as the king makes a justice of peace.

5. Christ himself was a great observer of the civil power, and did many things only justifiable because the state required it[1], which were things merely temporary for the time that state stood; but divines make use of them to gain power to themselves; as, for example, that of *Dic ecclesiæ*, Tell the church; there was then a Sanhedrim, a court to tell it to, and therefore they would have it so now.

6. Divines ought to do no more than what the state permits. Before the state became Christian, they made their own laws, and those that did not observe them, they excommunicated, [naughty men] they suffered them to

---

[1] *Required it*, H. 2] required, H.

l. 8. *Syllables govern the world*] Conf. 'Considerare debemus quod verba habent maximam potestatem; et omnia miracula facta a principio mundi fere facta sunt per verba. Et opus animae rationalis precipuum est verbum.' R. Bacon, Opus Tertium, cap. 26 (p. 96, Brewer's ed.).

come no more amongst them. But if they would come amongst them, could they hinder them? By what law? By what power? They were still subject unto the state, which was heathen. Nothing better expresses the condition of the Christians in those times, than one of the meetings you have in London, of men of the same country, of Sussex-men, or Bedfordshire-men; they appoint their meeting, and they agree, and make laws amongst themselves [*he that is not there shall pay double, &c.*], and if any one mis-behave himself, they shut him out of their 10 company; but can they recover a forfeiture made concerning their meeting by any law? Have they any power to compel one to pay? But afterwards when the state became Christian, all the power was in them, and they gave the church as much, or as little as they pleased; took away when they pleased, and added when they pleased.

7. The church is not only subject to the civil power with us that are protestants, but also in Spain, if the church does excommunicate a man for what it should not, the civil power will take him out of their hands. So in 20 France, the bishop of Angers altered something in the

l. 19. *but also in Spain*] Selden, in his treatise De Synedriis veterum Ebraeorum, offers full proof of the supremacy of the Civil Power in France and Spain as well as in England. See Works, i. 975 ff. In the Preuves des Libertez de l'Eglise Gallicane, a work to which Selden refers as a leading authority, there are numerous instances given in which French excommunications, illegally pronounced, have been annulled by the civil power, or in which their authors have been forced to revoke them. See ch. vi. p. 92 f., and the Traitez des droits et libertez de l'Eglise Gallicane (a companion volume to the Preuves), in which the subject is discussed at length by several writers.

l. 22. *the bishop of Angers* &c.] This was in 1602. See 'Arrest de la Cour donné en l'audience, sur l'appel comme d'abus du changement du Breviaire d'Anjou, ordonné par l'Evesque d'Angers en l'Eglise de la Trinité audit Angers, de l'injonction par luy faite d'user de celui du Concile de Trente.'

The case was heard on complaint by the Canons and Chaplains of the Church, and the decree of the Court, as entered on the Registres

Breviary; they complained to the parliament at Paris, that made him alter it again, with a *comme d'abus*[1].

8. The parliament of England has no arbitrary power in point of judicature, but in point of making law.

9. If the prince be *servus natura*, of a servile base spirit, and the subjects *liberi*, free and ingenuous, often-times they depose their prince, and govern themselves. On the contrary, if the people be *servi natura*, and some one amongst them of an ingenuous[2] free spirit, he makes himself king of the rest; and this is the cause of all changes in state, commonwealths into monarchies, and monarchies into commonwealths.

10. In a troubled state we must do as in foul weather upon the Thames, not think to cut directly through; so, the boat may be quickly full of water; but rise and fall as the waves do, give as much as conveniently we can.

---

[1] *Comme d'abus*] the MSS. and printed editions go wild here; comine abuse, H., come abuse, H. 2, cõm è abuse, S., comme abuse, 1st and 2nd editions.

[2] *Ingenuous*] H. reads free and ingenious, but gives 'ingenuous' a line or two afterwards. The words are confused here and elsewhere in the MSS.

---

de Parlement, was 'La Cour . . . . ordonne que le service divin ordinaire en l'eglise de la Trinite soit continué; et a fait et fait inhibitions et defenses audit Evesque d'innover aucune chose en l'exercise et celebration du service divin aux eglises de son diocese sans l'authorité du Roi.' Preuves des Libertez de l'Eglise Gallicane, ch. xxxi. p. 842.

The chapter is headed 'Que le changement des Missels et Breviaires des Eglises particulières de France, ne se peut faire sans ordre et permission du Roy.' It gives several instances in which an attempted change had been annulled.

l. 2. *with a comme d'abus.*] The appeal from the spiritual to the temporal power is known as *l'appel comme d'abus*: the person pleading it is described as *appellant comme d'abus*. Preuves des Libertez, p. 104 and *passim*.

CIX.

PRAYER.

1. IF I were a minister, I should think myself most in my office, reading of prayers, and dispensing the sacraments; and 'tis ill done to put one to officiate in the Church, whose person is contemptible out of it. Should a great lady that was invited to be a gossip, in her place send her kitchen-maid, 'twould be ill taken; yet she is a woman as well as she; let her send her gentle-woman at least.

2. *You shall pray*, is the right way, because according as the Church is settled, no man may make a prayer in public of his own head.

3. 'Tis not the original Common-prayer Book. Why, shew me an original Bible, or an original Magna Charta.

4. Admit the preacher prays by the spirit, yet that very prayer is common-prayer to the people; they are tied as much to his words, as in saying *Almighty and most merciful Father*. Is it then unlawful in the minister, but not unlawful in the people?

5. There were some mathematicians, that could with one fetch of their pen make an exact circle, and with the next touch, point out the centre; is it therefore reasonable to banish all use of the compasses? Set forms are a pair of compasses.

6. *God hath given gifts unto men*. General texts prove nothing: let him shew me John, William, or Thomas in the text, and then I will believe him. If a man has a voluble tongue, we say, he hath the gift of prayer. His gift is to pray long, that I see; but does he pray better?

7. We take care what we speak to men, but to God we may say any thing.

8. The people must not think a thought towards God,

but as their pastors will put it into their mouths. They will make right sheep of us.

9. The English priests would do that in English, which the Romish do in Latin, keep the people in ignorance ; but some of the people out-do them at their own game.

10. Prayer should be short, without giving God Almighty reasons why he should grant this, or that ; he knows best what is good for us. If your boy should ask you a suit of clothes, and give you reasons (otherwise he cannot wait upon you, he cannot go abroad but he shall discredit you) would you endure it ? You know it better than he ; let him ask a suit of clothes.

11. If a servant that has been fed with good beef, goes into that part of England where salmon is plenty, at first he is pleased with his salmon, and despises his beef; but after he has been there awhile, he grows weary of his salmon, and wishes for his good beef again. We have awhile been much taken with this praying by the spirit, but in time we may grow weary of it, and wish for our Common-prayer.

12. 'Tis hoped we may be cured of our extemporary prayers, the same way the grocer's boy is cured of his eating plums, when we have had our bellies full of them.

CX.

PREACHING.

1. Nothing is more mis-taken than that speech, *preach the gospel ;* for 'tis not to make long harangues, as they do now-a-days, but to tell the news of Christ's coming into the

l. 23. *Preaching.*] There are frequent instances of a demand for 'preaching ministers,' and of complaints that ministers do not preach often enough, and that some, bishops especially, do not preach at all. See, e. g. a formal complaint in the House of Commons that there was a deficiency of preaching ministers, a matter which was thought

world ; and when that is done, or where 'tis known already, the preacher's work is done.

2. Preaching, in the first sense of the word, ceased as soon as ever the gospels were written.

3. When the preacher says, this is the meaning of the Holy Ghost in such a place, in sense he can mean no more but this; that is, I by studying of the place, by comparing one place with another, by weighing what goes before, and what comes after, think this is the meaning of the Holy Ghost; and for shortness of expression I say, the Holy Ghost says thus, or this is the meaning of the Spirit of God. So the judge speaks concerning the king's proclamation, this is the intention of the king ; not that the king has any other way declared his intention to the judge, but the judge examining the contents of the proclamation, gathers by the purport of the words the king's intention, and then for shortness of expression says, this is the king's intention.

4. Nothing is text but as it was spoken in the Bible, and meant there for person and place ; the rest is application, which a discreet man may do well ; but 'tis his scripture, not the Holy Ghost's.

5. Preaching by the spirit, as they call it, is most esteemed by the common people, because they cannot abide art or learning, which they have not been bred up in. Just as in the business of fencing ; if one country fellow amongst the rest, has been at school, the rest will undervalue his skill, or tell him he wants valour [You come with your school-tricks : there's Dick Butcher has ten times more mettle in him]. So they say to the preachers, You come with your school-learning : there's such a one has the spirit.

so important and so pressing that a Committee of the House was appointed to enquire about and to find a remedy for it. Commons Journals, ii. p. 54. See also note on 'Lecturers,' p. 103.

6. The tone in preaching does much in working on the people's affections. If a man should make love in an ordinary tone, his mistress would not regard him: and therefore he must whine. If a man should cry fire, or murder, in an ordinary voice, nobody would come out to help him.

7. Preachers will bring any thing into the text. The young masters of arts preached against non-residency in the university; whereupon the heads made an order, that no man should meddle with any thing but what was in his text. The next day one preached upon these words, *Abraham begat Isaac ;* when he had gone a good way, at last he observed, that Abraham was resident, for if he had been non-resident, he could never have begot Isaac; and so fell foul upon the non-residents.

8. I could never tell what often preaching meant, after a church is settled, and we know what is to be done : 'tis just as if a husbandman should once tell his servants what they are to do, when to sow, when to reap ; and afterwards one should come and tell them twice or thrice a day what they know already ; You must sow your wheat in October, you must reap your wheat in August, &c.

9. The main argument why they would have two sermons a day, is, because they have two meals a day ; the soul must be fed as well as the body. But I may as well argue, I ought to have two noses, because I have two eyes ; or two mouths, because I have two ears. What have meals and sermons to do one with another ?

10. The things between God and man are but a few, and those, forsooth, we must be told often of; but the things between man and man are many; those I hear not of above twice a year, at the assizes, or once a quarter at a sessions ; but few come then, nor does the minister ever exhort the people to go at these times to learn their duty towards their neighbour. Often

preaching is, sure, to keep the minister in countenance, that he may have something to do.

11. In preaching, they say more to raise men to love virtue than men can possibly perform, to make them do their best : as if you would teach a man to throw the bar; to make him put out his strength, you bid him throw further than 'tis possible for him, or any man else: throw over yonder house.

12. In preaching, they do by men as writers of romances do by their chief knights, bring them into many dangers, but still fetch them off: so they put men in fear of hell, but at last they bring them to heaven.

13. Preachers say, Do as I say, not as I do. But if the physician had the same disease upon him that I have, and he should bid me do one thing, and himself do quite another, could I believe him?

14. Preaching the same sermon to all sorts of people, is as if a school-master should read the same lesson to his several forms: if he read *amo, amas, amavi,* the highest form laugh at him ; the younger admire him. So it is in preaching to a mixed auditory.

Question. But it cannot be otherwise; the parish cannot be divided into several forms : what must the preacher then do in discretion ?

Answer. Why then let him use some expressions by which this or that condition of people may know such doctrine does more especially concern them ; it being so delivered that the wisest may be content to hear it. For if he delivers it all together, and leaves it to them to single out what belongs to themselves (which is the usual way) 'tis as if a man would bestow gifts upon children of several ages, two years old, four years old, ten years old, &c., and there he brings tops, pins, points, ribbands, and casts them all in a heap together upon a table before them : though the boy of ten years old can tell how to choose his top, yet the child of two years old, that should have a ribband, takes a pin, and the pin ere he be aware pricks his fingers, and then all's out of order, &c. Preaching, for the most part, is the glory of the preacher, to shew himself a fine man. Catechising would be more beneficial.

15. Use the best arguments to persuade, though but few understand; for the ignorant will sooner believe the judicious of the parish, than the preacher himself; and they teach when they dissipate what he has said, and be-
lieve it the sooner, confirmed by men of their own side; for betwixt the laity and the clergy there is, as it were, a continual driving of a bargain; something the clergy would still have us be at, and therefore many things are heard at first from the preacher with suspicion [they are afraid of some ends] which are easily assented to, when they have it from one of themselves. 'Tis with a sermon as 'tis with a play; many come to see it, which do not under-stand it; and yet hearing it cried up by one, whose judg-ment they cast themselves upon, and of power with them, they swear and will die in it, that 'tis a very good play, which they would not have done if the priest himself had told them so. As in a great school, 'tis not the master that teaches all; the monitor does a great deal of work; it may be the boys are afraid to see their master: so in a parish 'tis not the minister does all; the greater neigh-bours teach the lesser, the master of the house teaches his servant, &c.

16. First in your sermons use your logic, and then your rhetoric. Rhetoric without logic is like a tree with leaves and blossoms, but no root; yet I confess more are taken with rhetoric than logic, because they are catched with a free expression, when they understand not reason. Logic must be natural, or 'tis not at all: your rhetoric figures may be learned. That rhetoric is best which is most seasonable and most catching. An instance we

have in that old blunt commander at Cadiz, who shewed himself a good orator, being to say something to his soldiers (which he was not used to do) he made them a speech to this purpose: What a shame will it be, you Englishmen, that feed upon good beef and brewess, to let those rascally Spaniards beat you, that eat nothing but oranges and lemons: and so put more courage into his men than he could have done with a more learned oration. Rhetoric is either very good, or stark naught: there's no medium in rhetoric. If I am not fully persuaded, I laugh 10 at the orator.

17. 'Tis good to preach the same thing again, for that's the way to have it learned. You see a bird, by often whistling to, learns a tune, and a month after records to herself.

18. 'Tis a hard case a minister should be turned out of his living for something they inform he should say in his pulpit. We can no more know what a minister said in his sermon[1] by two or three words picked out of it, than we can tell what tune a musician played last upon the 20 lute, by two or three single notes.

CXI.

PREDESTINATION.

1. Is a point inaccessible, out of our reach; we can make no notion of it, 'tis so full of intricacy, so full of contradiction; 'tis in good earnest, as we state it, half a dozen bulls one upon another.

2. They that talk nothing but predestination, and will not proceed in the way of heaven till they be satisfied in that point, do as if a man would not come to London,

---

[1] *His sermon*] his sermons, H. and H. 2.

unless at his first step he might set his foot upon the top of Paul's.

3. Doctor Prideaux in his lectures, several days used arguments to prove predestination; at last tells his auditory they are damned if they do not believe it; doing herein just as school-boys; when one of them has got an apple,

l. 4. *at last tells his auditory* &c.] This is not quite so. Dr. Prideaux gave a series of nine lectures on Romans ix. 10, 11, 12. The first three treat of predestination, and several of the others touch upon it. In none of these does he tell his auditory that they are damned that do not believe it. But in the last lecture of the series, against the Roman Catholics, he is provoked by their assertion that he himself, as a Protestant, must be damned, and he retorts accordingly, with some warmth of expression, that the fate in question is much more likely to be theirs.

His imaginary opponent has been arguing (Dr. Prideaux, it will be seen, conducts both sides of the dispute) as a point in favour of the Roman Catholic Church, 'Fatentur Protestantes sub Papismo quam plurimos salutem consequi. At Papistae damnatos pronuntiant omnes Protestantes.' Dr. Prideaux rejoins, 'Respondeo. Hoc ipsum arguit Protestantes non tantùm Religionis puritate, sed charitate etiam esse adversariis superiores, qui distinguunt tamen inter se-ductores et seductos, et inter seductos rursus in simplicitate cordium, ante Lutheri reformationem, et obstinatos sequentis seculi, qui moniti ad obortam lucem claudunt oculos. Nam ut de istis dictat charitas ut speremus optima; ita de hisce nihil possumus praeter horrenda polliceri, quamdiù characterem Bestiae in frontibus aut dextris prae-ferunt. Inter sordes autem istas, ista quae summo cum periculo expectetur salus, non ipsorum additamentis sed iis quae nobis habent communia fundamentis, est attribuenda.' Lectures by John Prideaux (Bishop of Worcester), p. 143 (ed. 3, 1648).

It seems probable from 'Church of Rome,' sec. 2, that Selden may have had this passage in his mind.

Prideaux's first lecture on predestination ends, not with damnatory threats, but with a defence of the doctrine of reprobation, attacking no one in particular, and proceeding somewhat after the fashion of Rabbi Busy with the puppet. 'Si cui haec sententia de absoluta reprobatione videatur asperior, possem respondere cum Augustino. . . . . Hoc scio, neminem contra istam praedestinationem, quam secundùm Scripturas sanctas defendimus, nisi errando disputare posse.' p. 14. But he does not press this, and it cannot be the passage to which Selden is referring.

or something the rest have a mind to, they use all the
arguments they can to get some of it from him [I gave you
some th' other day : you shall have some with me another
time]; when they cannot prevail, they tell him he is a
jackanapes, a rogue, and a rascal.

CXII.

PREFERMENT.

1. WHEN you would have a child go to such a place,
and you find him unwilling, you tell him he shall ride a
cock-horse, and then he will go presently: so do those
that govern the state deal by men, to work them to their
ends ; they tell them they shall be advanced to such or
such a place, and then they will do any thing they will
have them.

2. A great place strangely qualifies. John Read was
in the right [groom of the chamber to my lord of Kent].
Attorney Noy being dead, some were saying, How will the
king do for a fit man ? Why, any man, says John Read,
may execute the place. I warrant (says my lord) thou
thinkest thou understandest enough to perform it. Yes,
quoth John, let the king make me Attorney, and I would
fain see that man that durst tell me, there's anything I
understand not.

3. When the pageants are a coming, there's great thrusting and riding upon one another's backs, to look out at the
windows; stay a little and they will come just to you, you
may see them quietly. So 'tis when a new statesman or
officer is chosen ; there's great expectation and listening
who it should be ; stay but awhile, and you shall know
quietly.

4. Missing preferment makes the presbyters fall foul

upon the bishops. Men that are in hopes and in the way of rising, keep in the channel, but they that have none, seek new ways. 'Tis so amongst lawyers; he that has the judge's ear will be very observant of the way of the court; but he that has no regard will be flying out.

5. My lord Digby having spoken something in the House of Commons, for which they would have questioned him, was presently called to the upper house. He did by the parliament as an ape when he has done some 10 waggery; his master spies him, and looks for his whip, but before he can come at him, whip says he to the top of the house.

l. 6. *My lord Digby* &c.] Lord Digby, who had been one of the accusers of the Earl of Strafford, afterwards, just before the final vote, spoke strongly in his favour, declaring that he did, with a clear conscience, wash his hands of that man's blood, and protesting: 'that my vote goes not to the taking of the Earl of Strafford's life.' Exception was taken to this speech at the time when it was made (April, 1641): the speech afterwards, by order of the House, was burnt by the hand of the common hangman. Nalson, Collections, ii. 160.

Clarendon adds that when Lord Digby was questioned in the House about his speech, he defended himself so well, and so much to the disadvantage of those who were concerned, that from that time they prosecuted him with an implacable rage and uncharitableness upon all occasions. Hist. i. 359.

Clarendon's further account of his call to the Upper House and of the reasons for it, will throw some light on this. He had made private and secret offers of his service to the King, and the King being satisfied both in the discoveries he had made of what had passed, and in his professions for the future, called him by writ to the House of Peers, from which time forward he did visibly advance the King's service. i. 534, 535.

Forster thinks that Selden's image, of the ape who has done some waggery, may have been suggested by the apish tricks of Lord Digby's younger brother, member for Milborn Port. This young gentleman had perched himself upon a ladder in the House of Commons, and was called to by the Speaker and ordered to come down and not sit on the ladder as if he were going to be hanged. This happened on the day when his brother would have been expelled the House, if the King's letters patent had not issued the night before calling him to the Lords. Forster, The Grand Remonstrance, p. 279.

6. Some of the parliament were discontented that they wanted places at court which others had got; but when they had them once, then they were quiet. Just as at a christening, some that get no sugar-plums, when the rest have, mutter and grumble; presently the wench comes again with her basket of sugar-plums, and then they catch and scramble, and when they have got them, you hear no more of them.

CXIII.

PRÆMUNIRE.

THERE can be no *præmunire*. A *præmunire* (so called 10 from the word *præmunire facias*) was when a man laid an action in an ecclesiastical court, for which he could have remedy in any of the king's courts; that is, in the courts of common law; by reason the ecclesiastical courts before Henry the 8th were subordinate to the pope, and so it was

l. 10. *There can be no præmunire*] This statement, as reported, is wider than the facts warrant; and as the rest of the chapter shows, is wider than Selden meant it to be. He is probably arguing against Coke's opinion that a suitor in an ecclesiastical court might still incur the penalties of a præmunire. The first Statute of Præmunire, that of 27 Edward III (A. D. 1353), headed 'Statutum contra adnullatores judiciorum curiae Regis,' enacts that all subjects suing in a foreign court for matters cognizable in the King's court, or questioning else-where the judgments of the King's court, shall have warning to answer for such contempt, and on non-appearance shall be outlawed, forfeit their land and goods and be imprisoned. This Act was repeated in more stringent form by 38 Edward III (1363-4), but the offence against which the two Acts were directed was substantially the same, and it was one which, as Selden points out, had become impossible in his time. But a præmunire there still was, for several other named offences, to which the old penalties of a præmunire had been attached in express words. See Blackstone's Comm. Bk. IV. ch. viii.

contra coronam et dignitatem regis ; but now the ecclesiastical courts are equally subordinate to the king. Therefore
it cannot be *contra coronam et dignitatem regis,* and so no
præmunire.

CXIV.

PREROGATIVE.

1. PREROGATIVE is something that can be told what it is,
not something that has no name. Just as you see the
archbishop has his prerogative court, but we know what is
done in that court. So the king's prerogative is not his
10 will, or what divines make it, a power to do what he lists.

2. The king's prerogative ; that is, the king's law. For
example, if you ask if a patron may present to a living
after six months by law? I answer, No. If you ask
whether the king may ? I answer he may by his prerogative ; that is, by the law that concerns him in that case.

CXV.

PRESBYTERY.

1. THEY that would bring in a new government, would
very fain persuade us they meet it in antiquity ; thus they

l. 13. *If you ask whether the king may* &c.] In a case decided
2 James I, it was held that the King, as to the advowson, hath no
greater privilege than another person. This judgment was reversed
two years afterwards on the ground that the King had special privilege.
Croke, Reports, vol. ii. pp. 54, 123.

This later decision seems to be based on the general principle
that 'in the King can be no negligence or *laches,* and therefore no
delay will bar his right. *Nullum tempus occurrit regi* has been the
standing maxim upon all occasions.' Blackstone, Comm. Bk. I.
ch. vii.

interpret presbyters, when they meet the word in the
fathers.   Other professions likewise pretend to antiquity.
The alchymist will find his art in Virgil's *aureus ramus*,
and he that delights in optics, will find them in Tacitus.
When Cæsar came into England they would persuade us
they had perspective glasses, by which he could discover
what they were doing upon the land ; because it is said,
positis speculis: the meaning is, his watch or his sentinel
discovered this and this unto him.

l. 3.   Virgil's *aureus ramus*]   Aeneid, vi. 136–148.

Robertus Vallensis, in his De Veritate et Antiquitate Artis Chemicae
(Paris, 1561, the book is not paged), quotes this passage, together with
some others from Virgil, as if it proved or illustrated something in his
alchemical art, but he gives no precise interpretation to it.

Borrichius, writing a little before Selden's day, says of the lines:
' Haec de materiâ chemici magisterii fudisse cumaeam vatem opinio
est variorum, quos inter Robertus Vallensis, Glauberus, aliique ; nec
inficiendum sub illo fabulae involucro arcanum sensum delitescere,
forsan Virgilio ipsi, qui ex alio haec mutuatus est, incognitum.'   The
golden bough reminds him of a passage in Acosta (Hist. Nat. lib. iv.
cap. 1), in which the veins of metal are compared to the boughs of
plants, in their form and in the manner of their growth.   De Ortu et
Progressu Chemicae, p. 101.

Wedel, a later writer, mentions and approves the alchemical interpretation of the lines: ' Majori fide et applausu ad se nos vocant
chimicorum filii, qui suum faciunt hunc locum.   Hos inter praecipuus
Robertus Wallensis . . . . quem secuti hinc non pauci alii.   Instar
omnium sit Borrichius, chimicae decus summum.'   See Georgii
Wolffgangi Wedelii propempticum inaugurale de aureo ramo
Virgilii.

l. 5.   *When Cæsar came into England* &c.]   See 'Possunt sic figurari
perspicua ut longissime posita appareant propinquissima . . . . Sic
enim aestimatur Julius Caesar super littus maris in Galliis, deprehen-
disse per ingentia specula dispositionem et situm castrorum et
civitatum Britanniae majoris.'   R. Bacon, Epistola de secretis operibus
artis et naturae, cap. 5, Brewer's edition of Bacon's Opera inedita.
And again : ' Sic enim Julius Caesar, quando voluit Angliam expugnare,
repertur maxima specula erexisse, ut a Gallicano littore dispositionem
civitatum et castrorum Angliae praevideret.'   R. Bacon, Opus Majus,
pars v. p. 357.

l. 8.   *positis speculis*]   There is some difficulty about these words.
As the text stands, Selden quotes them as having been misinterpreted

2. Presbyters have the greatest power of any clergy in the world, and gull the laity most : for example, admit there be twelve laymen to six presbyters, the six shall govern the rest as they please. First, because they are constant, and the others come in like churchwardens in their turns, which is a huge advantage. Men will give way to those that have been there before them. Next, the laymen have other professions to follow; the presbyters make it their sole business ; and besides too, they learn and study the art of persuading; some of Geneva have confessed as much.

3. The presbyter, with his elders about him, is like a young tree fenced about with three or four stakes ; the stakes defend it, and hold it up; but the tree only prospers and flourishes ; it may be some willow-stake may bear a leaf or two, but it comes to nothing. Lay-elders are stakes, the presbyter the tree that flourishes.

4. When the queries were sent to the assembly con-

by Roger Bacon, or by some other writer, and he then adds what he considers to be their true sense. But the words do not occur in any history of Caesar's invasion that I have seen, and I have searched for them with some care. Nor do they seem to admit of the sense which Selden is reported as putting upon them. I think it likely that there has been some error in the report, and that the words in question are a free rendering of what Roger Bacon himself says, and that the rest of the clause ought to appear as Selden's own statement of the real facts of the case, not as his interpretation of what '*positis speculis*' means.

l. 18. *When the queries were sent* &c.] The power of the Presbytery to pass sentence of excommunication had been limited by the final appeal which the Parliament allowed to a body of lay commissioners of its own appointment. The Westminster Assembly of Divines petitioned against this appeal, and claimed *jure divino* a right to un-controlled spiritual jurisdiction. The Parliament in reply sent them a number of very searching queries, drawn up by a Committee of the House, touching the point of *jus divinum*, and demanding exact scriptural proofs for it (see Excursus E). The Assembly, however, had no scriptural proofs ready, and they were in a great fright to know what to do. They held a consultation, they proclaimed a fast,

cerning the *jus divinum* of presbytery, their asking time to
answer them, was a satire upon themselves. For if it were
to be seen in the text, they might quickly turn to the place
and shew us it. Their delaying to answer makes us think
there's no such thing there. They do just as you have
seen a fellow do at a tavern reckoning, when he should
come to pay his share; he puts his hands into his pockets,
and keeps a grabling and a fumbling and shaking, at last
tells you he has left his money at home; when all the
company knew at first he had no money there; for every
man can quickly find his own money.

CXVI.

PRIESTS OF ROME.

1. THE reason of the statute against priests, was this; in
the beginning of Queen Elizabeth, there was a statute

and appointed committees of their own body to prepare an answer.
When the questions came before the committees, first the Independents withdrew, then the Erastians entered their dissent from the
answer proposed to question 1, and at length a form of words was
agreed upon by a majority vote. The rest of the questions were
discussed from May till late in July, but the answers, if any, were
never sent to Parliament, and the matter practically dropped, as far
as the Assembly had to do with it. Neal, Hist. of Puritans, iii. 253
and 278. See Appendix, Excursus E.

l. 14. *in the beginning of Queen Elizabeth &c.*] The statutes, of
which Selden speaks, strengthen and grow precise as they proceed.
By 1 Elizabeth, ch. 1, sec. 27, penalties are fixed on those who
maintain or depend or endeavour to advance any foreign authority in
the Queen's dominions. To do this is made high treason on the third
offence. Then, 5 Elizabeth, ch. 1, sec. 2 enacts more particularly
that any person maintaining the authority of the Bishop of Rome, in
any part of the Queen's dominions, shall come under the pains, &c.,
of the statute of provisions and præmunire; and shall on the second
offence (secs. 10 and 11) be guilty of high treason. Next, 13 Elizabeth, ch. 2 declares that, notwithstanding the above statute, divers

made, that he that drew men from their civil obedience was a traitor. It happened this was done in privacies and confessions, when there could be no proof; therefore they made another act, that for a priest to be in England was treason, because they presumed that was his business here, to fetch men off from their allegiance.

2. When Queen Elizabeth died, and king James came in, an Irish priest does thus express it: *Elizabethâ in orcum detrusâ, successit Jacobus, alter hæreticus.*

10   You will ask why they do use such language in their church?

Answer. Why does the nurse tell the child of raw-head and bloody-bones? To keep it in awe.

3. The queen-mother and count Rosset are to the priests and Jesuits like the honey-pot to the flies.

seditious and very evil-disposed people have procured bulls and writings from the Bishop of Rome to absolve all those that will be content to forsake their due obedience to the Queen; and enacts that such people shall be deemed and adjudged high traitors to the Queen and the realm and shall be punished by death and forfeiture. Then, 23 Elizabeth, ch. 1 makes it treason for any one to withdraw any or to be himself withdrawn to the Romish religion. Lastly, 27 Elizabeth, ch. 2 declares that divers jesuits, seminary priests and other priests have come to this country for the purpose of withdrawing men from their due obedience to her Majesty; and enacts that all such persons are to leave the country, and that if being natural born subjects of the Queen, they are found here or come here, they shall suffer the penalties of high treason.

l. 14.   *The queen-mother and count Rosset* &c.] i. e. Mary de Medici, the French Queen-mother, who had sought a refuge at the English Court. In May 1641 the Commons resolved to suggest to the King—'That her Majesty be moved to depart this kingdom, the rather for the quieting of those jealousies in the hearts of his Majesty's well-affected subjects, occasioned by some ill instruments about the Queen's person, by the flowing of priests and papists to her house,' &c., &c. House of Commons' Journals, ii. 149.

Hobbes, in the Behemoth (pt. ii. beginning), after speaking of the belief, encouraged by the Parliamentary party, that it was the King's purpose to introduce popery, goes on to say that—'the colour they had for this slander was, first that there was one Rosetti, resident, at

4. The priests of Rome aim but at two things, to get power from the king, and money from the subject.

5. When the priests come into a family, they do as a man that would set fire on a house : he does not put fire to the brick-wall, but thrusts it into the thatch. They work upon the women and let the men alone.

6. For a priest to turn a man when he lies a dying, is just like one that has a long time solicited a woman, and cannot obtain his end; at length makes her drunk, and so lies with her.   10

CXVII.

PROPHECIES.

DREAMS and prophecies do thus much good ; they make a man go on with boldness and courage, upon a danger or a mistress; if he obtain, he attributes much to them ; if he miscarries, he thinks no more of them, or is no more thought of himself.

CXVIII.

PROVERBS.

THE proverbs of several nations were much studied by bishop Andrews ; and the reason he gave was, because by

and a little before that time, from the Pope, with the Queen . . . .
Also the resort of English Catholics to the Queen's chapel, gave them colour to blame the Queen herself, not only for that, but also for all the favours that had been shown to the Catholics.'

See also a letter from Secretary Windebank to the King (Sep. 7, 1640). 'I most humbly beseech your Majesty to give me leave to propose your writing to the Queen that Rosetti may be advised to retire into France, or some other foreign part, for awhile, and that the Capuchins may likewise disperse,' &c. Clarendon's State Papers, vol. ii. p. 113.

them he knew the minds of several nations, which is a
brave thing : as we count him a wise man that knows the
minds and insides of men, which is done by knowing what
is habitual to them. Proverbs are habitual to a nation
being transmitted from father to son.

CXIX.

QUESTION.

When a doubt is propounded, you must learn to distinguish, and shew wherein a thing holds, and wherein
it does not hold. Aye, or no[1], never answered any ques-
10 tion. The not distinguishing where things should be distinguished, and the not confounding, where things should
be confounded, is the cause of all the mistakes in the
world.

CXX.

REASON.

1. In giving reasons, men commonly do with us as the
woman does with her child ; when she goes to market
about her business, she tells it she goes to buy it a fine
thing, to buy it a cake, or some plums. They give us
such reasons as they think we will be catched withal, but
20 never let us know the truth.

2. When the schoolmen talk of *recta ratio* in morals,

[1] *Aye or no*] I or no, MSS.

l. 21. *When the schoolmen talk* &c.] Selden follows here the same
line of thought as when he says that the Law of Nature means only
the Law of God (p. 101). He urges, in effect, that moral rules must be
based on positive law, human or divine, and that without this they
have no sanction or meaning.

either they understand reason, as 'tis governed by
a command from above; or else they say no more than
a woman, when she says a thing is so, because it is so;
that is, her reason persuades her it is so. The other
acception has sense in it. As take a law of the land, I
must not depopulate; my reason tells me so. Why?
because if I do, I incur the detriment.

3. The reason of a thing is not to be enquired after, till
you are sure the thing itself is so. We commonly are at
what's the reason of it? before we are sure of the thing. 10
It was an excellent question of my lady Cotton, when Sr
Robert Cotton was magnifying of a shoe, which was Moses's
or Noah's, and wondering at the strange shape and fashion
of it: But, Mr. Cotton, says she, are you sure it is a shoe?

CXXI.

RELIGION.

1. KING James said to the fly, Have I three kingdoms,
and thou must needs fly into my eye? Is there not enough
to meddle withal upon the stage, or in love, or at the table,
but religion?

2. Religion amongst men appears to me like the learning 20
they got at school. Some men forget all, others spend
upon the stock, and some improve it. So some men forget
all the religion that was taught them when they were young,
others spend upon that stock, and some improve it.

3. Religion is like the fashion; one man wears his
doublet slashed, another laced, another plain; but every
man has a doublet: so every man has his religion. We
differ about the trimming.

4. Men say they are of the same religion for quietness'
sake; but if the matter were well examined, you would 30

M

scarce find three anywhere of the same religion in all points.

5. Every religion is a getting religion; for though I myself get nothing, I am subordinate to them that do. So you may find a lawyer in the Temple that gets little for the present; but he is fitting himself to be in time one of those great ones that do get.

6. Alteration of religion is dangerous, because we know not where it will stay; it is like a millstone that lies upon 10 the top of a pair of stairs; 'tis hard to remove it, but if it once be thrust off the first stair, it never stays till it comes to the bottom.

7. *Question.* Whether is the church or the scripture judge of religion ?

Answer. In truth neither, but the state. I am troubled with a boil; I call a company of surgeons about me; one prescribes one thing, another another; I single out some- thing I like, and ask you that stand by, and are no surgeon, what you think of it: you like it too; you and I are the 20 judges of the plaister, and we bid them prepare it, and there's an end. Thus 'tis in religion; the protestants say they will be judged by the scripture; the papists they say so too; but that cannot speak. A judge is no judge, except he can both speak and command execution: but the truth is, they never intend to agree. No doubt the pope, where he is supreme, is to be judge; if he says we in England ought to be subject to him, then he must draw his sword and make it good.

8. By the law was the Manual received in the church

---

l. 29. *the Manual*] was one of the many service-books in use before the Reformation. See e. g. a decree of a synod at Exeter (1287), giving a list of books with which every church was to be furnished, viz. missale bonum, gradale, troparium, manuale bonum, legenda, anti- phonale, psalteria, ordinale, venitare ympnare, collectare. Wilkins, Concilia, ii. 139.

The manual contained the offices and rites and ceremonies which

before the Reformation. Not by the civil law, that had
nothing to do with it; nor by the canon law, for that
Manual that was here, was not in France, nor in Spain;
but by custom, which is the common law of England ; and
custom is but the elder brother to a parliament ; and so it
will fall out to be nothing that the papists say ; that ours is
a parliamentary religion, by reason the service-book was
established by act of parliament, and never any service-
book was so before. That will be nothing that the pope
sent the Manual. 'Twas ours, because the state received :o
it. The state still makes the religion, and receives into it,
what will best agree with it. Why are the Venetians
Roman Catholics ? Because the state likes the religion.
All the world knows they care not three-pence for the pope.
The Council of Trent is not admitted at this day in France.

9. *Papist.* Where was your religion before Luther, an
hundred years ago ?

Protestant. Where was America an hundred or six-score
years ago? Our religion was where the rest of the Christian
Church was. 20

Papist. Our religion continued ever since the Apostles,
and therefore 'tis the better.

Protestant. So did ours. That there was an interruption
in it, will fall out to be nothing; no more than if another
earl should tell one of the earls of Kent; He is a better
earl than he, because there was one or two of the family of

a parish priest in the discharge of his ordinary duties would be called
upon to perform, and a variety of other offices less frequently needed.
Maskell, in the preface to his Monumenta Ritualia, ch. v, gives a
copy of the table of contents of the manual according to the Salisbury
use. They were not quite the same as those in use elsewhere, but
the claim and belief of Roman Catholic writers is that together with
the other devotional books in public use, they represent, substantially
and very closely, the forms which Augustine received from Pope
Gregory, when he set out on his English mission.

Selden appears to use the word 'manual' here as equivalent to
service-book of every kind.

Kent did not take the title upon them ; yet all that while they were really earls; and afterwards a great prince declared them to be earls of Kent, as he that made the other family an earl.

10. Disputes in religion will never be ended, because there wants a measure by which the business should be decided. The Puritan would be judged by the word of God : if he would speak clearly, he means himself, but that he is ashamed to say so ; and he would have me believe
10 him before a whole church, that have read the word of God as well as he. One says one thing, and another another ; and there is, I say, no measure to end the controversy. 'Tis just as if two men were at bowls, and both judged by the eye : one says 'tis his cast, the other says 'tis my cast ; and having no measure, the difference is eternal. Ben Jonson satirically expressed the vain disputes of divines by Rabbi Busy disputing with a puppet in his Bartholomew

l. 2.   *a great prince*] so in MSS. and early editions.   Some later editions read 'as great a prince.'

l. 17.   *Rabbi Busy disputing* &c.] The dispute referred to is between Rabbi Busy and a puppet belonging to Lanthorn Leatherhead, see Barthol. Fair, Act v. sc. 3.   There are various readings of the text of the Table Talk.   The Harleian MS. 690, gives—'Inigo Lanthorne disputing with a puppet in Bartholomew Fair.'   The Sloane MS. 2513 reads, 'in his Bartholomew Fair,' but otherwise agrees with Harleian 690.   The early printed editions read—'Inigo Lanthorne disputing with his puppet in a Bartholomew Fair.'   The reading which I have followed—that of Harleian MS. 1315—is the only one which is not obviously incorrect.   I am inclined to think that the original reading may have been 'Rabbi Busy disputing with Inigo Lanthorne his puppet, in his (sc. Ben Jonson's) Bartholomew Fair,' and that this has been cut down and changed into the various forms given above.   Inigo Lanthorne is of course a half-way name between Lanthorne Leatherhead and Inigo Jones, who is assumed to have been satirized by Jonson under the name of Lanthorne Leatherhead. Ben Jonson and Inigo Jones were for many years fellow-workers for the stage, Jonson contributing the words of the masque or play, and Jones undertaking the scenery and stage-properties.   This unequal partnership lasted for more than ten years after Bartholomew Fair was brought out (1614).   How sharply they quarrelled afterwards,

fair. It is so: it is not so: it is so: it is not so; crying thus
one to another a quarter of an hour together.

11. In matters of religion, to be ruled by one that writes
against his adversary, and throws all the dirt he can in his
face, is, as if in point of good manners a man should be
governed by one whom he sees at cuffs with another, and
thereupon thinks himself bound to give the next man he
meets a box on the ear.

12. It is to no purpose to labour to reconcile religions,
when the interest of princes will not suffer it. 'Tis well if 10
they would be reconciled so far, that they should not cut
one another's throats.

13. There is all the reason in the world divines should
not be suffered to go a hair's breadth beyond their bounds,
for fear of breeding confusion, since there now be so many
religions on foot.   The matter was not so narrowly to be
looked after when there was but one religion in Christendom; the rest would cry him down for an heretic, and there
was nobody to side with him.

14. We look after religion, as the butcher did after his 20
knife, when he had it in his mouth.

15. Religion is made a juggler's paper; now 'tis a horse,
now 'tis a lanthorn, now 'tis a boat, now 'tis a man.   To
serve ends, religion is turned into all shapes.

16. Some men's pretending religion, is like the roaring
boys' way of challenges: (their reputation is dear, it cannot

and what a mean opinion Ben Jonson had of his old partner, may be
seen from *inter alia* his 'Expostulation with Inigo Jones' and his
verses 'To Inigo Marquis-would-be,' in which Inigo Jones is held up
to ridicule as a mere stage-property-man and puppet-play presenter
and would-be poet, very much as Lanthorn Leatherhead is shown in
Bartholomew Fair. The resemblance between the two, as Ben Jonson
has drawn them, is certain; their intended identification is almost
certain. Selden knew Ben Jonson intimately, and if the words ' Inigo
Lanthorne' ever came from Selden's mouth, the proof may be
regarded as complete.

l. 25. *like the roaring boys* &c.] In Overbury's Characters, 'A roaring

stand with the honour of a gentleman :) when, God knows, they have neither reputation nor honour about them.

17. Pretending religion and the law of God, is to set all things loose. When a man has no mind to do something he ought to do by his contract with man, then he gets a text, and interprets it as he pleases, and so thinks to get loose.

18. We talk much of settling religion. Religion is well enough settled already, if we would let it alone. Methinks 10 we might look after, &c.

19. If men should say they took arms for anything

Boy' is represented as a bullying cheating fellow. 'He sends challenges by word of mouth ; for he protests (as he is a gentleman and brother of the sword) he can neither read nor write . . . . Soldier he is none, for he cannot distinguish between onion-seed and gunpowder : if he has worn it in his hollow tooth for the tooth-ache, and so come to the knowledge of it, that's all.' Overbury, Miscell. Works, p. 173 (ed. 1756).

In the old play, Amends for Ladies, Act iii. sc. 4, Whorebang, Bots, Tearchaps, and Spillblood appear as 'Roarers,' i.e. as noisy, cowardly bullies. Hazlitt's Old English Plays, vol. xi.

In the Dramatis Personae of Bartholomew Fair, Val. Cutting is described as a Roarer or Bully.

His honour, his reputation, are words frequently in Bobadil's mouth (Every man in his Humour).

l. 11. *If men should say* &c.] A care for religion was a chief reason alleged in the Declaration of the Kingdom of Scotland to justify their expedition into England in 1643. They said 'It was most necessary that every one, against all doubting, should be persuaded in his mind . . . . of the goodness of the cause maintained by him ; which they said was no other than the good of religion in England, and the deliverance of their brethren out of the depths of affliction ; the preservation of their own religion, and of themselves from the extremity of misery.' They trusted, therefore, 'that the Lord would save them from the curse of Meroz, who came not to help the Lord against the mighty.' There is much more to the same effect in this Declaration, and in a joint Declaration put out at the same time in the name of both kingdoms, England and Scotland. 'Their confidence was in God Almighty, the Lord of Hosts . . . It was his own truth and cause which they maintained against the heresy, superstition, and tyranny of Anti-Christ : the glory of his name, the exaltation of the kingdom

but religion, they might be beaten out of it by reason; out of that they never can, for they will not believe you whatever you say.

20. The very *arcanum* of pretending religion in all wars is, that something may be found out in which all men may have interest. In this the groom has as much interest as the lord. Were it for land, one has one thousand acres, and the other but one; he would not venture so far, as he that has a thousand. But religion is equal to both. Had all men land alike, by a *lex agraria*, then all 10 men would say they fought for land.

CXXII.

NON-RESIDENCY.

1. THE people thought they had a great victory over the clergy, when in Henry 8th's[1] time they got their bill passed, that a clergyman should have but two livings; before, a man might have twenty or thirty; 'twas but getting a dispensation from the pope's limitor, or gatherer of the Peter-

[1] *Henry 8th's*, H. 2] H. 8th's in H.

of his Son, and the preservation of his church, was their aim, and the end which they had before their eyes.' Clarendon, Hist. ii. 667 ff.

l. 4. *The very arcanum* &c.] 'The great pretences (in an alleged design against episcopacy and monarchy) were liberty, property and religion; for, as Mr. Hambden, one of the principal grandees of the faction, told a private friend, without that they could not draw the people to assist them.' Nalson, Collections, ii. 234.

l. 15. *that a clergyman should have* &c.] The Act against pluralities (21 Henry VIII, ch. 13) enacts that if a clerk, holding a living worth £8 a year, takes another cure, his original living becomes *ipso facto* void. But there are numerous exceptions to this rule. Vested rights are respected in the case of actual holders of not more than four cures; and certain named classes and orders are allowed for the future to hold, some three, some two cures.

pence, which was as easily got, as now you may have a licence to eat flesh.

2. As soon as a minister is made, he hath power to preach all over the world; but the civil power restrains him; he cannot preach in this parish or in that; there is one already appointed. Now if the state allows him two livings, then he has two places where he may exercise his function, and so has the more power to do his office, which he might do every where if he were not restrained.

CXXIII.

RETALIATION.

An eye for an eye, and a tooth for a tooth. That does not mean, that if I put out another man's eye, therefore I must lose one of my own, (for what is he the better for that?) though this be commonly received; but it means, that I shall give him what satisfaction an eye shall be judged to be worth.

CXXIV.

REVERENCE.

'Tis sometimes unreasonable to look after respect and reverence, either from a man's own servants, or from other inferiors. A great lord and a gentleman talking together, there came a boy by, leading a calf with both his hands; says the lord to the gentleman, You shall see me make the boy let go his calf; with that he came towards him, thinking

l. 3. *As soon as a minister is made* &c.] See 'Minister Divine,' sec. 4.

the boy would have put off his hat, but the boy took no
notice of him. The lord seeing that, Sirrah, says he, do
not you know me, that you use no reverence? Yes, says
the boy, if your lordship will hold my calf, I will put off
my hat.

CXXV.

SABBATH.

WHY should I think all the fourth commandment belongs to me, when all the fifth does not? What land will

l. 7. *Why should I think* &c.] The right way of keeping Sunday
was among the standing points of dispute between High and Low
Church, between the Anglican party and the Puritans. Selden, who
belonged to neither side, follows his usual rule—περὶ παντὸς τὴν ἐλευ-
θερίαν, and pronounces against strict Sabbath observances. The
controversy had become marked towards the latter part of Queen
Elizabeth's reign, when Sunday, which used to be the regular day
for games, dances and sports, began to be kept more precisely. The
governing clergy exclaimed against the change. Archbishop Whitgift
and Chief Justice Popham did what they could to put down current
Sabbatarian writings, and declared that the Sabbath doctrine agreed
neither with the teaching of the Church nor with the laws and orders
of the kingdom. In 1618, James put out his declaration concerning
lawful sports to be used on Sundays after divine service; and in 1635
it was ratified and republished by Charles, at Laud's instigation, and
encouragement was given to May Games, Whitsun Ales, and the like.
But with the rise of the Presbyterian party, all this was changed.
On March 5, 1641, Dr. Bray was sent for to the bar of the House of
Lords for having licensed Dr. Pocklington's books, called Sunday no
Sabbath and Altare Christianum, and he acknowledged his offence
and expressed regret for it. The obnoxious books were ordered
to be publicly burned. On May 5, 1643, it was ordered by the Lords
and Commons in Parliament that the book, concerning the enjoining
and tolerating sports on the Lord's day, be forthwith burned by the
hand of the common hangman in Cheapside and other usual places.
That this was in agreement with the popular sentiment of the day is
clear from Baxter's statement, that the publication of this book by the
Bishops was one of the reasons why ' serious godly people had been
alienated from them, and had thought that they concurred with the
profane.' Laud's share in publishing this book and in punishing

the Lord give me for honouring my father? It was spoken to the Jews with reference to the land of Canaan; but the meaning is, if I honour my parents, God will also bless me. We read the commandments in the church-service, as we do David's Psalms; not that all there concerns us, but a great deal of them does.

CXXVI.

SACRAMENT.

1. CHRIST suffered Judas to take the communion. Those ministers that keep their parishioners from it, because they will not do as they will·have them, revenge, rather than reform.

2. No man living can tell whether I am fit to receive the sacrament; for though I were fit the day before, when he examined me, at least appeared so to him, yet how can he tell what sin I have committed that night, or the next morning, or what impious atheistical thoughts I may have about me, when I am approaching to the very table?

CXXVII.

SALVATION.

WE may best understand the meaning of σωτηρία, salvation, from the Jews, to whom the Saviour was promised. They held that themselves should have the chief place of happiness in the other world; but the gentiles that were

ministers for not reading it in church, was among the charges brought against him at his trial. See Rushworth, Collections, ii. 193, iv. 207, v. 317. Fuller, Hist. of Church, xvii. xi. 32. Baxter's Life, p. 33. Laud's Works, iv. 251-3.

good men, should likewise have their portion of bliss there
too. Now by Christ the partition-wall is broken down,
and the gentiles that believe in him, are admitted to the
same place of bliss with the Jews. And why then should
not that portion of happiness still remain to them who do
not believe in Christ, so they be morally good? This is
a charitable opinion.

CXXVIII.

SHIP-MONEY.

1. MR. Noy brought in ship-money first for maritime
towns; but that was like putting in a little auger, that
afterwards you may put in a greater. He that pulls down
the first brick, does the main work, afterwards 'tis easy to
pull down the wall.

2. They that at first would not pay ship-money, till it
was decided, did like brave men, though perhaps they did
no good by the trial; but they that stand out since, and
suffer themselves to be distrained, never questioning those
that do it, do pitifully; for so they only pay twice as much
as they should.

CXXIX.

SIMONY.

THE name of simony was begot in the canon law: the

l. 9. *Mr. Noy brought in* &c.] 'The King required a loan of money
and sent to London and the port towns to furnish ships for guard of
the sea. Noy, his attorney, a great antiquary, had much to do in this
business of ship-money.' Whitelock's Memorials, p. 7, in ann. 1626

Next, 'by advice of his privy council and council learned, the King
requires ship-money. The writ for it was at first but to maritime
towns and counties; but that not sufficing, other writs were issued
out to all counties to levy ship-money.' Ib., p. 22, in ann. 1634.

first statute against it was in Queen Elizabeth's time.
Since the reformation simony has been frequent: one
reason why it was not practised in time of popery, was the
pope's provisions: no man was sure to bestow his own
benefice.

CXXX.

STATE.

In a troubled state save as much of your own as you
can. A dog had been at market to buy a shoulder of
mutton; coming home, he met two dogs by the way, that
10 quarrelled with him; he laid down his shoulder of mutton,
and fell to fighting with one of them; in the meantime the
other dog fell to eating his mutton; he seeing that, left
the dog he was fighting with, and fell upon him that was
eating; then the other dog fell to eat; when he perceived
there was no remedy, but which of them soever he was
fighting withal, his mutton was in danger, he thought he
would save as much of it as he could; and thereupon
gave over fighting, and fell to eating himself.

l. 1. *the first statute against it* &c.] This was 31 Elizabeth, ch. 6,
secs. 4 and 5, which declares void all simoniacal presentations to
benefices: and enacts, further, that in case of simony, the presentation devolves to the crown, and that both parties to the transaction
incur a fine of double the yearly value of the benefice.

l. 2. *one reason why* &c.] That the Pope used to present to
benefices in this country appears by, e. g., the Statutes passed to
forbid it. The Statute of Provisors, 25 Edward III, enacts that if the
Pope tries to appoint, the King shall present, and counterclaimants
to the King's presentment are made liable to fine and imprisonment.
So in 16 Richard II, the Pope is said to have proposed *inter alia* to
translate prelates out of the realm, or from one living to another.
All procuring such translations are put out of the King's protection,
forfeit lands and goods, and are brought to answer for it under former
statutes.

CXXXI.

SUBSIDIES.

1. HERETOFORE the parliament was wary what subsidies they gave to the king, because they had no accounts ; but now they care not how much they give of the subjects' money, because they give it with one hand and receive it with the other ; and so upon the matter give it themselves. In the meantime what a case the subjects of England are in! If the men they have sent to the parliament misbehave themselves, they cannot help it, because the parliament is eternal. 10

2. A subsidy was counted the fifth part of a man s estate, and so fifty subsidies is five and forty times more than a man is worth.

CXXXII.

SUPERSTITION.

1. THEY that are against superstition, oftentimes run

l. 3. *but now they care not* &c.] This change was one of the first acts of the second Parliament of 1640. When they raised money they did not follow what had been the usual way, of giving it immediately to the King, to be paid into the exchequer, but provided for its payment into the hands of members of the House, named by them, who were to take care to discharge all public engagements. The King allowed the first money bill to pass with the names of Commissioners inserted in it, who were to receive and dispense the money; and from that time there was no bill passed for the raising of money, but it was disposed of in like manner, so that none of it could be applied to the King's use, or by his direction. Clarendon, Hist. vol. i. pp. 321-2 and 678.

l. 6. *upon the matter*] i.e. in strict fact: really. See 'Philosophy' and note.

into it on the wrong side.   If I will wear all colours but black, then am I superstitious in not wearing black.

2. They pretend not to abide the cross, because 'tis superstitious; for my part I will believe them, when I see them throw away their money out of their pockets, and not till then.

3. If there be any superstition truly and properly so called, 'tis their observing the sabbath after the Jewish manner.

CXXXIII.

SYNOD. ASSEMBLY.

1. WE have had no national synod since the kingdom hath been settled, as now it is, only provincial; and there

---

l. 4.   *when I see them throw away their money* &c.]   'The Parliament's gold coins are just like their silver ones, viz. on one side two shields with the cross and harp.' Abp. Sharpe, Dissertation on the Golden Coins of England, sec. 6.

The cross was a common impress on earlier English coins.

l. 7.   *If there be any* &c.]   See 'Sabbath' and note.

l. 11.   *We have had no national synod* &c.]   The London ministers, in their petitions in 1641, prayed the Houses of Parliament to be mediators to his Majesty for a free Synod.   Neal, Hist. of Puritans, iii. 43.   The Commons accordingly included this among the requests in the grand Remonstrance of December 1, 1641 :—'We desire that there may be a general synod of the most grave, pious, learned, and judicious divines of this island, assisted with some from foreign parts professing the same religion with us, who may consider of all things necessary for the peace and good government of the church.'   Rushworth, iv. 450.

Selden's objections to the calling so many divines together, and to the forming of a Synod to do work which could be done by the existing Convocation, seem to have been directed against this request. It was not granted by the King; but the Commons finally took the matter into their own hands, and summoned, in 1643, the Westminster Assembly of Divines to advise with Parliament on the points for which a general Synod had been prayed for.   But it was not sum-

will be this inconveniency, to call so many divines together; it will be to put power in their hands, who are too
apt to usurp it, as if the laity were bound by their deter-
minations. No; let the laity consult with the divines on
all sides, hear what they say, and make themselves masters
of their reasons; as they do by any other profession, when
they have a difference before them. For example, gold-
smiths; they enquire of them, if such a jewel be of such a
value, and such a stone of such a value; hear them, and
then, being rational men, judge themselves. 10

2. Why should you have a synod, when you have a
convocation already, which is a synod? Would you have
a superfetation of another synod? The clergy of England, when they cast off the pope, submitted themselves
to the civil power, and so have continued; but these
challenge to be *jure divino*, and so to be above the civil
power: these challenge power to call before their presbyteries all persons for all sins directly against the law of
God, as proved to be sins by necessary consequence. If
you would buy gloves, send for a glover or two, not 20
Glovers' hall: consult with some divines, not send for
a body.

3. There must be some laymen in the synod, to over-

moned under the name of a Synod, indeed it was expressly claimed
for it that it was not a national Synod or representative body of the
clergy, but only a body to deliberate on matters submitted to it by
the House. Neal, Hist. of Puritans, iii. 43, 44, 49.

On the claim of the Presbyterian clergy of this body 'to be *jure
divino*, and so above the civil power,' see note on ' Presbytery,' sec. 4.

1. 23. *There must be some laymen* &c.] This takes us to a time, at
or about 1643, when the constitution of the Assembly of Divines had
not been finally settled, and when its name had not yet been fixed.
The next section shows that the point insisted upon in sec. 3 had
been so determined when the Assembly actually met. The Ordinance
(June, 1643) is termed : 'an ordinance for the calling of an assembly of
learned and godly divines *and others*'; but in the ordinance itself the
assembly is said to be : 'of learned, godly, and judicious divines.'

look the clergy, lest they spoil the civil work. Just as
when the good woman puts a cat into the milk-house to
kill a mouse; she sends her maid to look after the cat,
lest the cat should eat up the cream.

4. In the ordinance for the assembly, the lords and commons go under the names of learned, godly, and judicious
divines; there is no difference put betwixt them, and the
ministers in the context.

5. It is not unusual in the assembly to revoke their votes,
by reason they make such haste, but 'tis that will make
them scorned.   You never heard of a council revoked an
act of its own making.   They have been wary of that, to
keep up their infallibility; if they did anything, they took
away the whole council; and yet we would be thought as
infallible as anybody.   It is not enough to say, the House
of Commons revokes their votes, for theirs are but civil
truths, which they by agreement create, and uncreate,
as they please; but the truths the synod deals in are
divine; and when they have voted a thing, if it be then
true, 'twas true before, not true because they voted it;
nor does it cease to be true, because they vote it otherwise.

6. Subscribing in a synod, or to the articles of a synod,
is no such terrible thing as they make it; because, if I am
of a synod, 'tis agreed, either tacitly or expressly, that which
the major part determines, the rest are involved in; and
therefore I subscribe, though my own private opinion be
otherwise; and upon the same ground, I may without
scruple subscribe to what these have determined, whom
I sent, though my private opinion be otherwise; having
respect to that which is the ground of all assemblies, The
major part carries it.

Selden, who was a member of the assembly, must have been a little
amused to find himself included in the description.   Rushworth,
v. 337.

CXXXIV.

THANKSGIVING.

AT first we gave thanks for every victory as soon as e'er 'twas obtained; but since we have had many, now we can stay a good while. We are just like a child; give him a plum, he makes his leg; give him a second plum, he makes another leg: at last when his belly is full, he forgets what he ought to do; then his nurse, or somebody else that stands by him, puts him in mind of his duty, *Where's your leg?*

CXXXV.

TITHES.

1. TITHES are more paid in kind in England, than in all Italy and France. In France they have had impropriations a long time; we had none in England till Henry the 8th.

l. 13. *we had none in England*] They were, Selden shows, not common in England till Henry VIII, but he mentions them as occasionally found. Conf. 'Although in other states these infeodations or conveyances of the perpetual right of tythes to laymen be very ancient and frequent also, yet no such certain and obvious testimony of their antiquity is in the monuments of England as can enough assure us that they were before the statute of dissolutions in any common use here. But some were, and, for ought appears in the practice of the time, many more might equally have been. . . . In sum then we may affirm that some such ancient infeodations have been in England as in other states.' Works, iii. 1274 ff.

'Neither hath the canon law wrought otherwise in Italy, but that there also particular customs, as well of *non decimando* as in the *modus*, are frequent. *Multis Italiae locis*, says Cajetan, *contingit ex consuetudine* that nothing at all is paid. And so is the practice there for the most part at this day, the parish priests being sufficiently maintained by manse and glebe, and the revenues that are in some places paid as according to a *modus.*' iii. 1174.

'In that state (sc. France), against the whole course of the canon law in this kind, they have, what by reason of ancient infeodations still continuing, what through customs, allowed divers lands to be not at

N

2. To make an impropriation, there was to be the consent of the incumbent, the patron, and the king; and then 'twas confirmed by the pope: without all this the pope could make no impropriation.

3. Or what if the pope gave the tithes to any man, must they therefore be taken away? If the pope gives me a jewel, will you therefore take it from me?

4. Abraham paid tithes to Melchizedec; what then? 'Twas very well done of him: it does not follow therefore 10 that I must pay tithes, no more than I am bound to imitate any other action of Abraham's.

5. 'Tis ridiculous to say, the tithes are God's part, and

all subject to any tythes payable to the Church. For their infeoda-tions . . are to this day remaining, and are conveyed and descend as other lay inheritances. . . . Those infeodations of tythes are there very frequent, and in very many parishes the tythes are taken only by laymen.' iii. 1169.

'J'oseray encor mettre entre les privileges, mais non Ecclesiastiques, le droict de tenir dixmes en fief par gens pur laics. Ce qu'on ne peut nier avoir prins son origine d'une licence et abuz commencé soubs Charles Martel, Maire du Palais, et continué principalement soubs les Rois de sa race.' Pithou, printed in Libertez de l'Eglise Gallicane, vol. i. p. 19.

l. 2. *then 'twas confirmed by the pope*] The consent of the provin-cial primate was anciently needed for the alienation of Church property. See ' Placuit etiam ut rem ecclesiae nemo vendat, Quod si aliqua necessitas cogit, hanc insinuendam esse primati provinciae ipsius, ut cum statuto numero episcoporum, utrum faciendum sit arbitretur.' Canon of the 5th Council of Carthage, quoted by Bingham, Christian Antiquities, Bk. V. ch. vi. sec. 7.

In pre-Reformation days, when the Pope had an admitted primacy in the Western Church, this right of final judgment naturally devolved on him. That he could not move in the matter by his own mere will was effectually settled in this country by the Statutes of Provisors.

l. 12. *'Tis ridiculous to say*, &c.] Selden's view is not that of the sacerdotal champions of the Romish or of the English Church. See e. g. Decrees of Pope Boniface I, sec. 3 : ' Nulli liceat ignorare quod omne quod domino consecratur ... ad jus pertinet sacerdotum.' Labbé, Conciliorum Collectio, vol. iv. p. 397; and Laud's argument to prove that the payment of tithes to the ministers under the Gospel is due *jure divino*. Laud, Works, vi. 159.

therefore the clergy must have them: why, so they are if the layman has them. 'Tis as if one of my Lady Kent's maids should be sweeping this room, and another of them should come and take away the broom, and tell for a reason, why she should part with it; 'Tis my lady's broom: as if it were not my lady's broom, which of them soever had it.

6. They consulted in Oxford where they might find the best arguments for their tithes, setting aside the *jus divinum;* they were advised to my History of Tithes, a book so much cried down by them formerly (in which, I dare boldly say, 10

---

l. 9. *they were advised to my History of Tithes*] by Gerard Langbaine, Provost of Queen's, who wrote the letter to which Selden here refers:

'HOND. SIR,

'Upon occasion of the businesse of Tythes now under consideration, some whom it more nearly concerns, have been pleased to enquire of me what might be said as to the civil right of them; to whom I was not able to give any better direction than by sending them to yowr History. Happily it may seem strange to them; yet I am not out of hopes but that work (like Pelias hasta) which was lookt upon as a piece that struck deepest against the divine, will afford the strongest arguments for the civil right: and if that be made the issue, I do not despair of the cause....

GER. LANGBAINE.

Queen's Coll., Oxon.,
22 Aug. 1653.'
— Leland's Collectanea, Hearne, vol. v. p. 291 (ed. 1770).

l. 9. *a book so much cried down by them formerly*] Selden's History of Tythes was published in 1617, and roused the anger of the whole clerical party, mainly by its treatment of the tithe as a matter of variable civil right, and not as due to the clergy *jure divino.* So strong was the feeling against Selden that he found it necessary, in order to escape being called before the Court of High Commission —if indeed he did escape, which Dr. Tillesley denies—to express in writing his sense of the error which he had committed in publishing his History, and his grief that he had thereby incurred the King's displeasure and that of the bishops and lay officials to whom his ' retractation' was addressed. The History was vehemently attacked. in print by champions of the *jure divino* right, a right which Selden had ignored but had not denied, his end and purpose being ' to leave that question of divine right to divines, to whom it properly pertains.'

there are more arguments for them than are extant together anywhere): upon this, one writ me word, that my history of tithes was now become like *Pelias hasta*[1], to wound and to heal. I told him in my answer, I thought I could fit him with a better instance. 'Twas possible it might undergo

---

[1] *Pelias hasta*] Peleus's hasta, MSS.

These numerous attacks Selden was for the time forced to suffer in silence, for King James had told him that he would put him in prison if he or any of his friends made any answer to them. But as he insists, when he was at length able to reply to Dr. Tillesley's 'Animadversions,' he had been careful in making his submission to retract nothing. ' I was and am,' he says, 'sorry that I published it, and that I so gave occasion to others to abuse my history, by their false application of some arguments.' A full account of the whole matter will be found in Works, vol. i. Vita Authoris, p. v-viii. See also vol. iii. pp. 1370, 1394 and 1452 ff.

l. 3.   *like Pelias hasta*]
       ' Vulnus in Herculeo quae quondam fecerat hoste,
         Vulneris auxilium Pelias hasta tulit.'
                         Ovid, Remedium Amoris, 47.

l. 4.   *I could fit him with a better instance*]   See ' Ante annos scilicet ccclx, aut circiter . . . prorsus damnati sunt ejusdem libri illi (sc. Aristotelis physices et metaphysices libri) ut Christianismo nimis dissoni ; quod a Rogero Bachone Franciscano, qui paulo post id tempus floruit philosophus et mathematicus summus, didici. . . . Theologi, inquit, Parisiis, et episcopus, et omnes sapientes jam ab annis circiter quadraginta damnaverunt et excommunicaverunt libros naturales et metaphysicae Aristotelis, qui nunc ab omnibus recipiuntur. Et alibi idem—Scimus enim quod temporibus nostris Parisiis diu fuit contradictum philosophiae naturali et metaphysicae Aristotelis per Avicennam et Averroym expositis, et ob densam ignorantiam fuere libri eorum excommunicati, et utentes eis, per tempora satis longa.' De Jure Naturali et Gentium, lib. i. cap. 2 ; Works, i. pp. 98 and 947.

   The former of these passages occurs in Roger Bacon's Opus Tertium, p. 28 (Brewer's ed. 1859), the latter in the Opus Majus, cap. 9, p. 14. The Opus Tertium was written in 1267, as Bacon expressly states (p. 278). The sentence of excommunication, therefore, must have been about 1227, and could not have been pronounced by ' Stephen, Bishop of Paris,' who did not become bishop until 1268, i. e. a year after the Opus Tertium was written, and some forty years after the sentence. See Ecclesia Parisiensis, in Sainte Marthe's Gallia Christiana, vol. vii. p. 108.

Bishop Stephen's name must have been introduced through some

the same fate that Aristotle, Avicen, and Averroes did in
France, some five hundred years ago, which was excommunicated by Stephen, bishop of Paris, (by that very
name, *excommunicated*,) because that kind of learning puz-
zled and troubled[1] their divinity: but finding themselves
at a loss, some forty years after (which is much about the
time since I writ my history), they were called in again,
and so have continued ever since.

CXXXVI.

TRADE.

1. THERE is no prince in Christendom but is directly
a tradesman, though in another way than an ordinary
tradesman. For the purpose, I have a man; I bid him
lay out twenty shillings in such a commodity; but I tell

------

[1] *Troubled*, H. 2] trouble, H.

confusion on the part of Selden's reporter, Milward. The controversy
in which Stephen figures had to do with the nature and origin of the
higher form of intelligence. Aristotle's νοῦς ποιητικός, Roger Bacon's
intellectus agens. The authority of Aristotle and of his Arabian commentators, Avicenna, Averroes, and others, had been used, not
unfairly, to support the theory that this intelligence was no constituent
part of each human mind, but that it was of a divine nature, infused
into the mind, and the same in all minds, being a pre-existent entity
distinct from the human faculties properly so called, and quickening
them to the discovery of truth. This, which had long been the
accepted view, began to be called in question in the thirteenth
century, and was publicly condemned at Paris by Bishop Stephen in
1270. The objections made to it, and the terms of compromise by
which the dispute was finally adjusted, are very fully set down in
Selden's De Jure Naturali et Gentium, lib. i. cap. 9 (Works, i. 154-
157).
It is clear, from Langbaine's letter, that the discourse reported in
the text must have been towards the close of 1653 or in 1654, the year
of Selden's death.

him for every shilling he lays out I will have a penny: I trade as well as he. This every prince does in his customs.

2. That which a man is bred up in, he thinks no cheating; as your tradesman thinks not so of his profession, but calls it a mystery. Whereas if you would teach a mercer some other way to make his silks heavy than what he has been used to, he would peradventure think that to be cheating.

3. Every tradesman professes to cheat me, that asks for his commodity twice as much as 'tis worth.

CXXXVII.

TRADITION.

Say what you will against tradition, we know the signification of words by nothing but tradition. You will say the Scripture was written by the Holy Spirit, but do you understand that language 'twas writ in? No. Then for example, take these words, *In principio erat verbum.* How do you know those words signify, *In the beginning was the word,* but by tradition, because somebody has told you so?

CXXXVIII.

TRANSUBSTANTIATION.

1. The fathers using to speak rhetorically, brought up transubstantiation: as if because 'tis commonly said, *amicus est alter idem,* one should go about to prove that a man and his friend are all one. That opinion is only rhetoric turned into logic.

2. There is no greater argument (though not used) against transubstantiation, than the Apostles, at their first council,

forbidding blood and suffocation. Would they forbid blood, and yet enjoin the eating of blood too?

3. The best way for a pious man [1] is to address himself to the sacrament with that reverence and devotion, as if Christ were really there present.

CXXXIX.

TRAITOR.

'Tɪs not seasonable to call a man traitor, who has an army at his heels. One with an army is a gallant man. My Lady Cotton was in the right, when she laughed at the Duchess of Richmond for taking such state upon her, when she could command no forces. She a duchess! there is in Flanders a duchess indeed; meaning the arch-duchess.

CXL.

TRIAL.

1. TRIALS are one of these three ways; by confession; or by demurrer, that is, confessing the fact, but denying it to be that wherewith a man is charged; for example, denying it to be treason, if a man be charged with treason: or by a jury.

2. *Ordalium* was a trial, and was either by going over

---

[1] *The best way for a pious man*, &c.] This section appears in H. under heading 'Sacrament.' In H. 2, it appears as an appendix to the MS. with heading 'Transubstantiation' to which subject it seems more properly to belong.

l. 19. *Ordalium was a trial*] There were several forms of the ordeal. In the aquae frigidae judicium—una ex purgationibus vulgaribus quas judicia Dei appellabant—the suspected or accused person was plunged into deep water; if he swam he was held guilty, if he sank innocent. In the aquae ferventis judicium, the accused had

nine red hot ploughshares, (as in the case of Queen Emma, accused for lying with the bishop of Winchester, over which she being led blindfold, and having passed all her irons, asked when she should come to her trial;) or 'twas by taking a red. hot coulter in a man's hand, and carrying it so many steps, and then casting it from him. As soon as this was done, the feet or the hands were to be bound up, and certain charms to be said, and a day or two after to be opened; if the parts were whole, the party was judged
10 to be innocent; and so on the contrary.

3. The rack is used nowhere as in England. In other countries 'tis used in judicature, when there is a *semiplena probatio*, a half proof against a man; then to see if they can make it full, they rack him if he will not confess. But here in England they take a man and rack him, I do not

to plunge his bare hand and arm into boiling water. Of the same kind was the judgment by hot iron, to which Selden here refers. See Ducange, Gloss., under Aquae and Ferrum Candens.

Muratori adds, under 'Judicium ferri candentis,' the passing blindfold over hot ploughshares, and a further form known as the judicium crucis, in which the accused had to stand with his arms held out in the form of a cross, while a chapter in the Bible or some of the Psalms were read. If he could maintain the posture he was pronounced innocent, if he gave way he was guilty. See Muratori, Antiq. Ital. Dissert. 38, p. 611 ff.

l. 1. *as in the case of Queen Emma*] The account of Queen Emma's trial is given, as in the text, in Fabyan's Chronicle, pp. 224-5 (Ellis's ed. 1811). The ordeal, as might be assumed, was under the management of her episcopal friends. The Archbishop, Robert, who had declared against her, was not present.

l. 14. *But here in England they take a man* &c.] The infliction of torture was certainly against the English common law and against the Magna Charta, but it was no less certainly of regular and frequent occurrence. As to its illegality, we have, e.g., the statement of Chief Justice Fortescue, quoted and endorsed by Coke, and we have the declared opinion of the judges in Felton's case (November, 1628): 'That he ought not by the law to be tortured by the rack, for no such punishment is known or allowed by our law.' 'And yet' (says Jardine, in his Reading on the use of torture in England) 'it is an historical fact that, anterior to the Commonwealth, torture was

know why, nor when ; not in time of judicature, but when somebody bids.

4. Some men before they come to their trial, are cozened to confess upon examination, upon this trick. They are made to believe somebody has confessed before them; and then they think it a piece of honour to be clear and ingenuous[1], and that destroys them.

CXLI.

TRINITY.

THE Second Person is made of a piece of bread by the Papist; the Third Person is made of his own frenzy, malice, ignorance and folly, by the Roundhead. To all these the spirit is intituled[2]. One the baker makes, the other the cobbler; and betwixt these two, I think the First Person is sufficiently abused.

[1] *Ingenuous*] ingenious, MSS.   [2] *Intituled*, H. 2] intitled, H.

always used, as a matter of course, in all grave accusations, at the mere discretion of the King and the Privy Council, and uncontrolled by any law besides the prerogative of the sovereign.' He traces the practice from Henry VIII's reign down to May 1640, Archer's case, which is (he says) 'the last recorded instance of the infliction of torture in England, and as far as I have been able to discover the last instance of its occurrence.' Jardine holds that, though not lawful by the common law, it was lawful as an act of prerogative, a power superior to the laws and able to suspend the laws; but it may be fairly questioned whether this strain of prerogative over law can be allowed to have been lawful in any sense. See ' Prerogative,' sec. 1.

It is curious to find Grotius and other foreign jurists praising the law of England for its singular humanity in conducting criminal proceedings without the use of torture, and devising ingenious reasons to account for it; while Selden, well acquainted with the facts, compares English practice disadvantageously with that of other countries —an opinion which Jardine confirms by contrasting in detail the arbitrary and uncontrolled licence of the English method with the limitations and definite rules which prevailed in countries whose code was based on the Roman law. Reading, &c., p. 67.

CXLII.

TRUTH.

1. THE Aristotelians say, all truth is contained in Aristotle, in one place or another. Galileo makes Simplicius say so, but shews the absurdity of that speech, by answering, that all truth is contained in a lesser compass, vizt. in the alphabet. Aristotle is not blamed for mistaking sometimes, but Aristotelians for maintaining those mistakes. They should acknowledge the good they have from him, and leave him when he is in the wrong. 10 There never breathed that person to whom mankind was more beholden.

2. The way to find out the truth is by others' mistakings: for if I was to go to such a place, and one had gone before me on the right hand, and he was out; another had gone on the left hand, and he was out; this would direct me to keep the middle way, that peradventure would bring me to the place I intended to go.

l. 3. *Galileo makes Simplicius say so*, &c.] The passage occurs in the second of a series of imaginary conversations on mathematical and physical science, between Salviati and Sagredo, the spokesmen for modern science, and Simplicius, the Aristotelian commentator. Simplicius asserts that, with the aid of the syllogistic method, the man who can make a proper use of Aristotle's writings 'saprà cavar da' suoi libri le dimostrazioni di ogni scibile, perchè in essi è ogni cosa.'

Sagredo replies, banteringly, ' Ma, Signor Simplicio mio . . . questo che voi, e gli altri filosofi bravi, farete con i testi d'Aristotile, farò io con i versi di Virgilio, o di Ovidio. . . . Ma che dico io di Virgilio, o di altro poeta? io ho un libretto assai più breve di Aristotile e d'Ovidio, nel quale si contengono tutte le scienze . . . e questo è l' alfabeto; e non è dubbio che quello, che saprà ben accoppiare e ordinare questa e quella vocale con quelle consonanti o con quell' altre, ne caverà le risposte verissime a tutti i dubbj, e ne trarrà gli insegnamenti di tutte le scienze e di tutte le arti.' Opere di Galilei, vol. xi. p. 266 (Classici Italiani, Milan, 1808–1811, in 13 vols.).

3. In troubled water you can scarce see your face; or
see it very little, till the water be quiet and stand still.
So in troubled times you can see little truth. When
times are quiet and settled, then truth appears.

CXLIII.

UNIVERSITY.

1. THE best argument why Oxford should have precedence of Cambridge, is the act of parliament, by which
Oxford is made a body; made what it is; and Cambridge
is made what it is; and in that act it takes place. Besides,
Oxford has the best monuments to show.

2. 'Twas well said of one, hearing of a history lecture
to be founded in the university; Would to God, says he,
they would erect a lecture of discretion there, this would
do more good an hundred times.

3. He that comes from the university to govern the state,

---

l. 6. *The best argument why Oxford* &c.] This question of precedence was raised in the House of Commons in January, 1640-1, when
'the Bill of four subsidies for the relief of the King's army and the
northern counties having been drawn by a Committee, Cambridge
was placed before Oxford in the same.' This gave rise to a hot and
prolonged debate. Sir Simonds D'Ewes spoke at length in favour of
giving Cambridge the precedence, on the ground that Cambridge was
a renowned city before Oxford, and a nursery of learning before
Oxford, so that Cambridge was in all respects the elder sister. So
sharp was the contention that on that day 'the House came not to a
final determination in the reading of the Bill.' See, Two Speeches
by Sir S. D'Ewes (printed in 1642), and Nalson, Collections, i. 703.

l. 7. *the act of parliament* &c.] This is 13 Elizabeth, ch. 29, 'An
Act concerning the incorporations of the Universities of Oxford
and Cambridge,' in which Oxford is named before Cambridge in
several places. Once only, towards the end of the Act, we have 'the
said Universities of Cambridge and Oxford.'

before he is acquainted with the men and manners of the place, does just as if he should come into the presence all dirty, with his boots on, his riding-coat, and his hat all daubed. They may serve him well enough in the way, but when he comes to court, he must conform to the place.

CXLIV.

VOWS.

Question. Suppose a man find by his own inclination he has no mind to marry, may he not then vow chastity ?

10 *Answer.* If he does, what a fine thing has he done ? 'Tis as if a man did not love cheese; and then he would vow to God Almighty never to eat cheese. He that vows can mean no more in sense than this; to do his utmost endeavour to keep his vow.

CXLV.

USURY.

1. THE Jews were forbidden to take use one of another, but they were not forbidden to take it of other nations. That being so, I see no reason why I may not as well take use for my money as rent for my house. 'Tis a vain thing

20 to say, money begets not money; for that no doubt it does [1].

2. Would it not look oddly to a stranger, that should

---

[1] *No doubt it does*, H. 2] no doubt is does, H.

come into this land, and hear in our pulpits usury preached against; and yet the law allow it? Many men use it, perhaps some churchmen themselves. No bishop nor ecclesiastical judge, that pretends power to punish other faults, dares punish, or at least does punish, any man for doing it.

CXLVI.

PIOUS USES.

THE ground of the ordinary's taking part of a man's estate, who died without a will, to pious uses, was this ; to give it somebody to pray that his soul might be delivered out of purgatory. Now the pious uses come into his own pocket. 'Twas well expressed by John o' Powls in the play, who acted the priest ; one that was to be hanged, being brought to the ladder, would fain have given something to the poor ; he feels for his purse, (which John o' Powls had picked out of his pocket a little before) missing it, cries out, he had lost his purse now he intended to have given something to the poor: John o' Powls bid him be pacified, for the poor had it already.

l. 12. *'Twas well expressed* &c.] The same incident occurs in the following, which is probably the passage which Selden had in mind :—
  '*Malheureux (pinioned and led out to execution)* :
    My endless peace is made ; and to the poor—
    My purse, my purse ! '
  Cocledemoy (who has just picked Malheureux' pocket) :
    Ay, sir ; and it shall please you, the poor has your purse already.'
—Marston, Dutch Courtezan, Act v. sc. 3 (vol ii. p. 98 in Bullen's ed. of Marston's works).
  I am indebted to Mr. P. A. Daniel for this reference.

CXLVII.

WAR.

1. Do not undervalue an enemy by whom you have been worsted. When our countrymen came home from fighting against the Saracens, and were beaten by them, they pictured them with huge, big, terrible faces, (as you still see the sign of the Saracen's head is) when in truth they were like other men. But this they did to save their own credits.

2. Martial law in general, means nothing but the martial law of this or that place; with us 'tis to be used in *fervore belli*, in the face of the enemy, not in time of peace; then they can take away neither limb nor life. The commanders need not complain for want of it, because our ancestors have done gallant things without it.

l. 11. *In the face of the enemy, not in time of peace*] The billeting of great companies of soldiers and mariners, and the appointment of special commissioners to deal summarily, 'as is agreeable to martial law,' with them or with other dissolute persons joining with them to commit murder, robbery, felony, mutiny, or other outrage or misdemeanour, are among the grievances set down in the 'Petition of Right' of 1628. The result of them is said to have been the illegal execution of some persons by the commissioners, and the escape of 'sundry grievous offenders,' against whom the judges refused to proceed 'upon pretence that the said offenders were punishable only by martial law,' &c. Somers, Historical Tracts, vol. iv. pp. 118, 119.

There are several speeches of Selden's on this matter, in which he argues and brings proof that in time of peace there can be no martial law; that wherever the sheriff in the county can execute the king's writs, there it is time of peace, though in other parts there be war; that in time of peace, so defined, soldiers are under the common law; and that martial law, where it legitimately exists, is not the abrogation of law but proceeds by settled rules. Works, iii. 1986 ff.

The subject was fully discussed in Parliament by several other speakers, and the proclamation of martial law in time of peace was condemned as unconstitutional and illegal. Rushworth, Collections, vol. iii. Appendix, p. 76.

3. *Question*. Whether may subjects take up arms against their prince ?

Answer. Conceive it thus; here lies a shilling betwixt you and me; tenpence of the shilling is yours, twopence is mine by agreement : I am as much king of my twopence, as you of your tenpence : if you therefore go about to take away my twopence, I will defend it; for there you and I are equal, both princes.

4. ·Or thus; two supreme princes meet; one says to the other, Give me your land ; if you will not, I will take it from you : the other, because he thinks himself too weak to resist him, tells him, Of nine parts I will give you three, so I may quietly enjoy the rest, and I will become your tributary. Afterwards the prince comes to exact six parts, and leaves but three; the contract then is broken, and they are in parity again.

5. To know what obedience is due to the prince, you must look into the contract betwixt him and his people ; as if you would know what rent is due from the tenant to the landlord, you must look into the lease. Where the contract is broken, and there is no third person to judge, then the decision is by arms. And this is the case between the prince and the subject.

l. 1. *Whether may subjects* &c.] The right of subjects to take up arms against their Prince was a natural subject of discussion in Selden's day. The clergy pronounced against it. The new Canons of 1640, put out by the two Synods and accepted and endorsed by the King, speak very decidedly about it. 'For subjects to bear arms against their Kings, offensive or defensive, upon any pretence whatsoever, is at least to resist the powers which are ordained of God; and though they do not invade, but only resist, St. Paul tells them plainly, they shall receive to themselves damnation.' Constitutions and Canons Ecclesiastical, sec. 1. Wilkins, Concilia, iv. 545.

It was one of the charges against Archbishop Laud that he had ordered the clergy to preach in the above sense four times in the year. This order appears in the preface to the first Canon, and the doctrine thus approved is defended at length in Laud's own history of his troubles and trial. Conf. Laud's Works, vol. iii. pp. 366-370.

6. *Question.* What law is there to take up arms against the prince, in case he break his covenant?

Answer. Though there be no written law for it, yet there is custom, which is the best law of the kingdom; for in England they have always done it. There is nothing expressed between the king of England and the king of France, that if either invades the other's territory, the other shall take up arms against him; and yet they do it upon such an occasion.

7. 'Tis all one to be plundered by a troop of horse, or to have a man's goods taken from him by an order from the Council-table. To him that dies, 'tis all one whether it be by a penny halter, or a silk garter; yet I confess the silk garter pleases more; and, like trouts, we love to be tickled to death.

8. The soldiers say they fight for honour; when the truth is they have their honour in their pocket. And they mean the same thing that pretend to fight for religion. Just as a parson goes to law with his parishioners, he says, for the good of his successor, that the church may not lose its right; when the meaning is to get the tithe into his own pocket.

9. We govern this war as an unskilful man does a casting-net; if he has not the right trick to cast the net off of his shoulder, the leads will pull him into the river. I am afraid we shall pull ourselves into destruction.

10. We look after the particulars of a battle, because we live in the very time of the war. Whereas of battles past, we hear nothing but the number slain. Just so for the death of a man; when he is sick, we talk how he slept this night, and that night; what he eat, and what he drank: but when he is dead, we only say, he died of a fever, or name his disease; and there's an end.

11. Boccaline has this passage of soldiers; they came to

l. 34. *Boccaline has this passage* &c.] This is not quite correct.

Apollo to have their profession made the eighth[1] liberal science, which he granted. As soon as it was noised up and down, in came the butchers, and they desired their profession might be made the ninth: for, say they, the soldiers have this honour for killing of men ; now we kill as well as they; but we kill beasts for the preserving of men, and why should not we have honour likewise done us ? Apollo could not answer their reasons, so he reversed his sentence, and made the soldier's trade a mystery, as the butcher's is.

[1] *The eighth*] the eigth, H. and H. 2.

The passage is as follows :—'The precedency between Arms and Learning is still obstinately disputed on both sides, between the Literati and Military men in Parnassus. And it was resolved in the last *Ruota* that the question should be argued if at least the name of Science and Discipline might be attributed to the exercise of war. . . . The business was very subtilly canvassed and argued, and the Court seemed wholly to incline to the Literati; but the Princes used such forcible arguments, as it was resolved that military men in their exercise of war might use the honourable names of science and discipline. The Literati were much displeased at this decision . . . when unexpectedly all the Butchers of the world were seen to appear in Parnassus; . . . all besmeared with blood, with hatchets and long knives in their hands. . . . Apollo, that he might know what they meant, sent some Deputies to them. To whom those butchers stoutly said, that hearing that the Court had decided that the art of sacking and firing of cities, of cutting their inhabitants in pieces . . . and of calling with sword in hand, mine thine, should be termed a science and discipline, they also, who did not profess the killing of men . . . but the killing of calves and muttons to feed men withal, demanded that their art might be honoured by the same illustrious names. . . . The same *Signori Auditori di ruota*, when they saw the butchers appear in the Palace, and heard their demand, they were aware of the injustice which but a little before they had done to all the Virtuosi by their decision; wherefore they again propounded the same question, and unanimously agreed, that the mysterie of War, though it were sometimes necessary, was notwithstanding so cruel and so inhumane, as it was impossible to honest it with civil terms.' Boccalini, Advertisements from Parnassus, Century 1. Advert. 75. Trans. by Henry, Earl of Monmouth, p. 143.

CXLVIII.

WIFE.

1. He that has a handsome wife, by other men is thought happy; 'tis a pleasure to look upon her, and be in her company; but the husband is cloyed with her. We are never content with what we have.

2. You shall see a monkey sometime that has been playing up and down the garden, at length leap up to the top of the wall, but his clog hangs a great way below on this side: the bishop's wife is like that monkey's clog; himself is got up very high, takes place of temporal barons; but his wife comes a great way behind.

3. 'Tis reason a man that will have a wife should be at the charge of all her trinkets, and pay all the scores she sets on him. He that will keep a monkey, 'tis fit he should pay for the glasses she breaks.

CXLIX.

WISDOM.

1. A wise man should never resolve upon anything, at least never let the world know his resolution; for if he cannot arrive at that, he is shamed. How many things did the king resolve in his declaration concerning Scotland, never to do, and yet did them all? A man must do according to accidents and emergences.

2. Never tell your resolution before-hand; but when the cast is thrown, play it as well as you can to win the game you are at. 'Tis but folly to study how to play size-ace, when you know not whether you shall throw it or no.

3. Wise men say nothing in dangerous times. The lion,

you know, called the sheep, to ask her if his breath smelt;
she said, Aye[1]; he bit off her head for a fool.   He called
the wolf, and asked him; he said, No; he tore him in pieces
for a flatterer.   At last he called the fox, and asked him;
Truly he had got a cold, and could not smell.   King James
was pictured, &c.

CL.

WITCHES.

THE law against witches does not prove that there be
any; but it punishes the malice of those people that use
such means to take away men's lives.   If one should profess that by turning his hat thrice, and crying buz, he could
take away a man's life (though in truth he could do nothing),
yet this were a just law made by the state, that whosoever
should turn his hat thrice, and cry buz, with an intention to
take away a man's life, shall be put to death.

CLI.

WIT.

1. WIT and wisdom differ; wit is upon the sudden turn,
wisdom is in bringing about ends.

2. Nature must be the ground-work of wit and art;
otherwise whatever is done will prove but jack-pudding's
work.

3. Wit must grow like fingers; if it be taken from
others, 'tis like plums stuck upon blackthorn; there they
are for awhile, but they come to nothing.

4. He that will give himself to all manner of ways to get

---

[1] *Aye*] I, MSS.

money may be rich ; so he that will let fly all he knows or thinks, may by chance be sarcastically witty.   Honesty sometimes keeps a man from being rich ; and civility from being witty.

5. Women ought not to know their own wit, because then they will still be shewing it, and so spoil it ; like a child that will be continually shewing its fine new coat, till at length it all bedaubs it with its pah hands.

6. Fine wits destroy themselves with their own plots, in ₁₀ meddling with great affairs of state.   They commonly do as the ape that saw the gunner put bullets in the cannon, and was pleased with it, and he would be doing so too ; at last he puts himself into the piece, and so both ape and bullet were shot away together.

CLII.

WOMEN.

1. *Let the woman*[1] *have power on her head, because of the angels.*   The reason of the words, *because of the angels*, is this ; the Greek Church held an opinion that the angels fell in love with women ; an opinion grounded upon that ₂₀ in Genesis vi, The sons of God saw the daughters of men that they were fair.   This fancy St. Paul discreetly catches, and uses it as an argument to persuade them to modesty.

2. The grant of a place is not good by the canon law before a man be dead ; upon this ground, that some mischief might be plotted against him in present possession, by poisoning or some other way.   Upon the same reason a contract made with a woman during her husband's life, was not valid.

---

[1] *Let the woman*, H. 2 and S.] Let the women, H.

3. Men are not troubled to hear a man dispraised, be-cause they know, though he be naught, there's worth in others. But women are mightily troubled to hear any of them spoken against, as if the sex itself were guilty of some unworthiness.

4. Women and princes must both trust somebody; and they are happy or unhappy, according to the desert of those under whose hands they fall. If a man knows how to manage the favour of a lady, her honour is safe; and so is a prince.   10

CLIII.

YEAR.

1. It was the manner of the Jews (if the year did not fall out right, but that it was dirty for the people to come up to Jerusalem at the passover, or that their corn was not ripe for their first-fruits) to intercalate a month, and so to have, as it were, two Februaries; thrusting up the year still higher, March into April's place, April into May's place, &c. Whereupon it is impossible for us to know when our Saviour was born, or when he died.

l. 18. *Whereupon it is impossible for us* &c.] Selden, in his review of the 4th ch. of his book on Tithes, says:—'The learned know that until about cccc years after Christ . . . that day (sc. Dec. 25, as the day of the Nativity) was not settled, but variously observed in the Eastern Church. . . . And S. Chrysostom then learned the time of the 25th of December (which yet most think not to be the exact time) from the Western or Latin Church.' Works, iii. 1314.

This passage gave great offence to King James; and Selden, after several interviews with the King, wrote at his command a further tract on the subject. In this, after discussing the authorities at length, he concludes on a balance of evidence, ' It rests that we resolve on it (sc. on the 25th of December being the correct day) upon as certain and clear a truth of tradition, as by rational inference, by express testimony of the ancients, by common and continual practice of

2. The year is either the year of the moon, or the year of the sun; there is not above eleven days' difference. Our moveable feasts are according to the year of the moon; else they should be fixed.

3. Though they reckon ten days sooner beyond sea, yet it does not follow their spring is sooner than ours; we keep the same time in natural things, and their ten days sooner, and our ten days later in those things, mean the self-same time; just as twelve sous in French, are ten-pence in English.

4. The lengthening of days is not suddenly perceived, till they are grown a pretty deal longer; because the sun, though it be in a circle, yet it seems for a while to go in a right line. For take a segment of a great circle especially, and you shall doubt whether it be straight[1] or no. But when the sun is got past that line, then you presently perceive the days lengthened. Thus it is in the winter and summer solstice; which is indeed the true reason of them.

5. The eclipse of the sun is, when it is new moon; the eclipse of the moon, when it is full. They say Dionysius

---

[1] *Be straight*, H. 2] be not straight, H. and S.

---

several churches, and by accurate inquiry, may be discovered.' Works, iii. 1450.

The remark in the Table Talk shows that this forced retractation was not seriously made.

l. 11. *The lengthening of days* &c.] The sense of this passage is not clear. Selden's meaning perhaps is that in winter so small a part of the sun's orbit is visible above the horizon, that the sun appears to the eye to be travelling in a right line. In the much larger summer orbit, the curvature is distinctly seen. But that the lengthening of the days is on this account suddenly perceived, does not seem to follow. It is likely enough that the passage has been incorrectly reported.

l. 21. *They say Dionysius* &c.] The story is found in a letter written as from Dionysius the Areopagite to Polycarp, Bishop of Smyrna. It says that he and the Sophist Apollophanes were together at Heliopolis at the time of the Crucifixion, and that they then was converted by the eclipse that happened at our Saviour's death, because it was neither of these, and so could not be natural.

CLIV.

ZEALOTS.

ONE would wonder Christ should whip the buyers and sellers out of the temple, and nobody offer to resist him, considering what opinion they had of him ; but the reason was, they had a law, that whosoever did profane *sanctitatem Dei, aut templi*, the holiness of God, or the temple, before ten persons, it was lawful for any of them to kill him, or to do any thing on this side killing him, as whipping him, or the like. And hence it was, that when one struck our Saviour before a judge, (where it was not lawful to strike,

and there observed the moon pass in an unaccountable way over the face of the sun, and so remain from the sixth hour until the evening. Apollophanes, he remarks, must know that such an event as this, happening out of the ordinary course of nature, must have been due to direct divine interposition. Indeed, Apollophanes himself had admitted this, for at the time of the eclipse he said to Dionysius that what they saw must be the consequence of matters which concerned the Gods (θείων ἀμοιβαὶ πραγμάτων). The actual conversion of Dionysius is ascribed to the preaching of St. Paul at Athens, Acts xvii. 34. The unseasonable eclipse is referred to by Dionysius in his letter as supplying an argument which Polycarp is to press on the scoffing sophist Apollophanes. The result is said to have been that Apollophanes too became a Christian. See S. Dionysii Epistola 7, in vol. iii. of Migne's Patrologiae Cursus Completus, Series Graeca, and Epistola 11, extant only in Latin and marked by Migne as spurious—as indeed the rest of the writings ascribed to Dionysius commonly are.

l. 7. *the reason was, they had a law* &c.] Selden, in his De Jure Naturali, refers at length to this law, and to its enforcement by the Zealots. He gives, among instances of its being put in force, the well-known case of Phineas, and the case of Mattathias who, inflamed with zeal, slew a Jew who was about, in the sight of all, to offer sacrifice on a pagan altar (1 Maccabees, ch. ii. 23–26). The stoning of Stephen, and the oath taken against Paul's life, are other instances in point. See Works, i. 456 ff.

as it is not with us at this day), he only replied, If I have spoken evil, bear witness of the evil; but if well, why smitest thou me? He says nothing against their smiting him, in case he had been guilty of speaking evil, that is, blasphemy, and they could have proved it against him. They that put this law in execution were called zealots; but afterwards they committed many villanies.

l. 7. *afterwards they committed many villanies*] See Josephus, Wars of the Jews, bk. iv. chs. 4, 5, 6, 7, for an account of the wholesale murders and robberies which they committed during the great war with the Romans.

APPENDIX

—+—

EXCURSUS A.

EXCOMMUNICATION : p. 66.

Note on sec. 4.   The evidence for this is found in a rescript, &c.

CONSTANTINE in this rescript states it as law, that in every cause the judgment pronounced by bishops is to hold good absolutely and without appeal, that either of two disputants may carry the case to the bishop's court, whether his opponent wishes it or not ; and further, that the evidence of any one bishop is to be accepted as final, and that when a bishop has given his testimony, no other witness is to be heard.

That there is fraud or error attaching to this rescript seems certain, for it is found inserted in the later Codex Theodosianus, which contains laws wholly inconsistent with it.   These show that if it was written by Constantine—and this is a disputed point—the law which it recites must have been abrogated some fifty years before the Codex Theodosianus was compiled. Sirmondi, however, includes it in his Appendix Codicis Theodosiani.   Selden, here and in his treatise De Synedriis Veterum Ebraeorum (Works, i. 956), accepts it as Constantine's, but he insists that it was fraudulently inserted in the Codex Theodosianus, of which it could not possibly have formed part.   See Works, ii. 830 and 1067.   Godefroy, in his edition of the Codex, prints it under the heading, Extravagans seu subdititius titulus de Episcopali Judicio, and he gives reasons (endorsed by Gibbon, Decline and Fall, ch. xx. sec. 4, note) for rejecting it as an entire forgery, vol. vi. 303–308 (ed. 1665 fol.).   Haenel does not include it in his edition of the Codex, but he prints it at the end of his volume as forming part of Sirmondi's

Appendix, and he prefaces the Appendix with a discussion of his own, concluding in favour of the rescript as the genuine work of Constantine, but rejecting it from the Theodosian Code. He adds also a list of the various authorities who may be con-sulted on the above points.

The rescript runs thus: 'Sanximus namque, sicut edicti nostri forma declarat, sententias episcoporum, quolibet genere latas, . . . inviolatas semper incorruptasque servari, scilicet ut pro sanctis semper ac venerabilibus habeatur quicquid episco-porum fuerit sententiâ terminatum. . . . Quicunque itaque litem habens, sive possessor sive petitor erit, . . . judicium eligit sacro-sanctae legis antistitis, illico sine aliquâ dubitatione, etiamsi alia pars refragatur, ad episcopum cum sermone litigantium dirigatur. . . . Omnes itaque causae, quae vel praetorio jure vel civili tractantur, episcoporum sententiis terminatae, perpetuo stabili-tatis jure firmentur, nec liceat ulterius retractari negotium, quod episcoporum sententia deciderit. Testimonium etiam, ab uno licet episcopo perhibitum, omnes judices indubitanter accipiant, nec alius audiatur cum testimonium episcopi a qualibet parte fuerit repromissum.' Constitutiones Sirmondi, Appendix, cap. 1. On the other hand, conf. e. g. a law of Arcadius and Honorius, which was certainly part of the Codex: 'Quoties de religione agitur, episcopos convenit agitare; ceteras vero causas, quae ad ordinarios cognitores, vel ad usum publici juris pertinent, legibus oportet audiri.' Codex, lib. xvi, tit. xi. sec. 1.

The Novels of Valentinian III, of later date than the Codex, are not less conclusive. 'Constat episcopos forum legibus non habere, nec de aliis causis (secundum Arcadii et Honorii divalia constituta) praeter religionem posse judicare.' Tit. xxxiv.

EXCURSUS B.

INCENDIARIES : p. 83.

l. 9. *They that first set it on fire* &c.] The King's chief advisers in the matters which brought about the conflict with the Parliamentary party were, or were assumed to have been, the Duke of Buckingham, the High Treasurer, Sir Richard Weston, the Earl of Strafford, and Archbishop Laud.   It is not clear to what time Selden is referring, when he says that they had now 'become regenerate'; it is perhaps to the early part of the second Parliament of 1640, when the punishment of Strafford and Laud had already been taken in hand, and when it was clear that the Commons were in no temper to be trifled with. The Duke of Buckingham and Sir Richard Weston were both dead—unregenerate in Selden's sense of the word. On the death of the High Treasurer, Laud had been made one of the Commissioners of the Treasury and Revenue, which (says Clarendon) he had reason to be sorry for, because it engaged him in civil business and matters of state, wherein he had little experience and which he had hitherto avoided. Hist. vol. i. 152.

It appears, however, from Whitelock's Memorials, that he had long before this been credited with interfering in matters of state. On the imprisonment of the members (3^{tio} Caroli), 'the people were discontented. Libels were cast abroad especially against Bishop Laud, and Weston the Treasurer. . . . My father (i. e. Justice Whitelock) said that if Bishop Laud went on in his way, he would kindle a flame in the nation,' p. 13. The charge of being an incendiary is urged again in 1640, by the same authority, on general and on special grounds. 'He (Laud) was more busy in temporal affairs and matters of state than his predecessors of later times had been. My father, who was anciently and thoroughly acquainted with him and knew his disposition, would say, "He was too full of fire, though a just and good man ; and that his want of experience in state matters, and his too much zeal for the Church, and heat, would set this nation on fire."

'By his council chiefly (as it was fathered upon him) the Parliament being dissolved,' &c. Whitelocke, Memorials, p. 34.

Curiously, too, in the same year, we find the term 'incendiary' used about him by the Scotch Commissioners, and a charge brought by them in the Upper House in proof of it. Laud's Works, iii. 238.

l. 9. *Monopolies*] How numerous these monopolies had been will appear from the King's proclamation (April 15, 1639) revoking some of them. See also Sir John Culpeper's speech in the Parliament which met on November 3, 1640 : ' I have but one grievance more to offer unto you, but this one comprizeth

many.   It is a nest of wasps or swarm of vermin which have
overcrept the land.   I mean the monopolies and polers of the
people ; these, like the frogs of Egypt, have gotten possession
of our dwellings, and we have scarce a room free from them.
They sup in our cup.   They dip in our dish.   They sit by our
fire.   We find them in the Dye-fat, Wash-bowl, and Powdring-
tub.   They share with the butler in his box.   They have marked
and sealed us from head to foot.   Mr. Speaker, they will not
bate us a pin.   We may not buy our own cloaths without their
brokage.   These are the leeches that have sucked the commonwealth so hard that it is almost become hectical,' &c.   Rushworth, Collections, ii. 915–917.

Clarendon, like Selden, traces the troubles of his day to the
arbitrary and unwise proceedings in the early years of Charles's
reign.   'And here I cannot but let myself loose to say that no
man can shew me a source from whence those waters of bitterness we now taste have more probably flowed, than from these
unreasonable, unskilful, and precipitate dissolutions of Parliaments . . . And whoever considers the acts of power and injustice
of some of the ministers in those intervals of parliament, will
not be much scandalized at the warmth and vivacity of those
meetings.'   Clarendon, Hist. vol. i. p. 6.

These points, with many others, are referred to in the
'Remonstrance' of 1641.   They reproached his Majesty . . .
'with the enlargements of forests, and compositions thereupon ;
the ingrossing gunpowder and suffering none to buy it without
licence ; with all the most odious monopolies of soap, wine, salt,
leather, sea-coal and the rest.'   They remembered 'the dissolution of the Parliament in the fourth year of his reign . . . the
imprisoning divers members of that Parliament after the dissolution, and detaining them close prisoners for words spoken in
Parliament; sentencing and fining them for those words.'
Clarendon, Hist. i. 492, 493.

l. 9. *forest business*] This was the extortion in 1630 and
subsequent years of large sums of money on account of alleged
encroachments on the royal forests, although the lands thus
reclaimed for the King had been held without dispute under an
adverse title dating back for three or four centuries.   In 1630,
Clarendon says, 'the old laws of the forest were revived, by
which not only great fines were imposed, but great annual rents

intended and like to be settled by way of contract, which burden
lighted most upon persons of quality and honour, who thought
themselves above ordinary oppressions, and were therefore
likely to remember it with more sharpness.' Clarendon, Hist.
i. 105.

This grievance was finally put an end to by the Act of 1640,
'that from henceforth the Meets, Meers, Limits, and Bounds of
all and every the Forests shall be adjudged and taken to extend
no further respectively than the Meets, Meers, Limits, and
Bounds in the several counties respectively, wherein the said
Forests were commonly known, reputed, used, or taken, in the
20th year of the reign of the late king James and not beyond, &c.'
Rushworth, Collections, iii. 1386.

l. 10. *parliament men* 3° *Caroli*] Whitelocke in his Memorials
for this year speaks of 'Warrants of the Council issued for Hollis,
Selden, Hobert, Elliot, and other Parliament men to appear
before them ; Hollis, Curriton, Elliot, and Valentine appeared,
and refusing to answer out of Parliament, they were committed
close prisoners to the Tower, and a Proclamation for appre-
hending others went out, and some of their studies were sealed
up. All the judges were contented that the prisoners should be
bailed, but they must also find sureties for their good behaviour.
This, at Selden's instance, they refuse to do, and are remanded
to the Tower.' Memorials, pp. 13 and 14.

EXCURSUS C.

THE KING'S CHAPEL ESTABLISHMENT : p. 92. sec. 4.

l. 12. *'Twas the old way* &c.] In the Ordinances for the Government of the Royal Household (1790, 4°), there are frequent
references to the King's Chapel establishment. In the household
of Henry VI it consisted of 1 dean, 20 chaplains and clerks, and
7 children, p. 17. In the Liber Niger Domûs Regis Edw. IV,
the duties, &c. of the dean, chaplains, yeomen and children of
the chapel are set out, pp. 49, 50. The whole subject is
treated at length in the Ordinances made at Eltham in 1526.
'The King's pleasure is that at all times when his Highness
shall lie in his castle of Windsor, his Manors of Bewlye, Rich-

mond, and Hampton Court, Greenwich, Eltham or Woodstock, his hall shall be ordinarily kept and continued, and at all such times of keeping the said hall, the King's noble chapel to be kept in the same place. Nevertheless, forasmuch as . . . it would not only be a great annoyance, but also excessive labour, travell, charge and pain, to have the King's whole chapel continually attendant upon his person . . . specially in riding journeys and progresses it is . . . ordained that the master of the children, and six men with some officers of the vestry, shall give their continual attendance in the King's court . . . for which purpose no great carriage either of vestments or books shall be required,' p. 160. See, too, Jebb, Choral Service of the Church (1843), pp. 147, 148.

l. 14. *In St. Stephen's Chapel* &c.] On the 6th of August, 1348, 22 Edward III, that King, by his royal charter recited, 'that a spacious chapel, situate within the palace of Westminster, in honour of St. Stephen, protomartyr, had been nobly begun by his progenitors and had been completed at his own expense—which he appointed to be collegiate; and that there should be established therein a dean, twelve secular canons, with the same number of vicars and other sufficient ministers, to celebrate divine service for the King, his progenitors and successors for ever.' A statement follows of the endowments successively granted to the above-named dean, canons, and college. 'Canon Row, since by corruption called Channel Row, belonged also to the said dean and canons, where they had sometimes lodged.' This college was suppressed and surrendered in 1 Edward VI. The chapel was soon afterwards fitted up for the meeting of the House of Commons, which had before usually assembled in the Chapter House of the Abbey of Westminster. Dugdale, Monasticon, vi. 1348-49. The chapel was burnt in the fire of 1835.

EXCURSUS D.

LORDS BEFORE THE PARLIAMENT: p. 106. sec. 2.

l. 4. *The Prior of St. John* &c.] 'The Lord Prior here' (i. e. of the Hospital of St. John of Jerusalem near Clerkenwell) 'had precedence of all the lay barons in Parliament, and chief power over all the Preceptories and lesser Houses of this order throughout England.' Dugdale, Monasticon, vi. 799.

In Camden's Britannia (Gough's trans.), the list of abbots who were barons of Parliament ends with 'the Prior of St. John of Jerusalem, commonly called Grand Master of the Knights of St. John, and claiming to be the first baron of England.' Introduction, cap. on Orders in England.

In the sixteenth century, this claim had certainly been admitted. In the Journals of the House of Lords, giving a list of the Lords present at each Parliament in the reign of Henry VIII, the Prior of St. John of Jerusalem appears always among the temporal peers, immediately after the Earls and higher nobles, and above the Barons. This order is invariably observed down to 1536, the date at which the Priory was suppressed, after which the Prior's name disappears from the lists. In 1556 (4 & 5 Phil. and Mary) it reappears in its old place, the Priory having been restored by the Queen, and it finally disappears in the course of 1558 after the accession of Elizabeth. Conf. Journals of the House of Lords, vol. i.

At an earlier date, the Prior's position is not thus fixed. In the Parliamentary Roll of 13 Edward III his name comes last but one in the list of spiritual peers ; the Abbot of Westminster is below him. Conf. Rotuli Parliamentorum, printed by order of the Lords. In the writ of summons to Parliament of 23 Edward I it is clear that the Prior was then included among the spiritual peers. Conf. Dugdale : A perfect copy of all the summonses of the nobility, p. 8 (ed. 1685). In 13 and 49 Henry VI, he is the last of the spiritual barons, and he is addressed as they are in the summons to Parliament—*in fide et dilectione quibus nobis tenemini*; the form for the temporal barons being *in fide et homagio*, p. 161. But, as the head of a military order, his office must at all times have been lay rather than clerical. 'The Templars and Hospitalers,' says Selden, 'were devout soldiers only. . . . Their prayers or devotions in private were not the services expected from them in the Church, but their swords and valour only gave the desert.' Hist. of Tythes, vol. iii. p. 1140.

EXCURSUS E.

Presbytery, sec. 4.   When the queries were sent to the Assembly.

The questions sent (April 1646) were as follows :—

'The House of Commons desires to be satisfied by the Assembly of Divines in the questions following :—

' 1. Whether the Parochial and Congregational Elderships, appointed by ordinance of Parliament, or any other Congregational or Presbyterial Elderships are *jure divino*, and by the will and appointment of Jesus Christ ? and whether any particular Church Government be *jure divino* ? and what that government is ?

' 2. Whether all the members of the said Elderships, as members thereof, or which of them, are *jure divino*, and by the will and appointment of Jesus Christ ?

' 3. Whether the superior Assemblies or Elderships, viz. the Classical, Provincial, and National, whether all, or any of them, and which of them are *jure divino*, and by the will and appointment of Jesus Christ ?

' 4. Whether the appeals from Congregational Elderships to the Classical, Provincial, and National assemblies, or any of them, and to which of them are *jure divino*, and by the will and appointment of Jesus Christ ?

' 5. Whether Œcumenical assemblies are *jure divino* ? and whether there be appeals from any of the former assemblies to the said Œcumenical, *jure divino*, and by the will and appointment of Jesus Christ ?

' 6. Whether by the Word of God the power of judging and declaring what are such notorious and scandalous offences, for which persons guilty thereof are to be kept from the Sacrament of the Lord's Supper, and of conventing before them, trying, and actual suspending from the Sacrament of the Lord's Supper such offenders accordingly, is either in the Congregational Eldership or Presbytery, or in any other Eldership, Congregation, or persons ; and whether such powers are in them only, or any of them, and in which of them, *jure divino*, and by the will and appointment of Jesus Christ ?

' 7. Whether there be any certain and particular rules expressed in the Word of God to direct the Elderships or Presbyteries, Congregations, or persons, or any of them, in the exercise and execution of the powers aforesaid, and what are those rules?

'8. Is there anything contained in the Word of God that the supreme magistracy in a Christian State may not judge and determine what are the aforesaid notorious and scandalous offences, and the manner of suspension for the same ; and in what particulars concerning the premisses is the said supreme magistracy by the Word of God excluded?

'9. Whether the provision of Commissioners to judge of scandals not enumerated (as they are authorized by the ordinance of Parliament) be contrary to that way of government which Christ has appointed in his Church, and wherein are they so contrary?

' In answer to these particulars, the House of Commons desires of the Assembly of Divines their proofs from Scripture, and to set down the several texts of Scripture in the express words of the same : and there were orders added that every Minister present at the debate of any of these questions, shall put his Christian name to the answer, in the affirmative or negative ; and that those who dissent from the major part shall set down their positive opinions, with express texts in proof of them.' Rushworth, Collections, vi. 260.

Selden, who had had a hand in framing these queries, was well aware that search as they would, they would never find answers to them in the text of Scripture.

EXCURSUS F.

ERRORS IN FORMER TEXTS.

I APPEND some instances of obvious blunders in former texts, which have been corrected in this edition on the authority of the Harleian MSS. In 'Holy-Days,' for example, the old reading is: ' Yet that has relation to an Act of Parliament which forbids the keeping of any Holy-days in time of popery.' There is no such Act, and the alleged prohibition is, on the face of it, absurd. The reading, as restored from the MS., is : ' Yet that has relation to an Act of Parliament which forbids the keeping of any other Holy-days. The ground thereof was the

P

multitude of Holy-days in time of popery.' This makes sense, and is in agreement with the language of the Act. Again, in ' King of England,' sec. 5, the old editions of 1689 read : 'The three estates are the Lords Temporal, the Bishops are the clergy, and the Commons, as some would have it [take heed of that] for then if two agree the third is involved, but he is king of the three estates.' This jumble of nonsense is cured in the MS. by the insertion of a full stop after 'Commons.' Then follows : ' The King is not one of the three estates, as some would have it [take heed of that] for then,' &c., &c. In sec. 3 of the same discourse, the reading 'they did *not* much advance the king's supremacy' makes the statement at once incorrect and irrelevant. Again in ' Bishops out of the Parliament ' sec. 13, we have : ' If the *Parliament* and Presbyterian party should dispute, who should be the judge ? ' a question which Selden would certainly never have asked, and which was answered effectively more than once when such a dispute did happen. The reading should be : 'If the Prelatical and Presbyterian party' &c., for, as Selden says (Religion, sec. 10), ' Disputes in religion will never be ended, because there wants a measure by which the business should be decided . . . . One says one thing, and one another: and there is, I say, no measure to end the controversy.'

In 'Learning,' sec. 2, the old reading is : ' Most men's learning is nothing but history duly taken up.' It should be 'dully taken up.'

In ' Oaths,' sec. 3.—' 'Tis to me but reading a paper in *their* own sense ' corrected to ' in *my* own sense,' as the argument clearly requires.

In ' Devils,' sec. 2—' and so all of them *ought* to be of the same trade,' an absolutely unmeaning remark, is corrected in the Harleian MS. 1315 to 'thought to be of the same trade.' But the reading of MS. 690, 'and so think all of them to be of the same trade,' seems preferable here.

In several places a faulty punctuation has marred the sense, as e.g. in ' Devils,' sec. 2—' Why in the likeness of a bat or a rat or some creature ? That is, why not in some shape we paint him in,' &c. This should be ' Why in the likeness of a bat, or a rat, or some creature that is ? ' i.e. some creature that exists and that could therefore be more easily produced on occasion than a real live Devil with claws and horns.

So, too, in 'Bible,' sec. 3, we have: 'There is no book so translated as the Bible for the purpose.' Here the full stop should come after 'the Bible,' and 'For the purpose,' a regular Seldenian phrase = 'for example,' should begin the next clause. Again, in 'Preaching,' sec. 15, we have : ' many things are heard from the preacher with suspicion. They are afraid of some ends, which are easily assented to when they have it from some of themselves.' This piece of nonsense is cured in the MS., which puts a comma after 'suspicion,' brackets off the words [they are afraid of some ends] and thus makes the things easily assented to not 'some ends,' but the things which had been heard from the preacher with suspicion.

There are other changes introduced in the present text, but most of them are wholly unimportant, and adopted only because the MSS. so read. One or two are doubtful, as e.g. 'Treaty' for 'Laity' in 'Clergy,' sec. 6.

EXCURSUS G.

Testimonies to Selden, and Criticisms of Selden's Style.

Dr. Wilkins, in the preface to his edition of Selden's Works, and in his life of the author, has collected proofs of the high esteem in which Selden was held, not only by his own countrymen, but by the learned of all countries.

The following are among the notices which he quotes: 'Grotius eum *honorem Britanniae* appellat. Conringius vocat *virum stupendae lectionis.* Boeclerus ita—*Equidem Seldeni opera laudare velle, nihil aliud esset quam Soli testimonium splendoris meditari.* In Lexico Historico Universali Germanico, quod a J. F. Buddeo appellari solet, dicitur communiter appellatus *magnus dictator doctrinae gentis Anglorum.*' Other testimonies follow. See Works, vol. i. *Præfatio,* pp. 1 & 11, and *Vita authoris,* p. xlix.

If I have ventured in my Introduction to speak disparagingly of Selden's style and method, I have good warrant for what I have said. Clarendon, e.g., writes,—'His style in all his writings seems harsh and sometimes obscure : which is not wholly to be imputed to the abstruse subjects of which he commonly treated, out of the paths trod by other men ; but to a little undervaluing the beauty of a style, and too much propensity to the language of antiquity.'   Clarendon, Life, i. p. 35.

Le Clerc writes more severely—'*Selden, un des plus savans que l'Angleterre ait eus, est l'un de ceux qui gardoit le moins ce que l'on a dit touchant l'ordre, ce qui fait que ses écrits, quoique savans et utiles, sont lus par peu de gens d'un bout à l'autre*' : and again—'*Quoique je ne voulusse pas imiter la methode confuse, ni le stile de Selden . . . . les bonnes choses qu'il dit, et l'erudition qu'il fait paroitre par tout, surpassent de beaucoup en utilité ce qu'il y a d'ailleurs defectueux dans ses ouvrages.*'   Most severe of all is the judgment in the Ars Critica—'Apparet eum ita studia sua perturbasse, ut eodem tempore de rebus toto genere diversis cogitaret ; digressiones enim captat adeo remotas, et interdum tam longas, ut nisi ita studia instituisset, non potuisset tantam ordinis et rerum perturbationem ferre.   Ac sane dum ordinem et perspicuitatem negligit, non parum taedii lectoribus creat.'   And Le Clerc goes on to complain that where Selden errs, as he is said to do in some parts of the De Synedriis Veterum Ebraeorum, it is hardly possible to trace out how he has got wrong, since ' confusio, digressiones, testimonia aliena, et immensa illa eruditionis congesta farrago, facile fucum faciunt, et perspicaces etiam obruunt.'   Quoted in Works, vol. i. *Prefatio*, p. 2.

INDEX

THE END.

Clarendon Press, Oxford.

I. LITERATURE AND PHILOLOGY.

SECTION I.

DICTIONARIES, GRAMMARS, &c.

ANGLO-SAXON. An Anglo-Saxon Dictionary, based on the MS. Collections of the late JOSEPH BOSWORTH, D.D., Professor of Anglo-Saxon, Oxford. Edited and enlarged by Prof. T. N. TOLLER, M.A. Parts I–III. A—SAR. 4to, 15*s.* each. Part IV. Sect. I. SAR–SWIDRIAN. 8*s.* 6*d.*

ARABIC. A Practical Arabic Grammar. Part I. Compiled by A. O. GREEN, Brigade Major, Royal Engineers. *Second Edition, Enlarged.* Crown 8vo, 7*s.* 6*d.*

BENGALI. Grammar of the Bengali Language; Literary and Colloquial. By JOHN BEAMES. Crown 8vo, cloth, 4*s.* 6*d.*

CELTIC. Ancient Cornish Drama. Edited and translated by E. NORRIS, with a Sketch of Cornish Grammar, an Ancient Cornish Vocabulary, &c. 2 vols. 8vo, 1*l.* 1*s.*
> The Sketch of Cornish Grammar separately, stitched, 2*s.* 6*d.*

CHINESE. A Handbook of the Chinese Language. By JAMES SUMMERS. 8vo, half-bound, 1*l.* 8*s.*

ENGLISH. A New English Dictionary, on Historical Principles: founded mainly on the materials collected by the Philological Society. Vol. I. A and B. Imperial 4to, half-morocco, 2*l.* 12*s.* 6*d.*
> Part IV. Section II. C—CASS (beginning of Vol. II). 5*s.*
> Part V. CAST—CLIVY. 12*s.* 6*d.*
> Part VI. CLO—CONSIGNER. 12*s.* 6*d.*
Edited by JAMES A. H. MURRAY, LL.D.

Vol. III. Part I. E—EVERY. Edited by H. BRADLEY, M.A. 12*s.* 6*d.*

Oxford: Clarendon Press. London: HENRY FROWDE, Amen Corner, E.C
14.9.92.   B

ENGLISH (*continued*).

ENGLISH. An Etymological Dictionary of the English Language. By W. W. Skeat, Litt.D. *Second Edition.* 4to, 2l. 4s.

—— A Concise Etymological Dictionary of the English Language. By W. W. Skeat, Litt.D. *Fourth Edition.* Crown 8vo, 5s. 6d.

—— A Concise Dictionary of Middle English, from A.D. 1150 to 1580. By A. L. Mayhew, M.A., and W. W. Skeat, Litt. D. Crown 8vo, half-roan, 7s. 6d.

—— A Middle English Dictionary. By Francis Henry Stratmann. *A New Edition*, Re-arranged, Revised, and Enlarged by Henry Bradley, M.A. Small 4to, 1l. 11s. 6d.

—— A Primer of Spoken English. By Henry Sweet, M.A., Ph.D. Extra fcap. 8vo, 3s. 6d.

—— A New English Grammar, Logical and Historical. By Henry Sweet, M.A., Ph.D. Part I. Introduction, Phonology, and Accidence. Crown 8vo, 10s. 6d.

—— A Primer of Phonetics. By Henry Sweet, M.A., Ph.D. Extra fcap. 8vo, 3s. 6d.

—— Elementarbuch des Gesprochenen Englisch. Grammatik, Texte und Glossar. By Henry Sweet, M.A., Ph.D. *Second Edition.* Extra fcap. 8vo, stiff covers, 2s. 6d.

FINNISH. A Finnish Grammar. By C. N. E. Eliot, M.A. Crown 8vo, roan, 10s. 6d.

GOTHIC. A Primer of the Gothic Language; with Grammar, Notes, and Glossary. By Joseph Wright, Ph.D. Extra fcap. 8vo, cloth, 4s. 6d.

GREEK. A Greek-English Lexicon, by H. G. Liddell, D.D., and Robert Scott, D.D. *Seventh Edition, Revised and Augmented throughout.* 4to, 1l. 16s.

—— An Intermediate Greek-English Lexicon, founded upon the Seventh Edition of the above. Small 4to, 12s. 6d.

—— A Greek-English Lexicon, abridged from Liddell and Scott's 4to edition, chiefly for the use of Schools. Square 12mo, 7s. 6d.

GREEK. **A Concordance to the Septuagint** and the other Greek Versions of the Old Testament (including the Apocryphal Books). By the late EDWIN HATCH, M.A., and HENRY REDPATH, M.A. Part I. A–ΒΩΡΙ'Θ. Imperial 4to, 21s. Part II. *In the Press.*

—— A copious Greek-English Vocabulary, compiled from the best authorities. 24mo, 3s.

—— **Etymologicon Magnum.** Ad Codd. mss. recensuit et notis variorum instruxit T. GAISFORD, S.T.P. 1848. fol. 1l. 12s.

—— **Suidae Lexicon.** Ad Codd. mss. recensuit T. GAISFORD, S.T.P. Tomi III. 1834. fol. 2l. 2s.

HEBREW. **Gesenius' Hebrew and English Lexicon** of the Old Testament, with an Appendix containing the Biblical Aramaic. Translated and Edited by E. ROBINSON, FRANCIS BROWN, S. R. DRIVER, and C. A. BRIGGS. Part I (Aleph). Small 4to, 2s. 6d.—Part II. *Immediately.*

—— The Book of Hebrew Roots, by ABU 'L-WALÎD MARWÂN IBN JANÂH, otherwise called RABBÎ YÔNÂH. Now first edited, with an Appendix, by AD. NEUBAUER. 4to, 2l. 7s. 6d.

—— A Treatise on the use of the Tenses in Hebrew. By S. R. DRIVER, D.D. *Third Edition.* Crown 8vo, 7s. 6d.

ICELANDIC. An Icelandic-English Dictionary, based on the MS. collections of the late RICHARD CLEASBY. Enlarged and completed by G. VIGFÚSSON, M.A. 4to, 3l. 7s.

—— A List of English Words the Etymology of which is illustrated by comparison with Icelandic. Prepared in the form of an Appendix to the above. By W. W. SKEAT, Litt.D. Stitched, 2s.

—— An Icelandic Primer, with Grammar, Notes, and Glossary. By HENRY SWEET, M.A., Ph.D. Extra fcap. 8vo, 3s. 6d.

——An Icelandic Prose Reader, with Notes, Grammar, and Glossary, by Dr. GUDBRAND VIGFÚSSON and F. YORK POWELL, M.A. Extra fcap. 8vo, 10s. 6d.

LATIN. A Latin Dictionary, founded on Andrews' edition of Freund's Latin Dictionary, revised, enlarged, and in great part rewritten by CHARLTON T. LEWIS, Ph.D., and CHARLES SHORT, LL.D. 4to, 1l. 5s.

—— A School Latin Dictionary. By CHARLTON T. LEWIS, Ph.D. Small 4to, 18s.

—— An Elementary Latin Dictionary. By CHARLTON T. LEWIS, Ph.D. Square 8vo, 7s. 6d.

London : HENRY FROWDE, Amen Corner, E.C.

LATIN. Scheller's Dictionary of the Latin Language, revised and translated into English by J. E. RIDDLE, M.A. 1835. fol. 1*l.* 1*s.*

—— Contributions to Latin Lexicography. By HENRY NETTLESHIP, M.A. 8vo, 21*s.*

MELANESIAN. The Melanesian Languages. By ROBERT H. CODRINGTON, D.D., of the Melanesian Mission. 8vo, 18*s.*

RUSSIAN. A Grammar of the Russian Language. By W. R. MORFILL, M.A. Crown 8vo, 6*s.*

SANSKRIT. A Practical Grammar of the Sanskrit Language, arranged with reference to the Classical Languages of Europe, for the use of English Students, by Sir M. MONIER-WILLIAMS, D.C.L. *Fourth Edition.* 8vo, 15*s.*

—— A Sanskrit-English Dictionary, Etymologically and Philologically arranged, with special reference to Greek, Latin, German, Anglo-Saxon, English, and other cognate Indo-European Languages. By Sir M. MONIER-WILLIAMS, D.C.L. 4to, 4*l.* 14*s.* 6*d.*

—— Nalopákhyánam. Story of Nala, an Episode of the Mahá-Bhárata : the Sanskrit text, with a copious Vocabulary, and an improved version of Dean MILMAN's Translation, by Sir M. MONIER-WILLIAMS, D.C.L. *Second Edition, Revised and Improved.* 8vo, 15*s.*

—— Sakuntalá. A Sanskrit Drama, in Seven Acts. Edited by Sir M. MONIER-WILLIAMS, D.C.L. *Second Edition.* 8vo, 21*s.*

SYRIAC. Thesaurus Syriacus: collegerunt Quatremère, Bernstein, Lorsbach, Arnoldi, Agrell, Field, Roediger: edidit R. PAYNE SMITH, S.T.P. Vol. I, containing Fasc. I–V, sm. fol. 5*l.* 5*s.*
　　Fasc. VI, 1*l.* 1*s.* Fasc. VII, 1*l.* 11*s.* 6*d.* Fasc. VIII, 1*l.* 16*s.*

TAMIL. First Lessons in Tamil. By G. U. POPE, D.D. *Fifth Edition.* Crown 8vo, 7*s.* 6*d.*

BIBLIOGRAPHICAL DICTIONARIES.

Cotton's Typographical Gazetteer. 1831. 8vo, 12*s.* 6*d.*

—— Typographical Gazetteer. Second Series. 1866. 8vo, 12*s.* 6*d.*

Ebert's Bibliographical Dictionary, translated from the German. 4 vols. 1837. 8vo, 1*l.* 10*s.*

SECTION II.

ANGLO-SAXON AND ENGLISH.

—•◦•—

HELPS TO THE STUDY OF THE LANGUAGE AND LITERATURE.

—•◦•—

A NEW ENGLISH DICTIONARY on Historical Principles, founded mainly on the materials collected by the Philological Society. Imperial 4to. Parts I–IV, price 12s. 6d. each.

Vol. I (A and B), half-morocco, 2l. 12s. 6d.

Vol. II (C and D). *In the Press.*

Part IV, Section 2, **C—CASS**, beginning Vol. II, price 5s.

Part V, **CAST—CLIVY**, price 12s. 6d.

Part VI, **CLO—CONSIGNER**, price 12s. 6d.

Edited by JAMES A. H. MURRAY, LL.D.

Vol. III. Part I. **E—EVERY**. Edited by H. BRADLEY, M.A. 12s. 6d.

Bosworth and Toller. An Anglo-Saxon Dictionary, based on the MS. collections of the late JOSEPH BOSWORTH, D.D. Edited and enlarged by Prof. T. N. TOLLER, M.A. Parts I–III. A—SAR. 4to, stiff covers, 15s. each. Part IV. Sect. I. SÁR—SWÍDRIAN. 8s. 6d.

Earle. A Book for the Beginner in Anglo-Saxon. By JOHN EARLE, M.A. *Third Edition.* Extra fcap. 8vo, 2s. 6d.

—— The Philology of the English Tongue. *Fifth Edition, Newly Revised.* Extra fcap. 8vo, 8s. 6d.

Mayhew. Synopsis of Old English Phonology. By A. L. MAYHEW, M.A. Extra fcap. 8vo, bevelled boards, 8s. 6d.

Mayhew and Skeat. A Concise Dictionary of Middle English, from A.D. 1150 to 1580. By A. L. MAYHEW, M.A., and W. W. SKEAT, Litt.D. Crown 8vo, half-roan, 7s. 6d.

London : HENRY FROWDE, Amen Corner, E.C.

Skeat. An Etymological Dictionary of the English Language, arranged on an Historical Basis. By W. W. SKEAT, Litt.D. *Second Edition.* 4to, 2*l.* 4*s.*

    A Supplement to the First Edition of the above. 4to, 2*s.* 6*d.*

—— A Concise Etymological Dictionary of the English Language. *Fourth Edition.* Crown 8vo, 5*s.* 6*d.*

—— Principles of English Etymology. First Series. *The Native Element.* Second Edition. Crown 8vo, 10*s.* 6*d.*

—— Principles of English Etymology. Second Series. *The Foreign Element.* Crown 8vo, 10*s.* 6*d.*

—— A Primer of English Etymology. Extra fcap. 8vo, stiff covers, 1*s.* 6*d.*

—— Twelve Facsimiles of Old English Manuscripts, with Transcriptions and an Introduction. 4to, paper covers, 7*s.* 6*d.*

Stratmann. A Middle English Dictionary, containing Words used by English Writers from the Twelfth to the Fifteenth Century. By FRANCIS HENRY STRATMANN. *A New Edition*, Re-arranged, Revised, and Enlarged by HENRY BRADLEY, M.A. Small 4to, 1*l.* 11*s.* 6*d.*

Sweet. An Anglo-Saxon Primer, with Grammar, Notes, and Glossary. By HENRY SWEET, M.A., Ph.D. *Second Edition.* Extra fcap. 8vo, 2*s.* 6*d.*

—— An Anglo-Saxon Reader. In Prose and Verse. With Grammatical Introduction, Notes, and Glossary. *Sixth Edition, Revised and Enlarged.* Extra fcap. 8vo, 8*s.* 6*d.*

—— A Second Anglo-Saxon Reader. Extra fcap. 8vo, 4*s.* 6*d.* ·

—— Old English Reading Primers :

    I. Selected Homilies of Ælfric. Stiff covers, 1*s.* 6*d.*
    II. Extracts from Alfred's Orosius. Stiff covers, 1*s.* 6*d.*

—— First Middle English Primer, with Grammar and Glossary. Extra fcap, 8vo, 2*s.*

—— Second Middle English Primer. Extracts from Chaucer, with Grammar and Glossary. *Second Edition.* Extra fcap. 8vo, 2*s.* 6*d.*

—— History of English Sounds from the Earliest Period. With full Word-Lists. 8vo, 14*s.*

Oxford : Clarendon Press.

Sweet. A Primer of Spoken English. Extra fcap. 8vo, 3*s*. 6*d*.

—— A New English Grammar, Logical and Historical. Part I. Introduction, Phonology, and Accidence. Crown 8vo, 10*s*. 6*d*.

—— A Primer of Phonetics. Extra fcap. 8vo, 3*s*. 6*d*.

—— Elementarbuch des Gesprochenen Englisch. Grammatik, Texte und Glossar. *Second Edition.* Extra fcap. 8vo, stiff covers, 2*s*. 6*d*.

Tancock. An Elementary English Grammar and Exercise Book. By O. W. TANCOCK, M.A. *Second Edition.* Extra fcap. 8vo, 1*s*. 6*d*.

—— An English Grammar and Reading Book, for Lower Forms in Classical Schools. *Fourth Edition.* Extra fcap. 8vo, 3*s*. 6*d*.

Saxon Chronicles. Two of the Saxon Chronicles Parallel; with Supplementary Extracts from the others. A Revised Text. Edited, with Introduction, Notes, Appendices, and Glossary. By C. PLUMMER, M.A., and J. EARLE, M.A. Vol. I. Text, Appendices, and Glossary. 10*s*. 6*d*.

—— —— (787–1001 A.D.) Crown 8vo, stiff covers, 3*s*.

Specimens of Early English. A New and Revised Edition. With Introduction, Notes, and Glossarial Index.

Part I. From Old English Homilies to King Horn (A.D. 1150 to A.D. 1300). By R. MORRIS, LL.D. *Second Edition.* Extra fcap. 8vo, 9*s*.

Part II. From Robert of Gloucester to Gower (A.D. 1298 to A.D. 1393). By R. MORRIS, LL.D., and W. W. SKEAT, Litt. D. *Third Edition.* Extra fcap. 8vo, 7*s*. 6*d*.

Specimens of English Literature, from the 'Ploughman's Crede' to the 'Shepheardes Calender' (A.D. 1394 to A.D. 1579). With Introduction, Notes, and Glossarial Index. By W. W. SKEAT, Litt.D. *Fifth Edition.* Extra fcap. 8vo, 7*s*. 6*d*.

Typical Selections from the best English Writers, with Introductory Notices. In 2 vols. Extra fcap. 8vo, 3*s*. 6*d*. each.

Vol. I. Latimer to Berkeley.   Vol. II. Pope to Macaulay.

A SERIES OF ENGLISH CLASSICS.

Beowulf, The Deeds of. An English Epic of the Eighth Century done into Modern Prose. With an Introduction and Notes, by JOHN EARLE, M.A. Crown 8vo, 8*s*. 6*d*.

Ormulum, The, with the Notes and Glossary of Dr. R. M. WHITE. Edited by R. HOLT, M.A. 2 vols. Extra fcap. 8vo, 1*l*. 1*s*.

CHAUCER.

I. The Prologue to the Canterbury Tales. (School Edition.) Edited by W. W. SKEAT, Litt.D. Extra fcap. 8vo, 1*s*.

II. The Prologue, the Knightes Tale, The Nonne Preestes Tale; from the Canterbury Tales. Edited by R. MORRIS, LL.D. A New Edition, with Collations and Additional Notes by W. W. SKEAT, Litt.D. Extra fcap. 8vo, 2*s*. 6*d*.

III. The Prioresses Tale; Sir Thopas; The Monkes Tale; The Clerkes Tale; The Squieres Tale, &c. Edited by W. W. SKEAT, Litt.D. *Fifth Edition.* Extra fcap. 8vo, 4*s*. 6*d*.

IV. The Tale of the Man of Lawe; The Pardoneres Tale; The Second Nonnes Tale; The Chanouns Yemannes Tale. By W. W. SKEAT, Litt.D. *New Edition.* Extra fcap. 8vo, 4*s*. 6*d*.

V. Minor Poems. Edited by W. W. SKEAT, Litt.D. Crown 8vo, 10*s*. 6*d*.

VI. The Legend of Good Women. Edited by W. W. SKEAT, Litt.D. Crown 8vo, 6*s*.

Langland, W. The Vision of William concerning Piers the Plowman, in three Parallel Texts; together with Richard the Redeless. By WILLIAM LANGLAND (about 1362–1399 A.D.). Edited from numerous Manuscripts, with Preface, Notes, and a Glossary, by W. W. SKEAT, Litt.D. 2 vols. 8vo, 1*l*. 11*s*. 6*d*.

—— The Vision of William concerning Piers the Plowman, by WILLIAM LANGLAND. Edited, with Notes, by W. W. SKEAT, Litt.D. *Fourth Edition.* Extra fcap. 8vo, 4*s*. 6*d*.

Gamelyn, The Tale of. Edited, with Notes, Glossary, &c., by W. W. SKEAT, Litt.D. Extra fcap. 8vo, stiff covers, 1*s*. 6*d*.

Oxford: Clarendon Press.

WYCLIFFE.

I. The Books of Job, Psalms, Proverbs, Ecclesiastes, and the Song of Solomon: according to the Wycliffite Version made by NICHOLAS DE HEREFORD, about A.D. 1381, and Revised by JOHN PURVEY, about A.D. 1388. With Introduction and Glossary by W. W. SKEAT, Litt.D. Extra fcap. 8vo, 3*s. 6d.*

II. The New Testament in English, according to the Version by JOHN WYCLIFFE, about A.D. 1380, and Revised by JOHN PURVEY, about A.D. 1388. With Introduction and Glossary by W. W. SKEAT, Litt.D. Extra fcap. 8vo, 6*s.*

Minot (Laurence). Poems. Edited, with Introduction and Notes, by JOSEPH HALL, M.A., Head Master of the Hulme Grammar School, Manchester. Extra fcap. 8vo, 4*s. 6d.*

Spenser's Faery Queene. Books I and II. Designed chiefly for the use of Schools. With Introduction and Notes by G. W. KITCHIN, D.D., and Glossary by A. L. MAYHEW, M.A. Extra fcap. 8vo, 2*s. 6d.* each.

Hooker. Ecclesiastical Polity, Book I. Edited by R. W. CHURCH, M.A. Extra fcap. 8vo, 2*s.* [See also p. 53.]

OLD ENGLISH DRAMA.

I. York Plays.—The Plays performed by the Crafts or Mysteries of York, on the day of Corpus Christi, in the 14th, 15th, and 16th centuries; now first printed from the unique manuscript in the library of Lord Ashburnham. Edited, with Introduction and Glossary, by LUCY TOULMIN SMITH. 8vo, 1*l.* 1*s.*

II. English Miracle Plays, Moralities, and Interludes. Specimens of the Pre-Elizabethan Drama. Edited, with an Introduction, Notes, and Glossary, by ALFRED W. POLLARD, M.A. Crown 8vo, 7*s. 6d.*

III. The Pilgrimage to Parnassus, with the Two Parts of the Return from Parnassus. Three Comedies performed in St. John's College, Cambridge, A.D. MDXCVII-MDCI. Edited from MSS. by W. D. MACRAY, M.A., F.S.A. Medium 8vo, bevelled boards, gilt top, 8*s. 6d.*

IV. Marlowe's Edward II. With Introduction, Notes, &c. By O. W. TANCOCK, M.A. Extra fcap. 8vo, paper, 2*s.*; cloth, 3*s.*

V. Marlowe and Greene. Marlowe's Tragical History of Dr. Faustus, and Greene's Honourable History of Friar Bacon and Friar Bungay. Edited by A. W. WARD, Litt. D. *New and enlarged Edition.* Crown 8vo, 6*s. 6d.*

London : HENRY FROWDE, Amen Corner, E.C.

SHAKESPEARE. Select Plays. Extra fcap. 8vo, stiff covers.

Edited by W. G. CLARK, M.A., and W. ALDIS WRIGHT, D.C.L.

The Merchant of Venice. 1*s*.	Macbeth. 1*s*. 6*d*.
Richard the Second. 1*s*. 6*d*.	Hamlet. 2*s*.

Edited by W. ALDIS WRIGHT, D.C.L.

The Tempest. 1*s*. 6*d*.	Midsummer Night's Dream. 1*s*. 6*d*.
As You Like It. 1*s*. 6*d*.	Coriolanus. 2*s*. 6*d*.
Julius Caesar. 2*s*.	Henry the Fifth. 2*s*.
Richard the Third. 2*s*. 6*d*.	Twelfth Night. 1*s*. 6*d*.
King Lear. 1*s*. 6*d*.	King John. 1*s*. 6*d*.
	Henry the Eighth. 2*s*.

Shakespeare as a Dramatic Artist; a popular Illustration of the Principles of Scientific Criticism. By R. G. MOULTON, M.A. *Second Edition, Enlarged.* Crown 8vo, 6*s*.

Bacon.

I. Advancement of Learning. Edited by W. ALDIS WRIGHT, D.C.L. *Third Edition.* Extra fcap. 8vo, 4*s*. 6*d*.

II. The Essays. Edited, with Introduction and Illustrative Notes, by S. H. REYNOLDS, M.A. 8vo, half-bound, 12*s*. 6*d*.

MILTON.

I. Areopagitica. With Introduction and Notes. By JOHN W. HALES, M.A. *Third Edition.* Extra fcap. 8vo, 3*s*.

II. Poems. Edited by R. C. BROWNE, M.A. In two Volumes. *Fifth Edition.* Extra fcap. 8vo, 6*s*. 6*d*.
Sold separately, Vol. I, 4*s*.; Vol. II, 3*s*.

In paper covers:

Lycidas, 3*d*.   L'Allegro, 3*d*.   Il Penseroso, 4*d*.   Comus, 6*d*.

III. Paradise Lost. Book I. Edited by H. C. BEECHING, B.A. Extra fcap. 8vo, stiff covers, 1*s*. 6*d*.; in Parchment, 3*s*. 6*d*.

IV. Samson Agonistes. Edited, with Introduction and Notes, by J. CHURTON COLLINS, M.A. Extra fcap. 8vo, stiff covers, 1*s*.

Bunyan.

I. The Pilgrim's Progress, Grace Abounding, Relation of the Imprisonment of Mr. JOHN BUNYAN. Edited, with Biographical Introduction and Notes, by E. VENABLES, M.A. Extra fcap. 8vo, cloth, 3s. 6d.; in Parchment, 4s. 6d.

II. The Holy War, and The Heavenly Footman. Edited by MABEL PEACOCK. Extra fcap. 8vo, 3s. 6d.

Fuller. Wise Words and Quaint Counsels of Thomas Fuller. Selected by AUGUSTUS JESSOPP, D.D. Crown 8vo, 6s. *Immediately.*

Clarendon.

I. History of the Rebellion. Book VI. Edited by T. ARNOLD, M.A. Extra fcap. 8vo, 4s. 6d.

II. Characters and Episodes of the Great Rebellion. Selections from Clarendon. Edited by G. BOYLE, M.A., Dean of Salisbury. Crown 8vo, gilt top, 7s. 6d. [See also p. 56.]

Dryden. Select Poems. (Stanzas on the Death of Oliver Cromwell; Astraea Redux; Annus Mirabilis; Absalom and Achitophel; Religio Laici; The Hind and the Panther.) Edited by W. D. CHRISTIE, M.A. *Second Edition.* Extra fcap. 8vo, 3s. 6d.

—— An Essay of Dramatic Poesy. Edited, with Notes, by THOMAS ARNOLD, M.A. Extra fcap. 8vo, 3s. 6d.

Locke. Conduct of the Understanding. Edited, with Introduction, Notes, &c., by T. FOWLER, D.D. *Third Edition.* Extra fcap. 8vo, 2s. 6d.

Addison. Selections from Papers in the Spectator. With Notes. By T. ARNOLD, M.A. Extra fcap. 8vo, 4s. 6d.; in Parchment, 6s.

Steele. Selections from the Tatler, Spectator, and Guardian. Edited by AUSTIN DOBSON. Extra fcap. 8vo, 5s.; in Parchment, 7s. 6d.

Swift. Selections from his Works. Edited, with Life, Introductions, and Notes, by HENRY CRAIK. In two Volumes. Crown 8vo. Vol. I. Bevelled boards, gilt top, 7s. 6d. Vol. II. *Immediately.*

Pope. Select Works. With Introduction and Notes. By MARK PATTISON, B.D.

I. Essay on Man. Extra fcap. 8vo, 1s. 6d.

II. Satires and Epistles. Extra fcap. 8vo, 2s.

Parnell. The Hermit. Paper covers, 2d.

Thomson. The Seasons, and The Castle of Indolence. Edited by J. LOGIE ROBERTSON, M.A. Extra fcap. 8vo, 4s. 6d.

—— The Castle of Indolence. By the same Editor. Extra fcap. 8vo, 1s. 6d.

London : HENRY FROWDE, Amen Corner, E.C.

Gray. Selected Poems. Edited by EDMUND GOSSE, M.A.
Extra fcap. 8vo. In Parchment, 3*s.*

—— *The same*, together with Supplementary Notes for
Schools, by FOSTER WATSON, M.A. Stiff covers, 1*s.* 6*d.*

—— Elegy, and Ode on Eton College. Paper covers, 2*d.*

Chesterfield. Lord Chesterfield's Worldly Wisdom. Selections from his Letters and Characters. Edited by G. BIRKBECK HILL,
D.C.L. Crown 8vo, 6*s.*

Goldsmith.

    I. Selected Poems. Edited with Introduction and Notes, by
AUSTIN DOBSON. Extra fcap. 8vo, 3*s.* 6*d.* ; in Parchment, 4*s.* 6*d.*

    II. The Traveller. Edited by G. BIRKBECK HILL, D.C.L.
Stiff covers, 1*s.*

    III. The Deserted Village. Paper covers, 2*d.*

JOHNSON.

    I. Rasselas. Edited, with Introduction and Notes, by
G. BIRKBECK HILL, D.C.L. Extra fcap. 8vo, bevelled boards, 3*s.* 6*d.* ;
in Parchment, 4*s.* 6*d.*

    II. Rasselas ; Lives of Dryden and Pope. Edited by
ALFRED MILNES, M.A. (London). Extra fcap. 8vo, 4*s.* 6*d.* ; or Lives
of DRYDEN and POPE only, stiff covers, 2*s.* 6*d.*

    III. Life of Milton. Edited by C. H. FIRTH, M.A. Extra
fcap. 8vo, cloth, 2*s.* 6*d.* ; stiff covers, 1*s.* 6*d.*

    IV. Wit and Wisdom of Samuel Johnson. Edited by
G. BIRKBECK HILL, D.C.L. Crown 8vo, 7*s.* 6*d.*

    V. Vanity of Human Wishes. With Notes, by E. J.
PAYNE, M.A. Paper covers, 4*d.*

    VI. Letters of Samuel Johnson, LL.D. Collected and
Edited by G. BIRKBECK HILL, D.C.L. 2 vols. Medium 8vo, half-
roan, 28*s.*

BOSWELL.

    Boswell's Life of Johnson. With the Journal of a
Tour to the Hebrides. Edited by G. BIRKBECK HILL, D.C.L., Pem-
broke College. 6 vols. Medium 8vo, half-bound, 3*l.* 3*s.*

Cowper. Edited, with Life, Introductions, and Notes, by
H. T. GRIFFITH, B.A.

    I. The Didactic Poems of 1782, with Selections from
the Minor Pieces, A.D. 1779–1783. Extra fcap. 8vo, 3*s.*

    II. The Task, with Tirocinium, and Selections from the
Minor Poems, A.D. 1784–1799. *Second Edition.* Extra fcap. 8vo, 3*s.*

Burke. Select Works. Edited, with Introduction and Notes, by E. J. PAYNE, M.A.

    I. Thoughts on the Present Discontents; the two Speeches on America. *Second Edition.* Extra fcap. 8vo, 4*s*. 6*d*.

    II. Reflections on the French Revolution. *Second Edition.* Extra fcap. 8vo, 5*s*.

    III. Four Letters on the Proposals for Peace with the Regicide Directory of France. *Second Edition.* Extra fcap. 8vo, 5*s*.

Burns. Selected Poems. Edited, with Introduction, Notes, and a Glossary, by J. LOGIE ROBERTSON, M.A. Crown 8vo, 6*s*.

Keats. Hyperion, Book I. With Notes by W. T. ARNOLD, B.A. Paper covers, 4*d*.

Byron. Childe Harold. With Introduction and Notes, by H. F. TOZER, M.A. *Second Edition.* Extra fcap. 8vo, 3*s*. 6*d*.; in Parchment, 5*s*.

Scott. Lady of the Lake. Edited, with Preface and Notes, by W. MINTO, M.A. Extra fcap. 8vo,

—— Lay of the Last Mins̶t̶r̶e̶l̶. ̶B̶y̶ ̶t̶h̶e̶ same Editor. With Map. Extra fcap. 8vo, 2*s*. ; ̶ ̶ ̶ ̶ ̶ ̶ ̶ 6*d*.

—— Lay of the Last Mins̶t̶r̶e̶l̶. ̶I̶n̶t̶r̶o̶d̶u̶c̶t̶i̶o̶n̶ ̶a̶nd Canto I, with Preface and Notes, by the

—— Marmion. Edited, with Introduction and Notes, by T. BAYNE. Extra fcap. 8vo, 3*s*. 6*d*.

Shelley. Adonais. Edited, with Introduction and Notes, by W. M. ROSSETTI. Crown 8vo, 5*s*.

Campbell. Gertrude of Wyoming. Edited, with Introduction and Notes, by H. MACAULAY FITZGIBBON, M.A. Extra fcap. 8vo, 1*s*.

Wordsworth. The White Doe of Rylstone, &c. Edited by WILLIAM KNIGHT, LL.D. Extra fcap. 8vo, 2*s*. 6*d*.

Shairp. Aspects of Poetry; being Lectures delivered at Oxford, by J. C. SHAIRP, LL.D. Crown 8vo, 10*s*. 6*d*.

Palgrave. The Treasury of Sacred Song. With Notes Explanatory and Biographical. By F. T. PALGRAVE, M.A. *Thirteenth Thousand.* Extra fcap. 8vo, 4*s*. 6*d*.

London : HENRY FROWDE, Amen Corner, E.C.

SECTION III.

EUROPEAN LANGUAGES, MEDIAEVAL AND MODERN.

(1) FRENCH AND ITALIAN.

Brachet's Etymological Dictionary of the French Language. Translated by G. W. Kitchin, D.D. *Third Edition.* Crown 8vo, 7s. 6d.

—— Historical Grammar of the French Language. Translated by G. W. Kitchin, D.D. *Fourth Edition.* Extra fcap. 8vo, 3s. 6d.

Saintsbury. Primer of French Literature. By George Saintsbury, M.A. Extra fcap. 8vo, 2s.

—— Short History of French Literature. *Third Edition.* Crown 8vo, 10s. 6d.

—— Specimens of French Literature, from Villon to Hugo. *Second Edition.* Crown 8vo, 9s.

Song of Dermot and the Earl. An Old French Poem. Edited, with Translation, Notes, &c., by G. H. Orpen. Extra fcap. 8vo, 8s. 6d.

Toynbee. Specimens of Old French (ix–xv centuries). With Introduction, Notes, and Glossary. By Paget Toynbee, M.A. Crown 8vo, 16s.

Beaumarchais' Le Barbier de Séville. Edited, with Introduction and Notes, by Austin Dobson. Extra fcap. 8vo, 2s. 6d.

Corneille's Horace. Edited, with Introduction and Notes, by George Saintsbury, M.A. Extra fcap. 8vo, 2s. 6d.

Molière's Les Précieuses Ridicules. Edited, with Introduction and Notes, by Andrew Lang, M.A. Extra fcap. 8vo, 1s. 6d.

Musset's On ne badine pas avec l'Amour, and Fantasio. Edited, with Prolegomena, Notes, &c., by W. H. Pollock. Extra fcap. 8vo, 2s.

Racine's Esther. Edited, with Introduction and Notes, by GEORGE SAINTSBURY, M.A. Extra fcap. 8vo, 2s.

Voltaire's Mérope. Edited, with Introduction and Notes, by GEORGE SAINTSBURY, M.A. Extra fcap. 8vo, 2s.

*** *The above six Plays may be had in ornamental case, and bound in Imitation Parchment, price 12s. 6d.*

Molière. Le Misanthrope. Edited by W. H. G. MARKHEIM, M.A. Extra fcap. 8vo, 3s. 6d.

MASSON'S FRENCH CLASSICS.

Edited by Gustave Masson, B.A.

Corneille's Cinna. With Notes, Glossary, &c. Extra fcap. 8vo, 2s.; stiff covers, 1s. 6d.

Louis XIV and his Contemporaries; as described in Extracts from the best Memoirs of the Seventeenth Century. With English Notes, Genealogical Tables, &c. Extra fcap. 8vo, 2s. 6d.

Maistre, Xavier de, &c. Voyage autour de ma Chambre, by XAVIER DE MAISTRE; Ourika, by MADAME DE DURAS; Le Vieux Tailleur, by MM. ERCKMANN-CHATRIAN; La Veillée de Vincennes, by ALFRED DE VIGNY; Les Jumeaux de l'Hôtel Corneille, by EDMOND ABOUT; Mésaventures d'un Écolier, by RODOLPHE TÖPFFER. *Third Edition, Revised.* Extra fcap. 8vo, 2s. 6d.

—— Voyage autour de ma Chambre. Limp, 1s. 6d.

Molière's Les Fourberies de Scapin, and **Racine's** Athalie. With Voltaire's Life of Molière. Extra fcap. 8vo, 2s. 6d.

—— Les Fourberies de Scapin. With Voltaire's Life of Molière. Extra fcap. 8vo, stiff covers, 1s. 6d.

—— Les Femmes Savantes. With Notes, Glossary, &c. Extra fcap. 8vo, cloth, 2s.; stiff covers, 1s. 6d.

Racine's Andromaque, and **Corneille's** Le Menteur. With LOUIS RACINE's Life of his Father. Extra fcap. 8vo, 2s. 6d.

Regnard's Le Joueur, and **Brueys and Palaprat's** Le Grondeur. Extra fcap. 8vo, 2s. 6d.

Sévigné, Madame de, and her chief Contemporaries, Selections from their Correspondence. Extra fcap. 8vo, 3s.

London : HENRY FROWDE, Amen Corner, E.C.

Blouët. L'Éloquence de la Chaire et de la Tribune Françaises. Edited by PAUL BLOUËT, B.A. Vol. I. Sacred Oratory. Extra fcap. 8vo, 2s. 6d.

Gautier, Théophile. Scenes of Travel. Selected and Edited by GEORGE SAINTSBURY, M.A. Extra fcap. 8vo, 2s.

Perrault's Popular Tales. Edited from the Original Editions, with Introduction, &c., by A. LANG, M.A. Extra fcap. 8vo, 5s. 6d.

Quinet's Lettres à sa Mère. Selected and Edited by GEORGE SAINTSBURY, M.A. Extra fcap. 8vo, 2s.

Sainte-Beuve. Selections from the Causeries du Lundi. Edited by GEORGE SAINTSBURY, M.A. Extra fcap. 8vo, 2s.

Dante. Selections from the Inferno. With Introduction and Notes. By H. B. COTTERILL, B.A. Extra fcap. 8vo, 4s. 6d.

Tasso. La Gerusalemme Liberata. Cantos i, ii. With Introduction and Notes. By the same Editor. Extra fcap. 8vo, 2s. 6d.

(2) GERMAN AND GOTHIC.

Max Müller. The German Classics, from the Fourth to the Nineteenth Century. With Biographical Notices, Translations into Modern German, and Notes. By F. MAX MÜLLER, M.A. A New Edition, Revised, Enlarged, and Adapted to WILHELM SCHERER's 'History of German Literature,' by F. LICHTENSTEIN. 2 vols. Crown 8vo, 21s.

Scherer. A History of German Literature by WILHELM SCHERER. Translated from the Third German Edition by Mrs. F. C. CONYBEARE. Edited by F. MAX MÜLLER. 2 vols. 8vo, 21s.

—— A History of German Literature, from the Accession of Frederick the Great to the Death of Goethe. By the same. Crown 8vo, 5s.

Skeat. The Gospel of St. Mark in Gothic. By W. W. SKEAT, Litt.D. Extra fcap. 8vo, cloth, 4s.

Wright. An Old High German Primer. With Grammar, Notes, and Glossary. By JOSEPH WRIGHT, Ph.D. Extra fcap. 8vo, 3s. 6d.

—— A Middle High German Primer. With Grammar, Notes, and Glossary. By the same Author. Extra fcap. 8vo, 3s. 6d.

—— A Primer of the Gothic Language. With Grammar, Notes, and Glossary. By the same Author. Extra fcap. 8vo, 4s. 6d.

Oxford : Clarendon Press.

LANGE'S GERMAN COURSE.

By HERMANN LANGE, Lecturer on French and German at the Manchester
Technical School, and Lecturer on German at the Manchester Athenæum.

I. **Germans at Home**; a Practical Introduction to German
Conversation, with an Appendix containing the Essentials of German
Grammar. Third Edition. 8vo, 2s. 6d.

II. **German Manual**; a German Grammar, Reading Book,
and a Handbook of German Conversation. 8vo, 7s. 6d.

III. **Grammar of the German Language.** 8vo, 3s. 6d.

IV. **German Composition**; A Theoretical and Practical Guide
to the Art of Translating English Prose into German. *Second Edition.*
8vo, 4s. 6d.

*** *A Key to the above, price 5s.*

German Spelling; A Synopsis of the Changes which it
has undergone through the Government Regulations of 1880. 6d.

BUCHHEIM'S GERMAN CLASSICS.

Edited, with Biographical, Historical, and Critical Introductions, Arguments
(to the Dramas), and Complete Commentaries, by C. A. BUCHHEIM, Phil.
Doc., Professor in King's College, London.

Becker (the Historian). Friedrich der Grosse. Edited, with
Notes, an Historical Introduction, and a Map. 3s. 6d.

Goethe :
   (a) Egmont. A Tragedy. 3s.
   (b) Iphigenie auf Tauris. A Drama. 3s.

Heine :
   (a) Prosa : being Selections from his Prose Writings. 4s. 6d.
   (b) Harzreise. 2s. 6d.

Lessing :
   (a) Nathan der Weise. A Dramatic Poem. 4s. 6d.
   (b) Minna von Barnhelm. A Comedy. 3s. 6d.

Schiller :
   (a) Wilhelm Tell. A Drama. Large Edition. With Map. 3s. 6d.
   (b) Wilhelm Tell. School Edition. With Map. 2s.
   (c) Historische Skizzen. With Map. 2s. 6d.
   (d) Jungfrau von Orleans. 4s. 6d.

London : HENRY FROWDE, Amen Corner, E.C.

C

Modern German Reader. A Graduated Collection of Extracts from Modern German Authors :—
>   Part I. **Prose Extracts.** With English Notes, a Grammatical Appendix, and a complete Vocabulary. *Fourth Edition.* 2s. 6d.
>   Part II. **Extracts in Prose and Poetry.** With English Notes and an Index. *Second Edition.* 2s. 6d.

German Poetry for Beginners. Edited with English Notes and a complete Vocabulary, by EMMA S. BUCHHEIM. Extra fcap. 8vo, 2s.

Chamisso. Peter Schlemihl's Wundersame Geschichte. Edited with Notes and a complete Vocabulary, by EMMA S. BUCHHEIM. Extra fcap. 8vo, 2s.

Lessing. The Laokoon; with English Notes by A. HAMANN, Phil. Doc., M.A. Revised, with an Introduction, by L. E. UPCOTT, M.A. Extra fcap. 8vo, 4s. 6d.

Niebuhr: Griechische Heroen-Geschichten (Tales of Greek Heroes). With English Notes and Vocabulary, by EMMA S. BUCHHEIM. Second, Revised Edition. Extra fcap. 8vo, cloth, 2s.; stiff covers, 1s. 6d.
>   Edition A.   *Text in German Type.*
>   Edition B.   *Text in Roman Type.*

Riehl's Seines Vaters Sohn *and* Gespensterkampf. Edited with Notes by H. T. GERRANS. Extra fcap. 8vo, 2s.

Schiller's Wilhelm Tell. Translated into English Verse by E. MASSIE, M.A. Extra fcap. 8vo, 5s.

(3) SCANDINAVIAN.

Cloasby and Vigfússon. An Icelandic-English Dictionary, based on the MS. collections of the late RICHARD CLEASBY. Enlarged and completed by G. VIGFÚSSON, M.A. With an Introduction, and Life of Richard Cleasby, by G. WEBBE DASENT, D.C.L. 4to, 3l. 7s.

Sweet. Icelandic Primer, with Grammar, Notes, and Glossary. By HENRY SWEET, M.A. Extra fcap. 8vo, 3s. 6d.

Vigfússon. Sturlunga Saga, including the Islendinga Saga of Lawman STURLA THORDSSON and other works. Edited by GUDBRAND VIGFÚSSON, M.A. In 2 vols. 8vo, 2l. 2s.

Vigfússon and Powell. Icelandic Prose Reader, with Notes, Grammar, and Glossary. By G. VIGFÚSSON, M.A., and F. YORK POWELL, M.A. Extra fcap. 8vo, 10s. 6d.

—— Corpvs Poeticvm Boreale. The Poetry of the Old Northern Tongue, from the Earliest Times to the Thirteenth Century. Edited, classified, and translated, with Introduction, Excursus, and Notes, by GUDBRAND VIGFÚSSON, M.A., and F. YORK POWELL, M.A. 2 vols. 8vo, 2l. 2s.

Oxford : Clarendon Press.

SECTION IV.

CLASSICAL LANGUAGES.

(1) LATIN.

STANDARD WORKS AND EDITIONS.

King and **Cookson.** The Principles of Sound and Inflexion, as illustrated in the Greek and Latin Languages. By J. E. KING, M.A., and CHRISTOPHER COOKSON, M.A. 8vo, 18s.

Lewis and **Short.** A Latin Dictionary, founded on Andrews' edition of Freund's Latin Dictionary, revised, enlarged, and in great part rewritten by CHARLTON T. LEWIS, Ph.D., and CHARLES SHORT, LL.D. 4to, 1l. 5s.

Merry. Selected Fragments of Roman Poetry. Edited with Introduction and Notes by W. W. MERRY, D.D. Crown 8vo, 6s. 6d.

Nettleship. Contributions to Latin Lexicography. By HENRY NETTLESHIP, M.A. 8vo, 21s.

—— Lectures and Essays on Subjects connected with Latin Scholarship and Literature. Crown 8vo, 7s. 6d.

—— The Roman Satura. 8vo, sewed, 1s.

—— Ancient Lives of Vergil. 8vo, sewed, 2s.

Papillon. Manual of Comparative Philology. By T. L. PAPILLON, M.A. *Third Edition.* Crown 8vo, 6s.

Pinder. Selections from the less known Latin Poets. By NORTH PINDER, M.A. 8vo, 15s.

Sellar. Roman Poets of the Republic. By W. Y. SELLAR, M.A. *Third Edition.* Crown 8vo, 10s.

—— Roman Poets of the Augustan Age. VIRGIL. *New Edition.* Crown 8vo, 9s.

—— —— HORACE and the ELEGIAC POETS. With a Memoir of the Author by ANDREW LANG, M.A., and a Portrait. 8vo, cloth, 14s.

Wordsworth. Fragments and Specimens of Early Latin. With Introductions and Notes. By J. WORDSWORTH, D.D. 8vo, 18s.

London: HENRY FROWDE, Amen Corner, E.C.

C 2

Avianus. The Fables. Edited, with Prolegomena, Critical
Apparatus, Commentary, &c., by R. ELLIS, M.A., LL.D. 8vo, 8s. 6d.

Catulli Veronensis Liber. Iterum recognovit, apparatum
criticum prolegomena appendices addidit, ROBINSON ELLIS, A.M. 8vo, 16s.

Catullus, a Commentary on. By ROBINSON ELLIS, M.A.
Second Edition. 8vo, 18s.

Cicero. De Oratore Libri Tres. With Introduction and Notes.
By A. S. WILKINS, Litt.D. 8vo, 18s.

Also separately:—

Book I, 7s. 6d.   Book II, 5s.   Book III, 6s.

—— Philippic Orations. With Notes. By J. R. KING, M.A.
Second Edition. 8vo, 10s. 6d.

—— Select Letters. With English Introductions, Notes, and
Appendices. By ALBERT WATSON, M.A. *Fourth Edition.* 8vo, 18s.

Horace. With a Commentary. Vol. I. The Odes, Carmen
Seculare, and Epodes. By E. C. WICKHAM, M.A. *Second Edition.* 8vo, 12s.

—— Vol. II. The Satires, Epistles, and De Arte Poetica. By
the same Editor. 8vo, 12s.

Livy, Book I. With Introduction, Historical Examination,
and Notes. By J. R. SEELEY, M.A. *Second Edition.* 8vo, 6s.

Manilius. Noctes Manilianae; sive Dissertationes in Astro-
nomica Manilii. Accedvnt Coniectvrae in Germanici Aratea. Scripsit
R. ELLIS. Crown 8vo, 6s.

Ovid. P. Ovidii Nasonis Ibis. Ex Novis Codicibus edidit,
Scholia Vetera Commentarium cum Prolegomenis Appendice Indice
addidit, R. ELLIS, A.M. 8vo, 10s. 6d.

—— P. Ovidi Nasonis Tristium Libri V. Recensuit S. G.
OWEN, A.M. 8vo, 16s.

Persius. The Satires. With a Translation and Commentary. By JOHN CONINGTON, M.A. Edited by HENRY NETTLESHIP,
M.A. *Second Edition.* 8vo, 7s. 6d.

Plautus. Rudens. Edited, with Critical and Explanatory
Notes, by E. A. SONNENSCHEIN, M.A. 8vo, 8s. 6d.

—— Bentley's Plautine Emendations. From his copy of
Gronovius. By E. A. SONNENSCHEIN, M.A. (Anecdota Oxon.) 2s. 6d.

Quintilian. Institutionis Oratoriae Liber X. Edited by
W. PETERSON, M.A. 8vo, 12s. 6d.

Scriptores Latini rei Metricae. Ed. T. GAISFORD, S.T.P. 8vo, 5s.

Oxford: Clarendon Press.

Tacitus. The Annals. Books I–VI. Edited, with Introduction and Notes, by H. Furneaux, M.A. 8vo, 18*s*.

—— Books XI–XVI. By the same Editor. 8vo, 20*s*.

LATIN EDUCATIONAL WORKS.

Grammars, Exercise Books, &c.

ALLEN.

Rudimenta Latina. Comprising Accidence, and Exercises of a very Elementary Character, for the use of Beginners. By John Barrow Allen, M.A. Extra fcap. 8vo, 2*s*.

An Elementary Latin Grammar. By the same Author. *Ninety-Seventh Thousand.* Extra fcap. 8vo, 2*s*. 6*d*.

A First Latin Exercise Book. By the same Author. *Sixth Edition.* Extra fcap. 8vo, 2*s*. 6*d*.

A Second Latin Exercise Book. By the same Author. Extra fcap. 8vo, 3*s*. 6*d*.

  *** A Key to First and Second Latin Exercise Books, in one volume, price 5*s*. Supplied *to Teachers only*, on application to the Secretary, Clarendon Press.

An Introduction to Latin Syntax. By W. S. Gibson, M.A. Extra fcap. 8vo, 2*s*.

First Latin Reader. By T. J. Nunns, M.A. *Third Edition.* Extra fcap. 8vo, 2*s*.

A Latin Prose Primer. By J. Y. Sargent, M.A. Extra fcap. 8vo, 2*s*. 6*d*.

Passages for Translation into Latin. Selected by J. Y. Sargent, M.A. *Seventh Edition.* Extra fcap. 8vo, 2*s*. 6*d*.

  *** A Key to the above, price 5*s*. Supplied *to Teachers only*, on application to the Secretary, Clarendon Press.

Latin Prose Composition. By G. G. Ramsay, M.A., LL.D. *Third Edition.* Vol. I, containing *Syntax, Exercises with Notes, &c.* Extra fcap. 8vo, 4*s*. 6*d*.

  *** A Key to the above, price 5*s*. Supplied *to Teachers only*, on application to the Secretary, Clarendon Press.

Hints and Helps for Latin Elegiacs. By H. Lee-Warner, M.A. Extra fcap. 8vo, 3*s*. 6*d*.

  *** A Key to the above, price 4*s*. 6*d*. Supplied *to Teachers only*, on application to the Secretary, Clarendon Press.

London: Henry Frowde, Amen Corner, E.C.

Reddenda Minora; or, Easy Passages, Latin and Greek, for Unseen Translation. For the use of Lower Forms. Composed and selected by C. S. Jerram, M.A. Extra fcap. 8vo, 1s. 6d.

Anglice Reddenda; or, Extracts, Latin and Greek, for Unseen Translation. By C. S. Jerram, M.A. *Fourth Edition.* Extra fcap. 8vo, 2s. 6d.

Anglice Reddenda. *Second Series.* By the same Editor. Extra fcap. 8vo, 3s.

Models and Exercises in Unseen Translation. By H. F. Fox, M.A., and T. M. Bromley, M.A. Extra fcap. 8vo, 5s. 6d.

*** A Key to Passages quoted in the above, price 6d. Supplied *to Teachers only,* on application to the Secretary, Clarendon Press.

An Elementary Latin Dictionary. By Charlton T. Lewis, Ph.D. Square 8vo, 7s. 6d.

A School Latin Dictionary. By Charlton T. Lewis, Ph.D. Small 4to, 18s.

An Introduction to the Comparative Grammar of Greek and Latin. By J. E. King, M.A., and C. Cookson, M.A. Extra fcap. 8vo, 5s. 6d.

Latin Classics for Schools.

Caesar. The Commentaries (for Schools). With Notes and Maps. By Charles E. Moberly, M.A.

The Gallic War. *Second Edition.* Extra fcap. 8vo.

—— Books I and II, 2s.; III–V, 2s. 6d.; VI–VIII, 3s. 6d.

—— Books I–III, *stiff cover,* 2s.

The Civil War. Extra fcap. 8vo, 3s. 6d.

Catulli Veronensis Carmina Selecta, secundum recognitionem Robinson Ellis, A.M. Extra fcap. 8vo, 3s. 6d.

CICERO. Selection of Interesting and Descriptive Passages. With Notes. By Henry Walford, M.A. In three Parts. *Third Edition.* Extra fcap. 8vo, 4s. 6d.

Each Part separately, limp, 1s. 6d.

Part I.   Anecdotes from Grecian and Roman History.
Part II.   Omens and Dreams: Beauties of Nature.
Part III. Rome's Rule of her Provinces.

Oxford : Clarendon Press.

Cicero. De Senectute. Edited, with Introduction and Notes, by L. HUXLEY, M.A. Extra fcap. 8vo, 2*s.*

—— pro Cluentio. With Introduction and Notes. By W. RAMSAY, M.A. Edited by G. G. RAMSAY, M.A. *Second Edition.* Extra fcap. 8vo, 3*s.* 6*d.*

—— pro Milone. With Notes, &c. By A. B. POYNTON, M.A. Extra fcap. 8vo, 2*s.* 6*d.*

—— pro Roscio. With Notes. By ST. GEORGE STOCK, M.A. Extra fcap. 8vo, 3*s.* 6*d.*

—— Select Orations (for Schools). In Verrem Actio Prima. De Imperio Gn. Pompeii. Pro Archia. Philippica IX. With Introduction and Notes by J. R. KING, M.A. *Second Edition.* Extra fcap. 8vo, 2*s.* 6*d.*

—— In Q. Caecilium Divinatio, and In C. Verrem Actio Prima. With Introduction and Notes, by J. R. KING, M.A. Extra fcap. 8vo, limp, 1*s.* 6*d.*

—— Speeches against Catilina. With Introduction and Notes, by E. A. UPCOTT, M.A. Extra fcap. 8vo, 2*s.* 6*d.*

—— Selected Letters (for Schools). With Notes. By the late C. E. PRICHARD, M.A., and E. R. BERNARD, M.A. *Second Edition.* Extra fcap. 8vo, 3*s.*

—— Select Letters. Text. By ALBERT WATSON, M.A. *Second Edition.* Extra fcap. 8vo, 4*s.*

Cornelius Nepos. With Notes. By OSCAR BROWNING, M.A. *Third Edition.* Revised by W. R. INGE, M.A. Extra fcap. 8vo, 3*s.*

Horace. With a Commentary. (In a size suitable for the use of Schools.) Vol. I. The Odes, Carmen Seculare, and Epodes. By E. C. WICKHAM, M.A. *Second Edition.* Extra fcap. 8vo, 6*s.*

—— Odes, Book I. By the same Editor. *Immediately.*

—— Selected Odes. With Notes for the use of a Fifth Form. By E. C. WICKHAM, M.A. Extra fcap. 8vo, 2*s.*

Juvenal. Thirteen Satires. Edited, with Introduction and Notes, by C. H. PEARSON, M.A., and HERBERT A. STRONG, M.A., LL.D. *Second Edition.* Crown 8vo, 9*s.*

London : HENRY FROWDE, Amen Corner, E.C.

Livy. Books V–VII. With Introduction and Notes. By A. R. Cluer, B.A. *Second Edition.* Revised by P. E. Matheson, M.A. Extra fcap. 8vo, 5*s.*

——— Book V. By the same Editors. Extra fcap. 8vo, 2*s.* 6*d.*

——— Book VII. By the same Editors. Extra fcap. 8vo, 2*s.*

——— Books XXI–XXIII. With Introduction and Notes. By M. T. Tatham, M.A. *Second Edition, Enlarged.* Extra fcap. 8vo, 5*s.*

——— Book XXI. By the same Editor. Extra fcap. 8vo, 2*s.* 6*d.*

——— Book XXII. With Introduction, Notes, and Maps. By the same Editor. Extra fcap. 8vo, 2*s.* 6*d.*

——— Selections (for Schools). With Notes and Maps. By H. Lee-Warner, M.A. Extra fcap. 8vo. In Parts, limp, each 1*s.* 6*d.*

   Part I. The Caudine Disaster.
   Part II. Hannibal's Campaign in Italy.
   Part III. The Macedonian War.

Ovid. Selections for the use of Schools. With Introductions and Notes, and an Appendix on the Roman Calendar. By W. Ramsay, M.A. Edited by G. G. Ramsay, M.A. *Third Edition.* Extra fcap. 8vo, 5*s.* 6*d.*

——— Tristia. Book I. The Text revised, with an Introduction and Notes. By S. G. Owen, B.A. Extra fcap. 8vo, 3*s.* 6*d.*

——— Tristia. Book III. With Introduction and Notes. By the same Editor. Extra fcap. 8vo, 2*s.*

Plautus. Captivi. Edited by Wallace M. Lindsay, M.A. Extra fcap. 8vo, 2*s.* 6*d.*

——— Trinummus. With Notes and Introductions. (Intended for the Higher Forms of Public Schools.) By C. E. Freeman, M.A., and A. Sloman, M.A. Extra fcap. 8vo, 3*s.*

Pliny. Selected Letters (for Schools). With Notes. By C. E. Prichard, M.A., and E. R. Bernard, M.A. Extra fcap. 8vo, 3*s.*

Sallust. With Introduction and Notes. By W. W. Capes, M.A. Extra fcap. 8vo, 4*s.* 6*d.*

Tacitus. The Annals. Books I–IV. Edited, with Introduction and Notes (for the use of Schools and Junior Students), by H. Furneaux, M.A. Extra fcap. 8vo, 5*s.*

Oxford : Clarendon Press.

Tacitus. The Annals. Book I. With Introduction and Notes, by the same Editor. Extra fcap. 8vo, limp, 2s.

Terence. Andria. With Notes and Introductions. By C. E. FREEMAN, M.A., and A. SLOMAN, M.A. Extra fcap. 8vo, 3s.

—— Adelphi. With Notes and Introductions. (Intended for the Higher Forms of Public Schools.) By A. SLOMAN, M.A. Extra fcap. 8vo, 3s.

—— Phormio. With Notes and Introductions. By A SLOMAN, M.A. Extra fcap. 8vo, 3s.

Tibullus and Propertius. Selections. Edited by G. G. RAMSAY, M.A. (In one or two parts.) Extra fcap. 8vo, 6s.

Virgil. Text, with Introduction. By T. L. PAPILLON, M.A. Crown 8vo, 4s. 6d.

—— Aeneid. Text and Notes. Edited by T. L. PAPILLON, M.A., and A. E. HAIGH, M.A. In Four Parts. Crown 8vo, 3s. each.

—— Bucolics and Georgics. By the same Editors. Crown 8vo, 3s. 6d.

—— Bucolics. Edited by C. S. JERRAM, M.A. Extra fcap. 8vo, 2s. 6d.

—— Georgics, Books I, II. By the same Editor. Extra fcap. 8vo, 2s. 6d.

—— Aeneid I. With Introduction and Notes, by the same Editor. Extra fcap. 8vo, limp, 1s. 6d.

—— Aeneid VI. With Notes, &c. By J. B. ALLEN, M.A. *Immediately.*

—— Aeneid IX. Edited, with Introduction and Notes, by A. E. HAIGH, M.A. Extra fcap. 8vo, limp, 1s. 6d. In two Parts, 2s.

(2) GREEK.

STANDARD WORKS AND EDITIONS.

Allen. Notes on Abbreviations in Greek Manuscripts. By T. W. ALLEN, M.A., Queen's College, Oxford. Royal 8vo, 5s.

Chandler. A Practical Introduction to Greek Accentuation, by H. W. CHANDLER, M.A. *Second Edition.* 10s. 6d.

Haigh. The Attic Theatre. A Description of the Stage and Theatre of the Athenians, and of the Dramatic Performances at Athens. By A. E. HAIGH, M.A. 8vo, 12s. 6d.

Head. Historia Numorum: A Manual of Greek Numismatics. By BARCLAY V. HEAD. Royal 8vo, half-bound, 2l. 2s.

Hicks. A Manual of Greek Historical Inscriptions. By E. L. HICKS, M.A. 8vo, 10s. 6d.

King and Cookson. The Principles of Sound and Inflexion, as illustrated in the Greek and Latin Languages. By J. E. KING, M.A., and CHRISTOPHER COOKSON, M.A. 8vo, 18s.

Liddell and Scott. A Greek-English Lexicon, by H. G. LIDDELL, D.D., and ROBERT SCOTT, D.D. *Seventh Edition, Revised and Augmented throughout.* 4to, 1l. 16s.

Papillon. Manual of Comparative Philology. By T. L. PAPILLON, M.A. *Third Edition.* Crown 8vo, 6s.

Paton and Hicks. The Inscriptions of Cos. By W. R. PATON and E. L. HICKS. Royal 8vo, linen, with Map, 28s.

Veitch. Greek Verbs, Irregular and Defective. By W. VEITCH, LL.D. *Fourth Edition.* Crown 8vo, 10s. 6d.

Vocabulary, a copious Greek-English, compiled from the best authorities. 24mo, 3s.

Aeschinem et Isocratem, Scholia Graeca in. Edidit G. DINDORFIUS. 1852. 8vo, 4s.

Aeschines. See under **Oratores Attici,** and **Demosthenes.**

Aeschyli quae supersunt in Codice Laurentiano quoad effici potuit et ad cognitionem necesse est visum typis descripta edidit R. MERKEL. Small folio, 1l. 1s.

Aeschylus: Tragoediae et Fragmenta, ex recensióne GUIL. DINDORFII. *Second Edition.* 1851. 8vo, 5s. 6d.

—— Annotationes GUIL. DINDORFII. Partes II. 1841. 8vo, 10s.

Anecdota Graeca Oxoniensia. Edidit J. A. CRAMER, S.T.P. Tomi IV. 1835. 8vo, 1l. 2s.

—— Graeca e Codd. MSS. Bibliothecae Regiae Parisiensis. Edidit J. A. CRAMER, S.T.P. Tomi IV. 1839. 8vo, 1l. 2s.

Apsinis et Longini Rhetorica. E Codicibus MSS. recensuit JOH. BAKIUS. 1849. 8vo, 3s.

Oxford: Clarendon Press.

Aristophanes. A Complete Concordance to the Comedies and Fragments. By HENRY DUNBAR, M.D. 4to, 1*l.* 1*s.*

—— J. Caravellae Index in Aristophanem. 8vo, 3*s.*

—— Comoediae et Fragmenta, ex recensione GUIL. DINDORFII. Tomi II. 1835. 8vo, 11*s.*

—— Annotationes GUIL. DINDORFII. Partes II. 8vo, 11*s.*

—— Scholia Graeca ex Codicibus aucta et emendata a GUIL DINDORFIO. Partes III. 1838. 8vo, 1*l.*

ARISTOTLE.

—— Ex recensione IMMANUELIS BEKKERI. Accedunt Indices Sylburgiani. Tomi XI. 1837. 8vo, 2*l.* 10*s.*

The volumes (except vol. IX) may be had separately, price 5*s.* 6*d.* each.

—— **Ethica Nicomachea,** recognovit brevique Adnotatione critica instruxit I. BYWATER. 8vo, 6*s.*

—— **The same,** on 4to paper, for Marginal Notes, 10*s.* 6*d.*

—— Contributions to the Textual Criticism of Aristotle's **Nicomachean Ethics.** By INGRAM BYWATER. Stiff cover, 2*s.* 6*d.*

—— Notes on the Nicomachean Ethics. By J. A. STEWART, M.A. 2 vols. *Immediately.*

—— **The Politics,** with Introductions, Notes, &c., by W. L. NEWMAN, M.A., Fellow of Balliol College, Oxford. Vols. I and II. Medium 8vo, 28*s.*

—— **The Politics,** translated into English, with Introduction, Marginal Analysis, Notes, and Indices, by B. JOWETT, M.A. Medium 8vo. 2 vols. 21*s.*

—— **Aristotelian Studies.** I. On the Structure of the Seventh Book of the Nicomachean Ethics. By J. C. WILSON, M.A. 8vo, stiff covers, 5*s.*

—— The English Manuscripts of the **Nicomachean Ethics,** described in relation to Bekker's Manuscripts and other Sources. By J. A. STEWART, M.A. (Anecdota Oxon.) Small 4to, 3*s.* 6*d.*

—— On the History of the process by which the **Aristotelian** Writings arrived at their present form. By R. SHUTE, M.A. 8vo, 7*s.* 6*d.*

—— **Physics.** Book VII. Collation of various MSS.; with Introduction by R. SHUTE, M.A. (Anecdota Oxon.) Small 4to, 2*s.*

London : HENRY FROWDE, Amen Corner, E.C.

Choerobosci Dictata in Theodosii Canones, necnon Epimerismi in Psalmos. E Codicibus mss. edidit Thomas Gaisford, S.T.P. Tomi III. 8vo, 15*s*.

Demosthenes. Ex recensione Guil. Dindorfii. Tomi IX. 8vo, 2*l*. 6*s*.

Separately:—

Textus, 1*l*. 1*s*.   Annotationes, 15*s*.   Scholia, 10*s*.

Demosthenes and Aeschines. The Orations of Demosthenes and Aeschines on the Crown. With Introductory Essays and Notes. By G. A. Simcox, M.A., and W. H. Simcox, M.A. 8vo, 12*s*.

Euripides. Tragoediae et Fragmenta, ex recensione Guil. Dindorfii. Tomi II. 1833. 8vo, 10*s*.

—— Annotationes Guil. Dindorfii. Partes II. 8vo, 10*s*.

—— Scholia Graeca, ex Codicibus aucta et emendata a Guil. Dindorfio. Tomi IV. 8vo, 1*l*. 16*s*.

—— Alcestis, ex recensione G. Dindorfii. 8vo, 2*s*. 6*d*.

Harpocrationis Lexicon. Ex recensione G. Dindorfii. Tomi II. 8vo, 10*s*. 6*d*.

Hephaestionis Enchiridion, Terentianus Maurus, Proclus, &c. Edidit T. Gaisford, S.T.P. Tomi II. 10*s*.

Heracliti Ephesii Reliquiae. Recensuit I. Bywater, M.A. Appendicis loco additae sunt Diogenis Laertii Vita Heracliti, Particulae Hippocratei De Diaeta Lib. I, Epistolae Heracliteae. 8vo, 6*s*.

HOMER.

—— A Complete Concordance to the Odyssey and Hymns of Homer; to which is added a Concordance to the Parallel Passages in the Iliad, Odyssey, and Hymns. By Henry Dunbar, M.D. 4to, 1*l*. 1*s*.

—— Seberi Index in Homerum. 1780. 8vo, 6*s*. 6*d*.

—— A Grammar of the Homeric Dialect. By D. B. Monro, M.A. *Second Edition.* 8vo, 14*s*.

—— Ilias, cum brevi Annotatione C. G. Heynii. Accedunt Scholia minora. Tomi II. 8vo, 15*s*.

—— Ilias, ex rec. Guil. Dindorfii. 8vo, 5*s*. 6*d*.

Oxford: Clarendon Press.

HOMER (*continued*).

—— Scholia Graeca in Iliadem. Edited by W. DINDORF, after a new collation of the Venetian mss. by D. B. MONRO, M.A., Provost of Oriel College. 4 vols. 8vo, 2*l.* 10*s.*

—— Scholia Graeca in Iliadem Townleyana. Recensuit ERNESTUS MAASS. 2 vols. 8vo, 1*l.* 16*s.*

—— **Odyssea**, ex rec. G. DINDORFII. 8vo, 5*s.* 6*d.*

—— Scholia Graeca in Odysseam. Edidit GUIL. DINDORFIUS. Tomi II. 8vo, 15*s.* 6*d.*

—— **Odyssey**. Books I–XII. Edited with English Notes, Appendices, &c. By W. W. MERRY, D.D., and the late JAMES RIDDELL, M.A. *Second Edition.* 8vo, 16*s.*

Oratores Attici, ex recensione BEKKERI:

    I. Antiphon, Andocides, et Lysias. 8vo, 7*s.*

    II. Isocrates. 8vo, 7*s.*

    III. Isaeus, Aeschines, Lycurgus, Dinarchus, &c. 8vo, 7*s.*

Paroemiographi Graeci, quorum pars nunc primum ex Codd. mss. vulgatur. Edidit T. GAISFORD, S.T.P. 8vo, 5*s.* 6*d.*

PLATO.

—— **Apology**, with a revised Text and English Notes, and a Digest of Platonic Idioms, by JAMES RIDDELL, M.A. 8vo, 8*s.* 6*d.*

—— **Philebus**, with a revised Text and English Notes, by EDWARD POSTE, M.A. 8vo, 7*s.* 6*d.*

—— **Sophistes** and **Politicus**, with a revised Text and English Notes, by L. CAMPBELL, M.A. 8vo, 18*s.*

—— **Theaetetus**, with a revised Text and English Notes, by L. CAMPBELL, M.A. *Second Edition.* 8vo, 10*s.* 6*d.*

—— **The Dialogues**, translated into English, with Analyses and Introductions, by B. JOWETT, M.A. *Third Edition.* 5 vols. medium 8vo, 4*l.* 4*s.* In half-morocco, 5*l.*

—— **The Republic**, translated into English, with Analysis and Introduction, by B. JOWETT, M.A. Medium 8vo, 12*s.* 6*d.*; half-roan, 14*s.*

—— Index to Plato. Compiled for Prof. Jowett's Translation of the Dialogues. By EVELYN ABBOTT, M.A. 8vo, paper covers, 2*s.* 6*d.*

Plotinus. Edidit F. CREUZER. Tomi III. 4to, 1*l.* 8*s.*

London : HENRY FROWDE, Amen Corner, E.C.

Polybius. Selections. Edited by J. L. Strachan-Davidson, M.A. With Maps. Medium 8vo, buckram, 21s.

SOPHOCLES.

——— The Plays and Fragments. With English Notes and Introductions, by Lewis Campbell, M.A. 2 vols.

> Vol. I. Oedipus Tyrannus. Oedipus Coloneus. Antigone. 8vo, 16s.

> Vol. II. Ajax. Electra. Trachiniae. Philoctetes. Fragments. 8vo, 16s.

——— Tragoediae et Fragmenta, ex recensione et cum commentariis Guil. Dindorfii. *Third Edition.* 2 vols. Fcap. 8vo, 1l. 1s.
> Each Play separately, limp, 2s. 6d.

——— The Text alone, with large margin, small 4to, 8s.

——— The Text alone, square 16mo, 3s. 6d.
> Each Play separately, limp, 6d.

——— Tragoediae et Fragmenta cum Annotationibus Guil. Dindorfii. Tomi II. 8vo, 10s.
> The Text, Vol. I, 5s. 6d.   The Notes, Vol. II, 4s. 6d.

Stobaei Florilegium. Ad MSS. fidem emendavit et supplevit T. Gaisford, S.T.P. Tomi IV. 8vo, 1l.

——— Eclogarum Physicarum et Ethicarum libri duo. Accedit Hieroclis Commentarius in aurea carmina Pythagoreorum. Ad MSS. Codd. recensuit T. Gaisford, S.T.P. Tomi II. 8vo, 11s.

Thucydides. Translated into English, with Introduction, Marginal Analysis, Notes, and Indices. By B. Jowett, M.A., Regius Professor of Greek. 2 vols. Medium 8vo, 1l. 12s.

XENOPHON. Ex rec. et cum annotatt. L. Dindorfii.

> I. Historia Graeca. *Second Edition.* 8vo, 10s. 6d.

> II. Expeditio Cyri. *Second Edition.* 8vo, 10s. 6d.

> III. Institutio Cyri. 8vo, 10s. 6d.

> IV. Memorabilia Socratis. 8vo, 7s. 6d.

> V. Opuscula Politica Equestria et Venatica cum Arriani Libello de Venatione. 8vo, 10s. 6d.

GREEK EDUCATIONAL WORKS.

GRAMMARS, EXERCISE BOOKS, &c.

Chandler. The Elements of Greek Accentuation: abridged
from his larger work by H. W. CHANDLER, M.A. Extra fcap. 8vo, 2s. 6d.

King and Cookson. An Introduction to the Comparative
Grammar of Greek and Latin. By J. E. KING, M.A., and C. COOKSON,
M.A. Extra fcap. 8vo, 5s. 6d.

Liddell and Scott. An Intermediate Greek - English
Lexicon, founded upon the Seventh Edition of LIDDELL and SCOTT'S
Greek Lexicon. Small 4to, 12s. 6d.

Liddell and Scott. A Greek-English Lexicon, abridged
from LIDDELL and SCOTT'S 4to edition. Square 12mo, 7s. 6d.

Miller. A Greek Testament Primer. An Easy Grammar
and Reading Book for the use of Students beginning Greek. By the
Rev. E. MILLER, M.A. Extra fcap. 8vo, 3s. 6d.

Moulton. The Ancient Classical Drama. A Study in Literary
Evolution. Intended for Readers in English and in the Original. By
R. G. MOULTON, M.A. Crown 8vo, 8s. 6d.

Wordsworth. A Greek Primer, for the use of beginners in
that Language. By the Right Rev. CHARLES WORDSWORTH, D.C.L.
Seventh Edition. Extra fcap. 8vo, 1s. 6d.

—— Graecae Grammaticae Rudimenta in usum Scholarum.
Auctore CAROLO WORDSWORTH, D.C.L. *Nineteenth Edition.* 12mo, 4s.

A Primer of Greek Prose Composition. By J. Y. SARGENT,
M.A. Extra fcap. 8vo, 3s. 6d.
*** A Key to the above, price 5s. Supplied *to Teachers only,* on appli-
cation to the Secretary, Clarendon Press.

Passages for Translation into Greek Prose. By J. YOUNG
SARGENT, M.A. Extra fcap. 8vo, 3s.

Exemplaria Graeca. Being Greek Renderings of Selected
" Passages for Translation into Greek Prose." By the same Author. Extra
fcap. 8vo, 3s.

London : HENRY FROWDE, Amen Corner, E.C.

Models and Materials for Greek Iambic Verse. By J. Y. SARGENT, M.A. Extra fcap. 8vo, 4s. 6d.

Graece Reddenda. By C. S. JERRAM, M.A. Extra fcap. 8vo, 2s. 6d.

Reddenda Minora; or, Easy Passages, Latin and Greek, for Unseen Translation. By C. S. JERRAM, M.A. Extra fcap. 8vo, 1s. 6d.

Anglice Reddenda; or, Extracts, Latin and Greek, for Unseen Translation. By C. S. JERRAM, M.A. Extra fcap. 8vo, 2s. 6d.

Anglice Reddenda. *Second Series.* By the same Author. Extra fcap. 8vo, 3s.

Models and Exercises in Unseen Translation. By H. F. FOX, M.A., and T. M. BROMLEY, M.A. Extra fcap. 8vo, 5s. 6d.

　** A Key to Passages quoted in the above, price 6d. Supplied *to Teachers only*, on application to the Secretary, Clarendon Press.

Golden Treasury of Ancient Greek Poetry. By R. S. WRIGHT, M.A. *Second Edition.* Revised by EVELYN ABBOTT, M.A., LL.D. Extra fcap. 8vo, 10s. 6d.

Golden Treasury of Greek Prose, being a Collection of the finest passages in the principal Greek Prose Writers, with Introductory Notices and Notes. By R. S. WRIGHT, M.A., and J. E. L. SHADWELL, M.A. Extra fcap. 8vo, 4s. 6d.

GREEK READERS.

Easy Greek Reader. By EVELYN ABBOTT, M.A. In one or two Parts. Extra fcap. 8vo, 3s.

First Greek Reader. By W. G. RUSHBROOKE, M.L. *Second Edition.* Extra fcap. 8vo, 2s. 6d.

Second Greek Reader. By A. M. BELL, M.A. *Second Edition.* Extra fcap. 8vo, 3s.

Specimens of Greek Dialects; being a Fourth Greek Reader. With Introductions, &c. By W. W. MERRY, D.D. Extra fcap. 8vo, 4s. 6d.

Selections from Homer and the Greek Dramatists; being a Fifth Greek Reader. With Explanatory Notes and Introductions to the Study of Greek Epic and Dramatic Poetry. By EVELYN ABBOTT, M.A. Extra fcap. 8vo, 4s. 6d.

Oxford : Clarendon Press.

GREEK CLASSICS FOR SCHOOLS.

Aeschylus. In Single Plays. Extra fcap. 8vo.

I. Agamemnon. With Introduction and Notes, by ARTHUR SIDGWICK, M.A. *Third Edition.* 3s.

II. Choephoroi. By the same Editor. 3s.

III. Eumenides. By the same Editor. 3s.

IV. Prometheus Bound. With Introduction and Notes, by A. O. PRICKARD, M.A. *Second Edition.* 2s.

Aristophanes. In Single Plays. Edited, with English Notes, Introductions, &c., by W. W. MERRY, D.D. Extra fcap. 8vo.

I. The Acharnians. *Third Edition,* 3s.

II. The Clouds. *Third Edition,* 3s.

III. The Frogs. *Second Edition,* 3s.

IV. The Knights. *Second Edition,* 3s.

V. The Birds. 3s. 6d.

Cebes. Tabula. With Introduction and Notes. By C. S. JERRAM, M.A. Extra fcap. 8vo, 2s. 6d.

Demosthenes. Orations against Philip. With Introduction and Notes, by EVELYN ABBOTT, M.A., and P. E. MATHESON, M.A.

Vol. I. Philippic I. Olynthiacs I–III. Extra fcap. 8vo, 3s.

Vol. II. De Pace, Philippic II, De Chersoneso, Philippic III. Extra fcap. 8vo, 4s. 6d.

Euripides. In Single Plays. Extra fcap. 8vo.

I. Alcestis. Edited by C. S. JERRAM, M.A. 2s. 6d.

II. Cyclops. By W. E. LONG, M.A. 2s. 6d.

III. Hecuba. Edited by C. H. RUSSELL, M.A. 2s. 6d.

IV. Helena. Edited, with Introduction, Notes, &c., for Upper and Middle Forms. By C. S. JERRAM, M.A. 3s.

V. Heracleidae. By C. S. JERRAM, M.A. 3s.

VI. Iphigenia in Tauris. By the same Editor. 3s.

VII. Medea. By C. B. HEBERDEN, M.A. 2s.

London : HENRY FROWDE, Amen Corner, E.C.
D

Herodotus. Book IX. Edited, with Notes, by EVELYN ABBOTT, M.A. Extra fcap. 8vo, 3s.

—— Selections. Edited, with Introduction and Notes, by W. W. MERRY, D.D. Extra fcap. 8vo, 2s. 6d.

Homer.

I. For Beginners. Iliad, Book III. By M. T. TATHAM, M.A. Extra fcap. 8vo, 1s. 6d.

II. Iliad, Books I–XII. With an Introduction and a brief Homeric Grammar, and Notes. By D. B. MONRO, M.A. *Second Edition.* Extra fcap. 8vo, 6s.

III. Iliad, Books XIII–XXIV. With Notes. By the same Editor. Extra fcap. 8vo, 6s.

IV. Iliad, Book I. By the same Editor. *Second Edition.* Extra fcap. 8vo, 2s.

V. Iliad, Books VI and XXI. With Introduction and Notes. By HERBERT HAILSTONE, M.A. Extra fcap. 8vo, 1s. 6d. each.

VI. Odyssey, Books I–XII. By W. W. MERRY, D.D. *Forty-fifth Thousand.* Extra fcap. 8vo, 5s.

    Books I and II, separately, each 1s. 6d.

    Books VI and VII. Extra fcap. 8vo. 1s. 6d.

VII. Odyssey, Books VII–XII. By the same Editor. Extra fcap. 8vo, 3s.

VIII. Odyssey, Books XIII–XXIV. By the same Editor. Extra fcap. 8vo, 5s.

Lucian. Vera Historia. By C. S. JERRAM, M.A. *Second Edition.* Extra fcap. 8vo, 1s. 6d.

Lysias. Epitaphios. Edited, with Introduction and Notes, by F. J. SNELL, B.A. Extra fcap. 8vo, 2s.

Plato. With Introduction and Notes. By ST. GEORGE STOCK, M.A. Extra fcap. 8vo.

    The Apology, 2s. 6d.   Crito, 2s.   Meno, 2s. 6d.

—— Selections. With Introductions and Notes. By JOHN PURVES, M.A., and Preface by B. JOWETT, M.A. *Second Edition.* Extra fcap. 8vo, 5s.

Plutarch. Lives of the Gracchi. Edited, with Introduction, Notes, and Indices, by G. E. UNDERHILL, M.A. Crown 8vo. 5s.

Sophocles. Edited, with Introductions and English Notes, by LEWIS CAMPBELL, M.A., and EVELYN ABBOTT, M.A. *New Edition.* 2 vols. Extra fcap. 8vo, 10s. 6d.

> Sold separately: Vol. I, Text, 4s. 6d.; Vol. II, Explanatory Notes, 6s.
>
> *Or in single Plays:—*
>
> Oedipus Coloneus, Antigone, 1s. 9d. each; Oedipus Tyrannus, Ajax, Electra, Trachiniae, Philoctetes, 2s. each.

Sophocles. Oedipus Rex: Dindorf's Text, with Notes by the present Bishop of St. David's. Extra fcap. 8vo, limp, 1s. 6d.

Theocritus (for Schools). With English Notes. By H. KYNASTON, D.D. (late SNOW). *Fourth Edition.* Extra fcap. 8vo, 4s. 6d

XENOPHON. Easy Selections (for Junior Classes). With a Vocabulary, Notes, and Map. By J. S. PHILLPOTTS, B.C.L., and C. S. JERRAM, M.A. *Third Edition.* Extra fcap. 8vo, 3s. 6d.

—— Selections (for Schools). With Notes and Maps. By J. S. PHILLPOTTS, B.C.L. *Fourth Edition.* Extra fcap. 8vo, 3s. 6d.

—— Anabasis, Book I. Edited for the use of Junior Classes and Private Students. With Introduction, Notes, &c. By J. MARSHALL, M.A. Extra fcap. 8vo, 2s. 6d.

—— Anabasis, Book II. With Notes and Map. By C. S. JERRAM, M.A. Extra fcap. 8vo, 2s.

—— Anabasis, Book III. With Introduction, Analysis, Notes, &c. By J. MARSHALL, M.A. Extra fcap. 8vo, 2s. 6d.

—— Anabasis, Book IV. By J. MARSHALL, M.A. Extra fcap. 8vo, 2s.

—— Vocabulary to the Anabasis. By J. MARSHALL, M.A. Extra fcap. 8vo, 1s. 6d.

—— Cyropaedia, Book I. With Introduction and Notes. By C. BIGG, D.D. Extra fcap. 8vo, 2s.

—— Cyropaedia, Books IV and V. With Introduction and Notes. By C. BIGG, D.D. Extra fcap. 8vo, 2s. 6d.

—— Hellenica, Books I, II. With Introduction and Notes. By G. E. UNDERHILL, M.A. Extra fcap. 8vo, 3s.

—— Memorabilia. Edited with Introduction and Notes, &c., by J. MARSHALL, M.A. Extra fcap. 8vo, 4s. 6d.

SECTION V.

ORIENTAL LANGUAGES *.

THE SACRED BOOKS OF THE EAST.

TRANSLATED BY VARIOUS ORIENTAL SCHOLARS, AND EDITED BY
F. MAX MÜLLER.

First Series, Vols. I—XXIV. Demy 8vo, cloth.

Vol. I.   The Upanishads.   Translated by F. MAX MÜLLER.
Part I. 10s. 6d.

Vol. II.   The Sacred Laws of the Âryas, as taught in the
Schools of Âpastamba, Gautama, Vâsish*tha*, and Baudhâyana. Translated by Prof. GEORG BÜHLER.   Part I. 10s. 6d.

Vol. III.   The Sacred Books of China.   The Texts of Confucianism.   Translated by JAMES LEGGE.   Part I. 12s. 6d.

Vol. IV.   The Zend-Avesta.   Part I. The Vendidâd. Translated by JAMES DARMESTETER. 10s. 6d.

Vol. V.   The Pahlavi Texts.   Translated by E. W. WEST.
Part I. 12s. 6d.

Vols. VI and IX.   The Qur'ân.   Translated by E. H.
PALMER. 21s.

Vol. VII.   The Institutes of Vish*n*u.   Translated by JULIUS
JOLLY. 10s. 6d.

Vol. VIII.   The Bhagavadgîtâ, with The Sanatsu*g*âtîya, and
The Anugîtâ.   Translated by KÂSHINÂTH TRIMBAK TELANG. 10s. 6d.

Vol. X.   The Dhammapada, translated from Pâli by F. MAX
MÜLLER; and The Sutta-Nipâta, translated from Pâli by V. FAUSBÖLL;
being Canonical Books of the Buddhists. 10s. 6d.

Vol. XI.   Buddhist Suttas.   Translated from Pâli by T. W.
RHYS DAVIDS. 10s. 6d.

Vol. XII.   The *S*atapatha-Brâhma*n*a, according to the Text
of the Mâdhyandina School.   Translated by JULIUS EGGELING. Part I.
Books I and II. 12s. 6d.

Vol. XIII.   Vinaya Texts.   Translated from the Pâli by
T. W. RHYS DAVIDS and HERMANN OLDENBERG.   Part I. 10s. 6d.

---

* See also ANECDOTA OXON., Series II, III, pp. 41-42, below.

Oxford : Clarendon Press.

The Sacred Books of the East (*continued*).

Vol. XIV. The Sacred Laws of the Âryas, as taught in the Schools of Âpastamba, Gautama, Vâsish*th*a and Baudhâyana. Translated by GEORG BÜHLER. Part II. 10*s.* 6*d.*

Vol. XV. The Upanishads. Translated by F. MAX MÜLLER. Part II. 10*s.* 6*d.*

Vol. XVI. The Sacred Books of China. The Texts of Confucianism. Translated by JAMES LEGGE. Part II. 10*s.* 6*d.*

Vol. XVII. Vinaya Texts. Translated from the Pâli by T. W. RHYS DAVIDS and HERMANN OLDENBERG. Part II. 10*s.* 6*d.*

Vol. XVIII. Pahlavi Texts. Translated by E. W. WEST. Part II. 12*s.* 6*d.*

Vol. XIX. The Fo-sho-hing-tsan-king. A Life of Buddha by Asvaghosha Bodhisattva, translated from Sanskrit into Chinese by Dharmaraksha, A.D. 420, and from Chinese into English by SAMUEL BEAL. 10*s.* 6*d.*

Vol. XX. Vinaya Texts. Translated from the Pâli by T. W. RHYS DAVIDS and HERMANN OLDENBERG. Part III. 10*s.* 6*d.*

Vol. XXI. The Saddharma-pu*nd*arîka; or, the Lotus of the True Law. Translated by H. KERN. 12*s.* 6*d.*

Vol. XXII. *Gaina*-Sûtras. Translated from Prâkrit by HERMANN JACOBI. Part I. 10*s.* 6*d.*

Vol. XXIII. The Zend-Avesta. Part II. Translated by JAMES DARMESTETER. 10*s.* 6*d.*

Vol. XXIV. Pahlavi Texts. Translated by E. W. WEST. Part III. 10*s.* 6*d.*

Second Series.

Vol. XXV. Manu. Translated by GEORG BÜHLER. 21*s.*

Vol. XXVI. The *S*atapatha-Brâhma*n*a. Translated by JULIUS EGGELING. Part II. 12*s.* 6*d.*

Vols. XXVII and XXVIII. The Sacred Books of China. The Texts of Confucianism. Translated by JAMES LEGGE. Parts III and IV. 25*s.*

Vols. XXIX and XXX. The G*r*ihya-Sûtras, Rules of Vedic Domestic Ceremonies. Translated by HERMANN OLDENBERG.

Part I (Vol. XXIX). 12*s.* 6*d.*
Part II (Vol. XXX). 12*s.* 6*d.* *Just Published.*

London : HENRY FROWDE, Amen Corner, E.C.

The Sacred Books of the East (*continued*).

Vol. XXXI. The Zend-Avesta. Part III. Translated by
L. H. MILLS. 12s. 6d.

Vol. XXXII. Vedic Hymns. Translated by F. MAX
MÜLLER. Part I. 18s. 6d.

Vol. XXXIII. Nârada, and some Minor Law-books.
Translated by JULIUS JOLLY. 10s. 6d.

Vol. XXXIV. The Vedânta-Sûtras, with Sankara's Commentary. Translated by G. THIBAUT. 12s. 6d.

Vol. XXXV. Milinda. Translated by T. W. RHYS DAVIDS.
Part I. 10s. 6d.

Vols. XXXIX and XL. The Sacred Books of China. The
Texts of Tâoism. Translated by JAMES LEGGE. 21s.

Vol. XXXVII. Pahlavi Texts. Translated by E. W. WEST.
Part IV. 15s. *Just Published.*

In the Press :—

Vol. XXXVI. Milinda. Translated by T. W. RHYS DAVIDS.
Part II.

Vol. XLI. Satapatha-Brâhmaṇa. Translated by JULIUS
EGGELING. Part III.

ARABIC. A Practical Arabic Grammar. Part I. Compiled
by A. O. GREEN, Brigade Major, Royal Engineers. *Second Edition,
Enlarged.* Crown 8vo, 7s. 6d.

BENGALI. Grammar of the Bengali Language ; Literary
and Colloquial. By JOHN BEAMES. Crown 8vo, cloth, 4s. 6d.

CHINESE. The Chinese Classics : with a Translation,
Critical and Exegetical Notes, Prolegomena, and Copious Indexes. By
JAMES LEGGE, D.D., LL.D. In Seven Volumes. Royal 8vo.

Vol. I. Confucian Analects, &c. *Reprinting.*

Vol. II. The Works of Mencius. 1l. 10s.

Vol. III. The Shoo-King; or, The Book of Historical
Documents. In two Parts. 1l. 10s. each.

Vol. IV. The She-King ; or, The Book of Poetry. In
two Parts. 1l. 10s. each.

Vol. V. The Ch'un Ts'ew, with the Tso Chuen. In two
Parts. 1l. 10s. each.

CHINESE. The Nestorian Monument of Hsî-an Fû in Shen-hsî, China, relating to the Diffusion of Christianity in China in the Seventh and Eighth Centuries. By JAMES LEGGE, D.D., LL.D. *Paper covers,* 2s. 6d.

—— Record of Buddhistic Kingdoms; being an Account by the Chinese Monk FÂ-HIEN of his travels in India and Ceylon (A.D. 399-414) in search of the Buddhist Books of Discipline. Translated and annotated, with a Corean recension of the Chinese Text, by JAMES LEGGE, M.A., LL.D. Crown 4to, boards, 10s. 6d.

—— Catalogue of the Chinese Translation of the Buddhist Tripitaka, the Sacred Canon of the Buddhists in China and Japan. Compiled by BUNYIU NANJIO. 4to, 1l. 12s. 6d.

—— Handbook of the Chinese Language. Parts I and II. Grammar and Chrestomathy. By JAMES SUMMERS. 8vo, 1l. 8s.

CHALDEE. Book of Tobit. A Chaldee Text, from a unique MS. in the Bodleian Library; with other Rabbinical Texts, English Translations, and the Itala. Edited by AD. NEUBAUER, M.A. Crown 8vo, 6s.

COPTIC. Libri Prophetarum Majorum, cum Lamentationibus Jeremiae, in Dialecto Linguae Aegyptiacae Memphitica seu Coptica. Edidit cum Versione Latina H. TATTAM, S.T.P. Tomi II. 8vo, 17s.

—— Libri duodecim Prophetarum Minorum in Ling. Aegypt. vulgo Coptica. Edidit H. TATTAM, A.M. 8vo, 8s. 6d.

—— Novum Testamentum Coptice, cura D. WILKINS. 1716. 4to, 12s. 6d.

HEBREW. Psalms in Hebrew (without points). Cr. 8vo, 2s.

Driver. Notes on the Hebrew Text of the Books of Samuel. By S. R. DRIVER, D.D. 8vo, 14s.

—— Treatise on the use of the Tenses in Hebrew. By S. R. DRIVER, D.D. *Third Edition.* Crown 8vo, 7s. 6d.

—— Commentary on the Book of Proverbs. Attributed to Abraham Ibn Ezra. Edited from a Manuscript in the Bodleian Library by S. R. DRIVER, D.D. Crown 8vo, paper covers, 3s. 6d.

Gesenius' Hebrew and English Lexicon of the Old Testament, with an Appendix containing the Biblical Aramaic. Translated and Edited by E. ROBINSON, FRANCIS BROWN, S. R. DRIVER, and C. A. BRIGGS. Part I (Aleph). Small 4to. 2s. 6d.— Part II. *Immediately.*

Neubauer. Book of Hebrew Roots, by Abu 'l-Walid Marwân ibn Janâh, otherwise called Rabbi Yônâh. Now first edited, with an Appendix, by AD. NEUBAUER. 4to, 2l. 7s. 6d.

HEBREW (*continued*).

Spurrell. Notes on the Hebrew Text of the Book of
Genesis. By G. J. SPURRELL, M.A. Crown 8vo, 10*s.* 6*d.*

Wickes. Hebrew Accentuation of Psalms, Proverbs, and
Job. By WILLIAM WICKES, D.D. 8vo, 5*s.*

—— Hebrew Prose Accentuation. 8vo, 10*s.* 6*d.*

SANSKRIT.—Sanskrit-English Dictionary, Etymologically
and Philologically arranged, with special reference to Greek, Latin,
German, Anglo-Saxon, English, and other cognate Indo-European
Languages. By Sir M. MONIER-WILLIAMS, D.C.L. 4to, 4*l.* 14*s.* 6*d.*

—— Practical Grammar of the Sanskrit Language, arranged
with reference to the Classical Languages of Europe, by Sir M. MONIER-
WILLIAMS, D.C.L. *Fourth Edition.* 8vo, 15*s.*

—— Nalopákhyánam. Story of Nala, an Episode of the Mahá-
bhárata : Sanskrit Text, with a copious Vocabulary, and an improved
version of Dean Milman's Translation, by Sir M. MONIER-WILLIAMS,
D.C.L. *Second Edition, Revised and Improved.* 8vo, 15*s.*

—— Sakuntalá. A Sanskrit Drama, in seven Acts. Edited
by Sir M. MONIER-WILLIAMS, D.C.L. *Second Edition.* 8vo, 1*l.* 1*s.*

SYRIAC.—Thesaurus Syriacus : collegerunt Quatremère,
Bernstein, Lorsbach, Arnoldi, Agrell, Field, Roediger : edidit R. PAYNE
SMITH, S.T.P. Vol. I, containing Fasc. I-V. Sm. fol. 5*l.* 5*s.*
Fasc. VI, 1*l.* 1*s.* Fasc. VII, 1*l.* 11*s.* 6*d.* Fasc. VIII, 1*l.* 16*s.*

—— The Book of Kalilah and Dimnah. Translated from
Arabic into Syriac. Edited by W. WRIGHT, LL.D. 8vo, 1*l.* 1*s.*

—— Cyrilli Archiepiscopi Alexandrini Commentarii in Lucae
Evangelium quae supersunt Syriace. E MSS. apud Mus. Britan. edidit
R. PAYNE SMITH, A.M. 4to, 1*l.* 2*s.*

———— Translated by R. PAYNE SMITH, M.A. 2 vols. 8vo, 14*s.*

—— Ephraemi Syri, Rabulae Episcopi Edesseni, Balaei, &c.,
Opera Selecta. E Codd. Syriacis MSS. in Museo Britannico et Bibliotheca
Bodleiana asservatis primus edidit J. J. OVERBECK. 8vo, 1*l.* 1*s.*

—— John, Bishop of Ephesus. The Third Part of his Ecclesiastical History. [In Syriac.] Now first edited by WILLIAM CURETON,
M.A. 4to, 1*l.* 12*s.*

———— Translated by R. PAYNE SMITH, M.A. 8vo, 10*s.*

TAMIL. First Lessons in Tamil. By G. U. POPE, D.D.
Fifth Edition. Crown 8vo, 7*s.* 6*d.*

SECTION VI.

ANECDOTA OXONIENSIA.

(Crown 4to, stiff covers.)

I. CLASSICAL SERIES.

I.   The English Manuscripts of the Nicomachean Ethics.
By J. A. STEWART, M.A. 3*s.* 6*d.*

II.   Nonius Marcellus, de Compendiosa Doctrina, Harleian
MS. 2719. Collated by J. H. ONIONS, M.A. 3*s.* 6*d.*

III. Aristotle's Physics. Book VII. With Introduction by
R. SHUTE, M.A. 2*s.*

IV. Bentley's Plautine Emendations. From his copy of
Gronovius. By E. A. SONNENSCHEIN, M.A. 2*s.* 6*d.*

V.   Harleian MS. 2610; Ovid's Metamorphoses I, II, III.
1–622; XXIV Latin Epigrams from Bodleian or other MSS.; Latin
Glosses on Apollinaris Sidonius from MS. Digby 172. Collated and
Edited by ROBINSON ELLIS, M.A., LL.D. 4*s.*

VII. Collations from the Harleian MS. of Cicero 2682. By
ALBERT C. CLARK, M.A. 7*s.* 6*d.*

II. SEMITIC SERIES.

I.   Commentary on Ezra and Nehemiah. By Rabbi
Saadiah. Edited by H. J. MATHEWS, M.A. 3*s.* 6*d.*

II. The Book of the Bee. Edited by ERNEST A. WALLIS
BUDGE, M.A. 21*s.*

III. A Commentary on the Book of Daniel. By Japhet Ibn
Ali. Edited and Translated by D. S. MARGOLIOUTH, M.A. 21*s.*

IV. Mediaeval Jewish Chronicles and Chronological Notes.
Edited by AD. NEUBAUER, M.A. 14*s.*

London : HENRY FROWDE, Amen Corner, E.C.

ANECDOTA OXONIENSIA (*continued*).

III. ARYAN SERIES.

I.   Buddhist Texts from Japan. 1. Va*grakkh*edikâ. Edited
by F. Max Müller. 3*s. 6d.*

II.   Buddhist Texts from Japan. 2. Sukhâvatî Vyûha.
Edited by F. Max Müller, M.A., and Bunyiu Nanjio. 7*s. 6d.*

III.   Buddhist Texts from Japan. 3. The Ancient Palm-
leaves containing the Pra*gñâ*-Pâramitâ-H*ri*daya-Sûtra and the
Ush*ñ*isha-Vi*gaya*-Dhâra*ñ*î, edited by F. Max Müller, M.A., and
Bunyiu Nanjio, M.A. With an Appendix by G. Bühler. 10*s.*

IV.   Kâtyâyana's Sarvânukrama*ñ*î of the *Rig*veda. With
Extracts from Sha*d*gurusishya's Commentary entitled Vedârthadîpikâ.
Edited by A. A. Macdonell, M.A., Ph.D. 16*s.*

V.   The Dharma Sa*m*graha. Edited by Kenjiu Kasawara,
F. Max Müller, and H. Wenzel. 7*s. 6d.*

IV. MEDIAEVAL AND MODERN SERIES.

I.   Sinonoma Bartholomei. Edited by J. L. G. Mowat,
M.A. 3*s. 6d.*

II.   Alphita. Edited by J. L. G. Mowat, M.A. 12*s. 6d.*

III.   The Saltair Na Rann. Edited from a MS. in the
Bodleian Library, by Whitley Stokes, D.C.L. 7*s. 6d.*

IV.   The Cath Finntrága, or Battle of Ventry. Edited by
Kuno Meyer, Ph.D., M.A. 6*s.*

V.   Lives of Saints, from the Book of Lismore. Edited,
with Translation, by Whitley Stokes, D.C.L. 1*l.* 11*s. 6d.*

Oxford : Clarendon Press.

II. THEOLOGY.

A. THE HOLY SCRIPTURES, &c.

COPTIC. Libri Prophetarum Majorum, cum Lamentationibus Jeremiae, in Dialecto Linguae Aegyptiacae Memphitica seu Coptica. Edidit cum Versione Latina H. TATTAM, S.T.P. Tomi II. 8vo, 17s.

—— Libri duodecim Prophetarum Minorum in Ling. Aegypt. vulgo Coptica. Edidit H. TATTAM, A.M. 8vo, 8s. 6d.

—— Novum Testamentum Coptice, cura D. WILKINS. 1716. 4to, 12s. 6d.

ENGLISH. The Holy Bible in the Earliest English Versions, made from the Latin Vulgate by JOHN WYCLIFFE and his followers : edited by FORSHALL and MADDEN. 4 vols. Royal 4to, 3l. 3s.

Also reprinted from the above, with Introduction and Glossary by W. W. SKEAT, Litt.D.

I. The Books of Job, Psalms, Proverbs, Ecclesiastes, and the Song of Solomon. Extra fcap. 8vo, 3s. 6d.

II. The New Testament. Extra fcap. 8vo, 6s.

—— The Holy Bible : an exact reprint, page for page, of the Authorised Version published in the year 1611. Demy 4to, half-bound. 1l. 1s.

—— The Holy Bible, Revised Version*.

Cheap editions for School Use.

Revised Bible. Pearl 16mo, cloth boards, 1s. 6d.

Revised New Testament. Nonpareil 32mo, 6d. ; Brevier 16mo, 1s. ; Long Primer 8vo, 1s. 6d.

—— The Oxford Bible for Teachers, containing supplementary HELPS TO THE STUDY OF THE BIBLE, including Summaries of the several Books, with copious explanatory notes ; and Tables illustrative of Scripture History and the characteristics of Bible Lands, with a complete Index of Subjects, a Concordance, a Dictionary of Proper Names, and a series of Maps. Prices in various sizes and bindings from 3s. to 2l. 5s.

* *The Revised Version is the joint property of the Universities of Oxford and Cambridge.*

London : HENRY FROWDE, Amen Corner, E.C.

ENGLISH (*continued*).

—— **Helps to the Study of the Bible,** taken from the OXFORD BIBLE FOR TEACHERS. Crown 8vo, 3*s.* 6*d.*

—— **The Psalter, or Psalms of David, and certain Canticles,** with a Translation and Exposition in English, by RICHARD ROLLE of Hampole. Edited by H. R. BRAMLEY, M.A., Fellow of S. M. Magdalen College, Oxford. With an Introduction and Glossary. Demy 8vo, 1*l.* 1*s.*

—— **Studia Biblica et Ecclesiastica.** Essays in Biblical and Patristic Criticism, and kindred subjects. By Members of the University of Oxford. 8vo.

Vol. I, 10*s.* 6*d.*   Vol. II, 12*s.* 6*d.*   Vol. III, 16*s.*

—— **Lectures on the Book of Job.** Delivered in Westminster Abbey by the Very Rev. G. G. BRADLEY, D.D. Crown 8vo, 7*s.* 6*d.*

—— **Lectures on Ecclesiastes.** By the same Author. Cr. 8vo, 4*s.* 6*d.*

—— **The Book of Wisdom:** the Greek Text, the Latin Vulgate, and the Authorised English Version; with an Introduction, Critical Apparatus, and a Commentary. By W. J. DEANE, M.A. 4to, 12*s.* 6*d.*

—— **The Five Books of Maccabees,** in English, with Notes and Illustrations by HENRY COTTON, D.C.L. 8vo, 10*s.* 6*d.*

—— **List of Editions of the Bible in English.** By HENRY COTTON, D.C.L. *Second Edition.* 8vo, 8*s.* 6*d.*

—— **Rhemes and Doway.** An attempt to show what has been done by Roman Catholics for the diffusion of the Holy Scriptures in English. By HENRY COTTON, D.C.L. 8vo, 9*s.*

GOTHIC. Evangeliorum Versio Gothica, cum Interpr. et Annott. E. BENZELII. Edidit E. LYE, A.M. 4to, 12*s.* 6*d.*

—— **The Gospel of St. Mark in Gothic,** according to the translation made by WULFILA in the Fourth Century. Edited by W. W. SKEAT, Litt.D. Extra fcap. 8vo, 4*s.*

GREEK. Old Testament. Vetus Testamentum ex Versione Septuaginta Interpretum secundum exemplar Vaticanum Romae editum. Accedit potior varietas Codicis Alexandrini. Tomi III. 18mo, 18*s.*

—— Vetus Testamentum Graece cum Variis Lectionibus. Editionem a R. HOLMES, S.T.P. inchoatam continuavit J. PARSONS, S.T.B. Tomi V. folio, 7*l.*

Oxford: Clarendon Press.

GREEK (*continued*).

—— **A Concordance to the Septuagint** and the other Greek Versions of the Old Testament (including the Apocryphal Books). By the late EDWIN HATCH, M.A., and H. A. REDPATH, M.A. Part I, A–BΩPI'Θ. Imperial 4to, 21*s.* Part II. *In the Press.*

—— Origenis Hexaplorum quae supersunt; sive, Veterum Interpretum Graecorum in totum Vetus Testamentum Fragmenta. Edidit FREDERICUS FIELD, A.M. 2 vols. 1875. 4to, 5*l.* 5*s.*

—— Essays in Biblical Greek. By EDWIN HATCH, M.A., D.D. 8vo, 10*s.* 6*d.*

—— An Essay on the Place of Ecclesiasticus in Semitic Literature. By D. S. MARGOLIOUTH, M.A., Laudian Professor of Arabic in the University of Oxford. Small 4to, 2*s.* 6*d.*

—— New Testament. Novum Testamentum Graece. Antiquissimorum Codicum Textus in ordine parallelo dispositi. Edidit E. H. HANSELL, S.T.B. Tomi III. 8vo, 24*s.*

—— Novum Testamentum Graece. Accedunt parallela S. Scripturae loca, &c. Edidit CAROLUS LLOYD, S.T.P.R. 18mo, 3*s.* *On writing paper, with wide margin,* 7*s.* 6*d.*

> Critical Appendices to the above, by W. SANDAY, M.A. Extra fcap. 8vo, cloth, 3*s.* 6*d.*

—— Novum Testamentum Graece juxta Exemplar Millianum. 18mo, 2*s.* 6*d.* *On writing paper, with wide margin,* 7*s.* 6*d.*

—— Evangelia Sacra Graece. Fcap. 8vo, limp, 1*s.* 6*d.*

—— The Greek Testament, with the Readings adopted by the Revisers of the Authorised Version:—

> (1) Pica type, with Marginal References. Demy 8vo, 10*s.* 6*d.*
> (2) Long Primer type. Fcap. 8vo, 4*s.* 6*d.*
> (3) *The same, on writing paper, with wide margin,* 15*s.*

—— The New Testament in Greek and English. Edited by E. CARDWELL, D.D. 2 vols. 1837. Crown 8vo, 6*s.*

—— The Parallel New Testament, Greek and English; being the Authorised Version, 1611; the Revised Version, 1881; and the Greek Text followed in the Revised Version. 8vo, 12*s.* 6*d.*

—— Diatessaron; sive Historia Jesu Christi ex ipsis Evangelistarum verbis apte dispositis confecta. Ed. J. WHITE. 3*s.* 6*d.*

—— Outlines of Textual Criticism applied to the New Testament. By C. E. HAMMOND, M.A. *Fifth Edition.* Crown 8vo, 4*s.* 6*d.*

London : HENRY FROWDE, Amen Corner, E.C.

GREEK (*continued*).

—— A Greek Testament Primer. An Easy Grammar and Reading Book for the use of Students beginning Greek. By E. MILLER, M.A. Extra fcap. 8vo, 3s. 6d.

—— Canon Muratorianus. Edited, with Notes and Facsimile, by S. P. TREGELLES, LL.D. 4to, 10s. 6d.

HEBREW, &c. Gesenius' Hebrew and English Lexicon of the Old Testament, with an Appendix containing the Biblical Aramaic. Translated and Edited by E. ROBINSON, FRANCIS BROWN, S. R. DRIVER, and C. A. BRIGGS. Part I (Aleph). Small 4to, 2s. 6d.—Part II. *Immediately.*

—— Notes on the Hebrew Text of the Book of Genesis. By G. J. SPURRELL, M.A. Crown 8vo, 10s. 6d.

—— Notes on the Hebrew Text of the Books of Samuel. By S. R. DRIVER, D.D. 8vo, 14s.

—— The Psalms in Hebrew without points. Stiff covers, 2s.

—— A Commentary on the Book of Proverbs. Attributed to ABRAHAM IBN EZRA. Edited from a MS. in the Bodleian Library by S. R. DRIVER, D.D. Crown 8vo, paper covers, 3s. 6d.

—— The Book of Tobit. A Chaldee Text, from a unique MS. in the Bodleian Library; with other Rabbinical Texts, English Translations, and the Itala. Edited by AD. NEUBAUER, M.A. Crown 8vo, 6s.

—— Hebrew Accentuation of Psalms, Proverbs, and Job. By WILLIAM WICKES, D.D. 8vo, 5s.

—— Hebrew Prose Accentuation. By the same. 8vo, 10s. 6d.

—— Horae Hebraicae et Talmudicae, a J. LIGHTFOOT. A new Edition, by R. GANDELL, M.A. 4 vols. 8vo, 1l. 1s.

LATIN. Libri Psalmorum Versio antiqua Latina, cum Paraphrasi Anglo-Saxonica. Edidit B. THORPE, F.A.S. 8vo, 10s. 6d.

—— Nouum Testamentum Domini Nostri Iesu Christi Latine, secundum Editionem Sancti Hieronymi. Ad Codicum Manuscriptorum fidem recensuit IOHANNES WORDSWORTH, S.T.P., Episcopus Sarisburiensis; in operis societatem adsumto HENRICO IULIANO WHITE, A.M. 4to.

Fasc. I. *Euangelium secundum Mattheum.* 12s. 6d.
Fasc. II. *Euangelium secundum Marcum.* 7s. 6d.

Oxford: Clarendon Press.

LATIN (*continued*).

—— Old-Latin Biblical Texts: No. I. The Gospel according to St. Matthew, from the St. Germain MS. (g₁). Edited by JOHN WORDSWORTH, D.D. Small 4to, stiff covers, 6s.

—— Old-Latin Biblical Texts: No. II. Portions of the Gospels according to St. Mark and St. Matthew, from the Bobbio MS. (k), &c. Edited by JOHN WORDSWORTH, D.D., W. SANDAY, M.A., D.D., and H. J. WHITE, M.A. Small 4to, stiff covers, 21s.

—— Old-Latin Biblical Texts: No. III. The Four Gospels, from the Munich MS. (q), now numbered Lat. 6224 in the Royal Library at Munich. With a Fragment from St. John in the Hof-Bibliothek at Vienna (Cod. Lat. 502). Edited, with the aid of Tischendorf's transcript (under the direction of the Bishop of Salisbury), by H. J. WHITE, M.A. Small 4to, stiff covers, 12s. 6d.

OLD-FRENCH. Libri Psalmorum Versio antiqua Gallica e Cod. MS. in Bibl. Bodleiana adservato, una cum Versione Metrica aliisque Monumentis pervetustis. Nunc primum descripsit et edidit FRANCISCUS MICHEL, Phil. Doc. 8vo, 10s. 6d.

B. FATHERS OF THE CHURCH, &c.

St. Athanasius: Orations against the Arians. With an Account of his Life by WILLIAM BRIGHT, D.D. Crown 8vo, 9s.

—— Historical Writings, according to the Benedictine Text. With an Introduction by W. BRIGHT, D.D. Crown 8vo, 10s. 6d.

St. Augustine: Select Anti-Pelagian Treatises, and the Acts of the Second Council of Orange. With an Introduction by WILLIAM BRIGHT, D.D. Crown 8vo, 9s.

St. Basil: The Book of St. Basil on the Holy Spirit. A Revised Text, with Notes and Introduction by C. F. H. JOHNSTON, M.A. Crown 8vo, 7s. 6d.

Barnabas, The Editio Princeps of the Epistle of, by Archbishop Ussher, as printed at Oxford, A.D. 1642, and preserved in an imperfect form in the Bodleian Library. With a Dissertation by J. H. BACKHOUSE, M.A. Small 4to, 3s. 6d.

Canons of the First Four General Councils of Nicaea, Constantinople, Ephesus, and Chalcedon. With Notes, by W. BRIGHT, D.D. *Second Edition.* Crown 8vo, 7s. 6d.

Catenae Graecorum Patrum in Novum Testamentum. Edidit J. A. CRAMER, S.T.P. Tomi VIII. 8vo, 2l. 4s.

London: HENRY FROWDE, Amen Corner, E.C.

Clementis Alexandrini Opera, ex recensione Guil. Dindorfii. Tomi IV. 8vo, 3*l.*

Cyrilli Archiepiscopi Alexandrini in XII Prophetas. Edidit P. E. PUSEY, A.M. Tomi II. 8vo, 2*l.* 2*s.*

—— in D. Joannis Evangelium. Accedunt Fragmenta Varia necnon Tractatus ad Tiberium Diaconum Duo. Edidit post Aubertum P. E. PUSEY, A.M. Tomi III. 8vo, 2*l.* 5*s.*

—— Commentarii in Lucae Evangelium quae supersunt Syriace. E MSS. apud Mus. Britan. edidit R. PAYNE SMITH, A.M. 4to, 1*l.* 2*s.*

—— —— Translated by R. PAYNE SMITH, M.A. 2 vols. 8vo, 14*s.*

Dowling (J. G.). Notitia Scriptorum SS. Patrum aliorumque vet. Eccles. Mon. quae in Collectionibus Anecdotorum post annum Christi MDCC. in lucem editis continentur. 8vo, 4*s.* 6*d.*

Ephraemi Syri, Rabulae Episcopi Edesseni, Balaei, aliorumque Opera Selecta. E Codd. Syriacis MSS. in Museo Britannico et Bibliotheca Bodleiana asservatis primus edidit J. J. OVERBECK. 8vo, 1*l.* 1*s.*

Eusebii Pamphili Evangelicae Praeparationis Libri XV. Ad Codd. MSS. recensuit T. GAISFORD, S.T.P. Tomi IV. 8vo, 1*l.* 10*s.*

—— Evangelicae Demonstrationis Libri X. Recensuit T. GAISFORD, S.T.P. Tomi II. 8vo, 15*s.*

—— contra Hieroclem et Marcellum Libri. Recensuit T. GAISFORD, S.T.P. 8vo, 7*s.*

Eusebius' Ecclesiastical History, according to the text of BURTON, with an Introduction by W. BRIGHT, D.D. Crown 8vo, 8*s.* 6*d.*

—— —— Annotationes Variorum. Tomi II. 8vo, 17*s.*

Evagrii Historia Ecclesiastica, ex recensione H. VALESII. 1844. 8vo, 4*s.*

Irenaeus: The Third Book of St. Irenaeus, Bishop of Lyons, against Heresies. With short Notes and a Glossary by H. DEANE, B.D. Crown 8vo, 5*s.* 6*d.*

Origenis Philosophumena; sive omnium Haeresium Refutatio. E Codice Parisino nunc primum edidit EMMANUEL MILLER. 1851. 8vo, 10*s.*

Patrum Apostolicorum, S. Clementis Romani, S. Ignatii, S. Polycarpi, quae supersunt. Edidit GUIL. JACOBSON, S.T.P.R. Tomi II. *Fourth Edition.* 8vo, 1*l.* 1*s.*

Reliquiae Sacrae secundi tertiique saeculi. Recensuit M. J. ROUTH, S.T.P. Tomi V. *Second Edition.* 8vo, 1l. 5s.

Scriptorum Ecclesiasticorum Opuscula. Recensuit M. J. ROUTH, S.T.P. Tomi II. *Third Edition.* 8vo, 10s.

Socratis Scholastici Historia Ecclesiastica. Gr. et Lat. Edidit R. HUSSEY, S.T.B. Tomi III. 1853. 8vo, 15s.

Socrates' Ecclesiastical History, according to the Text of HUSSEY, with an Introduction by WILLIAM BRIGHT, D.D. Crown 8vo, 7s. 6d.

Sozomeni Historia Ecclesiastica. Edidit R. HUSSEY, S.T.B. Tomi III. 8vo, 15s.

Tertulliani Apologeticus adversus Gentes pro Christianis. Edited, with Introduction and Notes, by T. HERBERT BINDLEY, M.A. Crown 8vo, 6s.

Theodoreti Ecclesiasticae Historiae Libri V. Recensuit T. GAISFORD, S.T.P. 8vo, 7s. 6d.

—— Graecarum Affectionum Curatio. Ad Codices MSS. recensuit T. GAISFORD, S.T.P. 8vo, 7s. 6d.

C. ECCLESIASTICAL HISTORY, &c.

Baedae Historia Ecclesiastica. Edited, with English Notes, by G. H. MOBERLY, M.A. Crown 8vo, 10s. 6d.

Bigg. The Christian Platonists of Alexandria; being the Bampton Lectures for 1886. By CHARLES BIGG, D.D. 8vo, 10s. 6d.

Bingham's Antiquities of the Christian Church, and other Works. 10 vols. 8vo, 3l. 3s.

Bright. Chapters of Early English Church History. By W. BRIGHT, D.D. *Second Edition.* 8vo, 12s.

Burnet's History of the Reformation of the Church of England. *A new Edition.* Carefully revised, and the Records collated with the originals, by N. POCOCK, M.A. 7 vols. 8vo, 1l. 10s.

Cardwell's Documentary Annals of the Reformed Church of England; being a Collection of Injunctions, Declarations, Orders, Articles of Inquiry, &c., from 1546 to 1716. 2 vols. 8vo, 18s.

London : HENRY FROWDE, Amen Corner, E.C.

Councils and Ecclesiastical Documents relating to Great Britain and Ireland. Edited, after SPELMAN and WILKINS, by A. W. HADDAN, B.D., and W. STUBBS, D.D. Vols. I and III. Medium 8vo, each 1*l*. 1*s*.

> Vol. II, Part I. Medium 8vo, 10*s*. 6*d*.
>
> Vol. II, Part II. Church of Ireland; Memorials of St. Patrick. Stiff covers, 3*s*. 6*d*.

Formularies of Faith set forth by the King's authority during the Reign of Henry VIII. 8vo, 7*s*.

Fuller's Church History of Britain. Edited by J. S. BREWER, M.A. 6 vols. 8vo, 1*l*. 19*s*.

Gibson's Synodus Anglicana. Edited by E. CARDWELL, D.D. 8vo, 6*s*.

Hamilton's (Archbishop John) Catechism, 1552. Edited, with Introduction and Glossary, by THOMAS GRAVES LAW, Librarian of the Signet Library, Edinburgh. With a Preface by the Right Hon. W. E. GLADSTONE. Demy 8vo, 12*s*. 6*d*.

Hussey. Rise of the Papal Power, traced in three Lectures. By ROBERT HUSSEY, B.D. *Second Edition.* Fcap. 8vo, 4*s*. 6*d*.

Inett's Origines Anglicanae (in continuation of Stillingfleet). Edited by J. GRIFFITHS, M.A. 3 vols. 8vo, 15*s*.

John, Bishop of Ephesus. The Third Part of his Ecclesiastical History. [In Syriac.] Now first edited by WILLIAM CURETON, M.A. 4to, 1*l*. 12*s*.

—— The same, translated by R. PAYNE SMITH, M.A. 8vo, 10*s*.

Le Neve's Fasti Ecclesiae Anglicanae. Corrected and continued from 1715 to 1853 by T. DUFFUS HARDY. 3 vols. 8vo, 1*l*. 1*s*.

Noelli (A.) Catechismus sive prima institutio disciplinaque Pietatis Christianae Latine explicata. Editio nova cura GUIL. JACOBSON, A.M. 8vo, 5*s*. 6*d*.

Prideaux's Connection of Sacred and Profane History. 2 vols. 8vo, 10*s*.

Primers put forth in the Reign of Henry VIII. 8vo, 5*s*.

Records of the Reformation. The Divorce, 1527–1533. Mostly now for the first time printed from MSS. in the British Museum and other Libraries. Collected and arranged by N. POCOCK, M.A. 2 vols. 8vo, 1*l*. 16*s*.

Reformatio Legum Ecclesiasticarum. The Reformation of Ecclesiastical Laws, as attempted in the reigns of Henry VIII, Edward VI, and Elizabeth. Edited by E. CARDWELL, D.D. 8vo, 6s. 6d.

Shirley. Some Account of the Church in the Apostolic Age. By W. W. SHIRLEY, D.D. *Second Edition.* Fcap. 8vo, 3s. 6d.

Shuckford's Sacred and Profane History connected (in continuation of Prideaux). 2 vols. 8vo, 10s.

Stillingfleet's Origines Britannicae, with LLOYD's Historical Account of Church Government. Edited by T. P. PANTIN, M.A. 2 vols. 8vo, 10s.

Stubbs. Registrum Sacrum Anglicanum. An attempt to exhibit the course of Episcopal Succession in England. By W. STUBBS, D.D. Small 4to, 8s. 6d.

Strype's Memorials of Cranmer. 2 vols. 8vo, 11s.

Life of Aylmer. 8vo, 5s. 6d.

Life of Whitgift. 3 vols. 8vo, 16s. 6d.

General Index. 2 vols. 8vo, 11s.

Sylloge Confessionum sub tempus Reformandae Ecclesiae editarum. Subjiciuntur Catechismus Heidelbergensis et Canones Synodi Dordrechtanae. 8vo, 8s.

D. LITURGIOLOGY.

Cardwell's Two Books of Common Prayer, set forth by authority in the Reign of King Edward VI, compared with each other. *Third Edition.* 8vo, 7s.

—— History of Conferences on the Book of Common Prayer from 1551 to 1690. *Third Edition.* 8vo, 7s. 6d.

Hammond. Liturgies, Eastern and Western. Edited, with Introduction, Notes, and a Liturgical Glossary, by C. E. HAMMOND, M.A. Crown 8vo, 10s. 6d.

An Appendix to the above, crown 8vo, paper covers, 1s. 6d.

Helps to the Study of the Book of Common Prayer. Being a Companion to Church Worship. Crown 8vo, 3s. 6d.

Leofric Missal, The, as used in the Cathedral of Exeter during the Episcopate of its first Bishop, A.D. 1050-1072; together with some Account of the Red Book of Derby, the Missal of Robert of Jumièges, and a few other early MS. Service Books of the English Church. Edited, with Introduction and Notes, by F. E. WARREN, B.D., F.S.A. 4to, half-morocco, 1*l.* 15*s.*

Maskell. Ancient Liturgy of the Church of England, according to the uses of Sarum, York, Hereford, and Bangor, and the Roman Liturgy arranged in parallel columns, with preface and notes. By W. MASKELL, M.A. *Third Edition.* 8vo, 15*s.*

—— Monumenta Ritualia Ecclesiae Anglicanae. The occasional Offices of the Church of England according to the old use of Salisbury, the Prymer in English, and other prayers and forms, with dissertations and notes. *Second Edition.* 3 vols. 8vo, 2*l.* 10*s.*

Warren. The Liturgy and Ritual of the Celtic Church. By F. E. WARREN, B.D. 8vo, 14*s.*

E. ENGLISH THEOLOGY.

Beveridge's Discourse upon the XXXIX Articles. 8vo, 8*s.*

Biscoe's Boyle Lectures on the Acts of the Apostles. 8vo, 9*s.*6*d.*

Bradley. Lectures on the Book of Job. By GEORGE GRANVILLE BRADLEY, D.D., Dean of Westminster. Crown 8vo, 7*s.* 6*d.*

—— Lectures on Ecclesiastes. By G. G. BRADLEY, D.D. Crown 8vo, 4*s.* 6*d.*

Bull's Works, with NELSON's Life. Edited by E. BURTON, D.D. 8 vols. 8vo, 2*l.* 9*s.*

Burnet's Exposition of the XXXIX Articles. 8vo, 7*s.*

Burton's (Edward) Testimonies of the Ante-Nicene Fathers to the Divinity of Christ. 1829. 8vo, 7*s.*

—— Testimonies of the Ante-Nicene Fathers to the Doctrine of the Trinity and of the Divinity of the Holy Ghost. 1831. 8vo, 3*s.* 6*d.*

Butler's Works. 2 vols. 8vo, 11*s.*

—— Sermons. 5*s.* 6*d.* Analogy of Religion. 5*s.* 6*d.*

Chandler's Critical History of the Life of David. 8vo, 8*s.* 6*d.*

Chillingworth's Works. 3 vols. 8vo, 1*l.* 1*s.* 6*d.*

Clergyman's Instructor. *Sixth Edition.* 8vo, 6*s.* 6*d.*

Comber's Companion to the Temple ; or, A Help to Devotion in the use of the Common Prayer. 7 vols. 8vo, 1*l.* 11*s.* 6*d.*

Cranmer's Works. Collected and arranged by H. JENKYNS, M.A., Fellow of Oriel College. 4 vols. 8vo, 1*l.* 10*s.*

Enchiridion Theologicum Anti-Romanum.

    Vol. I. JEREMY TAYLOR'S Dissuasive from Popery, and Treatise on the Real Presence. 8vo, 8*s.*

    Vol. II. BARROW on the Supremacy of the Pope, with his Discourse on the Unity of the Church. 8vo, 7*s.* 6*d.*

    Vol. III. Tracts selected from WAKE, PATRICK, STILLINGFLEET, CLAGETT, and others. 8vo, 11*s.*

[Fell's] Paraphrase, &c., on the Epistles of St. Paul. 8vo, 7*s.*

Greswell's Harmonia Evangelica. *Fifth Edition.* 8vo, 9*s.* 6*d.*

—— Prolegomena ad Harmoniam Evangelicam. 8vo, 9*s.* 6*d.*

—— Dissertations on the Principles and Arrangement of a Harmony of the Gospels. 5 vols. 8vo, 3*l.* 3*s.*

Hall's Works. Edited by P. WYNTER, D.D. 10 vols. 8vo, 3*l.* 3*s.*

Hammond's Paraphrase on the Book of Psalms. 2 vols. 8vo, 10*s.*

—— Paraphrase, &c., on the New Testament. 4 vols. 8vo, 1*l.*

Heurtley. Harmonia Symbolica : Creeds of the Western Church. By C. HEURTLEY, D.D. 8vo, 6*s.* 6*d.*

Homilies appointed to be read in Churches. Edited by J. GRIFFITHS, M.A. 8vo, 7*s.* 6*d.*

HOOKER'S WORKS, with his Life by WALTON, arranged by JOHN KEBLE, M.A. *Seventh Edition.* Revised by R. W. CHURCH, M.A., Dean of St. Paul's, and F. PAGET, D.D. 3 vols. medium 8vo, 1*l.* 16*s.*

—— the Text as arranged by J. KEBLE, M.A. 2 vols. 8vo, 11*s.*

Hooper's Works. 2 vols. 8vo, 8*s.*

London : HENRY FROWDE. Amen Corner, E.C.

Jackson's (Dr. Thomas) Works. 12 vols. 8vo, 3*l.* 6*s.*

Jewel's Works. Edited by R. W. JELF, D.D. 8 vols. 8vo, 1*l.* 10*s.*

Martineau. A Study of Religion : its Sources and Contents. By JAMES MARTINEAU, D.D. *Second Edition.* 2 vols. crown 8vo, 15*s.*

Patrick's Theological Works. 9 vols. 8vo, 1*l.* 1*s.*

Pearson's Exposition of the Creed. Revised and corrected by E. BURTON, D.D. *Sixth Edition.* 8vo, 10*s.* 6*d.*

—— Minor Theological Works. Edited with a Memoir, by EDWARD CHURTON, M.A. 2 vols. 8vo, 10*s.*

Sanderson's Works. Edited by W. JACOBSON, D.D. 6 vols. 8vo, 1*l.* 10*s.*

Stanhope's Paraphrase and Comment upon the Epistles and Gospels. *A new Edition.* 2 vols. 8vo, 10*s.*

Stillingfleet's Origines Sacrae. 2 vols. 8vo, 9*s.*

—— Rational Account of the Grounds of Protestant Religion ; being a vindication of ARCHBISHOP LAUD's Relation of a Conference, &c. 2 vols. 8vo, 10*s.*

Wall's History of Infant Baptism. *A new Edition*, by HENRY COTTON, D.C.L. 2 vols. 8vo, 1*l.* 1*s.*

Waterland's Works, with Life, by Bp. VAN MILDERT. *A new Edition*, with copious Indexes. 6 vols. 8vo, 2*l.* 11*s.*

—— Review of the Doctrine of the Eucharist, with a Preface by the late Bishop of London. Crown 8vo, 6*s.* 6*d.*

Wheatly's Illustration of the Book of Common Prayer. 8vo, 5*s.*

Wyclif. A Catalogue of the Original Works of John Wyclif. By W. W. SHIRLEY, D.D. 8vo, 3*s.* 6*d.*

—— Select English Works. By T. ARNOLD, M.A. 3 vols. 8vo, 1*l.* 1*s.*

—— Trialogus. With the Supplement now first edited. By GOTTHARD LECHLER. 8vo, 7*s.*

Oxford : Clarendon Press.

III. HISTORY, BIOGRAPHY, &c.

Arbuthnot. The Life and Works of John Arbuthnot. By
GEORGE A. AITKEN. 8vo, cloth extra, with Portrait, 16*s.*

Baker's Chronicle. Chronicon Galfridi le Baker de Swyne-
broke. Edited with Notes by EDWARD MAUNDE THOMPSON, Hon. LL.D.
St. Andrews; Hon. D.C.L. Oxford and Durham; F.S.A.; Principal
Librarian of the British Museum. Small 4to, stiff covers, 18*s.*; cloth,
gilt top, 21*s.*

Bentham. A Fragment on Government. By JEREMY
BENTHAM. Edited, with an Introduction, by F. C. MONTAGUE, M.A.
8vo, 7*s.* 6*d.*

Bluntschli. The Theory of the State. By J. K. BLUNTSCHLI.
Translated from the Sixth German Edition. 8vo, half-bound, 12*s.* 6*d.*

Boswell's Life of Samuel Johnson, LL.D.; including Bos-
WELL'S Journal of a Tour to the Hebrides, and JOHNSON'S Diary of a
Journey into North Wales. Edited by G. BIRKBECK HILL, D.C.L. In
six volumes, medium 8vo. With Portraits and Facsimiles. Half-bound,
3*l.* 3*s.*

Burnet's History of James II, with Additional Notes. 8vo.
9*s.* 6*d.*

—— Life of Sir M. Hale, and Foll's Life of Dr. Hammond.
Small 8vo, 2*s.* 6*d.*

Calendar of the Clarendon State Papers, preserved in the
Bodleian Library. In three volumes. 1869–76.

Vol. I.   From 1523 to January 1649. 8vo, 18*s.*

Vol. II.   From 1649 to 1654. 8vo, 16*s.*

Vol. III.   From 1655 to 1657. 8vo, 14*s.*

Calendar of Charters and Rolls preserved in the Bodleian
Library. 8vo, 1*l.* 11*s.* 6*d.*

Carte's Life of James Duke of Ormond. A new Edition, carefully compared with the original MSS. 6 vols. 8vo, 1*l.* 5*s.*

Casaubon (Isaac), Life of, by MARK PATTISON, B.D. *Second
Edition.* 8vo, 16*s.*

Casauboni Ephemerides, cum praefatione et notis J. RUSSELL,
S.T.P. Tomi II. 8vo, 15*s.*

Chesterfield. Letters of Philip Dormer Fourth Earl of Chesterfield, to his Godson and Successor. Edited from the Originals, with a Memoir of Lord Chesterfield, by the late EARL OF CARNARVON. *Second Edition.* With Appendix of Additional Correspondence. Royal 8vo, cloth extra, 21*s.*

CLARENDON'S History of the Rebellion and Civil Wars in England. Re-edited from a fresh collation of the original MS. in the Bodleian Library, with marginal dates and occasional notes, by W. DUNN MACRAY, M.A., F.S.A. 6 vols. Crown 8vo, 2*l.* 5*s.*

—— History of the Rebellion and Civil Wars in England. To which are subjoined the Notes of BISHOP WARBURTON. 1849. 7 vols. Medium 8vo, 2*l.* 10*s.*

—— History of the Rebellion and Civil Wars in England. Also his Life, written by himself, in which is included a Continuation of his History of the Grand Rebellion. Royal 8vo, 1*l.* 2*s.*

Clarendon's Life, including a Continuation of his History. 2 vols. 1857. Medium 8vo, 1*l.* 2*s.*

Clinton's Fasti Hellenici. The Civil and Literary Chronology of Greece, from the LVIth to the CXXIIIrd Olympiad. *Third Edition.* 4to, 1*l.* 14*s.* 6*d.*

—— Fasti Hellenici. The Civil and Literary Chronology of Greece, from the CXXIVth Olympiad to the Death of Augustus. *Second Edition.* 4to, 1*l.* 12*s.*

—— Epitome of the Fasti Hellenici. 8vo, 6*s.* 6*d.*

—— Fasti Romani. The Civil and Literary Chronology of Rome and Constantinople, from the Death of Augustus to the Death of Heraclius. 2 vols. 4to, 2*l.* 2*s.*

—— Epitome of the Fasti Romani. 8vo, 7*s.*

Codrington. The Melanesians. Studies in their Anthropology and Folk-Lore. By R. H. CODRINGTON, D.D. 8vo, 16*s.*

Cramer's Geographical and Historical Description of Asia Minor. 2 vols. 8vo, 11*s.*

—— Description of Ancient Greece. 3 vols. 8vo, 16*s.* 6*d.*

Earle. Handbook to the Land-Charters, and other Saxonic Documents. By JOHN EARLE, M.A., Professor of Anglo-Saxon in the University of Oxford. Crown 8vo, 16*s.*

Finlay. A History of Greece from its Conquest by the Romans to the present time, B.C. 146 to A.D. 1864. By GEORGE FINLAY, LL.D. A new Edition, revised throughout, and in part re-written, with considerable additions, by the Author, and edited by H. F. TOZER, M.A. 7 vols. 8vo, 3*l*. 10*s*.

Fortescue. The Governance of England: otherwise called The Difference between an Absolute and a Limited Monarchy. By Sir JOHN FORTESCUE, Kt. A Revised Text. Edited, with Introduction, Notes, &c., by CHARLES PLUMMER, M.A. 8vo, half-bound, 12*s*. 6*d*.

Freeman. The History of Sicily from the Earliest Times. Vols. I and II. 8vo, 2*l*. 2*s*.

    Vol. III. The Athenian and Carthaginian Invasions. 1*l*. 4*s*.

—— History of the Norman Conquest of England; its Causes and Results. By E. A. FREEMAN, D.C.L. In Six Volumes, 8vo, 5*l*. 9*s*. 6*d*.

—— The Reign of William Rufus and the Accession of Henry the First. 2 vols. 8vo, 1*l*. 16*s*.

—— A Short History of the Norman Conquest of England. *Second Edition.* Extra fcap. 8vo, 2*s*. 6*d*.

French Revolutionary Speeches. See STEPHENS, H. Morse.

Gardiner. The Constitutional Documents of the Puritan Revolution. 1628–1660. Selected and Edited by SAMUEL RAWSON GARDINER, M.A. Crown 8vo, 9*s*.

Gascoigne's Theological Dictionary ('Liber Veritatum'): Selected Passages, illustrating the Condition of Church and State, 1403–1458. With an Introduction by JAMES E. THOROLD ROGERS, M.A. Small 4to, 10*s*. 6*d*.

George. Genealogical Tables illustrative of Modern History. By H. B. GEORGE, M.A. *Third Edition.* Small 4to, 12*s*.

Greswell's Fasti Temporis Catholici. 4 vols. 8vo, 2*l*. 10*s*.

—— Tables to Fasti, 4to, and Introduction to Tables, 8vo, 15*s*.

—— Origines Kalendariæ Italicæ. 4 vols. 8vo, 2*l*. 2*s*.

—— Origines Kalendariæ Hellenicæ. 6 vols. 8vo, 4*l*. 4*s*.

London: HENRY FROWDE, Amen Corner, E.C.

Greswell (W. Parr). History of the Dominion of Canada.
By W. PARR GRESWELL, M.A., under the Auspices of the Royal Colonial
Institute. With Eleven Maps. Crown 8vo, 7*s.* 6*d.*

—— Geography of the Dominion of Canada and Newfound-
land. By the same Author. With Ten Maps. Crown 8vo, 6*s.*

——- Geography of Africa South of the Zambesi. With
Maps. Crown 8vo, 7*s.* 6*d.*

Gross. The Gild Merchant: a Contribution to British
Municipal History. By C. GROSS, Ph.D. 2 vols. 8vo, half-bound, 24*s.*

Hastings. Hastings and The Rohilla War. By Sir JOHN
STRACHEY, G.C.S.I. 8vo, cloth, 10*s.* 6*d.*

Hodgkin. Italy and her Invaders. With Plates and Maps.
By THOMAS HODGKIN, D.C.L. Vols. I–IV, A.D. 376–553. 8vo, 3*l.* 8*s.*

—— The Dynasty of Theodosius; or, Seventy Years' Struggle
with the Barbarians. By the same Author. Crown 8vo, 6*s.*

Hume. Letters of David Hume to William Strahan. Edited
with Notes, Index, &c., by G. BIRKBECK HILL, D.C.L. 8vo, 12*s.* 6*d.*

Jackson. Dalmatia, the Quarnero, and Istria; with Cettigne
in Montenegro and the Island of Grado. By T. G. JACKSON, M.A.
3 vols. With many Plates and Illustrations. 8vo, half-bound, 2*l.* 2*s.*

Johnson. Letters of Samuel Johnson, LL.D. Collected
and Edited by G. BIRKBECK HILL, D.C.L. In two volumes. Medium
8vo, half-roan (uniform with Boswell's Life of Johnson,) 28*s.*

Kitchin. A History of France. With numerous Maps,
Plans, and Tables. By G. W. KITCHIN, D.D. In three Volumes.
Second Edition. Crown 8vo, each 10*s.* 6*d.*
　　Vol. I, to 1453.　　Vol. II, 1453–1624.　　Vol. III, 1624–1793.

Knight's Life of Dean Colet. 1823. 8vo, 7*s.* 6*d.*

Lloyd's Prices of Corn in Oxford, 1583–1830. 8vo, 1*s.*

Lewes, The Song of. Edited, with Introduction and Notes,
by C. L. KINGSFORD, M.A. Extra fcap. 8vo, 5*s.*

Lewis (Sir G. Cornewall). An Essay on the Government
of Dependencies. Edited by C. P. Lucas, B.A. 8vo, half-roan, 14*s.*

Oxford : Clarendon Press.

Lucas. Introduction to a Historical Geography of the British Colonies. By C. P. Lucas, B.A. With Eight Maps. Crown 8vo, 4s. 6d.

—— Historical Geography of the British Colonies. By the same Author:

> Vol. I. The Mediterranean and Eastern Colonies (exclusive of India). With Eleven Maps. 5s.

> Vol. II. The West Indian Colonies. With Twelve Maps. 7s. 6d.

Luttrell's (Narcissus) Diary. A Brief Historical Relation of State Affairs, 1678–1714. 6 vols. 8vo, 1l. 4s.

Machiavelli (Niccolò). Il Principe. Edited by L. Arthur Burd. With an Introduction by Lord Acton. 8vo, 14s.

Macray (W. Dunn). Annals of the Bodleian Library, Oxford, with a Notice of the Earlier Library of the University. By W. Dunn Macray, M.A., F.S.A. *Second Edition, enlarged and continued from* 1868 to 1880. Medium 8vo, half-bound, 25s.

Magna Carta, a careful Reprint. Edited by W. Stubbs, D.D., Lord Bishop of Oxford. 4to, stitched, 1s.

Metcalfe. Passio et Miracula Beati Olaui. Edited from a Twelfth-Century MS. by F. Metcalfe, M.A. Small 4to, 6s.

OXFORD, University of.

Oxford University Calendar for 1892. Crown 8vo, 6s.

The Historical Register of the University of Oxford. Being a Supplement to the Oxford University Calendar, with an Alphabetical Record of University Honours and Distinctions, completed to the end of Trinity Term, 1888. Crown 8vo, 5s.

Student's Handbook to the University and Colleges of Oxford. *Eleventh Edition.* Crown 8vo, 2s. 6d.

The Examination Statutes ; together with the present Regulations of the Boards of Studies and Boards of Faculties relating thereto. Revised to June 2, 1891. 8vo, paper covers, 1s.

Statuta Universitatis Oxoniensis. 1891. 8vo, 5s.

Statutes made for the University of Oxford, and the Colleges therein, by the University of Oxford Commissioners. 8vo, 12s. 6d. *Also separately*—University Statutes, 2s.; College Statutes, 1s. each.

London : Henry Frowde, Amen Corner, E.C.

OXFORD, University of (*continued*).

Supplementary Statutes made by the University of Oxford, and by certain of the Colleges therein, in pursuance of the Universities of Oxford and Cambridge Act, 1877; approved by the Queen in Council. 8vo, paper covers, 2*s.* 6*d.*

Statutes of the University of Oxford, codified in the year 1636 under the Authority of ARCHBISHOP LAUD, Chancellor of the University. Edited by the late JOHN GRIFFITHS, D.D. With an Introduction on the History of the Laudian Code by C. L. SHADWELL, M.A., B.C.L. 4to, 1*l.* 1*s.*

Enactments in Parliament, specially concerning the Universities of Oxford and Cambridge. Collected and arranged by J. GRIFFITHS, D.D. 1869. 8vo, 12*s.*

Catalogue of Oxford Graduates from 1659 to 1850. 8vo, 7*s.* 6*d.*

Index to Wills proved in the Court of the Chancellor of the University of Oxford, &c. Compiled by J. GRIFFITHS, D.D. Royal 8vo, 3*s.* 6*d.*

Manuscript Materials relating to the History of Oxford ; contained in the Printed Catalogues of the Bodleian and College Libraries. By F. MADAN, M.A. 8vo, 7*s.* 6*d.*

Pattison. Essays by the late MARK PATTISON, sometime Rector of Lincoln College. Collected and arranged by HENRY NETTLE-SHIP, M.A. 2 vols. 8vo, 24*s.*

—— Life of Isaac Casaubon (1559–1614). By the same Author. *Second Edition.* 8vo, 16*s.*

Payne. History of the New World called America. By E. J. PAYNE, M.A. Vol. I, 8vo, 18*s.*

Ralegh. Sir Walter Ralegh. A Biography. By W. STEBBING, M.A. 8vo, 10*s.* 6*d.*

Ramsay (Sir James H.). **Lancaster and York.** A Century of English History (A.D. 1399–1485). 2 vols. 8vo, 1*l.* 16*s.*

Ranke. A History of England, principally in the Seventeenth Century. By L. VON RANKE. Translated under the superintendence of G. W. KITCHIN, D.D., and C. W. BOASE, M.A. 6 vols. 8vo, 3*l.* 3*s.*

Rawlinson. A Manual of Ancient History. By GEORGE RAWLINSON, M.A. *Second Edition.* Demy 8vo, 14*s.*

Rhŷs. Studies in the Arthurian Legend. By JOHN RHŶS, M.A., Professor of Celtic in the University of Oxford. 8vo, 12*s.* 6*d.*

Ricardo. Letters of David Ricardo to T. R. Malthus (1810–1823). Edited by JAMES BONAR, M.A. 8vo, 10*s.* 6*d.*

Rogers. History of Agriculture and Prices in England, A.D. 1259–1793. By JAMES E. THOROLD ROGERS, M.A.

Vols. I and II (1259–1400). 8vo, 2*l.* 2*s.*

Vols. III and IV (1401–1582). 8vo, 2*l.* 10*s.*

Vols. V and VI (1583–1702). 8vo, 2*l.* 10*s.*

Vols. VII and VIII. *In the Press.*

—— First Nine Years of the Bank of England. 8vo, 8*s.* 6*d.*

—— Protests of the Lords, including those which have been expunged, from 1624 to 1874; with Historical Introductions. In three volumes. 8vo, 2*l.* 2*s.*

Smith's Wealth of Nations. A new Edition, with Notes, by J. E. THOROLD ROGERS, M.A. 2 vols. 8vo, 21*s.*

Sprigg's England's Recovery; being the History of the Army under Sir Thomas Fairfax. 8vo, 6*s.*

RULERS OF INDIA: The History of the Indian Empire in a carefully planned succession of Political Biographies. Edited by Sir WILLIAM WILSON HUNTER, K.C.S.I. In crown 8vo. Half-crown volumes.

Now Ready:

The Marquess of Dalhousie. By Sir W. W. HUNTER.

Akbar. By COLONEL MALLESON, C.S.I.

Dupleix. By COLONEL MALLESON, C.S.I.

Warren Hastings. By CAPTAIN L. J. TROTTER.

The Marquess of Cornwallis. By W. S. SETON-KARR.

The Earl of Mayo. By Sir W. W. HUNTER, K.C.S.I.

Viscount Hardinge. By his son, the Rt. Hon. VISCOUNT HARDINGE.

London : HENRY FROWDE, Amen Corner, E.C.

RULERS OF INDIA (*continued*).

Clyde and Strathnairn. By Major-General SIR OWEN TUDOR BURNE, K.C.S.I.

Earl Canning. By Sir H. S. CUNNINGHAM, K.C.I.E.

Mádhava Ráo Sindhia. By H. G. KEENE, M.A., C.I.E.

Mountstuart Elphinstone. By J. S. COTTON, M.A.

Lord William Bentinck. By DEMETRIUS C. BOULGER.

Ranjit Singh. By Sir LEPEL GRIFFIN, K.C.S.I.

Further volumes will be published at short intervals.

Stephens. The Principal Speeches of the Statesmen and Orators of the French Revolution, 1789–1795. With Historical Introductions, Notes, and Index. By H. MORSE STEPHENS, author of 'A History of the French Revolution.' 2 vols. Crown 8vo. 21*s.*

Stubbs. Select Charters and other Illustrations of English Constitutional History, from the Earliest Times to the Reign of Edward I. Arranged and edited by W. STUBBS, D.D., Lord Bishop of Oxford. *Seventh Edition.* Crown 8vo, 8*s.* 6*d.*

—— The Constitutional History of England, in its Origin and Development. *Library Edition.* 3 vols. Demy 8vo, 2*l.* 8*s.*

Also in 3 vols. crown 8vo, price 12*s.* each.

—— Seventeen Lectures on the Study of Mediaeval and Modern History, delivered at Oxford 1867–1884. *Second Edition.* Crown 8vo, 8*s.* 6*d.*

Tozer. The Islands of the Aegean. By H. FANSHAWE TOZER, M.A., F.R.G.S. Crown 8vo, 8*s.* 6*d.*

Vinogradoff. Villainage in England. Essays in English Mediaeval History. By PAUL VINOGRADOFF, Professor in the University of Moscow. 8vo, half-bound, 16*s.*

Wellesley. A Selection from the Despatches, Treaties, and other Papers of the MARQUESS WELLESLEY, K.G., during his Government of India. Edited by S. J. OWEN, M.A. 8vo, 1*l.* 4*s.*

Wellington. A Selection from the Despatches, Treaties, and other Papers relating to India of Field-Marshal the DUKE OF WELLINGTON, K.G. Edited by S. J. OWEN, M.A. 8vo, 1*l.* 4*s.*

Whitelock's Memorials of English Affairs from 1625 to 1660. 4 vols. 8vo, 1*l.* 10*s.*

Oxford: Clarendon Press.

IV. LAW.

Anson. Principles of the English Law of Contract, and of Agency in its Relation to Contract. By SIR W. R. ANSON, D.C.L. *Fifth Edition.* 8vo, 10s. 6d.

—— Law and Custom of the Constitution. In two Parts.
Part I. Parliament. *Second Edition.* 8vo, 12s. 6d.
Part II. The Crown. 8vo, 14s.

Baden-Powell. Land-Systems of British India; being a Manual of the Land-Tenures, and of the Systems of Land-Revenue Administration prevalent in the several Provinces. By B. H. BADEN-POWELL, C.I.E., F.R.S.E., M.R.A.S. 3 vols. 8vo, with Maps, 3l. 3s.

Bentham. An Introduction to the Principles of Morals and Legislation. By JEREMY BENTHAM. Crown 8vo, 6s. 6d.

Digby. An Introduction to the History of the Law of Real Property. By KENELM E. DIGBY, M.A. *Fourth Edition.* 8vo, 12s. 6d.

Grueber. Lex Aquilia. The Roman Law of Damage to Property: being a Commentary on the Title of the Digest 'Ad Legem Aquiliam' (ix. 2). With an Introduction to the Study of the Corpus Iuris Civilis. By ERWIN GRUEBER, Dr. Jur., M.A. 8vo, 10s. 6d.

Hall. International Law. By W. E. HALL, M.A. *Third Edition.* 8vo, 22s. 6d.

Holland. Elements of Jurisprudence. By T. E. HOLLAND, D.C.L. *Fifth Edition.* 8vo, 10s. 6d.

—— The European Concert in the Eastern Question, a Collection of Treaties and other Public Acts. Edited, with Introductions and Notes, by T. E. HOLLAND, D.C.L. 8vo, 12s. 6d.

—— Gentilis, Alberici, I.C.D., I.C.P.R., de Iure Belli Libri Tres. Edidit T. E. HOLLAND, I.C.D. Small 4to, half-morocco, 21s.

—— The Institutes of Justinian, edited as a recension of the Institutes of GAIUS, by T. E. HOLLAND, D.C.L. *Second Edition.* Extra fcap. 8vo, 5s.

London: HENRY FROWDE, Amen Corner, E.C.

Holland and **Shadwell.** Select Titles from the Digest of
Justinian. By T. E. HOLLAND, D.C.L., and C. L. SHADWELL, B.C.L.
8vo, 14*s.*
    Also sold in Parts, in paper covers, as follows:—
    Part I. Introductory Titles. 2*s.* 6*d.*
    Part II. Family Law. 1*s.*
    Part III. Property Law. 2*s.* 6*d.*
    Part IV. Law of Obligations (No. 1). 3*s.* 6*d.*
    Part IV. Law of Obligations (No. 2). 4*s.* 6*d.*

Markby. Elements of Law considered with reference to
Principles of General Jurisprudence. By Sir WILLIAM MARKBY, D.C.L.
Fourth Edition. 8vo, 12*s.* 6*d.*

Moyle. Imperatoris Iustiniani Institutionum Libri Quattuor; with Introductions, Commentary, Excursus, and Translation. By
J. B. MOYLE, D.C.L. *Second Edition.* 2 vols. 8vo, 22*s.*

—— Contract of Sale in the Civil Law. By J. B. MOYLE,
D.C.L. 8vo, 10*s.* 6*d.*

Pollock and **Wright.** An Essay on Possession in the Common
Law. By Sir F. POLLOCK, M.A., and Sir R. S. WRIGHT, B.C.L. 8vo,
8*s.* 6*d.*

Poste. Gaii Institutionum Juris Civilis Commentarii Quattuor;
or, Elements of Roman Law by Gaius. With a Translation and Commentary by EDWARD POSTE, M.A. *Third Edition.* 8vo, 18*s.*

Raleigh. An Outline of the Law of Property. By THOMAS
RALEIGH, M.A. 8vo, cloth, 7*s.* 6*d.*

Sohm. Institutes of Roman Law. By RUDOLPH SOHM,
Professor in the University of Leipzig. Translated (from the Fourth
Edition of the German) by J. C. LEDLIE, B.C.L., M.A. With an Intro-
ductory Essay by ERWIN GRUEBER, DR. JUR., M.A. 8vo, 18*s.*

Stokes. Anglo-Indian Codes. By WHITLEY STOKES, LL.D.
Vol. I. Substantive Law. 8vo, 30*s.* Vol. II. Adjective Law. 8vo, 35*s.*

—— First Supplement to the above, 1887, 1888. 2*s.* 6*d.*

—— Second Supplement, to May 31, 1891. 4*s.* 6*d.*

Twiss. The Law of Nations considered as Independent
Political Communities. By SIR TRAVERS TWISS, D.C.L.
    Part I. On the rights and Duties of Nations in time of
        Peace. New Edition, Revised and Enlarged. 8vo, 15*s.*
    Part II. On the Rights and Duties of Nations in time of
        War. Second Edition, Revised. 8vo, 21*s.*

V. PHILOSOPHY, LOGIC, &c.

Bacon. Novum Organum. Edited, with Introduction, Notes, &c., by T. FOWLER, D.D. *Second Edition.* 8vo, 15s.

—— Novum Organum. Edited, with English Notes, by G. W. KITCHIN, D.D. 8vo, 9s. 6d.

—— Novum Organum. Translated by G. W. KITCHIN, D.D. 8vo, 9s. 6d.

—— The Essays. Edited, with Introduction and Illustrative Notes, by S. H. REYNOLDS, M.A. Demy 8vo, half-bound, 12s. 6d.

Berkeley. The works of GEORGE BERKELEY, D.D., formerly Bishop of Cloyne; including many of his writings hitherto unpublished. With Prefaces, Annotations, and an Account of his Life and Philosophy, by ALEXANDER CAMPBELL FRASER, LL.D. 4 vols. 8vo, 2l. 18s.

The Life, Letters, &c., separately, 16s.

Berkeley. Selections. With Introduction and Notes. For the use of Students in the Universities. By ALEXANDER CAMPBELL FRASER, LL.D. *Third Edition.* Crown 8vo, 8s. 6d.

Bosanquet. Logic; or, The Morphology of Knowledge. By B. BOSANQUET, M.A. 8vo, 21s.

Butler's Works, with Index to the Analogy. 2 vols. 8vo, 11s.

Fowler. The Elements of Deductive Logic, designed mainly for the use of Junior Students in the Universities. By T. FOWLER, D.D. *Ninth Edition,* with a Collection of Examples. Extra fcap. 8vo, 3s. 6d.

Fowler. The Elements of Inductive Logic, designed mainly for the use of Students in the Universities. *Fifth Edition.* Extra fcap. 8vo, 6s.

—— The Principles of Morals (Introductory Chapters). By T. FOWLER, D.D., and J. M. WILSON, B.D. 8vo, boards, 3s. 6d.

—— The Principles of Morals. Part II. By T. FOWLER, D.D. 8vo, 10s. 6d.

Green. Prolegomena to Ethics. By T. H. GREEN, M.A. Edited by A. C. BRADLEY, M.A. *Third Edition.* 8vo, 12s. 6d.

Hegel. The Logic of Hegel; translated from the Encyclopaedia of the Philosophical Sciences. With Prolegomena by WILLIAM WALLACE, M.A. 8vo, 14s. *New Edition in the Press.*

Hume's Treatise of Human Nature. Reprinted from the Original Edition in Three Volumes, and Edited by L. A. Selby-Bigge, M.A. Crown 8vo, 9*s.*

Locke's Conduct of the Understanding. Edited by T. FOWLER, D.D. *Third Edition.* Extra fcap. 8vo, 2*s.* 6*d.*

Lotze's Logic, in Three Books; of Thought, of Investigation, and of Knowledge. English Translation; Edited by B. BOSANQUET, M.A. *Second Edition.* 2 vols. Crown 8vo, 12*s.*

—— Metaphysic, in Three Books; Ontology, Cosmology, and Psychology. English Translation; Edited by B. BOSANQUET, M.A. *Second Edition.* 2 vols. Crown 8vo, 12*s.*

Martineau. Types of Ethical Theory. By JAMES MARTINEAU, D.D. *Second Edition.* 2 vols. Crown 8vo, 15*s.*

—— A Study of Religion: its Sources and Contents. *A New Edition.* 2 vols. Crown 8vo, 15*s.*

VI. PHYSICAL SCIENCE AND MATHEMATICS, &c.

Acland. Synopsis of the Pathological Series in the Oxford Museum. By Sir H. W. ACLAND, M.D., F.R.S. 8vo, 2*s.* 6*d.*

Aldis. A Text-Book of Algebra: with Answers to the Examples. By W. S. ALDIS, M.A. Crown 8vo, 7*s.* 6*d.*

Aplin. The Birds of Oxfordshire. By O. V. APLIN. 8vo. with a Map and one coloured Plate, 10*s.* 6*d.*

Archimedis quae supersunt omnia cum Eutocii commentariis ex recensione J. TORELLI, cum nová versione Latiná. 1792. Fol. 1*l.* 5*s.*

Baynes. Lessons on Thermodynamics. By R. E. BAYNES, M.A. Crown 8vo, 7*s.* 6*d.*

BIOLOGICAL SERIES. (Translations of Foreign Memoirs.)

I.   Memoirs on the Physiology of Nerve, of Muscle, and of the Electrical Organ. Edited by J. BURDON-SANDERSON, M.D., F.R.SS.L. & E. Medium 8vo, 1*l.* 1*s.*

II. The Anatomy of the Frog. By Dr. ALEXANDER ECKER, Professor in the University of Freiburg. Translated, with numerous Annotations and Additions, by GEORGE HASLAM, M.D. Medium 8vo, 21*s.*

Biological Series (*continued*).

IV. Essays upon Heredity and kindred Biological Problems. By Dr. August Weismann, Professor in the University of Freiburg-in-Breisgau. Authorised Translation. Edited by Edward E. Poulton, M.A., F.R.S., Selmar Schönland, Ph.D., and Arthur E. Shipley, M.A., F.L.S. Crown 8vo. Vol. I, 7s. 6d.

> Vol. II. Edited by E. B. Poulton and A. E. Shipley. Crown 8vo, 5s. *Just Published.*

BOTANICAL SERIES.

History of Botany (1530–1860). By Julius von Sachs. Authorised Translation, by H. E. F. Garnsey, M.A. Revised by Isaac Bayley Balfour, M.A., M.D., F.R.S. Crown 8vo, 10s.

Comparative Anatomy of the Vegetative Organs of the Phanerogams and Ferns. By Dr. A. de Bary. Translated and Annotated by F. O. Bower, M.A., F.L.S., and D. H. Scott, M.A., Ph.D., F.L.S. Royal 8vo, half-morocco, 1l. 2s. 6d.

Outlines of Classification and Special Morphology of Plants. A new Edition of Sachs' Text-Book of Botany, Book II. By Dr. K. Goebel. Translated by H. E. F. Garnsey, M.A., and Revised by Isaac Bayley Balfour, M.A., M.D., F.R.S. Royal 8vo, half-morocco, 1l. 1s.

Lectures on the Physiology of Plants. By Julius von Sachs. Translated by H. Marshall Ward, M.A., F.L.S. Royal 8vo, half-morocco, 1l. 11s. 6d.

Comparative Morphology and Biology of Fungi, Mycetozoa and Bacteria. By Dr. A. de Bary. Translated by H. E. F. Garnsey, M.A., Revised by Isaac Bayley Balfour, M.A., M.D., F.R.S. Royal 8vo, half-morocco, 1l. 2s. 6d.

Lectures on Bacteria. By Dr. A. de Bary. Second Improved Edition. Translated by H. E. F. Garnsey, M.A. Revised by Isaac Bayley Balfour, M.A., M.D., F.R.S. Crown 8vo, 6s.

Introduction to Fossil Botany. By Count H. zu Solms-Laubach. Translated by H. E. F. Garnsey, M.A. Revised by Isaac Bayley Balfour, M.A., M.D., F.R.S. Royal 8vo, half-morocco, 18s.

Annals of Botany. Edited by Isaac Bayley Balfour, M.A., M.D., F.R.S., Sydney H. Vines, D.Sc., F.R.S., W. G. Farlow, M.D., and W. T. Thiselton-Dyer, C.M.G., M.A., F.R.S.; assisted by other Botanists. Royal 8vo, half-morocco, gilt top.

> Vol. I. Parts I–IV. 1l. 16s.
> Vol. II. Parts V–VIII. 2l. 2s.
> Vol. III. Parts IX–XII. 2l. 12s. 6d.
> Vol. IV. Parts XIII–XVI. 2l. 5s.
> Vol. V. Parts XVII–XX. 2l. 10s.
> Vol. VI. Part XXI. 12s.

Bradley's Miscellaneous Works and Correspondence. With an Account of Harriot's Astronomical Papers. 4to, 17*s.*

Chambers. A Handbook of Descriptive Astronomy. By G. F. CHAMBERS, F.R.A.S. *Fourth Edition.*

Vol. I. The Sun, Planets, and Comets. 8vo, 21*s.*
Vol. II. Instruments and Practical Astronomy. 8vo, 21*s.*
Vol. III. The Starry Heavens. 8vo, 14*s.*

Clarke. Geodesy. By Col. A. R. CLARKE, C.B., R.E. 8vo, 12*s. 6d.*

Cremona. Elements of Projective Geometry. By LUIGI CREMONA. Translated by C. LEUDESDORF, M.A. 8vo, 12*s. 6d.*

—— Graphical Statics. Two Treatises on the Graphical Calculus and Reciprocal Figures in Graphical Statics. By the same Author. Translated by T. HUDSON BEARE. Demy 8vo, 8*s. 6d.*

Daubeny's Introduction to the Atomic Theory. 16mo, 6*s.*

Dixey. Epidemic Influenza, a Study in Comparative Statistics. By F. A. DIXEY, M.A., D.M., Fellow of Wadham College. With Diagrams and Tables. Medium 8vo. Immediately.

Donkin. Acoustics. By W. F. DONKIN, M.A., F.R.S. *Second Edition.* Crown 8vo, 7*s. 6d.*

Emtage. An Introduction to the Mathematical Theory of Electricity and Magnetism. By W. A. T. EMTAGE, M.A. Crown 8vo, 7*s. 6d.*

Etheridge. Fossils of the British Islands, Stratigraphically and Zoologically arranged. Part I. PALAEOZOIC. By R. ETHERIDGE, F.R.SS.L. & E., F.G.S. 4to, 1*l.* 10*s.*

EUCLID REVISED. Containing the Essentials of the Elements of Plane Geometry as given by Euclid in his first Six Books. Edited by R. C. J. NIXON, M.A. *Second Edition.* Crown 8vo, 6*s.*

Supplement to *Euclid Revised.* 6*d.*

Sold separately as follows :—

Book I. 1*s.*   Books I, II. 1*s. 6d.*
Books I–IV. 3*s.*   Books V, VI. 3*s.*

Euclid. Geometry in Space. Containing parts of Euclid's Eleventh and Twelfth Books. By the same Editor. Crown 8vo, 3*s. 6d.*

Fisher. Class-Book of Chemistry. By W. W. FISHER, M.A., F.C.S. Crown 8vo, 4*s. 6d.*

Galton. The Construction of Healthy Dwellings. By Sir DOUGLAS GALTON, K.C.B., F.R.S. 8vo, 10*s. 6d.*

Greenwell. British Barrows, a Record of the Examination of Sepulchral Mounds in various parts of England. By W. GREENWELL, M.A., F.S.A. Together with Description of Figures of Skulls, General Remarks on Prehistoric Crania, and an Appendix by GEORGE ROLLESTON, M.D., F.R.S. Medium 8vo, 25*s.*

Gresswell. A Contribution to the Natural History of Scarlatina, derived from Observations on the London Epidemic of 1887–1888. By D. ASTLEY GRESSWELL, M.D. Medium 8vo, 10s. 6d.

Hamilton and Ball. Book-keeping. New and enlarged Edition. By Sir R. G. C. HAMILTON and JOHN BALL. Extra fcap. 8vo, limp cloth, 2s.

Ruled Exercise books adapted to the above may be had, price 1s. 6d.; also, adapted to the Preliminary Course only, price 4d.

Harcourt and Madan. Exercises in Practical Chemistry. Vol. I. Elementary Exercises. By A. G. VERNON HARCOURT, M.A., and H. G. MADAN, M.A. *Fourth Edition.* Crown 8vo, 10s. 6d.

Madan. Tables of Qualitative Analysis. By H. G. MADAN, M.A. Large 4to, paper covers, 4s. 6d.

Combination Chemical Labels. In Two Parts. Gummed ready for use, 3s. 6d.

Hensley. Figures made Easy. A first Arithmetic Book. By LEWIS HENSLEY, M.A. Crown 8vo, 6d.

—— Answers to the Examples in Figures made Easy, together with two thousand additional Examples, with Answers. Crown 8vo, 1s.

Hensley. The Scholar's Arithmetic. Crown 8vo, 2s. 6d.

—— Answers to Examples in Scholar's Arithmetic. 1s. 6d.

—— The Scholar's Algebra. Crown 8vo, 2s. 6d.

Hughes. Geography for Schools. By ALFRED HUGHES, M.A. Part I. Practical Geography. With Diagrams. Crown 8vo, 2s. 6d.

Maclaren. A System of Physical Education: Theoretical and Practical. By ARCHIBALD MACLAREN. Extra fcap. 8vo, 7s. 6d.

Maxwell. A Treatise on Electricity and Magnetism. By J. CLERK MAXWELL, M.A. *Third Edition.* 2 vols. 8vo, 1l. 12s.

A Supplementary Volume, by Professor J. J. THOMSON, is in the Press.

—— An Elementary Treatise on Electricity. Edited by WILLIAM GARNETT, M.A. 8vo, 7s. 6d.

Minchin. A Treatise on Statics with Applications to Physics. By G. M. MINCHIN, M.A. *Third Edition.* Vol. I. Equilibrium of Coplanar Forces. *Fourth Edition*, 10s. 6d. Vol. II. Statics. 8vo, 16s.

—— Uniplanar Kinematics of Solids and Fluids. Crown 8vo, 7s. 6d.

Müller. On certain Variations in the Vocal Organs of the Passeres. By J. MÜLLER. Translated by F. J. BELL, B.A., and edited by A. H. GARROD, M.A., F.R.S. With Plates. 4to, 7s. 6d.

London : HENRY FROWDE, Amen Corner, E.C.

Nixon. See Euclid Revised.

—— Elementary Plane Trigonometry, By R. C. J. Nixon, M.A. Crown 8vo, 7s. 6d.

Phillips. Geology of Oxford and the Valley of the Thames. By John Phillips, M.A., F.R.S. 8vo, 21s.

—— Vesuvius. Crown 8vo, 10s. 6d.

Prestwich. Geology, Chemical, Physical, and Stratigraphical. By Joseph Prestwich, M.A., F.R.S. In two Volumes.

Vol. I. Chemical and Physical. Royal 8vo, 1l. 5s.

Vol. II. Stratigraphical and Physical. With a new Geological Map of Europe. Royal 8vo, 1l. 16s.

New Geological Map of Europe. In case or on roller. 5s.

Price. Treatise on Infinitesimal Calculus. By Bartholomew Price, M.A., F.R.S.

Vol. I. Differential Calculus. *Second Edition.* 8vo, 14s. 6d.

Vol. II. Integral Calculus, Calculus of Variations, and Differential Equations. *Second Edition.* 8vo, 18s.

Vol. III. Statics, including Attractions; Dynamics of a Material Particle. *Second Edition.* 8vo, 16s.

Vol. IV. Dynamics of Material Systems. *Second Edition.* 8vo, 18s.

Pritchard. Astronomical Observations made at the University Observatory, Oxford, under the direction of C. Pritchard, D.D. No. 1. Royal 8vo, paper covers, 3s. 6d.

—— No. II. Uranometria Nova Oxoniensis. A Photometric determination of the magnitudes of all Stars visible to the naked eye, from the Pole to ten degrees south of the Equator. Royal 8vo, 8s. 6d.

—— No. III. Researches in Stellar Parallax by the aid of Photography. Royal 8vo, 7s. 6d.

Rigaud's Correspondence of Scientific Men of the 17th Century, with Table of Contents by A. de Morgan, and Index by J. Rigaud, M.A. 2 vols. 8vo, 18s. 6d.

Rolleston and Jackson. Forms of Animal Life. A Manual of Comparative Anatomy, with descriptions of selected types. By George Rolleston, M.D., F.R.S. *Second Edition.* Revised and enlarged by W. Hatchett Jackson, M.A. Medium 8vo, 1l. 16s.

Rolleston. Scientific Papers and Addresses. By George Rolleston, M.D., F.R.S. Arranged and edited by William Turner, M.B., F.R.S. With a Biographical Sketch by Edward Tylor, F.R.S. 2 vols. 8vo, 1l. 4s.

Smyth. A Cycle of Celestial Objects. Observed, Reduced, and Discussed by Admiral W. H. Smyth, R.N. Revised, condensed, and greatly enlarged by G. F. Chambers, F.R.A.S. 8vo, 12s.

Oxford : Clarendon Press.

Stewart. An Elementary Treatise on Heat, with numerous Woodcuts and Diagrams. By BALFOUR STEWART, LL.D., F.R.S. *Fifth Edition.* Extra fcap. 8vo, 7*s.* 6*d.*

Van 't Hoff. Chemistry in Space. Translated and Edited by J. E. MARSH, B.A. Crown 8vo, 4*s.* 6*d.*

Vernon-Harcourt. Treatise on Rivers and Canals, relating to Control and Improvement of Rivers, and Design, Construction, and Development of Canals. By L. F. VERNON-HARCOURT, M.A. 2 vols. 8vo, 1*l.* 1*s.*

—— Harbours and Docks; their Physical Features, History, Construction, Equipment, and Maintenance; with Statistics as to their Commercial Development. By the same Author. 2 vols. 8vo, 25*s.*

Walker. The Theory of a Physical Balance. By JAMES WALKER, M.A. 8vo, stiff cover, 3*s.* 6*d.*

Watson and Burbury.

I. A Treatise on the Application of Generalised Co-ordinates to the Kinetics of a Material System. By H. W. WATSON, D.Sc., and S. H. BURBURY, M.A. 8vo, 6*s.*

II. The Mathematical Theory of Electricity and Magnetism. Vol. I. Electrostatics. 8vo, 10*s.* 6*d.* Vol. II. Magnetism and Electrodynamics. 8vo, 10*s.* 6*d.*

Westwood. Thesaurus Entomologicus Hopeianus; or, A Description of the rarest Insects in the Collection given to the University by the Rev. William Hope. By J. O. WESTWOOD, M.A., F.R.S. With 40 Plates. Small folio, half-morocco, 7*l.* 10*s.*

Williamson. Chemistry for Students. With Solutions. By A. W. WILLIAMSON, Phil. Doc., F.R.S. Extra fcap. 8vo, 8*s.* 6*d.*

VII. ART AND ARCHAEOLOGY.

Butler. Ancient Coptic Churches of Egypt. By A. J. BUTLER, M.A., F.S.A. 2 vols. 8vo, 30*s.*

Head. Historia Numorum. A Manual of Greek Numismatics. By BARCLAY V. HEAD, Assistant-Keeper of the Department of Coins and Medals in the British Museum. Royal 8vo, half-morocco, 42*s.*

Jackson. Dalmatia, the Quarnero and Istria; with Cettigne in Montenegro and the Island of Grado. By T. G. JACKSON, M.A., Author of 'Modern Gothic Architecture.' In 3 vols. 8vo. With many Plates and Illustrations. Half-bound, 42*s.*

London : HENRY FROWDE, Amen Corner, E.C.

MUSIC.—Hullah. Cultivation of the Speaking Voice. By John Hullah. *Second Edition.* Extra fcap. 8vo, 2s. 6d.

Ouseley. Treatise on Harmony. By Sir F. A. Gore Ouseley, Bart. *Third Edition.* 4to, 10s.

—— Treatise on Counterpoint, Canon, and Fugue, based upon that of Cherubini. *Second Edition.* 4to, 16s.

—— Treatise on Musical Form and General Composition. *Second Edition.* 4to, 10s.

Troutbeck and Dale. Music Primer. By J. Troutbeck, D.D., and F. Dale, M.A. *Second Edition.* Crown 8vo, 1s. 6d.

Robinson. A Critical Account of the Drawings by Michel Angelo and Raffaello in the University Galleries, Oxford. By J. C. Robinson, F.S.A. Crown 8vo, 4s.

Tyrwhitt. Handbook of Pictorial Art. With Illustrations, and a chapter on Perspective by A. Macdonald. By R. St. J. Tyrwhitt, M.A. *Second Edition.* 8vo, half-morocco, 18s.

Upcott. Introduction to Greek Sculpture. By L. E. Upcott, M.A. Crown 8vo, 4s. 6d.

Vaux. Catalogue of the Castellani Collection in the University Galleries, Oxford. By W. S. W. Vaux, M.A. Crown 8vo, 1s.

VIII. PALAEOGRAPHY.

Allen. Notes on Abbreviations in Greek Manuscripts. By T. W. Allen, M.A., Queen's College, Oxford. Royal 8vo, 5s.

Gardthausen. Catalogus Codicum Graecorum Sinaiticorum. Scripsit V. Gardthausen Lipsiensis. With Facsimiles. 8vo, *linen,* 25s.

Fragmenta Herculanensia. A Descriptive Catalogue of the Oxford copies of the Herculanean Rolls, together with the texts of several papyri. Edited by Walter Scott, M.A. Royal 8vo, 21s.

—— Thirty-six Engravings of Texts and Alphabets from the Herculanean Fragments, taken from the original Copper-plates executed under the direction of the Rev. John Hayter, M.A., and now in the Bodleian Library. With an Introductory Note by Bodley's Librarian. Folio, *small paper,* 10s. 6d.; *large paper,* 21s.

Herculanensium Voluminum Partes II. 1824. 8vo, 10s.

Oxford:

AT THE CLARENDON PRESS.

LONDON: HENRY FROWDE,

OXFORD UNIVERSITY PRESS WAREHOUSE, AMEN CORNER, E.C.

www.ingramcontent.com/pod-product-compliance
Lightning Source LLC
Chambersburg PA
CBHW021033030726
47496CB00006B/1505